FLIRTING WITH
THE SOCIALITE DOC

BY

MELANIE MILBURNE

MILLS
BOON

Published in Great Britain 2014
by Mills & Boon, an imprint of Harlequin (UK) Limited,
Eton House, 18-24 Paradise Road, Richmond, Surrey, TW9 1SR

© 2014 Melanie Milburne

ISBN: 978 0 263 90758 2

Harlequin (UK) Limited's policy is to use papers that are natural,
renewable and recyclable products and made from wood grown in
sustainable forests. The logging and manufacturing processes conform
to the legal environmental regulations of the country of origin.

Printed and bound in Spain
by Blackprint CPI, Barcelona

Dear Reader

I love fish-out-of-water stories, where a character—usually the heroine!—is thrown into a situation or environment that is totally foreign to her. Like me right now! I am writing this on a four-wheel drive tour bus in The Kimberleys in Western Australia. The heat is intense, but the scenery and the small friendly communities we've travelled through are wonderful examples of the wild frontier of the Outback and the larger-than-life people who make it so special.

Lady Isabella (Izzy) Courtney has taken a four-week posting to Jerringa Ridge after the end of her four-year engagement. She's not looking for love, but Cupid has other plans.

Sergeant Zach Fletcher is the local cop, who also has a broken relationship behind him and has no interest in anything right now but helping his dad get back on his feet after a quad bike accident. But of course when Zach meets Izzy everything changes—for both of them.

They both learn—as I too have learnt over the years—that it doesn't matter where you live, as long as the one you love is with you.

I hope you enjoy Zach and Izzy's story.

Warmest wishes

Melanie Milburne

DEDICATION

To Alan and Sue Beswick for their continued support
of the Heart Foundation in Tasmania.

This one is for you. At last! XX

Praise for
Melanie Milburne:

'A tale of new beginnings, redemption and hope that
will make readers chuckle as well as wipe away a tear.
A compelling medical drama about letting go of the past
and seizing the day, it is fast-paced and sparkles with
mesmerising emotion and intense passion.'
—*Goodreads.com* on
THEIR MOST FORBIDDEN FLING

**These books are also available in eBook format
from www.millsandboon.co.uk**

CHAPTER ONE

EVEN THE DISTANCE of more than seventeen thousand kilometres that Izzy had put between herself and her best friend was not going to stop another Embarrassing Birthday Episode from occurring.

Oh, joy.

'I've got the perfect present winging its way to you,' Hannah crowed over the phone from London. 'You're going to get the biggest surprise. Be prepared. Be very prepared.'

Izzy gave a mental groan. Her closest friend from medical school had a rather annoying habit of choosing the most inappropriate and, on occasion, excruciatingly embarrassing birthday gifts. 'I know you think I'm an uptight prude but do you have to rub my nose in it every year? I'm still blushing from that grotesque sex toy you gave me last year.'

Hannah laughed. 'This is so much better. And it will make you feel a little less lonely. So how are you settling in? What's it like out there?'

'Out there' was Jerringa Ridge and about as far away from Izzy's life back in England as it could be, hot and dry with sunlight that wasn't just bright but violent. Unlike other parts of New South Wales, which had suffered unusually high levels of flooding, it hadn't rained, or at least with any significance, in this district for months.

And it looked like it.

A rust-red dust cloud had followed her into town like a dervish and left a fine layer over her car, her clothes, and had somehow even got into the small cottage she'd been assigned for her four-week locum.

'It's hot. I swear I got sunburnt walking from the car to the front door.' Izzy glanced down at the tiny white circle on her finger where her engagement ring had been for the last four years. *Not sunburnt enough.*

'Have you met any of the locals yet?'

'Just a couple of people so far,' Izzy said. 'The clinic receptionist, Margie Green, seems very nice, very motherly. She made sure the cottage was all set up for me with the basics. There's a general store run by a husband and wife team—Jim and Meg Collis—who are very friendly too. And the guy who owns and operates the local pub—I think his name is Mike something or other—has organised a welcome-drink-cum-party for me for tomorrow night. Apparently the locals grab at any excuse to party so I didn't like to say I'd prefer to lie low and find my feet first.'

'Perfect timing,' Hannah said. 'At least you won't be on your own on your birthday.'

On your own...

Izzy was still getting used to being single. She'd become so used to fitting in with Richard Remington's life—*his meticulously planned life*—that it was taking her a little while to adjust. The irony was she had been the one to end things. Not that he'd been completely devastated or anything. He'd moved on astonishingly quickly and was now living with a girl ten years younger than he was who had been casually employed to hand around drinks at one of his parents' soirees—another irony, as he had been so adamant about not moving in with Izzy while they'd been together.

This four weeks out at Jerringa Ridge—the first of six one-month locums she had organised in Australia—would give her the space to stretch her cramped wings, to finally fly free from the trappings and expectations of her aristocratic background.

Out here she wasn't Lady Isabella Courtney with a pedigree that went back hundreds of years.

She was just another GP, doing her bit for the Outback.

'Have you met the new doctor yet?' Jim Collis asked, as Zach Fletcher came into the general store to pick up some supplies the following day.

'Not yet.' Zach picked up a carton of milk and checked the use-by date. 'What's he like?'

'She.'

He turned from the refrigerated compartment with raised brows. 'No kidding?'

'You got something against women doctors?' Jim asked.

'Of course not. I just thought a guy had taken the post. I'm sure that's what William Sawyer said before he went on leave.'

'Yeah, well, it seems that one fell through,' Jim said. 'Dr Courtney stepped into the breach at the last minute. She's from England. Got an accent like cut glass.'

Zach grunted as he reached for his wallet. 'Hope she knows what she's in for.'

Jim took the money and put it in the till. 'Mike's putting on a welcome do for her tonight at the pub. You coming?'

'I'm on duty.'

'Doesn't mean you can't pop in and say g'day.'

'I'd hate to spoil the party by showing up in uniform,' Zach said.

'I don't know…' Jim gave him a crooked grin. 'Some women really get off on a guy in uniform. You could get lucky, Fletch. Be about time. How long's it been?'

Zach gave him a look as he stuffed his wallet in his back pocket. 'Not interested.'

'You're starting to sound like your old man,' Jim said. 'How is he? You haven't brought him into town for a while.'

'He's doing OK.'

Jim gave him a searching look. 'Sure?'

Zach steeled his gaze. 'Sure.'

'Tell him we're thinking of him.'

'Will do.' Zach turned to leave.

'Her name is Isabella Courtney,' Jim said. 'Got a nice figure on her and pretty too, in a girl-next-door sort of way.'

'Give it a break, Jim.'

'I'm just saying…'

'The tyres on your ute are bald.' Zach gave him another hardened look as he shouldered open the door. 'Change them or I'll book you.'

Zach's father Doug was sitting out on the veranda of Fletcher Downs homestead; the walking frame that had been his constant companion for the last eighteen months by his side. A quad-bike accident had left Doug Fletcher with limited use of his legs. It would have been a disaster for any person, but for a man who only knew how to work and live on the land it was devastating.

Seeing his strong and extremely physically active father struck down in such a way had been bad enough, but the last couple of months his dad had slipped into a funk of depression that made every day a nightmare of anguish for Zach. Every time he drove up the long drive to the homestead his heart rate would escalate in panic in case his dad had done something drastic in his absence, and it wouldn't slow down again until he knew his father had managed to drag himself through another day.

Popeye, the toy poodle, left his father's side to greet Zach with a volley of excited yapping. In spite of everything, he couldn't help smiling at the little mutt. 'Hey, little buddy.' He crouched down and tickled the little dog's soot-black fleecy ears. He'd chosen the dog at a rescue shelter in Sydney when he'd gone to bring his dad home from the rehabilitation centre. Well, really, it had been the other way around. Popeye had chosen him. Zach had intended to get a man's dog, a kelpie or a collie, maybe even a German shepherd like the one he'd worked with in the drug squad, but somehow the little black button eyes had looked at him unblinkingly as if to say, *Pick me!*

'Jim says hello,' Zach said to his father as he stepped into the shade of the veranda.

His father acknowledged the comment with a grunt as he continued to stare out at the parched paddocks, which instead of being lime green with fresh growth were the depressing colour of overripe pears.

'There's a new doctor in town—a woman.' Zach idly kicked a stray pebble off the floorboards of the veranda into the makeshift garden below. It had been a long time since flowers had grown there. Twenty-three years, to be exact. His English born and bred mother had attempted to grow a cottage garden similar to the one she had left behind on her family's country estate in Surrey, but, like her, none of the plants had flourished in the harsh conditions of the Outback.

'You met her?' His father's tone was flat, as if he didn't care one way or the other, but at least he had responded. That meant it was a good day. A better day.

'Not yet,' Zach said. 'I'm on duty this evening. I'm covering for Rob. I thought I'd ask Margie to come over and sit with—'

Doug's mouth flattened. 'How many times do I have to tell you I don't need a bloody babysitter?'

'You hardly see any of your old mates these days. Surely a quiet drink with—'

'I don't want people crying and wringing their hands and feeling sorry for me.' Doug pulled himself to his feet and reached for his walker. 'I'll see people when I can drive into town and walk into the pub on my own.'

Zach watched as his father shuffled back down the other end of the veranda to the French doors that led to his bedroom. The lace curtains billowed out like a ghostly wraith as the hot, dry northerly wind came through, before the doors closed with a rattling snap that made every weatherboard on the old house creak in protest.

These days it seemed every conversation he had with his dad ended in an argument. Moving back home after five years of living in the city had seemed the right idea at the time, but now he wondered if it had made things worse. It had changed their relationship too much. He'd always planned to come back to the country and run Fletcher Downs once his father was ready to retire, but the accident had thrown everything out of order. This far out in the bush it was hard to get carers to visit, let alone move in, and without daily support his father would have no choice but to move off the property that had been in the family for seven generations.

The day Zach's mother had left had broken his father's heart; leaving Fletcher Downs before his time would rip it right out of his chest.

Popeye gave a little whine at Zach's feet. He bent back down and the dog leapt up into his arms and proceeded to anoint his face with a frenzy of enthusiastic licks. He hugged the dog against his chest as he looked at the sunburnt paddocks. 'We'll get him through this, Popeye. I swear to God we will.'

The Drover's Rest was nothing like the pubs at home but the warm welcome Izzy received more than made up for it. Mike Grantham, the proprietor, made sure she had a drink in her hand and then introduced her to everyone who came in the door. She had trouble remembering all of their names, but she was sure it wouldn't be too long before she got to know them, as she was the only doctor serving the area, which encompassed over two hundred and fifty square kilometres.

Once everyone was inside the main room of the pub Mike tapped on a glass to get everyone's attention. 'A little bird told me it's Dr Courtney's birthday today, so let's give her a big Jerringa Ridge welcome.'

The room erupted into applause and a loud and slightly off-key singing of 'Happy Birthday' as two of the local ladies came out with a cake they had made, complete with candles and Izzy's name piped in icing over the top.

'How did you know it was my birthday?' Izzy asked Mike, once she'd blown out the candles.

'I got a call yesterday,' he said. 'A friend of yours from the old country. She gave me the heads up. Said she had a surprise lined up. It should be here any minute now. Why don't you go and wait by the door? Hey, clear a pathway! Let the doc get through.'

Izzy felt her face grow warm as she made her way through the smiling crowd of locals to the front door of the pub. *Why couldn't Hannah send her flowers or chocolate or champagne, like normal people did?*

And then she saw it.

Not it—*him*.

Tall. Muscled. Toned. Buffed. Clean-shaven. A jaw strong and square and determined enough to land a fighter jet on. A don't-mess-with-me air that was like an invisible wall of glass around him. Piercing eyes that dared you to outstare him.

A male stripper.

Dressed as a cop.

I'm going to kill you, Hannah.

Izzy went into damage control. The last thing she wanted was her reputation ruined before she saw her first patient. She could fix this. It would be simple. Just because Hannah had paid the guy—the rather gorgeous hot guy—to come out all this way and strip for her, it didn't mean she had to let him go through with it.

As long as he got his money, right?

'I'm afraid there's been a change of plan,' she said, before the man could put a foot inside the pub. 'I won't be needing your…er…services after all.'

The man—who had rather unusual grey-blue eyes—looked down at her from his far superior height. 'Excuse me?'

Izzy had to speak in a hushed tone as she could feel the crowd starting to gather behind her. 'Please, will you just leave? I don't want you here. It will spoil everything for me.'

One of the man's eyebrows lifted quizzically. 'Let me get this straight…you don't want me to step inside the pub?'

'No. Absolutely not.' Izzy adopted an adamant stance by planting her hands on her hips. 'And I strictly forbid you to remove any of your clothes in my presence. Do you understand?'

Something in those eyes glinted but the rest of his expression was still deadpan. 'How about if I take off my hat?'

She let out a breath and dropped her arms back by her sides, clenching her hands to keep some semblance of control. She *had* to get rid of him. *Now*. 'Are you *listening* to me? I don't want you here.'

'Last time I looked it was a free country.'

Izzy glowered at him. 'Look, I know you get paid to do this sort of stuff, but surely you can do much better? Don't you find this horribly demeaning, strutting around at parties, titillating tipsy women in a leather thong or whatever it is you get down to? Why don't you go out and get a real job?'

'I love my job.' The glint in his eyes made its brief appearance again. 'I've wanted to do it since I was four years old.'

'Then go and do your job someplace else,' she said

from behind gritted teeth. 'If you don't leave right now, I'm going to call the police.'

'He *is* the police,' Mike called out from behind the bar.

CHAPTER TWO

ZACH LOOKED DOWN at the pretty heart-shaped face that was now blushing a fire-engine-red. Her rosebud mouth was hanging open and her toffee-brown eyes were as wide as the satellite dish on the roof of the pub outside. He put out a hand, keeping his cop face on. 'Sergeant Zach Fletcher.'

Her slim hand quivered slightly as it slid into the cage of his. 'H-how do you do? I'm Isabella Court-ney…the new locum doctor…in case you haven't al-ready guessed.'

He kept hold of her hand a little longer than he needed to. He couldn't seem to get the message through to his brain to release her. The feel of her satin-soft skin against the roughness of his made something in his groin tighten like an over-tuned guitar string. 'Wel-come to Jerringa Ridge.'

'Thank you.' She slipped her hand away and used it to tuck an imaginary strand of hair behind her ear. 'I'm sorry. I expect you think I'm a complete fool but my friend told me she'd organised a surprise and I thought—well, I thought you were the surprise.'

'Sorry to disappoint you.'

'I'm relieved, not disappointed.' She blushed again.

'Quite frankly, I hate surprises. Hannah—that's my friend—thinks it's funny to shock me. Every year she comes up with something outrageous to make my birthday memorable.'

'I guess this will be one you won't forget in a hurry.'

'Yes...' She bit her lip with her small but perfectly aligned white teeth.

'Is there a Dr Courtney around here?' A young man dressed in a courier delivery uniform came towards them from the car park, his work boots crunching on the dusty gravel.

'Um, I'm Dr Courtney.' Isabella's blush had spread down to her décolletage by now, taking Zach's eyes with it. She was of slim build but she had all the right girly bits, a fact his hormones acknowledged with what felt like a stampede racing through his blood.

Cool it, mate.

Not your type.

'I have a package for you,' the delivery guy said. 'I need a signature.'

Zach watched as Isabella signed her name on the electronic pad. She gave the delivery guy a tentative smile as she took the package from him. It was about the size of a shoebox and she held it against her chest like a shield.

'Aren't you going to open it?' Zach asked.

Her cheeks bloomed an even deeper shade of pink. 'I think I'll wait until I'm...until later.'

There was a small silence...apart from the sound of forty or so bodies shuffling and jostling behind them to get a better view.

Zach had lived long enough in Jerringa Ridge to know it wouldn't take much to get the local tongues wagging. Ever since his fiancée Naomi had called off their relationship when he'd moved back home to take care of his father, everyone in town had taken it upon themselves to find him a replacement. He only had to look at a woman once and the gossip would run like a scrub fire. But whether he was in the city or the country, he liked to keep his private life off the grapevine. It meant for a pretty dry social life but he had other concerns right now.

'I'd better head back to the station. I hope you enjoy the rest of your birthday.' He gave Isabella Courtney a brisk impersonal nod while his body thrummed with the memory of her touch. 'Goodnight.'

Izzy watched Zach stride out of the reach of the lights of the pub to where his police vehicle was parked beneath a pendulous willow tree. *Argh!* If only she'd checked the car park before she'd launched into her I-don't-want-you-here speech. How embarrassing! She had just made an utter fool of herself, bad enough in front of *him* but practically the whole town had been watching. Would she ever live it down? Would everyone snigger at her now whenever they saw her?

And how would she face him again?

Oh, he might have kept his face as blank as a mask but she knew he was probably laughing his head off at her behind that stony cop face of his. Would he snigger as well with his mates at how she had mistaken him for a— Oh, it was too *awful* to even think about.

Of course he didn't look anything like a stripper, not that she had seen one in person or anything, only pictures of some well-built guys who worked the show circuit in Vegas. One of the girls she'd shared a flat with in London had hung their risqué calendar on the back of the bathroom door.

Idiot.

Fool.

Imbecile.

How could you possibly think he was—?

'So you've met our gorgeous Zach,' Peggy McLeod, one of the older cattleman's wives, said at Izzy's shoulder, with obvious amusement in her voice.

Izzy turned around and pasted a smile on her face. 'Um, yes… He seems very…um…nice.'

'He's single,' Peggy said. 'His ex-fiancée changed her mind about moving to the bush with him. He and his dad run a big property out of town—Fletcher Downs. Good with his hands, that boy. Knows how to do just about anything. Make someone a fine husband one day.'

'That's…um, nice.'

'His mum was English too, did you know?' Peggy went on, clearly not expecting an answer for she continued without pause. 'Olivia married Doug after a whirlwind courtship but she never could settle to life on the land. She left when Zach was about eight or nine…or was it ten? Yes, it was ten, I remember now. He was in the same class as one of my sister's boys.'

Izzy frowned. 'Left?'

Peggy nodded grimly. 'Yep. Never came back, not even to visit. Zach used to fly over to England for holidays occasionally. Took him ages to settle in, though. Eventually he stopped going. I don't think he's seen his mother in years. Mind you, he's kind of stuck here now since the accident.'

'The accident?'

'Doug Fletcher rolled his quad bike about eighteen

months back. Crushed his spinal cord.' Peggy shook her head sadly. 'A strong, fit man like that not able to walk without a frame. It makes you want to cry, doesn't it?'

'That's very sad.'

'Zach looks after him all by himself,' Peggy said. 'How he does it is anyone's guess. Doug won't hear of having help in. Too proud and stubborn for his own good. Mind you, Zach can be a bit that way too.'

'But surely he can't look after his father indefinitely?' Izzy said. 'What about his own life?'

Peggy's shoulders went up and down. 'Doesn't have one, far as I can see.'

Izzy walked back to her cottage a short time later. The party was continuing without her, which suited her just fine. Everyone was having a field day over her mistaking Zach Fletcher for a stripper. There was only so much ribbing she could take in one sitting. Just as well she was only here for a month. It would be a long time before she would be able to think about the events of tonight without blushing to the roots of her hair.

The police station was a few doors up from the clinic at the south end of the main street. She hadn't noticed it earlier but, then, during the day it looked like any other nondescript cottage. Now that it was fully dark the police sign was illuminated and the four-wheel-drive police vehicle Zach had driven earlier was parked in the driveway beside a spindly peppercorn tree.

As she was about to go past, Zach came out of the building. He had a preoccupied look on his face and almost didn't see her until he got to the car. He blinked and pulled up short, as if she had appeared from nowhere. He tipped his hat, his voice a low, deep burr in the silence of the still night air. 'Dr Courtney.'

'Sergeant Fletcher.' If he was going to be so formal then so was she. Weren't country people supposed to be friendly? If so, he was certainly showing no signs of it.

His tight frown put his features into shadow. 'It's late to be out walking.'

'I like walking.'

'It's not safe to do it on your own.'

'But it's so quiet out here.'

'Doesn't make it safe.' His expression was grimly set. 'You'd be wise to take appropriate measures in future.'

Izzy put her chin up pertly. 'I didn't happen to see a taxi rank anywhere.'

'Do you have a car?'

'Of course.'

'Next time use it or get a lift with one of the locals.' He opened the passenger door of the police vehicle. 'Hop in. I'll run you home.'

Izzy bristled at his brusque manner. 'I would prefer to walk, if you don't mind. It's only a block and I—'

His grey-blue eyes hardened. 'I do mind. Get in. That's an order.'

The air seemed to pulse with invisible energy as those strong eyes held hers. She held his gaze for as long as she dared, but in the end she was the first to back down. Her eyes went to his mouth instead and a frisson of awareness scooted up her spine to tingle each strand of her hair on her scalp. Something shifted in her belly...a turning, a rolling-over sensation, like something stirring after a long hibernation.

His mouth was set tightly, as tight and determined as his jaw, which was in need of a fresh shave. His eyes were fringed with dark lashes, his eyebrows the same rich dark brown as his hair. His skin was deeply tanned and it was that stark contrast with his eyes that was so heart-stopping. Smoky grey one minute, ice-blue the next, the outer rims of his irises outlined in dark blue, as if someone had traced their circumference with a fine felt-tip marker.

Eyes that had seen too much and stored the memories away somewhere deep inside for private reflection…or haunting.

'Fine, I'll get in,' Izzy said with bad grace. 'But you really need to work on your kerb-side manner.'

He gave her an unreadable look as he closed the door with a snap. She watched him stride around to the driver's side, his long legs covering the distance in no time at all. He was two or three inches over six feet and broad shouldered and lean hipped. When he joined her in the car she felt the space shrink alarmingly. She drew herself in tightly, crossing her arms and legs to keep any of her limbs from coming into contact with his powerfully muscled ones.

The silence prickled like static electricity.

'Peggy McLeod told me about your father's accident,' Izzy said as he pulled to the kerb outside her cottage half a minute later. She turned in her seat to look at him. 'I'm sorry. That must be tough on both of you.'

Zach's marble-like expression gave nothing away but she noticed his hands had tightened on the steering-wheel. 'Do you make house calls?'

'I…I guess so. Is that what Dr Sawyer did?'

'Once a week.'

'Then I'll do it too. When would you like me to come?'

Some of the tension seemed to leave his shoulders

but he didn't turn to look at her. 'I'll ring Margie and make an appointment.'

'Fine.'

Another silence.

'Look, about that little mix-up back at the pub—' she began.

'Forget it,' he cut her off. 'I'll wait until you get inside. Lock the door, won't you?'

Izzy frowned. 'You know you're really spooking me with this over-vigilance. Don't you know everyone in a town this size by name?'

'We have drive-throughs who cause trouble from time to time. It's best not to take unnecessary risks.'

'Not everyone is a big bad criminal, Sergeant Fletcher.'

He reached past her to open her door. Izzy sucked in a sharp breath as the iron bar of his arm brushed against her breasts, setting every nerve off like a string of fireworks beneath her skin.

For an infinitesimal moment her gaze meshed with his.

He had tiny blue flecks in that unreadable sea of grey and his pupils were inky-black. He smelt of lemons with a hint of lime and lemongrass and something else... something distinctly, arrantly, unapologetically male.

A sensation like the unfurling petals of a flower brushed lightly over the floor of her belly.

Time froze.

The air tightened. Pulsed. Vibrated.

'Sorry.' He pulled back and fixed his stare forward again, his hands gripping the steering-wheel so tightly his tanned knuckles were bone white.

'No problem.' Izzy's voice came out a little rusty. 'Thanks for the lift.'

He didn't drive off until she had closed the door of the cottage. She leant back against the door and let out a breath she hadn't realised she'd been holding, listening as his car growled away into the night.

'So what did your friend actually send you for your birthday?' Margie Green asked as soon as Izzy arrived at the clinic the next morning.

'I haven't opened it yet.' *Because I stupidly left it in Sergeant Fletcher's car last night.*

Margie's eyes were twinkling. 'What on earth made you think our Zach was a male stripper?'

Izzy cringed all over again. Was every person in town going to do this to her? Remind her of what a silly little idiot she had been? If so, four weeks couldn't go fast enough. 'Because it's exactly the sort of thing my friend Hannah would do. As soon as I saw him standing there I went into panic mode. I didn't stop to think that he could be a real cop. I didn't even know if Jerringa Ridge *had* a cop. I didn't have time to do much research on the post because the agency asked me to step in for someone at the last minute.'

'We have two cops…or one and a half really,' Margie said. 'We used to have four but with all the government cutbacks that's no longer the case. Rob Heywood is close to retirement so Zach does the bulk of the work. He's a hard worker is our Zach. You won't find a nicer man out in these parts.'

'I'm not here to find a man.' Why did every woman over fifty—including her own mother—seem to think younger women had no other goal than to get married? 'I'm here to work.'

Margie cocked her head at a thoughtful angle. 'You're here for four weeks. These days that's a long time for a young healthy woman like you to be without a bit of male company.'

Izzy's left thumb automatically went to her empty ring finger. It was a habit she was finding hard to break. It wasn't that she regretted her decision to end things with Richard. It was just strange to feel so...so unattached. She hadn't looked at another man in years. But now she couldn't get Zach Fletcher's eyes or his inadvertent touch out of her head...*or her body*. Even now she could remember the feel of that slight brush of his arm across her breasts—the electric, tingly feel of hard male against soft female...

She gave herself a mental shake as she picked up a patient's file and leafed through it. 'I'm not interested in a relationship. There'd be no point. I'm on a working holiday. I won't be in one place longer than a month.'

'Zach hasn't dated anyone since he broke up with his ex,' Margie said, as if Izzy hadn't just described her plans for the next six months. 'It'd be good for him to move on. He was pretty cut up about Naomi not wanting to come with him to the bush. Not that he's said anything, of course. He's not one for having his heart flapping about on his sleeve. He comes across as a bit arrogant at times but underneath all that he's a big softie. Mind you, you might have your work cut out for you, being an English girl and all.'

Izzy lowered the notes and frowned. 'Because his mother was English?'

'Not only English but an aristocrat.' Margie gave

a little sniff that spoke volumes. 'One of them blue-blooded types. Her father was a baron or a lord of the realm or some such thing. Olivia Hardwick was as posh as anything. Used to having servants dancing around her all her life. No wonder she had so much trouble adjusting to life out here. Love wasn't enough in the end.'

Izzy thought of the veritable army of servants back at Courtney Manor. They were almost part of the furniture, although she tried never to take any of them for granted. But now was probably not a good time to mention her background with its centuries-old pedigree.

Margie sighed as sat back in her chair. 'It broke Doug's heart when she left. He hasn't looked at another woman since…more's the pity. He and I used to hang out a bit in the old days. Just as friends.'

'But you would have liked something more?' Izzy asked.

Margie gave her a wistful smile. 'We can't always have what we want, can we?'

Izzy glanced at the receptionist's left hand. 'You never married?'

'Divorced. A long time ago. Thirty years this May. I shouldn't have married Jeff but I was lonely at the time.'

'I'm sorry.'

Margie shrugged.

'Did you have children?'

'A boy and a girl. They both live in Sydney. And I have three grandchildren who are the joy of my life. I'm hoping to get down to see them at Easter.'

Izzy wondered if Margie's marriage had come about because of Doug Fletcher's involvement with Olivia. How heartbreaking it must have been for her to watch him fall madly in love with someone else, and how sad for Doug to have the love of his life walk out on him and their young son.

Relationships were tricky. She knew that from her own parents, who had a functional marriage but not a particularly happy or fulfilling one. That was one of the reasons she had decided to end things with Richard. She hadn't wanted to end up trapped in an empty marriage that grumbled on just for the sake of appearances.

'Sergeant Fletcher asked me to make a house call on his father,' Izzy said. 'Has he rung to make an appointment yet?'

'Not yet,' Margie said. 'He might drop in on his way to the station. Ah, here he is now. Morning, Zach. We were just talking about you.'

Izzy turned to see Zach Fletcher duck his head slightly to come through the door. Her stomach did a little freefall as his eyes met hers. He looked incredibly commanding in his uniform; tall and composed with an air of untouchable reserve. How on earth she had mistaken him for anything other than a cop made her cheeks fire up all over again. She ran her tongue over her lips before she gave him a polite but distant smile. 'Good morning, Sergeant Fletcher.'

He dipped his head ever so slightly, his eyes running over her in a lazy, unreadable sweep that set her pulse rate tripping. 'Dr Courtney.'

Izzy's smile started to crack around the edges. Did he have to look at her so unwaveringly, as if he knew how much he unsettled her? Was he laughing at her behind that inscrutable cop mask? 'What can I do for you? Would you like to make an appointment for me to come out and see your father today? I could probably work something in for later this afternoon. I'm pretty solidly booked but—'

He handed her the package the delivery guy had delivered the night before, his eyes locking on hers in a way that made the base of her spine shiver and fizz. 'You left this in my car last night.'

Izzy could practically hear Margie's eyes popping out of her head behind the reception counter. 'Oh... right, thanks.' She took the package from him and held it against her chest, where her heart was doing double time.

'Aren't you going to open it?' Margie said.

'Um...not right now.'

Was that a hint of mockery glinting in Zach Fletcher's eyes? 'What time would suit you?' he asked.

'I...I think I'd rather do it when I get home.'

The glint in his eyes was unmistakable this time, so too was the slight curve at one side of his mouth. His version of a smile? It made her hungry to see a real one. Was he capable of stretching that grim mouth that far? 'I meant what time would suit you to see my father.'

Izzy's blush deepened. What was it about this man that made her feel about twelve years old? Well, maybe not twelve years old. Right now she was feeling *incredibly* adult. X-rated adult. Every particle of her flesh was shockingly aware of him. Her skin was tight, her senses alert, her pulse rate rising, her heart fluttering like a butterfly trapped in the narrow neck of a bottle. 'Oh...' She swung back to Margie. 'What time am I free?'

'Your last patient is at four forty-five. It's a twenty-minute drive out to Fletcher Downs so shall we say five-thirty, give or take a few minutes?' Margie said.

'I'll make sure I'm there to let you in,' Zach said.

'My father can be a bit grouchy meeting people for the first time. Don't let him get to you.'

Izzy raised her chin the tiniest fraction. 'I'm used to handling difficult people.'

His eyes measured hers for a pulsing moment. 'Margie will give you a map. If you pass Blake's waterhole, you've gone too far.'

'I'm sure I'll find it without any trouble,' Izzy said. 'I have satellite navigation in my car.'

He gave a brisk nod that encompassed the receptionist as well as Izzy and left the clinic.

'Are you going to tell me how you ended up in his car last night or am I going to have to guess?' Margie asked.

Izzy let out a breath as she turned back around. 'He gave me a lift home.'

Margie's eyes widened with intrigue. 'From the pub? It's like half a block by city standards.'

'Yes, well, apparently Sergeant Fletcher thinks it's terribly unsafe to walk home at night without an escort. Typical cop, they think everyone's a potential criminal. They never see the good in people, only the bad. They have power issues too. You can pick it up a mile off. I'd bet my bottom dollar Zach Fletcher is a total control freak. And a blind man could see he has a chip on his shoulder the size of a boulder.'

Margie smiled a knowing smile. 'You like him.'

'What on earth gives you that idea?' Izzy gave a scornful little laugh but even to her ears it sounded tinny. 'He's not my type.'

And I bet I'm not his either.

CHAPTER THREE

ZACH HAD BEEN at the homestead long enough to change out of his uniform, make his father a cup of tea, and take Popeye for a walk down to the dam and back when he saw Isabella Courtney coming up the driveway.

He waved a fly away from his face as he watched her handle the corrugations of the gravel driveway that was as long as some city streets. A dust cloud plumed out in her wake and a flock of sulphur-crested white cockatoos and salmon-pink corellas flew out of the gum trees that lined the driveway before settling in another copse of trees closer to the dam. The chorus of cicadas was loud in the oven-warm air and in the distance the grey kangaroo he'd rescued as a joey, and who now had a joey of her own, hopped towards a few tufts of grass that had pushed up through the parched ground around the home paddock's water trough.

Popeye gave a whine and looked up at Zach as his body did its little happy dance at the thought of a visitor. 'Cool it, buddy,' Zach said. 'She's not staying long.'

It was hard to ignore the stirring of male hormones in his body as he watched her alight from the car. She had a natural grace about her, lissom and lithe, like a ballerina or yoga enthusiast. She wasn't particularly tall, or at least not compared to him at six feet three in bare feet. She was about five-six or -seven with a waist he could probably span with his hands, and her features were classically beautiful but in a rather understated way. She wore little or no make-up and her mid-length chestnut hair was tied back in a ponytail she had wound around itself in a casual knot, giving her a fresh, youthful look.

But it was her mouth his gaze kept tracking to. It was soft and full and had an upward curve that made it look like she was always on the brink of smiling.

'Oh, what an adorable dog!' Her smile lit up her brown eyes so much that they sparkled as she bent down to greet Popeye. 'Oh, you darling little poppet. Who's a good boy? Hang on a minute—*are* you a boy? Oh, yes, you are, you sweet little thing. Yes, I love you too.' She laughed a tinkling-bell laugh and stood up again, her smile still stunningly bright as she stood and faced Zach. 'Is he yours?'

Zach had to take a moment to gather himself after being on the receiving end of that dazzling smile.

Earth to Zach. Do you read me?

He wondered if he should fob Popeye off as his father's but he had a feeling she wouldn't buy it for a moment. 'Yes.'

She angled her head at him in an appraising manner. 'Funny, I had you picked as a collie or kelpie man, or maybe a German shepherd or Doberman guy.'

He kept his expression blank. 'The station manager has working dogs. Popeye's just a pet.'

She brushed a tendril of hair away from her face that the light breeze had worked loose. 'This is a lovely property. I couldn't believe how many birds I saw coming up the driveway.'

'You're not seeing it at its best. We need rain.'

She scanned the paddocks with one of her hands shading her eyes against the sun. 'It's still beautiful—Oh, there's a kangaroo and it's got a joey! He just popped his head out. How gorgeous!'

'That's Annie,' Zach said.

She swung around to look at him again. 'Is she a pet too?'

'Not really.' He waved another fly away from his face. 'Her mother was killed on the highway. I reared her by hand and released her back into the wild a few years ago, but she hangs about a bit, mostly because of the drought.'

Her eyes widened in surprise. 'You reared her yourself?'

'Yeah.'

Her pretty little nose was wrinkled over the bridge from her small frown. 'Like with a bottle or something?'

'Yep. Six feeds a day.'

'How did you juggle that with work?'

'I took her with me in a pillowcase.'

She blinked a couple of times as if she couldn't quite imagine him playing wet-nurse. 'That's…amazing…' She looked back at the paddock where Annie was grazing. 'It must be wonderful to have all this space to yourself. To be this close to wildlife and to breathe in such fresh air instead of pollution.'

Zach saw her finely shaped nostrils widen to take in the eucalyptus scent of the bush. He picked up a faint trace of her fragrance in the air: a flowery mix that was redolent of gardenias and vanilla. The sun caught the golden highlights in her hair and he found himself wondering what it would feel like to run his fingers through those glossy, silky strands.

Get a grip.

He thrust his hands in his pockets, out of the way of temptation. She was a blow-in and would be gone before the first dust storm hit town. His track record with keeping women around wasn't flash. His mother had whinged and whined and then withdrawn into herself for ten years before she'd finally bolted and never returned. His fiancée hadn't even got as far as the Outback before the call of the city had drawn her back. Why would Isabella Courtney with her high-class upbringing have anything to offer him?

She turned back to look at him and a slight blush bloomed in her cheeks. 'I guess I should get on with why I came here. Is your father inside?'

'Yes. Come this way.'

Izzy stepped into the cool interior of the homestead but it took her eyes a moment to adjust to the dim interior after the assault of the bright sunlight outside. A man who was an older version of Zach sat in an armchair in the sitting room off the long, wide hallway; a walking frame was positioned nearby. He had steel-grey hair at his temples and his skin was weathered by long periods in the sun but he was still a fine-looking man. He had the same aura of self-containment his son possessed, and a strong uncompromising jaw, although his cheeks were hollowed by recent weight loss. His mouth had a downward turn and his blue eyes had damson-coloured shadows beneath them, as if he had trouble sleeping.

'Dad, Dr Courtney is here,' Zach said.

'Hello, Mr Fletcher.' Izzy held out her hand but dropped it back by her side when Doug Fletcher rudely ignored it.

He turned his steely gaze to his son. 'Why didn't you tell me she was a bloody Pom?'

Zach tightened his mouth. 'Because it has nothing to do with her ability as a medical practitioner.'

'I don't want any toffee-nosed Poms darkening my doorstep ever again. Do you hear me? Get her out of here.'

'Mr Fletcher, I—'

'You need to have regular check-ups and Dr Courtney is the only doctor in the region,' Zach said. 'You either see her or you see no one. I'm not driving three hundred kilometres each way to have your blood pressure checked every week.'

'My blood pressure was fine until you brought her here!' Doug snapped.

Izzy put a hand on Zach's arm. 'It's all right, Sergeant Fletcher. I'll come back some other time.'

Doug glared at her. 'You'll be trespassing if you do.'

'Well, at least the cops won't be far away to charge me, will they?' she said.

Doug's expression was as dark as thunder as he shuffled past them to exit the room. Izzy heard Zach release a long breath and turned to look at him. 'I'm sorry. I don't think I handled that very well.'

He raked a hand through his hair, leaving it sticking up at odd angles. 'You'd think after twenty-three years he'd give it a break, wouldn't you?'

'Is that how long it's been since your mother left?'

He gave her a grim look. 'Yeah. I guess you twigged she was English.'

'Peggy McLeod told me.'

He walked over to the open fireplace and kicked a gum nut back into the grate. His back and shoulders were so tense Izzy could see each muscle outlined by his close-fitting T-shirt. He rubbed the back of his neck before he turned back around to face her. 'I'm worried about him.'

'I can see that.'

'I mean *really* worried.'

Izzy saw the haunted shadows in his eyes. 'You think he's depressed?'

'Let's put it this way, I don't leave him alone for long periods. And I've taken all the guns over to a friend's place.'

She felt her heart tighten at the thought of him having to keep a step ahead of his father all the time. The pressure on the loved ones of people struggling with depression was enormous. And Zach seemed to be doing it solo. 'Has his mood dropped recently or has he been feeling low for a while?'

'It's been going down progressively since he came out of rehab.' He let out another breath as he dragged his hand over his face. 'Each day I seem to lose a little bit more of him.'

Izzy could just imagine the toll it was taking on him. He had so many responsibilities to shoulder, running his father's property as well as his career as a cop. 'Would he see someone in Sydney if I set up an appointment? I know it's a long trip but surely it would be worth it to get him the help he needs.'

'He won't go back to the city, not after spending three months in hospital. He won't even go as far as Bourke.'

'Does he have any friends who could spend time

with him?' she asked. 'It might help lift his mood to be more active socially.'

The look he threw her was derisive. 'My father is not the tea-party type.'

'What about Margie Green?'

His brows came together. 'What about her?'

'She's a close friend, isn't she? Or she was in the old days before your parents got together.'

His expression was guarded now; the drawbridge had come up again. 'You seem to have gained a lot of inside information for the short time you've been in town.'

Izzy compressed her lips. 'I can't help it if people tell me stuff. I can assure you I don't go looking for it.'

He curled his lip in a mocking manner. 'I bet you don't.'

She picked up her doctor's bag from the floor with brisk efficiency. 'I think it's time I left. I've clearly out-stayed my welcome.'

Izzy had marched to the front door before he caught up with her. 'Dr Courtney.' It was a command, not a request or even an apology. She drew in a tight breath and turned to face him. His expression still had that reserved unreadable quality to it but something about his eyes made her think he was not so much angry at her as at the situation he found himself in.

'Yes?'

He held her gaze for a long moment without speak-ing. It was as if he was searching through a filing drawer in his brain for the right words.

'Yes?' Izzy prompted.

'Don't give up on him.' He did that hair-scrape thing again. 'He needs time.'

'Will four weeks be long enough, do you think?' she asked.

He gave her another measured look before he opened the screen door for her. 'Let's hope so.'

'So, what did you call your new boyfriend I sent you?' Hannah asked when she video-messaged Izzy a couple of nights later.

Izzy looked at the blow-up male doll she had propped up in one of the armchairs in the sitting room. 'I've called him Max. He's surprisingly good company for a man. He doesn't hog the remote control and he doesn't eat all the chocolate biscuits.'

Hannah giggled. 'Have you slept with him?'

Izzy rolled her eyes. 'Ha-ha. I'm enjoying having the bed to myself, thank you very much.'

'So, no hot guys out in the bush?'

She hoped the webcam wasn't picking up the colour of her warm cheeks. She hadn't told Hannah about her case of mistaken identity with Zach Fletcher. She wasn't sure why. Normally she told Hannah everything that was going on in her life…well, maybe not *everything*. She had never been the type of girl to tell all about dates and boyfriends. There were some things she liked to keep private. 'I'm supposed to be using this time to sort myself out in the love department. I don't want to complicate my recovery by diving head first into another relationship.'

'You weren't in love with Richard, Izzy. You know you weren't. You were just doing what your parents expected of you. He filled the hole in your life after Jamie died. I'm glad you saw sense in time. Don't get me wrong—I really like Richard but he's not the one for you.'

Izzy knew what Hannah said was true. She had let things drift along for too long, raising everyone's hopes and expectations in the process. Her parents were still a little touchy on the subject of her split with Richard, whom they saw as the ideal son-in-law. The stand-in son for the one they had lost after a long and agonising battle with sarcoma.

Her decision to come out to the Australian Outback on a working holiday had been part of her strategy to take more control over her life. It was a way to remind her family that she was serious about her career. They still thought she was just dabbling at medicine until it was time to settle down and have a couple of children to carry on the long line of Courtney blood now that her older brother Jamie wasn't around to do it.

But she loved being a doctor. She loved it that she could help people in such a powerful way. Not just healing illnesses but changing lives, even saving them on occasion.

Like Jamie might have been saved if he had been diagnosed earlier...

Thinking about her brother made her heart feel like it had been stabbed. It actually seemed to jerk in her chest every time his name was mentioned, as if it were trying to escape the lunge of the sword of memory.

'Maybe you'll meet some rich cattleman out there and fall madly in love and never come home again, other than for visits,' Hannah said.

'I don't think that's likely.' Izzy couldn't imagine leaving England permanently. Her roots went down too deep. She even loved the capricious weather.

No, this trip out here was timely but not permanent.

Besides, with Jamie gone she was her parents' only child and heir. Not going home to claim her birthright would be unthinkable. She just needed a few months to let them get used to the idea of her living her own life and following her own dreams, instead of living vicariously through theirs.

Izzy's phone buzzed where it was plugged into the charger on the kitchen bench. 'Got to go, Han. I think that's a local call coming through. I'll call you in a day or two. Bye.' She picked up her phone. 'Isabella Courtney.'

'Zach Fletcher here.' Even the way he said his name was sharp and to the point.

'Good evening, Sergeant,' Izzy said, just as crisply. 'What can I do for you?'

'I just got a call about an accident out by the Honeywells' place. It doesn't sound serious but I thought you should come out with me to check on the driver. The volunteer ambos are on their way. I can be at your place in two minutes. It will save you having to find your way out there in the dark.'

'Fine. I'll wait at the front for you.'

Izzy had her doctor's bag at the ready when Zach pulled up outside her cottage. She got into the car and clipped on her seat belt, far more conscious than she wanted to be of him sitting behind the wheel with one of those unreadable expressions on his face.

Would it hurt him to crack a smile?

Say a polite hello?

Make a comment on the weather?

'Do you know who's had the accident?' she asked.

'Damien Redbank.' He gunned the engine once he

turned onto the highway and Izzy's spine slammed back against the seat. 'His father Charles is a big property owner out here. Loads of money, short on common sense, if you get my drift.'

Izzy sent him a glance. 'The son or the father?'

The top edge of his mouth curled upwards but it wasn't anywhere near a smile. 'The kid's all right. Just needs to grow up.'

'How old is he?'

'Eighteen and a train wreck waiting to happen.'

'What about his mother?'

'His parents are divorced. Vanessa Redbank remarried a few years ago.' He waited a beat before adding, 'She has a new family now.'

Izzy glanced at him again. His mouth had tightened into its default position of grim. 'Does Damien see his mother?'

'Occasionally.'

Occasionally probably wasn't good enough, Izzy thought. 'Where does she live?'

'Melbourne.'

'At least it's not the other side of the world.' She bit her lip and wished she hadn't spoken her thoughts out loud. 'I'm sorry…I hope I didn't offend you.'

He gave her a quick glance. 'Offend me how?'

Izzy tried to read his look but the mask was firmly back in place. 'It must have been really tough on you when your mother left. England is a long way away from here. It feels like *everywhere* is a long way away from here. It would've seemed even longer to a young child.'

'I wasn't a young child. I was ten.' His voice was stripped bare of emotion; as if he was reading from a script and not speaking from personal experience. 'Plenty old enough to take care of myself.'

Izzy could imagine him watching as his mother had driven away from the property for the last time. His face blank, his spine and shoulders stoically braced, while no doubt inside him a tsunami of emotion had been roiling. Had his father comforted him or had he been too consumed by his own devastation over the breakdown of his marriage? No wonder Zach had an aura of unreachability about him. It was a circle of deep loneliness that kept him apart from others. He didn't want to need people so he kept well back from them.

Unlike her, who felt totally crushed if everyone didn't take an instant shine to her. Doing and saying the right thing—*people-pleasing*—had been the script she had been handed from the cradle. It was only now that she had stepped off the stage, so to speak, that she could see how terribly lonely and isolated she had felt.

Still felt...

When had she not felt lonely? Being sent to boarding school hadn't helped. She had wanted to go to a day school close to home but her protests had been ignored. All Courtneys went to boarding school. It was a tradition that went back generations. It was what the aristocracy did. But Izzy had been too bookish and too shy to be the most popular girl. Not athletic enough to be chosen first, let alone be appointed the captain of any of the sporting teams. Too keen to please her teachers, which hadn't won her any friends. Too frightened to do the wrong thing in case she was made a spectacle of in front of the whole school. Until she'd met Hannah a couple of years later, her life had been terrifyingly, achingly lonely.

* * *

'When I was ten I still couldn't go to sleep unless all of my Barbie dolls were lined up in bed with me in exactly the right order.' *Why are you telling him this stuff?* 'I've still got them. Not with me, of course.'

Zach's gaze touched hers briefly. It was the first time she had seen a hint of a smile dare to come anywhere near the vicinity of his mouth. But just as soon as it appeared it vanished. He turned his attention back to the grey ribbon of road in front of them where in the distance Izzy could see the shape of a car wedged at a steep angle against the bank running alongside the road. Another car had pulled up alongside, presumably the person who had called for help.

'Damien's father's not going to be too happy about this,' Zach said. 'He's only had that car a couple of weeks.'

'But surely he'll be more concerned about his son?' Izzy said. 'Cars can be replaced. People can't.'

The line of his mouth tilted in a cynical manner as he killed the engine. 'Try telling Damien's mother that.'

CHAPTER FOUR

WHEN IZZY GOT to the car the young driver was sitting on the roadside, holding his right arm against his chest. 'Damien? Hi, I'm Isabella Courtney, the new locum doctor in town. I'm going to check you over. Is that OK?'

Damien gave her a belligerent look. 'I'm fine. I don't need a doctor. And before you ask—' he sent Zach a glance '—no, I wasn't drinking.'

'I still have to do a breathalyser on you, mate,' Zach said. 'It's regulation when there's been an accident.'

'A stupid wombat was in the middle of the road,' Damien said. 'I had to swerve to miss it.'

'That arm looks pretty uncomfortable,' Izzy said. 'How about I take a look at it and if it's not too bad we can send you home.'

He rolled his eyes in that universal teenage *this sucks* manner, but he co-operated while she examined him. He had some minor abrasions on his forehead and face but the airbag had prevented any major injury. His humerus, however, was angled and swollen, indicative of a broken arm. Izzy took his pulse and found it was very weak and the forearm looked dusky due to the artery being kinked at the fracture site.

'I'm going to have to straighten that arm to restore blood flow,' she said. 'I'll give you something to take the edge off it but it still might hurt a bit.' She took out a Penthrane inhalant, which would deliver rapid analgesia. 'Take a few deep breaths on this...yes, that's right. Good job.'

While Damien was taking deep breaths on the inhalant Izzy put traction on the arm and aligned it. He gave a yowl during the process but the pulse had come back into the wrist and the hand and forearm had pinked up.

'Sorry about that,' she said. 'You did really well. I'm going to put a splint on your arm so we can get you to hospital. You're going to need an orthopaedic surgeon to have a look at that fracture.'

Damien muttered a swear word under his breath. 'My dad is going to kill me.'

'I've just called him,' Zach said. 'He's on his way. The ambos are five minutes away,' he said to Izzy.

'Good,' Izzy said, as she unpacked the inflatable splint. The boy was shivering with shock by now so she gave him an injection of morphine. She was about to ask Zach to pass her the blanket out of the kit when he handed it to her. She gave him a smile. 'Mind-reader.'

He gave a shrug. 'Been at a lot of accidents.'

Izzy hated to think of how terrible some of them might have been. Cops and ambulance personnel were always at the centre of drama and tragedy. The toll it took on them was well documented. But out in the bush, where the officers often personally knew the victims, it was particularly harrowing.

The volunteer ambulance officers were two of the people Izzy had met the other night at the pub, Ken Gordon and Roger Parker. After briefing them on the boy's condition, she supervised them as they loaded Damien onto a stretcher, supporting his arm. And then, once he was loaded, she put in an IV and set some fluids running. The Royal Flying Doctor Service would take over once the ambulance had delivered the boy to the meeting point about eighty kilometres away.

Not long after the ambulance had left, a four-wheel-drive farm vehicle pulled up. A middle-aged man got out from behind the wheel and came over to where Zach was sorting out the towing of the damaged vehicle with the local farmer who had called in the accident.

'Is it a write-off?' Charles Redbank asked.

Izzy paused in the process of stripping off her sterile gloves. Although Zach had called Charles and told him Damien was OK, she still found it strange that he would want to check on the car before he saw his son. What sort of father was he? Was a car really more important to him than his own flesh and blood?

Zach put his pen back in his top pocket as he faced Charles. His mouth looked particularly grim. 'No.'

'Bloody fool,' Charles muttered. 'Was he drinking?' 'No.'

'He's not seriously hurt.' Izzy stepped forward. 'He has a broken arm that will need to be seen by an orthopaedic surgeon. I've arranged for him to be flown to Bourke. If you hurry you can catch up with the ambulance. It's only just left. You probably passed it on the road.'

'I came in on the side road from Turner's Creek,' Charles said. 'And you can think again if you think I'm going to chase after him just because he's got a broken arm. He can deal with it. He's an adult, or he's supposed to be.'

Yes, and he's had a great role model, Izzy thought. 'Damien will need a few things if he stays in hospital for a day or two. A change of clothes, a toothbrush, toiletries—that sort of thing.'

Charles gave her the once-over. 'Are you the new doctor?'

'Yes. Isabella Courtney.'

His eyes ran over her again, lingering a little too long on her breasts. 'Bit young to be a doctor, aren't you?'

Izzy had faced similar comments for most of her medical career. She did her best to not let it get to her. Just because she had a youthful appearance, it didn't mean she wasn't good at her job. 'I can assure you I am quite old enough and have all the necessary qualifications.'

'Your left brake light isn't working,' Zach said to Charles.

Charles rocked back on his heels, his gaze running between Izzy and Zach like a ferret's. 'So that's the way it is, is it? Well, well, well. You're a fast worker. She's only been in town, what, a couple of days?'

Zach's jaw looked like it had been set in place by an invisible clamp. 'I told you three weeks ago to get it fixed.'

Charles's smile was goading. 'She's a bit too upmarket for you, Fletch. And what would your old man say if you brought a posh Pommy girl home, eh? That'd go down a treat, wouldn't it?'

Izzy marvelled at Zach's self-control for even *she* felt like punching Charles Redbank. Zach looked down from his considerable height advantage at the farmer, his strong gaze unwavering. 'I'll give you twenty-four hours to get that light seen to. Ian Cooke is going to tow the car into Joe's workshop. He's gone back to town for the truck now. I'm heading to Bourke for a court appearance tomorrow. If you pack a few things for Damien, I'll swing by and pick them up before I leave in the morning.'

'Wouldn't want to put you to any trouble,' Charles said, with a deliberate absence of sincerity.

'It's no trouble,' Zach said. 'Damien's a good kid. He just needs a little direction.'

Charles's lip curled. 'What? And you think you're the one to give it to him?'

'That's your job,' Zach said, and turned away to leave. 'Coming, Dr Courtney?'

Izzy waited until they were in the car before she said, 'Is there a special section in the police training manual on how to handle jerks?'

He gave her a look as he started the engine. 'He's a prize one, isn't he?'

'You handled that situation so well. I was impressed.' She pulled down her seat belt and clicked it into place. 'Quite frankly, I wanted to punch him.'

'Two wrongs never make a right.'

Izzy studied him for a beat or two. 'Are you really going to Bourke for a court appearance tomorrow?'

He turned the car for town before he answered. 'I have the day off. It'll be an outing for my father if I can convince him to come. Take his mind off his own troubles for a change.'

'He's very lucky to have you.'

'He's a good dad. He's always tried to do his best, even under difficult circumstances.'

The township appeared in the distance, the sprinkling of lights glittering in the warm night air.

'You did a good job out there tonight.' Zach broke the silence that had fallen between them.

Izzy glanced at him again. 'You were expecting me not to, weren't you?'

'Have you worked in a remote region before?'

'I did a short stint in South Africa last year.'

His brows moved upwards. 'So why Outback Australia this year?'

'I've always wanted to come out here,' Izzy said. 'A lot of my friends had come out and told me how amazing it is. I spent a few days in Sydney on my way here. I'm looking forward to seeing a bit more after I finish my six months of locums. Melbourne, Adelaide, Perth, maybe a quick trip up to Broome and the Kimberleys.'

Another silence fell.

Izzy felt as if he was waiting for her to tell him her real reason for coming out here. It was what cops did. They waited. They listened. They observed. She had seen him looking at her ring hand while she'd been strapping up Damien. He'd been a cop too long to miss that sort of detail. 'I also wanted to get away from home for a while. My parents weren't too happy about me breaking off my engagement a couple of months ago.'

'How long were you engaged?'

'Four years.'

'Some people don't stay married that long.'

'True.' She waited a moment before saying, 'Margie told me you'd gone through a break-up a while back.'

'Yeah, well, I can't scratch my nose in this town without everyone hearing about it.' His tone was edgy, annoyed.

Izzy pushed on regardless. 'Were you together long?'

He threw her a hard glance. 'Why are you asking

me? Surely the locals have already given you all the gory details?'

'I'd like to hear it from you.'

He drove for another two kilometres or so before he spoke. 'We'd been seeing each other a year or so. We had only been engaged for a couple of months when my father had his accident.'

'So you came back home.'

'Yeah.'

'She didn't want to pull up stumps and come with you?'

'Nope.'

'I'm sorry.'

'Don't be. I'm not.' He pulled up in front of her cottage and swivelled in his seat to look at her. 'Was your fiancé a doctor?'

'A banker.' She put her hand on the door. 'Um, I should go in. It's getting late.'

'I'll walk you to the door.'

'That's not necessary…' It was too late. He was already out of the car and coming round to her side.

Izzy stepped out of the car but she misjudged the kerb and stumbled forward. Two iron-strong hands shot out and prevented her from falling. She felt every one of his fingers around her upper arms. That wasn't all she felt. Electric heat coursed through her from the top of her head to the balls of her feet. She could smell the scent of his skin, the sweat and dust and healthy male smell that was like a tantalising potion to her overly sanitised city nostrils. Her heart gave a skittish jump as she saw the way his grey-blue gaze tracked to her mouth. The pepper of his stubble was rough along his jaw, the vigorous regrowth a heady reminder of the potent hormones that marked him as a full-blooded man.

'You OK?' His fingers loosened a mere fraction as his eyes came back to hers.

'I—I'm fine…' She felt a blush run up over her skin, the heat coming from the secret core of her body. 'I'm not normally so clumsy.'

He released her and took a step backwards, his expression as unfathomable as ever. 'The ground is pretty rough out here. You need to take extra care until you find your feet.'

'I'll be careful.' Izzy pushed a strand of hair back off her face. 'Um, would you like to come in for a coffee?' *Oh. My. God. You just asked him in for coffee! What are you doing? Are you nuts?*

His brows twitched together. 'Coffee?'

'Don't all cops drink coffee? I have tea if you'd prefer. No doughnuts, I'm afraid. I guess it's kind of a cliché, you know, cops and doughnuts. I bet you don't even eat them.' *Stop talking!*

'Thanks, but no.'

No?

No?

It was hard not to feel slighted. Was she such hideous company that a simple coffee was out of the question? 'Fine.' Izzy forced a smile. 'Some other time, then.' She lifted a hand in a fingertip wave. 'Thanks for the lift. See you around.' She turned and walked quickly and purposefully to the cottage knowing he probably wouldn't drive away until she was safely inside.

'Dr Courtney.'

Izzy turned to see him holding her doctor's bag, which she had left on the back seat of his car. Her cheeks flared all over again. What was it about him that made her brain turn to scrambled mush? 'Oh... right. Might need that.'

He brought her bag to her on the doorstep, his fingers brushing against hers as he handed it over. The shock of his touch thrilled her senses all over again and her heart gave another skip-hop-skip inside her chest. The flecks of blue in his eyes seemed even darker than ever, his pupils black, bottomless inkwells.

'Thanks.' Her voice came out like a mouse squeak.

'You're welcome.'

The crackle of the police radio in the car sounded excessively loud. Jarring.

He gave her one of his curt nods and stepped down off the veranda, walking the short distance to his car, getting behind the wheel and driving off, all within the space of a few seconds.

Izzy slowly released her breath as she watched his taillights disappear into the distance.

Stop that thought.

You did not come all this way to make your life even more complicated.

Zach found his father sitting out on the southern side of the veranda when he got back to the homestead. He let out the tight breath he felt like he'd been holding all day and let his shoulders go down with it. 'Fancy a run out to Bourke tomorrow?'

'What for?'

'Damien Redbank had an accident this evening. He's fine, apart from a broken arm. He'll be in hospital a couple of days. I thought he could do with some company.'

'What's wrong with his father?'

'Good question.' Zach took off his police hat and raked his hands through his sweat-sticky hair.

Doug gave him a probing look. 'You OK?'

Zach tossed his hat onto the nearest cane chair. 'I've never felt more like punching someone's lights out.'

'Understandable. Charles has been pressing your buttons for a while now.'

'He's incompetent as a father,' Zach said. 'He's got no idea how to be a role model for that kid. No wonder the boy is running amok. He's crying out for someone to take notice of him. To show they care about him.'

'The boy hasn't been the same since his mother remarried.'

Zach grunted. 'Yeah, I know.'

The crickets chirruped in the garden below the veranda.

'What time are you thinking of heading out of town?' Doug asked.

'Sixish.'

A stone curlew let out its mournful cry and Popeye lifted his little black head off the faded cushion on the seat beside Zach's father's chair, but seeing Zach's stay signal quickly settled back down again with a little doggy sigh and closed his eyes.

'How'd the new doctor handle things?' Doug asked.

'Better than I thought she would, but it's still early days.'

His father slanted him a glance. 'Watch your step, son.'

'I'm good.'

'Yeah, that's we all say. Next thing you know she'll have your heart in a vice.'

'Not going to happen.' Zach opened and closed his

fingers where the tingling of Izzy's touch had lingered far too long. It had taken a truckload of self-control to decline her offer of coffee. Even if she had just been being polite in asking him in, he hadn't wanted to risk stepping over the boundaries.

His body had other ideas, of course. But he was going to have to tame its urges if he was to get through this next month without giving in to temptation. A fling with her would certainly break the dogged routine he'd slipped into but how would he feel when she packed her bags and drove out of town?

He had to concentrate on his father's health right now.

That was the priority.

Distractions—even ones as delightfully refreshing and dazzling as Izzy Courtney—would have to wait.

CHAPTER FIVE

IZZY REALISED ON her fourth patient the following morning that a rumour had been circulated about her and Zach Fletcher. Ida Jensen, a seventy-five-year-old farmer's wife, had come in to have her blood pressure medication renewed, but before Izzy could put the cuff on her arm to check her current reading, the older woman launched into a tirade.

'In my day a girl wouldn't dream of sleeping with a man before she was married, especially with a man she's only just met.' She pursed her lips in a disapproving manner. 'I don't know what the world's coming to, really I don't. Everyone having casual flings as if love and commitment mean nothing. It's shameful, that's what it is.'

'I guess not everyone shares the same values these days,' Izzy said, hoping to prevent an extended moral lecture.

'I blame the Pill. Girls don't have to worry about falling pregnant so they just do what they want with whoever they want. That boy needs a wife, not a mistress.'

'That…er, boy?'

'Zach Fletcher,' Ida said. 'Don't bother trying to deny it. Everyone knows you've got your eye on him, and him not even over the last one. Mind you, they do say you should get back on the horse, don't they? Never did like that saying. It's a bit coarse, if you ask me. But I think he needs more time. What if his ex changes her mind and comes out here to see you're involved with him?'

'I beg your pardon?'

Ida shifted in her chair like a broody hen settling on a clutch of eggs. 'Not that anyone could really blame you, of course. No one's saying he isn't good looking. Got a nice gentle nature too, when you get to know him.'

Izzy frowned. 'I'm sorry but I'm not sure where you got the idea that I'm involved with Sergeant Fletcher.'

'Don't bother denying it,' Ida said. 'I heard it from a very reliable source. Everyone's talking about it.'

'Then they can stop talking about it because it's not true!' Izzy was fast becoming agitated. 'Have you asked Sergeant Fletcher about this? I suggest you do so you can hear it from him as well that nothing is going on. This is nothing more than scurrilous gossip.' *And I have a feeling I know who started it.*

'Are you sure it's not true?' Ida looked a little uncomfortable.

'I think I would know who I was or wasn't sleeping with, don't you?' Izzy picked up the blood-pressure cuff. 'Now, let's change the subject, otherwise my blood pressure is going to need medication.'

'What? Don't you fancy him?' Ida asked after a moment.

Izzy undid the cuff from the older woman's arm and wrote the figure in her notes. 'I see here you're taking anti-inflammatories for your arthritis. Any trouble with your stomach on that dosage?'

'Not if I take them with food.'

'Is there anything else I can help you with?'

The older woman folded her lips together. 'I hope I haven't upset you.'

'Not at all,' Izzy lied.

'It's just we all love Zach so much. We want him to be happy.'

'I'm sure he appreciates your concern but he's a big boy and can surely take care of himself.'

'That's half the trouble…' Ida let out a heartfelt sigh. 'He's been taking care of himself for too long.'

Izzy stood up to signal the end of the consultation. 'Make another appointment to see me in a week. I'd like to keep an eye on your blood pressure. It was slightly elevated.'

Just like mine.

'Nice work, Fletch,' Jim Collis said, when Zach came in the next morning for the paper.

Zach didn't care for the ear-to-ear grin the storekeeper was wearing. 'What?'

Jim had hooked his thumbs in his belt and tilted backwards on his heels behind the counter. 'Getting it on with the new doctor. Talk about a fast mover. You want me to stock up on condoms?'

Zach kept his expression closed as he picked up a stock magazine his father enjoyed, as well as the paper. He put them both on the counter and took out his wallet. 'You should check your sources before you start spreading rumours like that.'

'You telling me it's not true?'

'Even if it was true, I wouldn't be standing here discussing it.'

'Charles Redbank seemed pretty convinced you two

were getting it on,' Jim said. 'Not that anyone would blame you for making a move on her. Be a good way to get that Naomi chick out of your system once and for all.'

Zach ground his molars together. It got under his skin that the whole town saw him as some sort of broken-hearted dude let down by his fiancée. He was over Naomi. It had been a convenient relationship that had worked well for both of them until he'd made the decision to come back to Jerringa Ridge to help his father. Yes, he was a little pissed off she hadn't wanted to come with him but that was her loss. In time he would find someone to fill her place, but he needed to get his father sorted out first.

'Anyway, way I see it,' Jim went on, 'if you don't hit on Izzy Courtney then you can bet your bottom dollar some other fella soon will.' He cleared his throat as the screen door opened. 'Hi, Dr Courtney, I got that honey and cinnamon yogurt you wanted.'

Zach hitched his hip as he put his wallet in his back pocket before turning to look at her. 'G'day.'

'Hello...' The blush on her cheeks was like the petals of a pink rose. She looked young and fresh, like a model from a fashion magazine. Her simple flowered cotton dress was cinched in at her tiny waist, her legs were bare and her feet in ballet flats. She had a string of pearls around her neck that were a perfect foil for her milk-pure skin. And even with all the other competing smells of the general store he could still pick up her light gardenia scent. It occurred to him to wonder why anyone would wear pearls in the Outback but it was something his mother had done and he knew from experience there was no explaining it.

'So, I'll get those condoms in for you, will I, Fletch?' Jim said with a cheeky grin. 'Extra-large, wasn't it?'

The blush on Izzy Courtney's cheeks intensified. Her eyes slipped out of reach of his and her teeth snagged at her full lower lip. 'Maybe I'll come back later...' She turned and went back out the screen door so quickly it banged loudly on its hinges.

Zach scooped up the paper and the magazine, giving Jim a look that would have cut through steel. 'You're a freaking jerk, you know that?'

Izzy turned at the sound of firm footsteps to find Zach coming towards her. That fluttery sensation she always got when she saw him tickled the floor of her stomach like an ostrich feather held by someone with a tremor. His mouth was tightly set, his expression formidable this time rather than masked. Her earlier blush still hadn't completely died down but as soon as his eyes met hers she felt it heat up another few degrees.

'We need to talk.' He spoke through lips so tight they barely moved.

'We do?' She saw his dark frown and continued, 'Yes, of course we do. Look, it's fine. It's just a rumour. It'll go away when they realise there's no truth in it.'

'I'm sorry but this is what happens in small country towns.'

'I realise that,' Izzy said. 'I've already had a couple of stern lectures from some of the more conservative elders in the community. It seems that out here it's still a sin for a woman to have sex before marriage. Funny, but they didn't mention it being a sin for men. That really annoys me. Why should you men have all the fun?'

His gaze briefly touched her mouth before glancing away to look at something in the distance, his eyes squinting against the brutal sunlight. 'Not all of us are having as much fun as you think.'

Izzy moistened her suddenly dry lips. 'How is your father? Did he go with you to Bourke?'

'Yes.'

'And how was Damien?'

'Feeling a bit sorry for himself.'

'Did his father end up going to see him?' Izzy brushed a wisp of hair away from her face.

He made a sound that sounded somewhere between a grunt and a laugh. 'No.'

'I guess he was too busy spreading rumours back here.'

His brooding frown was a deep V between his brows. 'I should've punched him when I had the chance.'

She studied Zach for a moment. Even without his uniform he still maintained that aura of command and control. She wondered what it would take to get under his skin enough to make him break out of that thick veneer of reserve. There was a quiet intensity about him, as if inside he was bottling up emotions he didn't want anyone to see. 'You don't seem the type of guy to throw the first punch.'

'Yeah, well, I don't get paid to pick fights.' He drew in a breath and released it in a measured way as if he was rebalancing himself. 'I'd better let you get to work. Have a good one.'

Izzy watched as he strode back to where his car was parked outside the general store. She too let out a long breath, but any hope of rebalancing herself was as likely as a person on crutches trying to ice-skate.

Not going to happen.

* * *

Almost a week went past before Izzy saw Zach again other than from a distance. Although they worked within a half a block of each other, he was on different shifts and she spent most days inside the clinic, other than a couple of house calls she had made out of town. But each time she stepped outside the clinic or her cottage or drove out along any of the roads she mentally prepared herself for running into him.

She had seen him coming out of the general store one evening as she'd been leaving work, but he'd been on the phone and had seemed preoccupied, and hadn't noticed her at all. For some reason that rankled. It didn't seem fair that she was suffering heart skips and stomach flips at the mere mention of his name and yet he didn't even sense her looking at him. Neither did he even glance at the clinic just in case she was coming out.

Izzy still had to field the occasional comment from a patient but she decided that was the price of being part of a small community. You couldn't sneeze in a town the size of Jerringa Ridge without everyone saying you had flu.

But on Saturday night, just as she was thinking about going to bed, she got a call from Jim Collis, who was down at the pub. 'Been a bit of trouble down here, Doc,' he said. 'Thought you might want to look in on Zach if you've got a minute. I reckon he might need a couple of stitches.'

'What happened?'

'Couple of the young fellas had too much to drink and got a bit lively. Zach's down at the station, waiting for the parents to show up. I told him to call you but he said it's just a bruise. Don't look like a bruise to me. He's lucky he didn't lose an eye, if you ask me.'

'I'll head down straight away.'

Izzy turned up the station just as a middle-aged couple came out with their son. The smell of alcohol was sour in the air as they walked past to bundle him into the car. The mother looked like she had been crying and the father looked angry enough to throw something. The son looked subdued but it was hard to tell if that was the excess alcohol taking effect or whether he'd faced charges.

When she went inside the building Zach was sitting behind the desk with a folded handkerchief held up to his left eye as he wrote some notes down on a sheet of paper. He glanced up and frowned at her. 'Who called you?'

'Jim Collis.'

He let out a muffled expletive. 'He had no right to do that.' He pushed back from the desk and stood up. 'It's nothing. Just a scratch.'

'Why don't you let me be the judge of that?' She held up her doctor's bag. 'I've come prepared.'

He let out a long breath as if he couldn't be bothered arguing and led the way out to the small kitchen area out the back. 'Make it snappy. I need to get home.'

Izzy pushed one of the two chairs towards him. 'Sit.'

'Can't you do it standing up?'

'I'm not used to doing it standing up...' A hot blush stormed into her cheeks when she saw the one-eyed glinting look he gave her. 'I mean...you're way too tall for me to reach you.' *God, that sounded almost worse!*

He sat in the chair with his long legs almost cutting

the room in half. She had nowhere to stand other than between them to get close enough to inspect his eye. She was acutely aware of the erotic undertones as his muscled legs bracketed her body. They weren't touching her at all but she felt the warmth of his thighs like the bars of a radiator. Her mind went crazy with images of him holding her between those powerful thighs, his body pumping into hers, those muscled arms pinning her against the bed, a wall, or some other surface. Scorching heat flowed through her veins even as she slammed the brakes on her wickedly wanton thoughts.

Doctor face. Doctor face. Mentally chanting it was the only way she could get herself back on track. She gently took the wadded handkerchief off his eye to find it bruised and swollen with a split in the skin above his eyebrow that was still oozing blood. 'You won't need stitches but you'll have a nice shiner by morning.'

He grunted. 'Told you it was nothing.'

Izzy's leg bumped against his as she reached for some antiseptic in her bag. It was like being touched with a laser—the tingles went right to her core. She schooled her features as she turned back to tend to his cut. *Cool and clinical. Cool and clinical.* She could do that. She always did that…well; she did when it was anyone other than Zach Fletcher.

She could hear his breathing; it was slow and even, unlike hers, which was shallow and picking up pace as every second passed.

His scent teased her nostrils, making her think of sun-warmed lemons. He had a decent crop of prickly stubble on his jaw. She felt it catch on the sensitive skin on the underside of her wrist as she dabbed at his wound. 'I'm sorry if this hurts. I'm just cleaning the area before I put on a Steri-strip to hold the edges of the wound together.'

'Can't feel a thing.'

She carefully positioned the Steri-strip over the wound. 'There. Now, all we need is some ice for that eye. Do you have any in the fridge?'

'I'll put some on at home.'

He got to his feet at the same time as she reached to dab at a smear of blood on his cheek. He put his hands on her each of her forearms, presumably to stop her fussing over him, but somehow his fingers slid down to her wrists, wrapping around them like a pair of hand-cuffs.

Izzy felt her breath screech to a halt as his hooded gaze went to her mouth. The tip of her tongue came out and moistened the sudden dryness of her lips. He was so close she could feel the fronts of his muscle-packed thighs against hers.

He looked at her mouth and her belly did a little somersault as she saw the way his eyes zeroed in on it, as if he was memorising its contours. 'This is a re-ally dumb idea.'

'It is? I mean, yes, *of course* it is,' Izzy said a little breathlessly. 'An absolutely crazy thing to do. What were we thinking? Hey, is that a smile? I didn't think you knew how to.'

'I'm a little out of practice.' He brought her even closer, his warm vanilla- and milk-scented breath skat-ing over the surface of her lips. 'Isn't there some rule about doctors getting involved with their patients?'

'I'm not really your doctor. Not officially. I mean I treated you, but *I* came to see you. You didn't come to see me. It's not the same as if you'd made an appointment and paid me to see you. I just saw you as a one-off. A favour, if you like. It's not even going on the record. All I did was put a Steri-strip on your head. You could have done it yourself.' She took a much-needed breath. 'Um…you're not really going to kiss me, are you?'

His grey-blue eyes smouldered. 'What do you think?'

Izzy couldn't think, or at least not once his mouth came down and covered hers. His mouth was firm and warm and tasted of salt and something unexpectedly sinful. His tongue flickered against the seam of her mouth, a teasing come-play-with-me-if-you-dare gesture that made her insides turn to liquid. She opened her mouth and he entered it with a sexy glide of his tongue that made the hairs on her scalp stand up on tiptoe, one by one. He found her tongue with devastating expertise, toying with it, cajoling it into a dance as old as time.

He put a hand on the small of her back and pressed her closer. The feel of his hot urgent male body against her called to everything that was female in her. She had always struggled with desire in the past. She could talk herself into it eventually, but it had never been an instantaneous reaction.

Now it was like a dam had burst. Desire flowed through her like a flash flood, making her flesh cry out for skin-on-skin contact. Her hands came up to link around his neck, her body pressing even closer against his. Her breasts tingled behind the lace of her bra; she had never been more aware of her body, how it felt, what it craved, how it responded.

He gave a low, deep sound of pleasure and deepened the kiss, his hands going to both of her hips and locking her against him. She felt the hardened ridge of him against her and a wave of want coursed through her so rampantly it took her breath away.

She started on his shirt, pulling it out of his trousers and snapping open the buttons so she could glide her hands over his muscled chest. She could feel his heart beneath her palm. Thud. Thud. Thud. She could feel where his heart had pumped his blood in preparation. It throbbed against her belly with a primal beat that resonated through her body like a deep echo, making her insides quiver and reverberate with longing.

He kept kissing her, deeply and passionately, as his hands ran up under her light cotton shirt. The feel of his broad, warm, work-roughened hands on her skin made her gasp out loud. Her blood felt like it was on fire as it raced through her veins at torpedo speed.

Her inner wild woman had been released. Uncaged. Unrestrained. And the wild man in him was more than up to the task of taming her. She felt it in the way he was kissing her.

This was a kiss that meant business.

This was a kiss that said sex was next.

His hands found her breasts, pushing aside the confines of her bra to cup her skin on skin. She shivered as his thumbs rolled each of her nipples in turn; all while his mouth continued its mind-blowing assault on her senses.

The sound of the door opening at the front had Izzy springing back from him as if someone had fired a gun. She assiduously avoided Zach's gaze as she tidied her clothes with fingers that refused to co-operate.

'You there, Fletch?' Jim Collis called out.

'Yeah. Won't be a tick.' Zach redid the buttons before tucking in his shirt. Izzy envied his cool cop composure as he went out to talk to Jim. Her nerves were in shreds at almost being discovered making out like teenagers in the back room.

'Is the doc still with you?' Jim asked.

There was a moment of telling silence.

'Yes, I'm still here.' Izzy stepped out, carrying her doctor's bag and what she hoped passed for doctor-just-finished-a-consult composure. 'I'm just leaving.'

Jim's eyes twinkled knowingly. 'So you've got him all sorted?'

'Er, yes.' She pasted on a tight smile. 'No serious damage done.'

'I hope you weren't annoyed with me, Fletch, for sending her over to patch you up?' Jim said.

Zach still had his cop face on. 'Not at all. She was very...professional.'

'Did you charge Adam Foster with assault?'

'Not this time. I gave him a warning.'

'You're too soft,' Jim said. 'Don't you think so, Dr Courtney?'

Izzy blushed to the roots of her hair. 'Um, it's late. I have to get home.' She gripped the handle of her bag and swung for the door. 'Goodnight.'

CHAPTER SIX

'WHAT HAPPENED TO your eye?' Doug Fletcher asked the following morning.

'I got in the way of Adam Foster's elbow.' Zach switched on the kettle. The less he talked about last night the better. The less *he thought* about last night the better. He had barely been able to sleep for thinking about Izzy Courtney's hot little mouth clamped to his, not to mention her hot little hands winding around his neck and smoothing over his chest. Even taking into account his eighteen-month sex drought, he couldn't remember ever being so turned on before. He had always prided himself on his self-control. But as soon as his mouth had connected with hers something had short-circuited in his brain.

He gave himself a mental shake and took out a couple of cups from the shelf above the sink. 'You want tea or coffee?'

'What did the doctor say?'

He frowned as he faced his father. 'What makes you think I saw the doctor? It's just a little cut and a black eye, for pity's sake. I don't know what all the fuss is about.'

His father gave him a probing look. 'Is it true?'

'Is what true?'

'The rumour going around town that you're sleeping with her.'

'Where'd you hear that?'

'Bill Davidson dropped in last night while you were at work. Said his wife Jean saw the doctor a couple of days back. She said the doctor blushed every time your name was mentioned.'

'Oh, for God's sake.' Zach wrenched open the fridge door for the milk.

'Find yourself another woman, by all means, but make sure she's a country girl who'll stick around,' his father said.

'Dad, give it a break. I'm not going to lose my head or my heart to Dr Courtney. She's not my type.'

'Your mother wasn't my type either but that didn't stop me falling in love with her, and look how that ended up.'

Zach let out a long breath. 'You really need to let it go. Mum's never coming back. You have to accept it.'

'She hasn't even called, not once. Not even an email or a get-well card.'

'That's because you told her never to contact you again after she forgot my thirtieth birthday, remember?'

His father scowled. 'What sort of mother forgets her own son's birthday?'

A mother who has two other younger sons she loves more, Zach thought. 'What do you want for breakfast?'

'Nothing.'

'Come on. You have to have something.'

'I'm not hungry.'

'Are you in pain?' Zach asked.

His father glowered. 'Stop fussing.'

'You must be getting pretty low on painkillers. You want me to get Dr Courtney to write a prescription for you?'

'I'll manage.'

He threw his father an exasperated look. 'How'd you get to be so stubborn? No wonder Mum walked out on you.'

His father's eyes burned with bitterness. 'That may be why she walked out on me but why'd she leave you?'

It was a question Zach had asked himself a thousand times. And all these years later he still didn't have an answer other than the most obvious.

She hadn't loved him enough to stay.

'So how are you and Zach getting on?' Margie asked on Monday morning.

Izzy worked extra-hard to keep her blush at bay. 'Fine.'

'Jim told me you saw to Zach's eye on Saturday night.'

'Yes.' Izzy kept her voice businesslike and efficient. 'Do you have Mrs Patterson's file there? I have to check on something.'

Margie handed the file across the counter. 'The Shearers' Ball is on the last weekend of your locum. Did Peggy tell you about it? It's to raise money for the community centre. It's not a glamorous shindig, like you'd have in England or anything. Just a bit of a bush dance and a chance to let your hair down. Will I put you down as a yes?'

It sounded like a lot of fun. Would Zach be there? Her insides gave a funny little skip at the thought of those strong arms holding her close to him in a waltz or a barn dance. 'I'll have a think about it.'

'Oh, but you must come!' Margie insisted. 'You'll have heaps of fun. People drive in from all over the district to come to it. We have a raffle and door prizes. It's the social event of the year. Everyone will be so disappointed if you don't show up. It'll be our way of thanking you for stepping in while William Sawyer and his wife were on holiday. They come every year without fail.'

Izzy laughed in defeat. 'All right. Sign me up.'

'Fabulous.' Margie grinned. 'Now I can twist Zach's arm.'

Izzy left the clinic at lunchtime to pick up the sandwich she'd ordered at the corner store. Jim gave her a wink and a cheeky smile as she came in. 'How's the patient?'

She looked at him blankly, even though she knew exactly which patient he meant. 'Which patient?'

'You don't have to be coy with me, Izzy. I know what you two were up to out back the other night. About time Zach got himself back out there. I bet that ex-fiancée of his hasn't spent the last eighteen months pining his absence.'

She kept her features neutral. 'Is my salad sandwich ready?'

'Yep.' He handed it over the counter, his grin still in place. 'Do me a favour?' He passed over another sandwich-sized package in a brown paper bag. 'Drop that in to Zach on your way past.'

Izzy took the package with a forced smile. 'Will do.'

Zach looked up when the door opened. Izzy was standing there framed by the bright sunlight. She was wearing trousers and a cotton top today but she looked no less feminine. Her hair was in one of those up styles that somehow managed to look makeshift and elegant at the same time. There was a hint of gloss on her lips, making them look even more kissable. He wondered what flavour it was today. Strawberry? Or was it raspberry again?

'Jim sent me with your lunch.' She passed it over the counter, her cheeks going a light shade of pink. He'd never known a woman to blush so much. What was going on inside that pretty little head of hers? Was she thinking of that kiss? Had she spent the night feeling restless and edgy while her body had throbbed with unmet needs, like his had?

'Thanks.' He stood up and put the sandwich to one side. 'I was going to call you about my father.'

'Oh?' Her expression flickered with concern. 'Is he unwell?'

'He's running out of prescription painkillers.'

She chewed at her lip. 'I'd have to officially see him before I'd write a script. There can be contraindications with other medications and so on.'

'Of course. I'll see if I can get him to come to the clinic.'

She shifted her weight from foot to foot. 'I could always come out again to the homestead, if you think he'd allow it. I know what it's like to have something unexpected sprung on you. Maybe if you told him ahead of time that I was coming out, he would be more amenable to seeing me.'

'I'll see what I can do.'

The elephant in the room was stealing all the oxygen out of the air.

'What about coming out for dinner tomorrow?' Zach

could hardly believe he had spoken the words until he heard them drop into the ringing silence.

Her eyes widened a fraction. 'Dinner?'

'It won't be anything fancy. I'm not much of a chef but I can rub a couple of ingredients together.'

'What about your dad?'

'He has to eat.'

'I know, but will he agree to eat if I'm there?'

He shrugged, as if he didn't care either way. 'Let's give it a try, shall we?'

Her eyes went to the Steri-strip above his eyebrow. 'Would you like me to check that wound for you?'

Zach wanted her to check every inch of his body, preferably while both of them were naked. He had to blink away the erotic image that flashed through his brain at that thought—her limbs entangled with his, his body plunging into hers. 'It's fine.'

Her gaze narrowed as she peered at him over the bridge of the desk. 'It looks a little red around the edges.'

So do your cheeks, he thought. Her eyes were remarkably steady on his, but he had a feeling she was working hard at keeping them there. 'It's not infected. I'm keeping an eye on it.'

'Right…well, if you think it's not healing properly let me know.'

Zach couldn't figure if it was her in particular or the thought of having sex again that was making him so horny. He had tried his best to avoid thinking about sex for months. But now Izzy Courtney, with her toffee-brown eyes and soft, kissable mouth, was occupying his thoughts and he was in a constant start of arousal. He could feel it now, the pulse of his blood ticking through his veins. His heightened awareness of her sweet, fresh scent, the way his hands wanted to stroke down the length of her arms, to encircle her slim wrists, to tug her up against him so she could feel the weight and throb of his erection before his mouth closed over hers.

Her gaze flicked to his mouth, as if she had read his mind, the point of her tongue sneaking out to moisten her plump, soft lips. 'Um… What time do you want me to come?' Her cheeks went an even darker shade of red. 'Er…tonight. For dinner. To see your dad.'

'Seven or thereabouts?'

'Lovely.' She backed out of the reception area but somehow managed to bump her elbow against the door as she turned on her way out. She stepped out into the bright sunshine and walked briskly down the steps and out of sight.

Zach didn't sit down again until the fragrance of her had finally disappeared.

'What do you mean, you're going out?' Zach asked his father that evening.

His father gave him an offhand glance. 'I'm entitled to a social life, aren't I?'

'Of course.' Zach raked a distracted hand through his hair. 'But tonight of all nights? You haven't been out for months.'

'It's been a while since I caught up with Margie Green. She invited me for dinner.'

'She's been inviting you for dinner for years and you've always declined.'

'Then it's high time I said yes. You're always on about me not socialising enough. I enjoyed that run up to Bourke. It made me realise I need to have a change of scene now and again.'

Zach frowned. 'Isabella Courtney is going to think I've set this up. I asked her to come out to see you, not me.'

'She can think what she likes,' his father said. 'Anyway, I don't want to cramp your style.'

'But what about your painkillers?' Zach asked. 'You know what your rehab specialist said. You have to stay in front of the pain, not chase it.'

Doug chewed that over for a moment. 'I'll think about going to the clinic in a day or two.' A car horn tooted outside. 'That's Margie now.' He shuffled to the door on his frame. 'Don't wait up.'

Within a few minutes of his father leaving with Margie, Izzy arrived. Zach held open the door for her while Popeye danced around her like he had springs on his paws. 'My father's gone out. You probably passed him on the driveway.'

'Yes, Margie waved to me on the way past. I bet she's pleased he finally agreed to have dinner with her.' She picked Popeye up and cuddled him beneath her chin. 'Hello, sweetie pie.'

Zach was suddenly jealous of his dog, who was nestled against the gentle swell of Izzy's breasts. He gave himself a mental kick. He had to stop thinking of that kiss. It was becoming an obsession. 'Why's that?'

'I think she's been in love with him for years,' she said, and Popeye licked her face enthusiastically, as if in agreement.

'She's wasting her time,' Zach said. 'My father is still in love with my mother.'

She put the dog back down on the floor before she faced him. 'Do you really think so?'

He looked into her beautiful brown eyes, so warm

and soft, like melted caramel. The lashes like minia-ture fans. She seemed totally unaware of how beautiful she was. Unlike his ex, Naomi, who hadn't been able to walk past a mirror or a plate of glass without check-ing her reflection to check that her hair and make-up were perfect.

Another mental kick.

Harder this time.

'He's never looked at anyone else since.'

'Doesn't mean he still loves her. Some men have a lot of trouble with letting go of bitterness after a break-up.'

Zach coughed out a disparaging laugh. 'How long does he need? Isn't a couple of decades long enough?'

She gave a little lip-shrug. 'I guess some men are more stubborn than others.'

He wondered if she was having a little dig at his own stubbornness. He knew he should have found some-one else by now. Most men would have done. It wasn't that he wasn't ready... He just hadn't met anyone who made him feel like...well, like Izzy did. Hot. Bothered. Hungry.

At this rate he was going to knock himself uncon-scious with all those mental kicks. 'What would you like to drink? I have white wine, red wine or beer...or something soft?'

'A small glass of white wine would be lovely.' She handed him a small container she was carrying. 'Um...I made these. I thought your father might enjoy them.'

He opened the plastic container to find home-baked chocolate-chip cookies inside. The smell of sugar and chocolate was like ambrosia. 'His favourite.' *And mine.* He met her gaze again. 'How'd you guess?'

She gave him a wry smile. 'I don't know too many men who would turn their nose up at home baking.'

'The way to a man's heart and all that.'

She looked taken aback. 'I wasn't trying to—'

'He'll love you for it. Eventually.'

After he'd put the cookies aside he handed her a glass of wine. 'Have you had the hard word put on you about the Shearers' Ball yet?'

'Margie twisted my arm yesterday to sign up. You?'

'I swear every year I'm not going to go and somehow someone always manages to convince me to show up if I'm in town. I try to keep a low profile. I'm seen as the fun police even when I'm not in uniform.'

'I've never been to a bush dance before. Is it very hard to learn the steps?'

'No, there's a caller. That's usually Bill Davidson. He's been doing it for years. His father did it before him. You'll soon get the hang of it.'

'I hope so…'

He couldn't stop looking at her mouth, how softly curved it was, how it had felt beneath the firm pressure of his. Desire was already pumping through his body. Just looking at her was enough to set him off. She was dressed in one of her simple dresses, black, sleeveless and just over the knee, with nothing but the flash of a small diamond pendant around her neck. There were diamond studs in her ears and her hair was in a high ponytail that swished from side to side when she walked. She had put on the merest touch of make-up: a neutral shade of eyeshadow with a fine line of kohl pencilled on her eyelids and beneath her eyes, emphasising the dark thickness of her lashes.

Zach cleared his throat. It was time to get the elephant on its way. 'Look, about the other night when I—'

'It's fine.' She gave him another little twisted smile. 'Really. It was just a kiss.'

'I wouldn't want you to get the wrong idea about me.' He pushed a hand through his hair. 'Contrary to what you might think, I'm not the sort of guy to feel up a woman as soon as he gets her alone.'

Her gaze slipped away from his. 'It was probably my fault.'

He frowned down at her. 'How was it *your* fault? I made the first move.'

'I kissed you back.' She bit her lower lip momentarily. 'Rather enthusiastically, if I recall.'

He *did* recall.

He could recall every thrilling moment of that kiss.

The trouble was he wanted to repeat it. But a relationship with Izzy would be distracting, to say the least. He had to concentrate on getting his dad as independent as he could before he spared a thought to what *he* wanted. He hadn't been that good at balancing the demands of a relationship and work in the past. It would be even worse now with his dad's needs front and centre. He couldn't spread himself any thinner than he was already doing.

His ex had always been on at him to give more of himself but he hadn't felt comfortable with that level of emotional intimacy. He had loved Naomi…or at least he thought he had. Sometimes he wondered if he'd just loved being part of a couple. That was a large part of the reason he'd agreed to her moving in with him. Having someone there to share the sofa with while he zoned out the harrowing demands of the day in front of the television or over a meal he hadn't had to cook.

He sounded like a chauvinist, but after living alone with his dad for all those years he'd snapped up Naomi's willingness to take over the kitchen. Asking her to marry him had been the logical next step. Her refusal to move to the country with him after his father's accident had been not so much devastating as disappointing. He was disappointed in himself. Why had he thought she would follow him wherever life took him? She had her own career. It was unfair of him to demand her to drop everything and come with him. And living in the dry, dusty Outback on a sheep property with a partially disabled and disgruntled father-in-law was a big ask.

Zach blinked himself out of the past. 'Do you want to eat outside? There's a nice breeze coming in from the south. Dad and I often eat out there when a southerly is due.'

'Lovely. Can I help bring anything out?'

He handed her a pair of salad servers and a bottle of dressing.

Her fingers brushed against his as she took the bottle from him and a lightning-fast sensation went straight to his groin. He felt the stirring of his blood; the movement of primal instinctive flesh that wanted something he had denied it for too long.

Her eyes met his, wide, doe-like, the pupils enlarged. Her tongue—*the tongue he had intimately stroked and sucked and teased*—darted out over her lips in a nervous sweeping action. He caught a whiff of her fragrance, wisteria this time instead of gardenias, but just as alluring.

But then the moment passed.

She seemed to mentally gather herself, and with another one of those short on-off smiles she turned in the direction of the veranda, her ponytail swinging behind her.

Zach looked down at Popeye, who was looking up at him with a quizzical expression in those black button eyes. 'Easy for you. You've had the chop. I have to suffer the hard way. No pun intended.'

CHAPTER SEVEN

IZZY PUT THE salad servers and the dressing on the glass-topped white cane table then turned and looked at the view from the veranda. The paddocks stretched far into the distance where she could see a line of trees where the creek snaked in a sinuous curve along the boundary of the property. The air was warm with that hint of eucalyptus she was coming to love. It was such a distinctive smell, sharp and cleansing. The setting sun had painted the sky a dusky pink, signalling another fine day for tomorrow, and a flock of kookaburras sounded in the trees by the creek, their raucous call fracturing the still evening air like the laughter of a gang of madmen.

She turned when she heard the firm tread of Zach's footsteps on the floorboards of the veranda. Popeye was following faithfully, his bright little eyes twinkling in the twilight. Zach looked utterly gorgeous dressed casually in blue denim jeans and a light blue cotton shirt that was rolled up to his forearms. The colour of his shirt intensified the blue rim in his grey eyes and the deep tan of his skin.

Her stomach gave a little flutter when he sent her a quick smile. He was so devastatingly attractive when he lost that grim look. The line of his jaw was still firm, he was too masculine for it ever to be described as anything but determined, but his mouth was sensual and sensitive rather than severe, as she had earlier thought.

Her mouth tingled in memory of how those lips had felt against hers. She remembered every moment of that heart-stopping kiss. It was imprinted on her memory like an indelible brand. She wondered if she would spend the rest of her life recalling it, measuring any subsequent kisses by its standard.

He had deftly changed the subject when she had stumblingly tried to explain her actions of the other night. He had given an apology of sorts for kissing her, but he hadn't said he wasn't going to do it again. She was not by any means a vain person but she was woman enough to know when a man showed an interest in her. He might be able to keep his expression masked and his emotions under lock and key but she had still sensed it.

She had *felt* it in his touch.

She had *tasted* it in his kiss.

She sensed it now as he handed her the glass of wine she had left behind. His eyes held hers for a little longer than they needed to, something passing in the exchange that was unspoken but no less real. She tried to avoid touching his fingers this time. It was increasingly difficult to disguise the way she reacted to him. Would any other man stir her senses quite the way he did? Her body seemed to have a mind of its own when he came near. It was like stepping inside the pull of a powerful magnet. She felt the tug in her flesh, the entire surface of her skin stretching, swelling to get closer to him.

'Thanks.' She took a careful sip of wine. 'Mmm... lovely. Is that a local one?'

He showed her the label. 'It's from a boutique vineyard a couple of hundred kilometres away. I went to boarding school with the guy who owns it.'

'How old were you when you went to boarding school?'

'Eleven.' He swirled the wine in his glass, watching as it splashed around the sides with an almost fierce concentration. 'It was the year after my mother left.' He raised the glass and took a mouthful, the strong column of his throat moving as he swallowed deeply.

'Were you dreadfully homesick?'

He glanced at her briefly before looking back out over the paddocks that were bathed in a pinkish hue instead of their tired brown. 'Not for long.'

Izzy suspected he had taught himself not to feel anything rather than suffer the pain of separation. Homesickness—like love—would be another emotion he had barred from his repertoire. His iron-strong reserve had come about the hard way—a lifetime of suppressing feelings he didn't want to own. She pictured him as an eleven-year-old, probably tall for his age, broad shouldered, whipcord lean and tanned, and yet inside just a little boy who had desperately missed his mother.

She pushed herself away from the veranda rail where she had been leaning her hip. 'I went to boarding school when I was eight. I cried buckets.'

'Eight is very young.' His voice had a gravelly sound to it and his gaze looked serious and concerned, as if he too was picturing her as a child—that small, inconsolable little pigtailed girl with her collection of Barbie dolls in a little pink suitcase.

'Yes…but somehow I got through it. I haven't got any sisters so the company of the other girls was a bonus.' *Or it was when I met Hannah.*

'Any brothers?'

Izzy felt that painful stab to her heart again. It didn't matter how many years went past, it was always the same. She found the question so confronting. It was like asking a first-time mother who had just lost her baby if she was still a mother. 'Not any more...' She swallowed to clear the lump in her throat. 'My brother Jamie died five years ago of sarcoma. He was diagnosed when he was fourteen. He was in remission for twelve years and then it came back.'

'I'm sorry.' The deep gravitas in his voice was strangely soothing.

'He wasn't diagnosed early enough.' She gripped the rails of the veranda so tightly the wood creaked beneath her hands. 'He would've had a better chance if he'd gone to a doctor earlier but he was at boarding school and didn't tell anyone about his symptoms until he came home for the holidays.' She loosened her grip and turned back to look at him. 'I think that's what tortures me most. The thought that he might've been saved.'

His eyes held hers in a silent hold that communicated a depth of understanding she hadn't thought him capable of on first meeting him. His quiet calm was a counterpoint to her inner rage at the cruel punch the fist of fate had given to her family and from which they had never recovered.

'Are your parents still together?'

'Yes, but they probably shouldn't be.' Izzy saw the slight questioning lift of his brow and continued. 'My father's had numerous affairs over the years. Even before Jamie's death. In fact, I think it started soon after Jamie was diagnosed. Mum's always clung to her comfortable life and would never do or say anything to jeopardise it, which is probably why she doesn't understand why I ended things with Richard.'

'Why *did* you break it off with him?'

Izzy looked into his blue-rimmed eyes and wondered if he was one of that increasingly rare breed of men who would take his marriage vows seriously, remaining faithful, loyal and devoted over a lifetime. 'I know this probably sounds ridiculously idealistic, romantic even, but I've always wanted to feel the sort of love that stops you in your tracks. The sort that won't go stale or become boring. The sort of love you just know is your one and only chance at happiness. The sort of love you would give everything up for. I didn't feel that for Richard. It wasn't fair to him to go on any longer pretending I did.'

His top lip lifted in a cynical manner. 'So in amongst all those medical textbooks and journals you've managed to sneak in a few romance novels, have you?'

Izzy could have chosen to be offended by his mockery but instead she gave a guilty laugh. 'One or two.' She toyed with the stem of her glass. 'My friend Hannah thinks I'm a bit of a romance tragic.'

'What did she send you in that package? A stack of sentimental books?'

'If only.' She laughed again to cover her embarrassment. Just as well it was dark enough for him not to see her blush.

'What, then?'

'*Please* don't make me tell you.'

'Come on.' His smile was back and it was just as spine-melting as before. 'You've really got my attention now.'

And you've got mine. 'Promise not to laugh?'

'Promise.'

She let out a breath in a rush. 'A blow-up doll. A male one. I've called him Max.'

He threw his head back and laughed. He had a nice-sounding laugh, rich and deep and genuine, not booming and raucous like Richard's when he'd had one too many red wines.

Izzy gave him a mock glare. 'You promised not to laugh!'

'Sorry.' He didn't look sorry. His lips were still twitching and his eyes twinkled with amusement.

'Hannah thought a stand-in boyfriend would stop me from being lonely. I think I already told you she has a weird sense of humour.'

'Are you going to take him with you when you move on?'

'I'm not sure the Sawyers will appreciate him as part of the furniture.'

'Where do you head after here?' The question was casual. Polite interest. Nothing more.

'Brisbane,' Izzy said. 'I've got a job lined up in a busy GP clinic. After that I have a stint in Darwin. The locum agency is pretty flexible. There's always somewhere needing a doctor, especially out in the bush. That's why I took this post. The guy they had lined up had to pull out at the last minute due to a family crisis. I was happy to step in. I'm enjoying it. Everyone's been lovely.'

Zach absently rubbed the toe of his booted foot against one of the uneven floorboards. 'Everyone, apart from my father.'

'I haven't given up on him.'

The silence hummed as their gazes meshed again.

Izzy's breath hitched on something, like a silk sleeve catching on a prickly bush. She moistened her lips as his gaze lowered to her mouth, her stomach feeling as if a tiny fist had reached through her clothes and clutched at her insides.

Male to female attraction was almost palpable in the air. She could feel it moving through the atmosphere like sonic waves. It spoke to her flesh, calling all the pores of her skin to lift up in a soft carpet of goosebumps, each hair on her head to stand up and tingle at the roots. A hot wire fizzed in her core, sparking a wave of restless energy unlike anything she had ever felt before. It moved through her body, making her as aware of her erogenous zones as if he had reached out and kissed and caressed each one in turn. Her neck, just below her ears, her décolletage, her breasts, the base of her spine, the backs of her knees, her inner thighs…

His eyes moved from her gaze to her mouth and back again. He seemed to be fighting an internal battle. She could see it being played out on his tightly composed features. Temptation and common sense were waging a war and it seemed he hadn't yet decided whose team he was going to side with.

'Are you still in love with your ex?' It was a question Izzy couldn't stop herself asking. Was a little shocked she had.

The night orchestra beyond the veranda filled the silence for several bars. The percussion section of insects. A chorus of frogs. A lonely solo from a stone curlew.

Izzy found herself holding her breath, hoping he wasn't still in love with his ex-fiancée. Why? She couldn't answer. Didn't want to answer. Wasn't ready to answer.

'No.' The word was final. Decisive. It was as if a line had been drawn in his head and he wasn't going back over it.

'But you were hurt when she ended things?'

He gave her a look she couldn't quite read. 'How did your ex take it when you broke things off?'

'Remarkably well.'

One of his brows lifted. 'Oh?'

'He found a replacement within a matter of days.' Izzy looked at the contents of her glass rather than meet his gaze. 'Don't get me wrong...I didn't want him to be inconsolable or anything, but it was a slap in the face when he found someone so completely the opposite of me and so quickly.'

'Why did you accept his proposal in the first place?' Was that a hint of censure in his tone?

Izzy thought back to the elaborate proposal Richard had set up. A very public proposal that had made her feel hemmed in and claustrophobic. She hadn't had the courage to turn him down and make him lose face in front of all of her friends and colleagues. The banner across the front of the hospital with *Will You Marry Me, Izzy?* emblazoned on it had come has a complete and utter shock to her on arriving at work. She could still see Richard down on bended knee, with the Remington heirloom engagement ring taken out of his family's bank vault especially for the occasion, his face beaming with pride and enthusiasm.

No had been on her tongue but hadn't made it past her embarrassed smile. She'd told herself it was the right thing to do. They'd known each other for years. They'd drifted into casual dating and then into a physical relationship. He had been one of Jamie's close friends and had stuck by him during every gruelling bout of chemo. Her parents adored him. He was part of the family. It was her way of staying connected with her lost brother. 'Lots of reasons.'

'But not love.'

'No.' Izzy let out a breath that felt like she had been holding it inside her chest for years. 'That's why I came out here, as far away from home as possible. I want to know who I am without Richard or my parents telling me what to do and how and when I should do it. My parents have expectations for me. I guess all parents do, but I've got my own life to live. They thought I was wasting my time going to medical school when I have enough money behind me to never have to work. But I want to make a difference in people's lives. I want to be the one who saves someone's brother for them, you know?'

Zach's gaze was steady on hers, his voice low and husky. 'I do know.'

Izzy bit her lip. Had she told him too much? Revealed too much? She put her glass down. 'Sorry. Two sips of wine and I'm spilling all my secret desires.' She gave a mental cringe at her choice of words. 'Maybe I should just leave before I embarrass you as well as myself.'

Zach blocked her escape by placing a hand on her arm. 'What do you think would happen if we followed through on this?'

Her skin sizzled where his hand lay on her arm. She could feel the graze of the rough callus on his fingers, reminding her he was a man in every sense of the word. 'Um…I'm not sure what you mean. Follow through on what?'

His eyes searched hers for a lengthy moment. 'So that's the way you're going to play it. Ignore it. Pretend it's not there.' He gave a little laugh that sounded very deep and very sexy. 'That could work.'

Izzy pressed her lips together, trying to summon up some willpower. Where had it gone? Had she left it behind in England? It certainly wasn't here with her now. 'I think it's for the best, don't you?'

'You reckon you've got what it takes to unlock this banged-up cynical heart of mine, Dr Courtney?' He was mocking her again. She could see it in the way the corner of his mouth was tilted and his eyes glinted at her in the darkness.

She gave him a pert look to disguise how tempted she was to take him on. 'I'm guessing I'd need a lot more than a month, that is if I could be bothered, which I can't.'

He brushed an idle fingertip underneath the base of her upraised chin. 'I would like nothing better right now than to take you inside and show you a good time.'

Izzy suppressed the shiver of longing his light touch evoked. 'What makes you think I'd be interested?'

His gaze moved between each of her eyes. 'Have you slept with anyone since your fiancé?'

'No, but I hardly see how that's got anything to do with anything.'

His fingertip moved like a feather over her lower lip. 'Might explain the fireworks the other night.'

'Just because I got a little excited about a kiss doesn't mean I'm going to jump into bed with you any time soon.' She knew she sounded a little schoolmarmish but she desperately wanted to hide how attracted she was to him. She had never felt such an intensely physical reaction to a man before. His very presence made every nerve in her body pull tight with anticipation.

His tall, firm body was not quite touching hers but was close enough for her to feel the warmth that emanated from him. He planted a hand on the veranda post just above the left side of her head. 'Thing is…' his eyes went to her mouth again '…everyone already thinks I'm doing you.'

A wave of heat coursed through her lower body as his eyes came back to burn into hers. The thought of him 'doing' her made her insides contort with lust. She could picture it in her mind, his body so much bigger and more powerfully made than her ex-fiancé's. Somehow she knew there would be nothing predictable or formulaic about any such encounter. She wouldn't be staring at the ceiling, counting the whorls on the ceiling rose to pass the time. It would be mind-blowing pleasure from start to finish.

'It's just gossip… I'm sure it'll go away once they see there's no truth in it…' If only she could get her voice to sound firm and full of conviction instead of that breathy, phone-sex voice that seemed to be coming out.

'Maybe.'

She saw his nostrils flare as he took in the fragrance of her perfume. She could smell his lemon-based aftershave and his own warm, male smell that was equally intoxicating. She could see the shadow of stubble that peppered his jaw and around his nose and mouth and remembered with another clench of lust how it had felt so sexily abrasive against her skin when he'd kissed her.

A wick of something dangerous lit his gaze. 'Ever had a one-night stand before?'

'No.' She swept her tongue over her lips. 'You?'

'Couple of times.'

'Before or after your fiancée?'

'Before.'

Izzy couldn't drag her gaze away from his mouth. She remembered how it had tasted. How it had felt. The way his firm lips had softened and hardened in turn. The way his tongue had seduced hers. Bewitching her. Giving her a hint of the thorough possession he would take of her if she allowed him. 'So...no one since?' She couldn't believe she was asking such personal questions. It was so unlike her.

'No.' He took a wisp of her hair and curled it around one of his fingers, triggering a sensual tug in her inner core. 'We could do it and get it over with. Defuse the bomb, so to speak.'

She moistened her lips again. She could feel herself wavering on a threshold she had never encountered before. Temptation lured her like a moth towards a light that would surely scorch and destroy. 'You're very confident of yourself, aren't you?'

His gaze had a satirical light as it tussled with hers. 'I recognise lust when I see it.'

Izzy felt the lust she was trying to hide crawl all over her skin, leaving it hot and flushed. She took an uneven breath, shocked at how much she wanted him. It was an ache that throbbed in her womb, prickling and swelling the flesh of her breasts until they felt twice their normal size. 'I'm not the sort of girl who jumps into bed with virtual strangers.' *Even if he was the most attractive and intriguing man she had ever met.*

His eyes held hers for a semitone of silence. 'You know my name. Where I live. What I do for a living. You've even met my father. That hardly makes me a stranger.'

'I don't know your values.'

His mouth kicked up wryly in one corner. 'I'm a cop. Can't get more value-driven than that.'

Izzy gave him an arch look. 'I've met some pretty nasty wolves in cops' clothing in my time.'

His hand was still pressed against the post of the veranda, his strongly muscled arm close enough for her cheek to feel its warmth. His warm breath with its hint of summer wine caressed her face as he spoke in that low, deep, gravel-rough voice. 'I only bat for the good guys.'

Izzy could feel herself melting. Her muscles softened, her ligaments loosened, her hands somehow came up to rest against the hard wall of his chest. His pectoral muscles flinched under the soft press of her palms as if he found her as electrifying as she found him. His eyes were locked on hers, a question burning in their grey-blue depths. An invitation. 'I don't normally do this sort of thing...' Her voice was not her own. It was barely a whisper of sound, and yet it was full of unspoken longing.

His eyes lowered to gaze at her mouth. 'Kiss men you hardly know?'

She looked at his mouth, her belly shifting like a foot stepping on a floating plank. He had a beautiful mouth, sensual and neatly sculpted, the lips neither too thick nor too thin. 'Is that all we're doing? Kissing?'

His gaze became sexily hooded. 'Let's start with that and see where it takes us.'

CHAPTER EIGHT

HIS MOUTH CAME down and covered hers in a kiss that tasted of wine and carefully controlled need. It was a slow kiss, with none of the hot urgency of the other night. This one was more languid, leisurely, a slow but thorough exploration of her mouth that made her pulse skyrocket all the same.

Her heart beat like a drum against her ribcage, her hands moving up his chest to link around his neck. He was much taller than her, so that she had to lift up on her toes, bringing her pelvis into intimate contact with his. The pressure of his kiss intensified, his tongue driving through the seam of her mouth in a commanding search of hers. She felt its sexy rasp, the erotic glide and thrusts that so brazenly imitated the act of human mating. Carnal needs surged like a wild beast in her blood; she felt them do the same in his. The throbbing pulse of his erection pounded against her belly; so thick, so strong, so arrantly male it made her desire race out of her control like a rabid dog slipping its leash.

She pressed herself closer, loving the feel of his chest against her breasts, the way the cotton of his shirt smelt, so clean and laundry fresh with that sexy understory of male body heat.

His tongue played with hers, light and teasing and playful at first, determined and purposeful the next. He drew her closer with a firm, warm hand in the small of her back, the other hand skimming over her right breast, the touch light but devastatingly arousing. Izzy liked it that he hadn't made a grab for her, squeezing too tightly or baring her flesh too quickly. His fainéant touch caused a sensual riot in her body, making her ache to feel his calloused palm on her soft skin. She made a murmur of assent against his mouth, reaching for his hand and bringing it back to the swell of her breast. He cupped her through her clothes; his large palm should have made her feel inadequately small but never had she felt more feminine.

His mouth moved down from hers, along the line of her jaw, lingering at the base of her ear where every sensitive nerve shrieked in delight as his tongue laved her flesh. 'You like that?' His voice came from deep within him, throaty, husky.

She sighed with pleasure. 'Hate it.'

He gave a little rumble of laughter as his lips moved to her collarbone. 'Let's see how much you hate this, then.' His hand released the zipper on the back of her dress just enough to uncover one of her shoulders. The feel of his lips and tongue on the cap of her shoulder made her spine soften like candlewax. For a man who hadn't had sex in a while he certainly hadn't lost his touch. Izzy had never been subjected to such a potent assault on her senses. Her body was a tingling matrix of over stimulated nerves, each one screaming out for assuagement.

He moved from her shoulder to the upper curve of her breast showing above her lowered dress. His lips left a quicksilver trail of fire over her flesh, causing her to whimper as the need tightened and pulled inside her.

He tugged her dress a little lower, not bothering to unclip her bra; he simply moved it out of his way and closed his mouth over her tightly budded nipple. The moist warmth of his mouth, the graze of his teeth and the salve of his tongue as he nipped and licked and sucked her in turn made her shudder with pleasure.

Izzy splayed her fingers through the thickness of his hair, holding him to her, prolonging the delicious sensations for as long as she could. His hand on the small of her back moved around her body to possess her hip. It was a strong alpha type of hold that thrilled her senses into overload. Her inner core moistened as he brought her hard against him.

He left her breast to lick the scaffold of her collarbone in one sexy sweep of his tongue. 'We should stop.'

'W-we should?' Izzy had to remind her good girl to get back inside her head and her body. 'Yes. Right. Of course we should.' She pulled her dress back up over her shoulder but she couldn't quite manage the zip with her fumbling fingers.

He turned her so her back was towards him, his fingers an electric shock against her skin as he dragged the zipper back up. His body brushed hers from behind, his hands coming to rest on the tops of her shoulders as if he couldn't quite bring himself to release her just yet. The temptation to lean back against his arousal, to feel him probe her in that sinfully erotic fashion was overwhelming. Just the thought of him there, so close, so thick and turgid with want, was enough to make her flesh hot all over.

'Um…you can let me go now.' Her voice was still that whisper-soft thread of sound.

His hands tightened for the briefest of moments before they fell away. He stepped back, the floorboards of the veranda creaking in protest as if they too felt her disappointment. 'You want a top-up of your drink before dinner?'

Izzy couldn't believe how even his tone was, so cool and calm and collected as if his senses hadn't been subjected to the biggest shake-up of all time. 'I'd better not. What I've had so far seems to have gone straight to my head.'

Even though most of his face was in shadow she caught a glimpse of a half-smile before he turned and went back to the kitchen to see to their meal.

Izzy looked at Popeye, who was looking up at her with bright button eyes. 'Don't look at me like that. I wasn't going to do it. I'm not a one-night stand sort of girl.'

Popeye barked and then jumped off the cane chair and trotted after his master.

Zach planted his hands on the kitchen bench and drew in a long, slow breath to steady himself. It had been a long time since he had let hot-blooded passion overrule common sense. That was the stuff of teenage hormones, not of a thirty-three-year-old man who had responsibilities and priorities.

But, damn it, Izzy Courtney was tempting. His body was thrumming with need, his mouth still savouring the sweetness of hers. Was he asking for trouble to indulge in a fling with her while she was here? It wasn't as if either of them would be making any promises.

She had an end point in sight. She had plans. Commitments elsewhere. He had responsibilities he couldn't leave. Wouldn't leave.

The trouble was he liked her. Not just sexual attraction. He actually *liked* her. She was intelligent, hard-working, committed to serving the community. Everyone was talking about how well she was fitting in. He hadn't heard a bad said word about her.

Zach heard the sound of a mobile phone ringing. He glanced at his phone lying on the bench but the screen was dark. He wasn't on duty tonight, Rob Heywood was.

Izzy came in from the veranda with an apologetic look on her face. 'I'm sorry, Zach. I have to leave. Caitlin Graham's little girl Skylar has fallen off a bed while playing with her older brothers and cut her forehead. It might not be much but with little kids you can never be sure. I'm going to meet them at the clinic.'

Zach snatched up his keys. 'I'll drive down with you.'

'But I've only had a couple of sips of wine.'

'It's not that. We can take both cars.' He turned off the oven on his way past. 'Caitlyn's new boyfriend, Wayne Brody, is a bit of a hot head, especially if he's been drinking.'

Izzy's eyes widened. 'Are you saying Skylar might not have fallen out of bed?'

Zach kept his expression cop neutral. 'Best we take a look at the evidence first.'

Zach and Izzy arrived at the clinic just as a young woman in her early to mid-twenties was getting out of a car that looked like it could do with a makeover. But then, Caitlyn Graham looked the same. Her skin was weathered by a combination of harsh sun and years of smoking, the tell-tale stain of nicotine on her fingers mirroring the rust on her car, her mouth downturned at the edges as if there wasn't much in her life to smile about. There was no sign of the boyfriend Zach had mentioned, which made Izzy wonder if what he had alluded to had any grounds in truth. Caitlyn carried a whimpering two-year-old girl in her arms and two little boys of about five and seven trailed in her wake, the younger one sucking his thumb, the older one carrying a toy dinosaur.

'I'm sorry to drag you out but I think she needs stitches,' Caitlin said, hitching her daughter to her other bony hip as she took the five-year-old's hand. The little girl buried her head against her mother's thin chest and gave another mewling cry.

'Let's go inside and take a look.' Izzy smiled at the boys. 'Hi, guys. Wow, that's a nice triceratops.'

The seven-year-old gave her a scornful look from beneath long spider leg eyelashes. 'It's a stegosaurus.'

'Oh, right. My mistake.' Izzy caught Zach's glinting glance as she led the way into the clinic.

On examination little Skylar had a gash on her forehead that had stopped bleeding due to the compress her mother had placed on it but still needed a couple of stitches to ensure it healed neatly. There were no other injuries that she could see and the child otherwise seemed in good health.

'I'll put some anaesthetic cream on her forehead before I inject some local,' Izzy said to Caitlyn. 'It'll still sting a bit but hopefully not too much.'

Once the stitches were in place, Izzy handed the little tot a choice of the lollipops she kept in a jar on her desk. 'What a brave little girl you've been.'

The little girl chose a red one and silently handed it to her mother to take the cellophane wrapping off.

'Can I have one too?' the five-year-old, called Eli, asked around his thumb.

'Of course. Here you go.' Izzy then passed the jar to the seven-year-old with the stegosaurus. The boy hesitated before finally burying his hand in the jar and taking out two lollipops.

'Only one, Jobe,' Caitlyn said.

The boy gave his mother a defiant look. 'I'm taking one for Dad.'

Caitlyn's lips tightened. 'It'll be stale before you see him again.'

Izzy watched as Jobe's dark eyes hardened. It was a little shocking to see such a young child exhibiting such depth of emotion. Not childlike emotion but emotion well beyond his years. 'I'd like to see Skylar in a couple of days to check those stitches,' she said to defuse the tense atmosphere. 'If it's tricky getting into town, I can always make a house call.'

'I can get here no trouble.'

Was it her imagination or had Caitlin been a little bit too insistent? Izzy shook off the thought. Zach's comments earlier had made her unnecessarily biased. Not every stepfather was a child abuser. Jobe was a tense child but that was probably because he missed his biological father, who apparently was no longer on the scene. 'Let's make an appointment now.' She reached for the computer mouse to bring up the clinic's electronic diary.

'I'll call Margie tomorrow,' Caitlin said. 'I'd better get back. My partner will wonder what's happened.'

'You can use the phone here if you like.'

Caitlyn was already at the door. 'Come on, boys. It's way past your bedtime.'

Jobe was looking at Zach with an intense look on his face. 'Do you always carry a gun?'

'Not always,' Zach said. 'Only when I'm on duty.'

'Are you on duty now?'

'No. Sergeant Heywood is.'

'What if a bad guy came to your house? Would you be allowed to shoot him if you're not on duty?'

Caitlyn came back over and grabbed Jobe by the back of his T-shirt. 'Come on. Sergeant Fletcher's got better things to do than answer your dumb questions.'

The little boy shrugged off his mother's hand and scowled. 'They're not dumb.'

'Don't answer back or I'll give you a clip across the ear.'

Zach crouched down to Jobe's level. 'Maybe you and your brother could drop into the station one day and have a look around. I can show you how the radio works and other cool stuff.' He glanced up at Caitlyn. 'That all right with you?'

Caitlyn's mouth was so tight her lips were white. 'Sure. Whatever.'

Izzy chewed at her lower lip as she began to tidy up the treatment area. Zach came back in from seeing the young family out to the car. She turned and looked at him. 'Cute kids.'

He was frowning in a distracted manner. 'Yeah.'

'You think she would hit Jobe or the other two?'

'A lot of parents do. It's called discipline.'

'There are much better ways to discipline a child than to hit them,' Izzy said. 'How can you teach a child not to hit others if you're hitting them yourself?'

'You're preaching to the choir,' he said. 'I don't agree with it either but some parents insist it's their right to use corporal punishment.'

'I didn't notice any bruises or marks on the little one but Jobe seems a very tense little boy. He doesn't seem to have a close relationship with his mother, does he?'

'He misses his dad.'

'Where is he?'

He shrugged. 'Who knows? Probably shacked up with some other woman with another brood of kids by now.'

Izzy washed her hands at the sink and then tore off a paper towel to dry them. 'Beats me why some people have kids if they're just going to abandon them when the going gets tough.'

'Tell me about it.'

She looked at him again. 'Did your mother remarry?'

'Yes. Got a couple of sons. They take up a lot of her time.'

'I'm sorry...I shouldn't have asked.'

'It was a long time ago.'

She put the used paper towel in the pedal bin. 'Do you want kids?' *Where on earth had that question come from?* 'Sorry.' She bit her lip again. 'None of my business.'

'I do, actually.' He picked up a drug company's promotional paperweight off her desk and smoothed his right thumb over its surface. 'Not right now, though.

Maybe in a couple of years or so. I have to get a few things straightened out first.'

'Your father?'

He put the paperweight down and met her gaze. 'It's a good sign he went out tonight.'

'Yes, I agree. Social isolation isn't good for someone suffering depression.'

There was a little silence.

'What about you?' he asked. 'Do you want kids or is your career your top priority?'

'I would hate to miss out on having a family. I love my career but I really want to be a mum one day.'

It was hard to tell if her answer met with his approval or not. He had his cop face on again. 'Caitlyn Graham had Jobe when she was fifteen. She was a kid with a kid.'

'It looks like she's had it tough,' Izzy said. 'Do all three kids have the same father?'

'No, Eli and Skylar are another guy's. A drifter who came into town for a couple of years before moving on again.'

'Does Caitlyn have any extended family to support her?'

'Her mother comes to visit from Nyngan now and again but she never stays long.' His mouth took on a cynical line. 'Just long enough to have a fight with Caitlyn's new boyfriend.'

'He doesn't sound like a good role model for the boys,' Izzy said.

He gave her a grim look. 'He's not. He's been inside for assault and possession and supply of illegal drugs. He's only just come off parole. Reckon it won't be long before he ends up back behind bars.'

'Once a criminal, always a criminal?'

'In my experience, most of the leopards I've met like to hang onto their spots.'

'Don't you think people can change if they're given some direction and support?' Izzy asked.

'Maybe some.'

She picked up her bag and hitched it over her shoulder. 'Were you always this cynical or has your job made you that way?'

He held the door open for her. 'I'll tell you over dinner.'

'You still want me to—?'

His look was unreadable. 'You're still hungry, aren't you?'

Izzy had a feeling he wasn't just talking about food. 'It's getting late. Maybe I should just head home. Your dad will be back soon in any case.'

'If that's what you want.' He sounded as if he didn't care either way.

It wasn't what she wanted but she wasn't quite ready to admit it. She wasn't sure how to handle someone as deep and complicated as Zach Fletcher. He was strong and principled, almost to the point of being conservative, which, funnily enough, resonated with her own homespun values. But she was only here for another three weeks. It wouldn't be fair to start something she had no intention of finishing. 'Thanks for coming down with me to see to little Skylar.'

'You'd better get Margie to give Caitlyn a call tomorrow. She's not good at following through on stuff.'

'Yes, I gathered that.'

Once she had locked the clinic and set the alarm, Zach walked her to her car. He waited until she was inside the car with her seat belt pulled down and clipped into place.

'Thanks again.'

He tapped the roof of her car with his hand. 'Drive safely.'

'Zach?'

He stopped and turned back to look at her. 'Yes?'

'Maybe I could cook dinner for you some time...to make up for tonight?'

He gave her the briefest of smiles. 'I'll get working on my appetite.'

CHAPTER NINE

'How did your evening go with Doug Fletcher?' Izzy asked Margie the next morning at the clinic.

'I was about to ask you the same question about yours with Zach.'

'It got cut short. I got called out to Caitlyn Graham's little daughter, who'd cut her forehead,' Izzy said. 'Can you call her to make a follow-up appointment? I'd like to see Skylar on Thursday. And can you check to see whether all three kids are up to date on their vaccinations?'

'Will do. Did Caitlyn's boyfriend come with her?'

'No, but Zach warned me about him. He came with me to the clinic.'

Margie's brows lifted. 'Did he, now?'

Izzy felt a blush creep over her cheeks. 'He's a bit of a stickler for safety.'

'Wayne Brody is a ticking time bomb,' Margie said. 'Wouldn't take much to set him off. Zach's got a good nose for sensing trouble.'

'Why would Caitlyn hook up with someone so unsavoury? There must be some other much nicer young man out here.'

Margie shrugged. 'Some girls would rather be with

anybody rather than nobody. Her mother's the same. Hooked up with one deadbeat after the other. I don't think Caitlyn has ever met her biological father. I'm not sure her mother even knows who it is. Caitlyn had one stepfather after the other. Now she's doing the same to her kids. It's a cycle that goes on one generation after another. It's a case of monkey see, monkey do.'

'Are there any playgroups or activities for young mums like her around here?' Izzy asked.

'Peggy McLeod tried to set one up a few years back but her arthritis set in and she had to give it up. No one's bothered to do anything since.'

'The community centre…do you think I could book it for one morning this week?' Izzy asked. 'I could re-arrange my clinic hours. I could get some toys donated or buy them myself if I have to. It'd be a place for the mums and kids to hang out and chat and play.'

'Sounds good, but who's going to take over when your time with us is up?'

'I could get one of the mums to take charge,' Izzy said. 'It might be a chance to get Caitlyn engaged in something that would build her self-esteem.'

Margie gave a snort. 'There's nothing wrong with that girl's self-esteem. It's her taste in men that's the problem.'

'But that's exactly my point,' Izzy said. 'She thinks so badly of herself that she settles for the first person who shows an interest in her. There's a saying I heard once. You get the partner in life you think you deserve.'

Margie gave her a twinkling look. 'And who do you think you deserve?'

Izzy felt that betraying blush sneak back into her

cheeks. 'Did you manage to convince Doug to book in for a check-up?'

Margie's twinkle dulled like a cloud passing over the sun. 'I'm working on it.'

'Are you going to see him again?'

'I'm working on that too,' Margie said. 'I mentioned the Shearers' Ball but he was pretty adamant he wasn't going to go.'

'I guess it's pretty hard to dance when you're on a walking frame.'

'It's not about the dancing.' Margie's eyes suddenly watered up. 'I couldn't give a toss about the dancing. I just want to be with him. I've waited so long for him but he's got this stupid idea in his head that no one could ever want him the way he is now.'

Izzy gave Margie's shoulder a gentle squeeze. 'I hope it works out for you and him. I really do.'

Margie popped a tissue out of the box on the reception counter and blew her nose. She tossed the tissue in the bin under the desk and assembled her features back into brisk receptionist mode. 'Silly fool. A woman of my age fancying herself in love. Phhfft. Ridiculous.'

'It's not ridiculous,' Izzy said. 'Falling in love isn't something you can control. It just happens—' she caught Margie's look '—or so I'm told,' she added quickly. She took the file for her first patient of the day from the counter as the front door of the clinic opened. 'Mrs Honeywell? Come this way.'

Zach was leaving the station a couple of days later when he saw Izzy coming out of the clinic and walking towards her car. It had been a brute of a day, hot and dry with a northerly wind that was gritty and relentless.

He could think of nothing better than a cool beer and a swim out at Blake's waterhole... Actually, he could think of something way better than that. Izzy Courtney lying naked underneath him while he—

She suddenly turned and looked at him as if she had felt his gaze on her. Or read his X-rated thoughts. 'Oh...hello.' She gave him a smile that looked beaten up around the edges.

'You look like you've had a tough day.'

Her mouth twisted as she scraped a few tendrils of sticky hair back behind her ear. 'Caitlyn didn't show up for Skylar's check-up. Margie confirmed it with her but she didn't come. I called her on the phone to offer to go out there but there was no answer.' She blew out a little breath of frustration. 'I can't force her to bring the child in. And I don't want to turn up at her house as if I'm suspicious of her.'

'I've got a couple of things for Jobe and Eli,' Zach said. 'Stuff I had when I was a kid. I found them in a cupboard in one of the spare rooms at home. We can drop them round now just to see if everything's OK. Better take your car, though. Might not get such a warm welcome, turning up in mine.'

Her caramel-brown eyes brightened. 'That was thoughtful of you. What sort of things? Toys?'

Zach found himself trying to disguise a sheepish look. 'I went through a dinosaur stage when I was about seven or eight. Got a bit obsessive there for a bit.'

She gave him a smile that loosened some of the tight barbed wire wrapped around his heart. 'So you can tell a stegosaurus from a triceratops?'

'Any fool can do that.'

She pursed her lips and then must have realised he

was teasing her for her sunny smile broke free again. 'You're a nice man, Sergeant Fletcher. I think I'm starting to like you after all.'

The house Caitlyn Graham was living in was on the outskirts of Jerringa Ridge. It was a stockman's cottage from the old days that looked like it hadn't had much done to it since. The rusty gate was hanging on one hinge and the once white but now grey picket fence had so many gaps it looked like a rotten-toothed smile. A dog of mixed breeding was chained near the tank stand and let out a volley of ferocious barking as Izzy pulled her car up in front of the house. 'Can he get off, do you think?' she asked, casting Zach a worried glance.

'I'll keep an eye on him.'

'Poor dog tied up like that in this heat.' She turned off the engine and unclipped her belt. 'Is anyone around? There's no car about that I can see.'

'Stay in the car and I'll have a mosey around.' Zach got out and closed the door with a snick. The dog put its ears back and brought its body low to the ground as it snarled and bared its teeth.

Izzy watched as Zach ignored the dog as he walked up the two steps of the bull-nosed veranda, opening the screen door to knock on the cracked paint of the front door. The dog was still doing its scary impersonation of an alien beast from a horror movie but Zach didn't seem the least put off by it. He left the bag of toys near the door and came back down the veranda steps. Apart from the dinosaurs, Izzy had spotted a set of toy cars and a doll that looked suspiciously new. She had seen one just like it in the corner store yesterday but it hadn't been there when she'd picked up her sandwich today at lunchtime.

Zach made a clicking sound with his tongue and the dog stopped growling and slunk down in a submissive pose. Zach picked up the dog's water dish, took it over to the tap on the base of the tank, rinsed the rusty water out of it and filled it with fresh, setting it down in a patch of shade next to the dog's kennel. The dog drank thirstily, so thirstily Zach had to refill the dish a couple of times.

He came back to the car after doing another round of the house. 'No one home.'

Izzy started the engine. 'You certainly have a way with wild animals.'

'He's not wild.' He leaned his arm along the back of her seat as she backed the car to turn around. 'He's scared. Probably had the boot kicked into his ribs a few too many times.'

Izzy could see the tightness around his jaw. That grim look was back. The look that was like a screen behind which the horrors and cruelty and brutal inhumanity he'd seen first hand were barricaded. 'How do you cope with it? The stuff you see, I mean. The bad stuff.'

'Reckon you've seen your share of bad stuff too.'

'Yes, but I'm not usually out on the coalface. Most of the stuff I see is in the controlled environment of a clinic or hospital. And mostly it's stuff I can fix.'

He didn't speak until Izzy had driven back to the road leading to town. 'It doesn't get any easier, that's for sure. Rocking up to someone's place to tell them their only kid is lying in the morgue after a high-speed accident is the kind of stuff that gets to even the toughest cops.' He paused for a beat. 'Anything to do with kids gets me. Abuse. Neglect. Murder. It's not something you can file away like the investigation report. It stays with you. For years.' He released a jagged breath. 'For ever.'

Izzy glanced at him. 'Did you think it would be as bad as it is when you first joined the force?'

He gave her a twisted smile that had nothing to do with humour. 'Most cops fresh out of the academy think they're going to be the one that changes the world. We all think we're going to make a difference. To help people. Trouble is, some people don't want to be helped.'

'I've been talking to Margie about setting up a playgroup in town,' Izzy said, 'for mums like Caitlyn and their kids. A place to hang out and chat and swap recipes and stuff. Do you think it's a good idea?'

'Who's going to run it?'

'I will, to start with.'

He flashed her an unreadable look. 'And who's going to take over when you drive off into the sunset in search of your next big adventure?'

Izzy pressed her lips together. Was he mocking her or was he thinking of the locals getting all excited about something only to have it fall flat once she left? A little flag of hope climbed up the flagpole of her heart. Was he thinking of how *he* would feel when she left? 'I'm going to be here long enough to get it up and running. After that it's up to the locals to keep things going, if that's what they want.'

He gave a noncommittal grunt, his eyes trained on the road ahead.

Izzy let a silence pass before she added, 'So what's wrong with looking for adventure?'

'Nothing, as long as you don't hurt others going in search of it.'

'I'm not planning on hurting anyone.' She found her fingers tightening on the steering-wheel and had to force herself to relax them. 'I suppose this attitude of yours is because of your mother leaving the way she did.'

She felt the razor-sharp blade of his gaze. 'You really think you've got what it takes to make a difference out here in a month? You haven't got a hope, sweetheart.'

'Don't patronise me by calling me sweetheart.'

He gave a sound midway between a laugh and a cynical snort. 'You flounce into town, sprinkling your fairy dust around, hoping some of it will stick, but you haven't got a clue. The country out here is tough and it needs tough people to work in it and survive. It's not the place for some pretty little blow-in who's looking for something to laugh about over a latte with her friends when she gets back from her big adventure with the rednecks in the antipodes.'

Izzy tried to rein in her anger but it was like trying to control a scrub fire with an eyedropper. The one thing she hated the most was people not taking her seriously. Thinking she was too much of a flake to get the job done. A silly little socialite playing at doctors and nurses. 'Thanks for the charming summation of my motives and character,' she said through tight lips.

'Pleasure.'

She pulled up outside the police station a few bristling minutes later. 'Have a nice evening, Sergeant,' she said, her voice dripping with sarcasm.

He didn't even bother replying, or at least not verbally. He shut the car door with a sharp click that could just as easily be substituted for an imprecation.

* * *

'What's got under your skin?' Doug asked Zach over dinner later that evening. 'You've been stabbing at that steak as if it's a mortal enemy.'

Zach pushed his plate away. 'It's too hot to eat.'

'Tell me about it.' Doug wiped the back of his hand over his forehead. 'Must be something wrong with the air-con. I'm sweating like a pig.'

Zach frowned as he saw his father's sickly colour. 'You all right?'

'Will be in a minute...' Doug gripped the arms of the standard chair. 'Just a funny turn. Had one earlier... just before you got home.'

'When was the last time you took a painkiller?'

'Ran out last night.'

Zach swore under his breath. 'You're not supposed to stop them cold turkey. You're supposed to wean yourself off them. You're probably having withdrawal symptoms. It can be dangerous to suddenly stop taking them.'

Doug winced as he pushed back from the table. 'Maybe you should call the doctor for me. Pain's pretty bad...' He sucked in a breath. 'Getting worse by the minute.'

Zach mentally rolled his eyes as he reached for his phone. The one time he wanted some distance from Izzy Courtney and his father springs a turnaround on him. He considered waiting it out to see if his father recovered without intervention but he knew he would never forgive himself if things took a turn for the worse. His father's health hadn't been checked since William Sawyer had left on holidays. He was supposed to be monitored weekly for his blood pressure. Severe pain could trigger heart attacks in some patients and the last thing Zach wanted was to be responsible for inaction just because of a silly little tiff with the locum doctor.

He was annoyed with himself for reacting the way he had. He didn't want Izzy thinking she had any hold over him. So what if she wanted to get a playgroup going before she left? It was a good idea—a *great* idea. It was exactly what the town needed. She was doing all she could in the short time she was here to make a difference. Once she was done waving her magic wand around he would wave her off without a flicker of emotion showing on his face.

That was one lesson he had learned and learned well.

Izzy arrived twenty-five minutes later, carrying her doctor's bag and a coolly distant manner Zach knew he probably deserved. 'He's in the bedroom, lying down,' he said.

'How long has he been feeling unwell?'

'Since before I got home. He's run out of pain meds. It's probably withdrawal.'

'Is he happy to see me?'

He inched up the corner of his mouth in a sardonic curl. 'You think I would've called you otherwise?'

Her brown eyes flashed a little arc of lightning at him. 'Lead the way.'

Zach knew he was acting like a prize jerk. He couldn't seem to help it. It was the only way to keep his distance. He was worried about complicating his life with a dalliance with her even though he could think of nothing he wanted more than to lose himself in a bit of mindless sex. He didn't have her pegged as the sort of girl who would settle for a fling. She'd been engaged to the same man for four years. That didn't sound like a girl who was eager to put out to the first guy who showed an interest in her.

And Zach was more than interested in her.

He couldn't stop thinking about her. How she'd felt in his arms, the way her mouth had met the passion of his, the softness of her breast in his mouth, the hard little pebble of her nipple against his tongue, the taste of the skin of her neck, that sweet, flowery scent of her that reminded him of an English cottage garden in spring.

'Hello, Mr Fletcher.' Izzy's voice broke through Zach's erotic reverie. 'Zach told me you're not feeling so good this evening.'

'Pain…' Doug gestured to his abdomen and his back; his breathing was ragged now, his brow sticky with sweat. 'Bad pain…'

Zach watched as she examined his father's chest and abdomen and then his back with gentle hands. He couldn't help feeling a little jealous. He would have liked those soft little hands running over his chest and abdomen and lower. His groin swelled at the thought and he had to think of something unpleasant to get control again.

She took his father's blood pressure, her forehead puckered in concentration as she listened to his account of how he had been feeling over the last few hours.

'Any history of renal colic?' she asked. 'Kidney stones?'

'A few years back,' his father said. 'Six or seven years ago, I think. Didn't need to go to hospital or anything. I passed them eventually. Hurt like the devil. None since.'

'I'll give you a shot of morphine for the pain but I think we should organise an IVP tomorrow if the pain doesn't go away overnight,' Izzy said. 'When was the last time you passed urine?'

'Not for a while, three hours ago maybe.'

'Any pain or difficulty?'

'A bit.'

'Do you think you could give me a urine sample if I leave you with a specimen bottle?' she asked as she administered the injection.

'I'll give it a try.'

'I'll wait in the kitchen to give you some privacy.' She clipped shut her bag and walked past Zach, her body brushing his in the doorway making him go hard all over again.

'Might need a hand getting to the bathroom, Zach,' his father said.

Zach blinked a couple of times to reorient himself. 'Right. Sure.'

CHAPTER TEN

Izzy was sitting on one of the kitchen chairs with Popeye on her lap when Zach came back in, carrying a urine sample bottle inside the press-lock plastic bag she'd provided. She put the dog on the floor and stood, taking the sample from him and giving it a quick check for blood or cloudiness that would suggest infection, before putting it next to her bag on the floor.

She straightened and kept her doctor face in place, trying to ignore the way her body was so acutely aware of the proximity of Zach's. 'Your father should be feeling a little better in the next half-hour or so. Make sure he drinks plenty of clear fluids over the next twenty-four hours. If he has any trouble passing urine, don't hesitate to call. If the bladder blocks I can insert a catheter to drain it until we can get him to hospital. But I don't think it will come to that. It seems a pretty standard case of renal colic. Being less active, he probably doesn't feel as thirsty as much as he used to. Older men often fail to keep an adequate intake of fluids.' She knew she was talking like a medical textbook but she couldn't seem to stop it. 'That's about it. I'll be on my way. Goodbye.'

'Izzy.' His hand was firm and warm on the bare skin of her arm. It sent a current of electricity to the secret heart of her.

Izzy met his gaze. It wasn't hard and cold with anger now but tired, as if he had grown weary of screening his inner turmoil from view. Her heart stepped off its high horse and nestled back down in her chest with a soft little sign. 'Are you OK?'

His mouth softened its grim line. 'Sorry about this afternoon. I was acting like a jerk.' His thumb started stroking the skin of her arm, a back-and-forth motion that was drugging her senses.

'You've got a lot on your mind right now with your dad and everything.'

'Don't make excuses for me.' His thumb moved to the back of her hand, absently moving over the tendons in a circular motion. 'I was out of line, snapping your head off like that.'

Izzy gave him a mock reproachful arch of her brow. 'Fairy dust?'

His thumb stalled on her hand and he looked down at it as if he'd only just realised he'd been stroking it. He released her and took a step backwards, using the same hand to score a crooked pathway through his hair. 'Thanks for coming out. I appreciate it. I think you've won my dad over.'

What about you? Have I won you over? Izzy studied his now closed-off expression. 'I hope he has a settled night. Call me if you're worried. I'll keep my phone on.'

He walked her out to the car but he hardly said a word. Izzy got the impression he couldn't wait for her to leave. It made her spirits plummet. She'd thought for a moment back there he'd been going to kiss her, maybe even take it a step further.

She hadn't realised how much she wanted him to until he hadn't.

Caitlyn Graham turned up at the clinic the following day with Skylar. 'Sorry about missing our appointment,' she said. 'I took the kids for a drive to see a friend of mine on a property out of town. I forgot to phone and cancel. There's no signal out there so I couldn't call even when I remembered.'

'No problem,' Izzy said. 'Just as long as Skylar's OK.' She inspected the little tot's forehead and asked casually, 'How are the boys?'

'They're at school,' Caitlyn said. 'Jobe made a fuss about going. He hates it. He has a tantrum about going just about every morning.'

'Is he being bullied?'

'What, at school? Nah, don't think so. Wayne would have a fit if he heard Jobe couldn't stand up for himself.'

'Did you get the bag of toys Zach dropped in for the kids?' Izzy asked.

Caitlyn's expression flickered with something before she got it under control. 'Wayne wasn't too happy about that. He doesn't think it's right to spoil kids, especially if they're not behaving themselves.'

'Does Wayne get on well with the kids?'

'All right, I guess.' Caitlyn brushed her daughter's fluffy blonde hair down into some semblance of order. 'They're not his. None of my kids are.'

'Do you have any contact with Jobe's father?' Izzy asked.

'No, and I don't want to.' Caitlyn's expression tightened like a fist. 'Jobe's got it in his head Connor is some sort of hero but he's just another loser. Connor caused a lot of trouble between Brad and me—that's Eli and Skylar's dad. It's what broke us up, actually.'

'What sort of trouble?'

'Picking fights. Saying things about Brad that weren't true. Punch-ups on the street. Making me look like trailer trash. I took a restraining order out on him. He can't come anywhere near me or Jobe.'

'What about Brad? Does he have contact with Eli and Skylar?'

'Now and again but Wayne's not keen on it. Thinks I might be tempted to go back to him or something. As if.' She rolled her eyes at the thought. 'Wayne's no prize but at least he brings in a bit of money.'

'What does he do?'

'He's a truck driver. He does four runs a week, sometimes more. He's the first man I've had who's held down a regular job.'

'It must get lonely out here for you with him away a lot,' Izzy said.

'It's no picnic with three kids, but, as my mum keeps saying, I made my bed so I have to lie in it.'

Izzy brought up the subject of a playgroup at the community centre. Caitlyn shrugged as if the thought held little appeal but Izzy knew apathy was a common trait amongst young women who felt the world was against them. 'I'll let you know once we get things sorted,' she said as Caitlyn left the consulting room. 'Skylar will enjoy it and we might even be able to do an after-school one if things go well so the boys can come too.'

'I'll think about it. See what Wayne says. I like to fit in with him. Causes less trouble that way.'

Izzy closed the door once Caitlyn had left. It was a shock to realise she had no right to criticise Caitlyn for accommodating her partner's unreasonable demands.

Hadn't she done more or less the same with Richard for the last four years?

Margie put the reception phone down just as Izzy came out of her room. 'That was Doug Fletcher. He passed a couple of kidney stones last night. He's feeling much better.'

'I'm glad to hear it.'

'Not only that,' Margie continued with a beaming smile, 'he asked me to go over there tonight. I'm going to make him dinner.'

'That's lovely. I'm pleased for you.'

'I have a favour to ask.'

'You want to leave early?' Izzy asked. 'Sure. I can do the filing and lock up.'

'No, not that.' Margie gave her a beseeching look. 'Would you be a honey and invite Zach to dinner at your place tonight?'

'Um…'

'Go on. He'll feel like a gooseberry hanging around with us oldies,' Margie said. 'A night out at your place will be good for him. It'll give him a break from always having to keep an eye on his dad.'

'I don't know…'

'Or ask him to join you for a counter meal at the pub if you're not much of a cook.'

'I can cook.'

'Then what's the problem?'

Izzy schooled her features into what she hoped

passed for mild enthusiasm. 'I'll give him a call. See what he's up to. He might be on duty.'

'He's not. I already checked.'

Zach was typing a follow-up email to his commander in Bourke when Izzy came into the station. He pressed 'Send' and got to his feet. 'I was going to call you. My dad's feeling a lot better.'

'Yes, Margie told me. He called the clinic earlier this morning.'

'You were spot on with your diagnosis.'

'I may not know a triceratops from a stegosaurus but I'm a whizz at picking up renal colic.'

Zach felt a smile tug at his mouth. 'You doing anything tonight?'

She gave him a wry look. 'Apparently I'm cooking dinner for you.'

'Yeah, so I heard. You OK with that?'

'Have I got a choice?'

Zach found it cute the way she arched her left eyebrow in that haughty manner. 'I wouldn't want to put you to any trouble. I can pick up a bite to eat at the pub. Mike hates it when I do, though. He says it puts his regulars off.'

'You don't have to go in uniform.'

'Wouldn't make a bit of difference if I went in stark naked.'

Her cheeks lit up like twin fires. 'Um…dinner's at seven.'

'I'll look forward to it.' She was at the door when he asked, 'Hey, will your stand-in boyfriend Max be joining us?'

She gave him a slitted look over her shoulder and then flounced out.

* * *

Izzy had cooked for numerous dinner parties for her friends when living in London and she'd never felt the slightest hint of nerves. She was an accomplished cook; she'd made it her business to learn as she'd grown up with cooks at Courtney Manor and wasn't content to sit back and watch, like her parents, while someone else did all the work. From a young age she had taken an interest in preparing food, getting to know the kitchen staff and talking to the gardeners about growing fresh vegetables and herbs.

But preparing a meal for Zach in an Outback town that had only one shop with limited fresh supplies was a challenge, so too was trying not to think about the fact she was sure that food was not the only thing they would be sharing tonight.

She put the last touches to the table, thinking wistfully of the fragrant roses of Courtney Manor as she placed an odd-looking banksia on the table in a jam jar, the only thing she could in the cottage that was close to a vase.

Izzy looked at Max sitting at the end of the table. It had taken her half an hour to blow him up manually as she didn't have a bicycle pump. He was leaning to one side, his ventriloquist dummy-like eyes staring into space. 'I hope you're going to behave yourself, Max.' *Why are you talking to a blow-up doll?* 'No talking with your mouth full or elbows on the table, OK?'

The doorbell sounded and Izzy quickly smoothed her already smooth hair as she went to answer it. Zach was standing on the porch, wearing an open-necked white shirt with tan-coloured chinos. His hair was still damp from a shower; she could see the grooves where his comb or brush had passed through it. Her first 'Hi…' came out croakily so she cleared her throat and tried again. 'Hi. Come on in.'

'Thanks.'

She could smell the clean fresh scent of fabric softener on his shirt as he came through the door, that and the hint of lemon and spice and Outback maleness that never failed to get her senses spinning.

'I brought wine.' He handed her a bottle, his eyes moving over her in a lazy sweep that made her insides feel hollow. 'Something smells good.'

Izzy took the wine, getting a little shock from his fingers as they brushed against hers. 'I hope you're hungry.'

'Ravenous.'

She swallowed and briskly turned to get the glasses, somehow managing to half fill two without spilling a drop in spite of hands that weren't too steady. 'Max decided to join us after all.' She handed Zach a glass of the white wine he had brought. 'I hope you don't mind.'

A hint of a smile played at the corners of his mouth. 'Aren't you going to introduce us?'

Izzy felt her own smile tug at her lips. 'He's not one for small talk.'

'I'm known to be a bit on the taciturn side myself.' The smile had travelled up to his eyes with a twinkle that was devastatingly attractive.

She led the way to the small eating area off the kitchen. 'Max, this is Sergeant Zach Fletcher.' She turned to Zach. 'Zach, this is Max.'

Zach rubbed at his chin thoughtfully. 'Mmm, I guess a handshake is out of the question?'

A laugh bubbled out of Izzy's mouth. 'This is ridiculous. I'm going to kill Hannah. I swear to God I will. Would you like some nibbles?' she asked as she thrust a plate of dips and crackers towards him. 'I have to check on the entrée.'

His eyes were still smiling but they had taken on a smouldering heat that made the backs of her knees feel tingly. 'Do you think Max would get jealous if I kissed you?'

Izzy's stomach hollowed out again. 'I don't know. I've never kissed anyone in front of him before.'

He put a hand to the side of her face, a gentle cupping of her cheek, the dry warmth and slight roughness of his palm making her inner core quiver like an unset jelly. 'I wouldn't want to cut in on him but I've been dying to do this since last night.' His mouth came down towards hers, his minty breath dancing over the surface of her lips in that tantalising prelude to take-off.

Izzy let out a soft sigh of delight as his mouth connected with hers, a velvet brush of dry male lips on moist, lip-gloss-coated female ones. The moment of contact made shivers flow like a river down her spine, the first electrifying sweep of his tongue over her lips parted them, inviting her to take him in. She opened to the commanding glide of his tongue, shuddering with need as he made contact with hers in a sexy tangle that drove every other thought out of her mind other than what she was feeling in her body. The stirring of her blood, the way her feminine folds pulsed and ached to be parted and filled, just like he was doing with her mouth. The way her breasts tingled and tightened, the nipples erect in arousal.

His hands grasped her by the hips, pulling her against his own arousal, the hard heat of him probing her intimately, reminding her of everything that was different between them and yet so powerfully, irresistibly attractive.

Izzy snaked her arms around his neck, stepping up on her toes so she could keep that magical connection with his mouth on hers. She kissed him with the passion that had been lying dormant inside her body, just waiting for someone like him to awaken it. She had never felt the full force of it before. She'd felt paltry imitations of it, but nothing like this.

This was fiery.

This was unstoppable.

This was inevitable.

'I want you.' Izzy couldn't believe she had said the words out loud, but even if she hadn't done so her body was saying them for her. The way she was clinging to him, draping her body over him like a second layer of skin, was surely leaving him in no doubt of her need for him. She pressed three hot little kisses, one after the other, on his mouth and repeated the words she had never said to anyone else and meant them quite the way she meant them now. 'I want you to make love to me.'

Zach brought his hands back up to cup her face. 'Sure?'

Izzy gazed into his beautiful haunted eyes. 'Don't you recognise consent when you see it?'

His thumbs stroked her cheeks, his eyes focused on her mouth as if it were the most fascinating thing he had ever seen. 'It's been a while for me.'

'I'm sure you still know the moves.'

One of his thumbs brushed over her lower lip in a caress that made the base of her spine shiver. 'Are we having a one-night stand or is this something else?'

'What do you want it to be?'

He took a while to answer, his gaze still homed in on her mouth, the pads of his thumbs doing that mesmerising stroking, one across her cheek, the other on her lower lip. 'You're only here for another couple of weeks. Neither of us is in the position to make promises.'

'I'm not asking for promises,' Izzy said. 'I had promises and they sucked.'

His mouth kicked up at the corner. 'Yeah, me too.'

She placed her fingertip on his bottom lip, caressing it the way he had done to hers. 'I've never had a fling with someone before.'

Something in his gaze smouldered. Simmered. Burned. 'Flings can be fun as long as both parties are clear on the rules.'

Izzy shivered as he took her finger in his mouth, his teeth biting down just firmly enough for her insides to flutter in anticipatory excitement. 'You're mighty big on rules, aren't you, Sergeant? I guess that's because of that gun you're wearing.'

His hands encircled her wrists like handcuffs, his pelvis carnally suggestive against hers. 'I'm not wearing my gun.'

Her brow arched in a sultry fashion. 'Could've fooled me.'

He scooped her up in his arms in an effortless lift, calling out over his shoulder as he carried her towards the bedroom, 'Start without us, Max. We've got some business to see to.'

Izzy quaked with pleasure when Zach slid her down the length of his body once he had her in the bedroom. And there was a *lot* of his body compared to hers. So tall, so lean and yet so powerfully muscled she barely came up to his shoulder once she'd kicked off her heels. His hands cupped her bottom and pulled her against him, letting her feel the weight and heft of his erection. Even through the barrier of their clothes it was the most erotic feeling to have him pulse and pound against her. He kissed her lingeringly, deeply, taking his time to build her need of him until she was whimpering, gasping, clawing at him to get him naked.

'What's the hurry?' he said against the side of her neck.

Izzy kissed his mouth, his chin, and then flicked the tip of her tongue into the dish below his Adam's apple. 'I've heard things go at a much slower pace in the Outback but I didn't realise that included sex.'

He gave a little rumble of laughter and pulled the zipper down the back of her dress in a single lightning-fast movement. 'You want speed, sweetheart?' He unclipped her bra and tossed it to the floor. 'Then let's see if we can pick up the pace a bit, shall we?'

Izzy whooshed out a breath as she landed on her back on the mattress with a little bounce. As quickly as he had removed her clothes, he got rid of his own, coming down over her, gloriously, deliciously naked.

The sexy entanglement of limbs, of long and hard and toned and tanned and hair-roughened muscles entwining with softer, smoother, shorter ones made everything that was feminine in her roll over in delight. His hands, those gorgeously manly hands, sexily grazed the soft skin of her breasts. That sizzling-hot male mouth with its surrounding stubble suckled on each one in turn, the right one first and then the left, the suction just right, the pressure and tug of his teeth perfect, the roll and sweep of his tongue mind-blowing.

Izzy had never been all that vocal during sex in the past. The occasional sigh or murmur perhaps—sometimes just to feed Richard's ego rather than from feeling anything spectacular herself—but nothing like the gasps and whimpers that were coming out of her now. It wasn't just Zach's mouth that was wreaking such havoc on her senses but the feel and shape of his body as it pinned hers to the bed. Not too heavy, not awkward or clumsy, but potent and powerful, determined and yet respectful.

He moved down from her breasts to sear a scorching pathway to her bellybutton and beyond. She automatically tensed when he came to the seam of her body, but immediately sensing her hesitation he placed his palm over her lower abdomen to calm her. 'Trust me, Izzy. I can make it good for you.'

Should she tell him she had never experienced such intimacy before? She didn't want to make Richard sound like a prude, but the truth was he had made it clear early on in their relationship that he found oral sex distasteful. In spite of her knowledge as a doctor to the contrary, his attitude had made her feel as if her body was unpleasant, unattractive and somehow defective. 'Um…I've never done it before… I mean no one's done it to me…'

He looked at her quizzically. 'Your ex didn't?'

She knew she was blushing. But rather than hide it she decided to be honest with him. 'It wasn't Richard's thing.'

He was still frowning. 'But it's one of the best ways for a woman to have an orgasm.'

Izzy was silent for just a second or two too long.

He cocked an eyebrow at her questioningly. 'You have had an orgasm, right?'

'Of course...' Majorly fiery blush this time. 'Plenty of times.'

'Izzy.' The way Zach said her name was like a parent catching a child out for lying.

'It was hard for me to get there...I always took too long to get in the mood and then Richard would pressure me and I...' Izzy gave him a helpless look '...I usually faked it.'

His frown had made a pleat between his grey eyes. 'Usually?'

'Mostly.' She bit her lip at his look. 'It was easier that way. I didn't want to hurt Richard's feelings or make him feel inadequate. Seems to me some men have such fragile egos when it comes to their sexual prowess.'

He stroked her face with his fingers. 'Being able to satisfy a partner is one of the most enjoyable aspects of sex. I want you to enjoy it, Izzy. Don't pretend with me. Be honest. Take all the time you need.'

Izzy pressed her lips against his. 'If we take too long Max might wonder what we're doing.'

He smiled against her mouth. 'I reckon he's got a pretty fair idea.' And then he kissed her.

CHAPTER ELEVEN

'THANK YOU so much for stepping in last night,' Margie said when Izzy arrived at work the next morning. 'Doug and I had the most wonderful time. It was as if the last twenty-three years hadn't happened. We talked for hours and hours. Just as well Zach didn't get back till midnight.' Her eyes twinkled meaningfully. 'Must have been a pretty decent dinner you cooked for him. He looked very satisfied.'

Izzy had all but given up on trying to disguise her blush. Her whole body was still glowing from the passionate lovemaking she had experienced in Zach's arms last night. He had been both tender and demanding, insisting on a level of physical honesty from her that was way outside her experience. But she had loved every earth-shattering second of it.

The things she had discovered about her body had amazed her. It was capable of intense and repeated orgasms. Zach had taught her how to relax enough to embrace the powerful sensations, to let her inhibitions go, to stop over-thinking and worrying she wasn't doing things according to a schedule. He had let her choose her own timetable and his pleasure when it had come had been just as intense as hers. That the pleasure had been mutual had given their sensual encounter a depth, an almost sacred aspect she'd found strangely moving.

The only niggling worry she had was how was she going to move on after their fling was over? Falling in love with him or anyone was not part of her plan for her six months away from home. She had only just extricated herself from a long-term relationship. The last thing she wanted was to tie herself up in another one, even if Zach was the most intriguing and attractive man she had met in a long time. Strike that—had *ever* met.

'Yes, well, there's certainly nothing wrong with his appetite,' Izzy said as she popped her bag into the cupboard next to the patients' filing shelves.

'Are you going to see him again?'

'I see him practically every day.' Izzy straightened her skirt as she turned round. 'In a town this size everyone sees everyone every day.'

Margie pursed her lips in a you-can't-fool-me manner. 'You know what I mean. Are you officially a couple? I know the gossip started the moment you showed up in town but that was Charles Redbank's doing. He just wanted to make trouble. He's never forgiven Zach for booking him for speeding a couple of months back.'

'We're not officially anything.' Izzy resented even having to say that much. She wasn't used to discussing her private life with anyone other than Hannah and even then there were some things she wasn't prepared to reveal. Even to herself.

'It'd be lovely if you stayed on a bit longer,' Margie said. 'Everyone loves you. Even that old sourpuss Ida Jensen thinks you're an angel now that you've sorted out her blood-pressure medication. And Peggy McLeod's thrilled you suggested she help start up the playgroup again. She's already got a heap of toys and play equipment donated from the locals. She even got Caitlyn Graham's boyfriend, Wayne Brody, to donate some. He dropped by a bag of stuff yesterday, most of it brand new. Wasn't that nice of him?'

Izzy kept her features schooled, even though inside she was fuming. 'Unbelievably nice of him.'

Margie glanced at the diary. 'Your first patient isn't until nine-thirty. You've got time for a coffee. Want me to make you one here or shall I run up to the general store and get you a latte from Jim's new machine?'

'I'll go,' Izzy said. 'There's something I want to see Sergeant Fletcher about on the way past.'

Zach was typing up an incident report on the computer at the station when he heard the sound of footsteps coming up the path. He knew it was Izzy even before he looked up to check. His skin started to tingle; it hadn't stopped tingling since last night, but it went up a gear when he caught a whiff of summer flowers. He had gone home last night with her fragrance lingering on his skin. He had even considered skipping a shower this morning to keep it there. The way she had come apart in his arms had not only thrilled him, it had made him feel something he hadn't expected to feel.

Didn't want to feel.

He stood as she came in. 'Morning.' He knew he sounded a bit formal but he was having trouble getting that feeling he didn't want to feel back in the box where he had stashed it last night.

His manner obviously annoyed her for her brow puckered in a frown and her lips pulled tight. 'Sorry to disturb you while you're busy, but I forgot to tell you something last night.'

Would this be the bit about how she didn't want to continue their fling? He mentally prepared himself, keeping his face as blank as possible. 'Fire away.'

Her hands were balled into tight little fists by her sides, her cheeks like two bright red apples, and her toffee-brown eyes flashing. 'The toys you left for Caitlyn's kids?' She didn't give him time to say anything in response but continued; 'Wayne wouldn't let her give them to the kids.'

Zach was so relieved her tirade wasn't about ending their affair it took him a moment to respond. 'There's not much I can do about that. They were a gift and if Caitlyn didn't want to accept—'

'You're not listening to me,' she said with a little stamp of her foot. 'Caitlyn would've loved them for the kids, I know she would, she's too frightened to stand up to Wayne. But even worse than that, he passed them off as his own donation to Peggy McLeod for the community centre playgroup. He's passing off *your* gift as his own largesse. It makes my blood boil so much I want to explode!'

He came round from behind the desk and took her trembling-with-rage shoulders in his hands. 'Hey, it's not worth getting upset about it. At least the kids will have a chance to play with the toys when they go to the centre.'

Her pretty little face was scrunched up in a furious scowl. 'If that control freak lets them go. He'll probably put a stop to that too. Can't you do something? Like arrest him for making a false declaration of generosity or something?'

Zach fought back a smile as he rubbed his hands up and down her silky arms. 'My experience with guys like him is that the more you show how much they get under your skin the more they enjoy it. Best thing you can do is support Caitlyn and the kids. Helping to build up her confidence as a parent is a great start.'

She let out a sign that released her tense shoulders. 'I guess you're right…'

He tipped up her chin and meshed his gaze with her still troubled one. 'Do you have any plans for tonight?'

Her eyes lost their dullness and began to sparkle. 'I don't know. I'll have to check what Max has got planned. He might want to hang out. Watch a movie or something. He gets lonely if he's left on his own too long.'

Zach had no hope of suppressing his smile. 'Then why don't we take him on a picnic out to Blake's waterhole? I'll bring the food. I'll pick you up at six-thirty so we can catch the sunset.'

She scrunched up her face again but her eyes were dancing. 'I'm not sure Max has a pair of bathers.'

Zach gave her a glinting smile as he brought his mouth down to hers. 'Tell him he won't need them.'

Izzy spread the picnic blanket down over a patch of sunburned grass near the waterhole while Zach brought the picnic basket and their towels from the car. The sun was still high and hot enough to crisp and crackle the air with the sound of cicadas. But down by the water's edge the smell of the dusty earth was relieved by the earthy scent of cool, deep water shadowed by the overhanging craggy-armed gums. Long gold fingers of sunlight were poking between the branches to gild the water, along with a light breeze that was playfully tickling the surface.

Zach put the picnic basket down on the blanket. 'Swim first or would you like a cold drink?'

Izzy looked at him, dressed in faded blue denim jeans with their one tattered knee, his light grey body-hugging T-shirt showcasing every toned muscle of his chest and shoulders and abdomen. He looked strong and fit and capable, the sort of man you would go to in a crisis. The sort of man you could depend on, a man who was not only strong on the outside but had an inner reserve of calm deliberation. He was the sort of man who wasn't daunted by hard work or a challenging task. The way he had moved back to the bush to help his father even though it had cost him his relationship with his fiancée confirmed it. He was a man of principles, conviction. Loyalty.

It made her think of Richard, who within a couple of days of her ending their relationship had found a replacement.

Zach, on the other hand, had spent the last eighteen months quietly grieving the loss of his relationship and the future he had planned for himself, devoting his time to his father and the community. Doing whatever it took, no matter how difficult, to help his father come to terms with the limitations that had been placed on him. He didn't complain. He didn't grouse or whinge about it. He just got on with it.

Zach must have mistaken her silence for something else. 'There are no nasties in the water, if that's what's putting you off. An eel or two, a few tadpoles and frogs but nothing to be too worried about.'

A shiver of unease slithered down her spine. 'Snakes?'

'They're definitely about but more will see you than you see them.' He gave her a quick grin. 'I'll go in first and scare them away, OK?'

'Big, brave man.'

He tugged his T-shirt over his head and tossed it onto one of the sun-warmed rocks nearby. 'Yeah, well, that's more than I can say about that roommate of yours squibbing at the last minute.'

Izzy feasted her eyes on his washboard stomach and then her heart gave a little flip as he reached for the zipper on his jeans. She disguised her reaction behind humour but was sure he wasn't fooled for a second. 'It wasn't that he was scared or anything. He's got very sensitive skin. He was worried about mosquitoes. One prick and he might never recover.'

Zach's smile made her skin lift up in goose-bumps as big as the gravel they had driven over earlier. He came and stood right in front of her, dressed in nothing but his shape-hugging black underwear. He flicked the collar of her lightweight cotton blouse with two of his fingers. 'Need some help getting your gear off?'

Izzy found it hard to breathe with him so deliciously close. The smell of him, the citrus and physically active man smell of him made her insides squirm with longing. His grey-blue eyes were glinting, his mouth slanted in a sexy smile that never failed to make her feminine core contract and release in want. Her body remembered every stroke and glide and powerful thrust of his inside hers last night. Her feminine muscles tightened in feverish anticipation, the musky, silky moisture of her body automatically activated in response to his intimate proximity. 'Are you offering to do a strip search, Sergeant Fletcher?' she asked with a flirty smile.

His eyes gleamed with sensual promise as his fingers went to the buttons on her shirt. 'Let's see what you've got hidden under here, shall we?'

One by one he undid each button, somehow making it into a game of intense eroticism. His fingers scorched her skin each time he released another button from its tiny buttonhole, the action triggering yet another pulse of primal longing deep in her flesh. He peeled the shirt off her shoulders, and then tracked his finger down between her breasts, still encased in her bra. 'Beautiful.'

How one word uttered in that deep, husky tone could make her feel like a supermodel was beyond her. It wasn't just a line, a throw-away comment to get what he wanted. She knew he meant it. She could feel it in his touch, the gentle way he had of cupping her breasts once he'd released her bra, the way his thumbs stroked over her nipples with a touch that was both achingly tender and yet tantalisingly arousing.

Her cotton summer skirt was next to go, the zip going down, the little hoop of fabric circling her ankles before he took her hand and helped her step away from it like stepping out of a puddle. He put a warm, work-roughened hand to the curve of her hip just above the line of her knickers, holding her close enough to the potent heat of his body for her to feel his reaction to her closeness.

He was powerfully erect. She could feel the thrum of his blood through the lace of her knickers, the hot, urgent pressure of him stirring her senses into frantic overload.

He touched her then, a single stroke down the lace-covered seam of her body, a teasing taste of the intimate invasion to come. She whimpered as he slid her knickers aside, waiting a heart-stopping beat before he touched her again, skin on skin.

Izzy tugged his underwear down so she could do the same to him, taking him in her hands, stroking him, caressing the silky steel of him until he was breathing as raggedly as she was.

He slipped a finger inside her, swallowing her gasp as his mouth came down on hers. His kiss was passionate, thorough, and intensely erotic as his tongue tangled with hers in a cat-and-mouse caper.

Izzy's caressing of him became bolder, squeezing and releasing, smoothing up and down his length, running her fingertip over the ooze of his essence, breathing in the musky scent of mutual arousal.

There was something wildly, deeply primitive about being naked with a man in the bush. No sounds other than their hectic breathing and those of nature. The distant warble of magpies, the throaty arck-arck of a crow flying overhead, the whisper of the breeze moving through the gum leaves, sounding like thousands of finger-length strips of tinsel paper being jostled together.

Zach pressed her down on the tartan blanket, pushing the picnic things out of the way with his elbow, quickly sourcing a condom before entering her with a thrust that made her cry out with bone-deep pleasure. He set a fast rhythm that was as primal as their surroundings, the intensity of it thrilling her senses in a way she had never thought possible just a few short weeks ago. Her life in England had never felt more distant. It was like having another completely different identity that belonged back there.

Over there she was a buttoned-up girl who had spent

years of her life pretending to be happy, pleasing others rather than pleasing herself.

Out here she was a wild and wanton woman, having smoking-hot sex with a man she hadn't known a fortnight ago.

And now...now she was rocking in his arms as if her world began and ended with him. The physicality of their relationship was shocking, the blunt, almost brutal honesty of the needs of their bodies as they strove for completion was as carnal as two wild animals mating. Even the sound of her cries as she came were those of a woman she didn't know, had never encountered before. Wild, shrieking cries that spoke of a depth of passion that had never been tapped into or expressed before.

Zach's release was not as vocal but Izzy felt the power of it as he tensed, pumped and then flowed.

He didn't move for a long moment. His body rested on hers in the aftermath, his breathing slowly returning to normal as she stroked her hands up and down his back and shoulders, their bodies still intimately joined.

'I think there's a pebble sticking into my butt,' Izzy finally said.

He rolled her over so she was lying on top of him, his eyes heavily lidded, sleepy with satiation. 'Better?'

'Much.'

He circled her right breast with a lazy finger. 'Ever skinny dipped before?'

'Not with a man present.' Izzy gave him a wry smile. 'I did it with Hannah and a couple of other girlfriends when we were thirteen at my birthday party. It was a dare.'

His finger made a slow, nerve-tingling circuit of her

other breast. 'Is that how the crazy birthday stuff with her started?'

Izzy sent her own fingers on an exploration of his flat brown nipple nestled amongst his springy chest hair. 'Come to think of it, yes. She was always on about me being too worried about what other people thought. She made it her mission in life to shock me out of my "aristocratic mediocrity", as she calls it.'

He stroked his hand over the flank of her thigh. 'Somehow mediocre isn't the first word that comes to mind when I think of you.'

Izzy angled her head at him. 'So what word does?'

He gave her a slow smile that crinkled up the corners of his eyes in a devastatingly attractive manner. 'Cute. Funny. Sexy.'

She traced the outline of his smile with her fingertip. 'I never felt sexy before. Not the way I do with you.' She bit down on her lip, wondering if she'd been too honest, revealed too much.

He brushed her lower lip with his thumb. 'You do that a lot.'

'What?'

'Bite your lip.'

Izzy had to stop her teeth from doing it again. 'It's a nervous habit. Half the time I'm not even aware I'm doing it.'

His thumb caressed her lip as if soothing it from the assault of her teeth. 'Why don't you come down here and bite mine instead?'

Izzy leaned down and started nibbling at his lower lip, using her teeth to tug and tease. She used her tongue to sweep over where her teeth had been, before starting the process all over again. Nip. Tug. Nip. Tug.

He gave little grunts of approval, one of his hands splayed in her hair as he held her head close to his. 'Harder,' he commanded.

A shudder of pleasure shimmied down her spine as his hand fisted in her hair. She pulled at his lip with her teeth, stroked it with her tongue and then pushed her tongue into his mouth to meet his. Zach murmured his pleasure and took control of the kiss, his masterful tongue darting and diving around hers.

It was an exhilarating kiss, wild and abandoned and yet still with an element of tenderness that ambushed her emotionally.

She wasn't supposed to be feeling anything but lust for this man.

This was a fling.

A casual hook-up like all her girlfriends experienced from time to time. It was a chance to own her sexuality, to express it without the confining and formal bounds of a relationship.

She was only here for another couple of weeks. She was moving on to new sights and experiences, filling her six months away from home with adventure and memories to look back on in the years to come.

Falling in love would be a crazy...a totally disastrous thing to do...

Izzy eased off Zach while he dealt with the condom. She gathered her tousled hair and tied it into a makeshift knot, using the tresses as an anchor. Her body tingled with the memory of his touch as she got to her feet, tiny aftershocks of pleasure rippling through her.

She was dazed by sensational sex, that's all it was.

It wasn't love. How could it be?

Maybe it was time to cool off.

'Are you sure it's safe to swim here?'

'Not for diving but it's fine for a dip.' He took her hand and led her down to the water. 'Not quite St Barts, is it?'

Izzy glanced at him. 'You've been there?'

'Once.' He looked out over the water as if he was seeing the exclusive Caribbean holiday destination in his mind's eye, his mouth curled up in a cynical arc. 'With my mother and her new family when I was fourteen. Cost her husband a packet. I'm sure he only took us all there to make a point of how good her life was with him instead of my father. I didn't go on holidays with them after that. I got tired of having all that wealth thrust in my face.'

Izzy moved her fingers against his. 'I hated most of my family holidays. I'm sure we only went to most of the places we went to because that's where my parents thought people expected to see us. Skiing at exclusive lodges in Aspen. Sailing around the Mediterranean on yachts that cost more than most people ever see in a lifetime. I would've loved to go camping under the stars in the wilderness but, no, it was butlers and chauffeurs and five stars all the way.'

He looked at her with a wry smile tilting his mouth. 'Funny, isn't it, that you always want what you don't have?'

I have what I want right now. Izzy quickly filed away the thought. She looked down at the mud that was squelching between her toes. The water was refreshingly cool against her heated skin. She went in a little further, holding Zach's hand for balance until she was waist deep. 'Mmm, that's lovely.' She went in a bit deeper but something cold and slimy brushed against her leg and she yelped and sprang back and clung to Zach like a limpet. 'Eeek! What was that?'

He held her against him, laughing softly. 'It was just a bit of weed. Nothing to worry about. You're safe with me.'

Her arms were locked around his neck, her legs wrapped around his waist and her mouth within touching distance of his. She watched as his gaze went to her mouth, the way his lashes lowered in that sleepily hooded way a man did when he was thinking about sex. A new wave of desire rolled through her as his mouth came down and fused with hers.

You're safe with me.

Izzy wasn't safe. Not the way she wanted to be. Not the way she needed to be.

She was in very great danger indeed.

CHAPTER TWELVE

As ZACH PACKED the picnic things back in the car Izzy looked up at the brilliant night sky with its scattering of stars like handfuls of diamonds flung across a bolt of dark blue velvet. The air was still warm and the night orchestra's chorus had recruited two extra voices: a tawny frogmouth owl and a vixen fox, looking for a mate.

That distinctive bark was a sound from home, making Izzy feel a sudden pang of homesickness. She wondered if sounds like those of a lonely feral fox had caused Zach's mother to grieve for the life she had left behind. Had the years fighting drought and dust and flies or floods and failed crops and flyblown sheep finally broken her spirit? Or had she simply fallen out of love with her husband? Leaving a husband one no longer loved was understandable, but leaving a child to travel to the other side of the world was something else again. Leaving Zach behind must have been a very difficult decision.

Izzy couldn't imagine a mother choosing her freedom over her child, but she recognised that not all mothers found the experience as satisfying and fulfilling as others.

Leaving Zach behind...

The words reverberated inside her head. That was what she would have to do in a matter of a fortnight. She would never see him again. He would move on with his life, no doubt in a year or two find a good, sensible, no-nonsense country girl to settle down with, raise a family and work the land as his father and grandfather and forebears had done before him. She imagined him sitting at the scrubbed pine kitchen table at Fletcher Downs homestead surrounded by his wife and children. He would make a wonderful father. She had seen him with Caitlyn's children, generous, gentle and calm.

Izzy heard his footfall on the gravel as he came to join her. 'Have you found the Southern Cross?' he asked.

'I think so.' She pointed to a constellation of stars in the south. 'Is that it there?'

He followed the line of her arm and nodded. 'Yep, that's it. Good work. You must've done your research.'

Izzy turned and looked at him, something in her heart contracting as if a hand had grabbed at it and squeezed. 'Would you ever consider living somewhere else?' she asked.

A frown flickered over his brow. 'You mean like back in the city?'

Izzy wasn't sure what she meant. She wasn't sure why she had even asked. 'Will you quit your work as a cop and take over Fletcher Downs once your father officially retires?'

He looked back at the dark overturned bowl of the sky, his gaze going all the way to the horizon, where a thin lip of light lingered just before the sun dipped to wake the other side of the world. 'I love my work as a cop...well, most of the time. But the land is in my blood. The Fletcher name goes back a long way in these parts, all the way back to the first European settlers. I'm my dad's only heir. I can't afford to pay a manager for ever. The property would have to be sold if I didn't take it on full time.'

'But is that what *you* want?'

He continued to focus on the distant horizon with a grim set to his features. 'What I want is my dad to get back to full health and mobility but that doesn't look like it's going to happen any time soon.'

'But at least he's becoming more socially active,' Izzy said. 'That's a great step forward. Margie's determined to get him out more. It would be so nice if they got together, don't you think?'

He looked back at her with that same grave look. 'My father will never get married again. He's been burned once. He would never go back for a second dose.'

'But that's crazy,' Izzy said. 'Margie loves him. She's loved him since she was a girl. They belong together. Anyone can see that.'

His lip curled upwards but it wasn't so much mocking as wry. 'Stick to your medical journals, Izzy. Those romance novels you read are messing with your head.'

It's not my head they're messing with, Izzy thought as she followed him back to the car.

It was her heart.

Zach brought a beer out to his father on the veranda a couple of days later. 'Here you go. But only the one. Remember what the doctor said about drinking plenty of clear fluids.'

'Thanks.' Doug took a long sip, and then let a silence slip past before asking, 'You seeing her tonight?'

Zach reached down to tickle Popeye's ears. 'Not tonight.'

'Wise of you.'

'What's that supposed to mean?'

Doug took another sip of his beer before answering. 'Better not get too used to having her around. She's going to be packing up and leaving before you know it.'

Zach tried to ignore the savage twist of his insides at the thought of Izzy driving out of town once her locum was up. He'd heard a whisper the locals were going to use the Shearers' Ball as a send-off for her. William Sawyer and his wife would be back from their trip soon and life would return to normal in Jerringa Ridge.

Normal.

What a weird word to describe his life. When had it ever been normal? Growing up since the age of ten without a mother. Years of putting up with his father's ongoing bitterness over his marriage break-up. For years he hadn't even been able to mention his mother without his father flinching as if he had landed a punch on him.

Dealing with the conflicted emotions of visiting his mother in her gracious home in Surrey, where he didn't fit in with the formal furniture or her even more formal ridiculously wealthy new husband who never seemed to wear anything but a suit and a silk cravat, even on St Barts. Those gut-wrenching where-do-I-belong feelings intensifying once her new sons Jules and Oliver had been born. Coming back home and feeling just as conflicted trying to settle back in to life at Fletcher Downs or at boarding school.

Always feeling the outsider.

'I know what I'm doing, Dad.'

His father glanced at him briefly before turning to look at the light fading over the paddocks. It was a full minute, maybe longer before he spoke. 'I'm not going to get any better than this, am I? No point pretending I am.'

Zach found the sudden shift in conversation disorienting. 'Sure you are. You're doing fine.' He was doing it again. It was his fall-back position. A pattern of the last twenty-three years he couldn't seem to get out of—playing Pollyanna to his father's woe-is-me moods. He could recall all the pep-talk phrases he'd used in the past: *Time heals everything. You'll find someone else. Take it one day at a time. Baby steps. Everything happens for a reason.*

Doug's hand tightened on his can of beer until the aluminium crackled. 'I should've married Margie. I should've done it years ago. Now it's too late.'

It's never too late was on the tip of Zach's tongue but he refrained from voicing it. 'Is that what Margie wants? Marriage?'

'It's what most women want, isn't it?' His father gave his beer can another crunch. 'A husband, a family, a home they can be proud of. Security.'

'Margie's already got a family and a house and her job is secure,' Zach said. 'Seems to me what she wants is companionship.'

His father's top lip curled in a manner so like his own it was disquieting to witness. 'And what sort of companion am I? I can't even get on a stepladder and change a bloody light bulb.'

'There's more to a relationship than who puts out the garbage or takes the dog for a walk,' Zach said.

His father didn't seem to be listening. He was still looking out over the paddocks with a frown between his eyes. 'I didn't see it at the time…all those years ago I didn't see Margie for who she was. She was always just one of the local girls, fun to be around but didn't stand out. Then I met your mother.' He made a self-deprecating sound. 'What a fool I was to think I could make someone like her happy. I tried for ten years to keep her. Ten years of living with the dread she would one day pack up and leave. And then she did.' He clicked his fingers. *Snap.* 'She was gone.'

Zach remembered it all too well. He could still remember exactly where he had been standing on the veranda as he'd watched his mother drive away. He had gripped the veranda rail so tightly his hands had ached for days. He had watched with his heart feeling as heavy as a headstone in his chest. His mouth had been as dry as the red dust his mother's car had stirred up as she'd wheeled away.

For weeks, months, even years every time he heard a car come up the long driveway he would feel his heart leap in hope that she was coming back.

She never did.

Doug looked at Zach. 'It wasn't her fault. Not all of it. I was fighting to keep this place going after your grandfather died and then your grandmother so soon after. I didn't give her the attention she needed. You can't take an orchid out of an English conservatory and expect it to survive in the Outback. You have to nurture it, protect it.'

'Do you still love her?'

Doug's mouth twisted. 'There's a part of me that will always love your mother. Maybe not the same way

I did. It's like keeping that old pair of work boots near the back door. I'm not quite ready to part with them yet.'

'I'm not sure Mum would appreciate being compared to a pair of your old smelly work boots,' Zach said wryly, thinking of his mother's penchant for cashmere and pearls and designer shoes.

A small sad smile skirted around the edges of Doug's mouth. 'No…probably not.'

A silence passed.

'Why's it too late for you and Margie?' Zach asked. 'You're only fifty-eight. She's, what? Fifty-two or -three? You could have a good thirty or forty years together.'

'Look at me, Zach.' His father's eyes glittered with tightly held-back emotion. 'Take a good look. I'm like this now, shuffling about like a man in his eighties. What am I going to be like in five or even ten years' time? You heard what the specialist said. I was lucky to get this far. I can't do it to Margie. I can't turn her into a carer instead of a wife and lover. It'd make her hate me.' His chin quivered as he fought to keep his voice under control. 'I couldn't bear to have another woman I love end up hating me.'

'I think you're underestimating Margie,' Zach said. 'She's not like Mum. She's strong and dependable and loyal.'

'And you're such a big expert on women, aren't you, Zach? You've got one broken engagement on the leader board already. How soon before there's another?'

'There's not going to be another.'

'Why?' His father's lip was still up in that nasty little curl. 'Because you won't risk asking her, will you?'

Zach could barely get the words out through his clenched teeth. 'Ask who?'

His father pushed himself to his feet, nailing Zach with his gaze. 'That toffee-nosed little doctor you spend every spare moment of your time with.'

'I'm not in love with Isabella Courtney.'

'No, of course you're not.' Doug gave a scornful grunt of laughter. 'Keep on telling yourself that, son. If nothing else, it'll make the day she leaves a little easier on you.'

Izzy knew it was cowardly of her to pretend to be busy with catching up on emails and work-related stuff two nights in a row but spending all her spare time with Zach was making it increasingly difficult for her to keep her emotions separate from the physical side of their relationship. No wonder sex was called making love. Every look, every touch, every kiss, every spine-tingling orgasm seemed to up the ante until she wasn't sure what she felt any more. Was it love or was it lust?

Had it been a mistake to indulge in an affair with him? She had spent four years making love—*having sex*—with Richard and had never felt anything like the depth of feeling she did with Zach, and she had only known him three weeks.

And there was only one to go.

Margie looked very downcast when Izzy got to the clinic the next morning. She was sitting behind the reception desk with red-rimmed eyes and her shoulders slumped. 'Don't ask.'

'Doug?'

Margie reached for a tissue from the box on her desk. 'He said it's best if we don't see each other any more, only as friends. I've been friends with him for most of my life but it's not enough. I want more.'

'Oh, Margie, I'm so sorry. I thought things were going so well.'

Margie dabbed at her eyes. 'It's my fault for thinking I could change his mind. I should have left well alone. Now he knows how I feel about him it makes me feel so stupid. Like a lovesick schoolgirl or something.'

'Is there anything I can do?'

'Not unless you can make him fall out of love with his ex-wife.'

Izzy frowned. 'Do you really think that's what it's about?'

'What else could it be? Olivia was his grand passion.' Margie plucked another tissue out of the box and blew her nose.

'What if it's more to do with his limitations? He's a proud man. Having to rely on others for help must be really tough on someone like him.'

'But I love him. I don't care if he can't get around the way he used to. Why can't he just accept that I love him no matter what?'

Izzy gave her a sympathetic look. 'Maybe he needs more time. From what I've read of his notes, his injuries were pretty severe. And this latest bout of renal colic has probably freaked him out a bit. It's very common for every ache or pain in someone who's suffered a major illness or trauma to get magnified in their head.'

Margie gave a sound of agreement. 'Well, enough about me and my troubles. How are you and Zach getting on?'

'Fine.'

'Just fine?'

Izzy picked off a yellowed leaf from the pot plant on

the counter. 'There's nothing serious going on between us. We both know and understand that.'

'Would you like it to be more?'

'I'm leaving at the end of next week.'

'That's not the answer I was looking for,' Margie said.

'It's the only one I'm prepared to give.'

Margie looked at her thoughtfully for a lengthy moment. 'Don't make the same mistake I made, Izzy. I should've told Doug years ago what I felt for him. Now it's too late.'

'I spent four years with a man and then realised I didn't love him enough to marry him,' Izzy said. 'What makes you think I would be so confident about my feelings after less than four weeks?'

Margie gave her a sage look. 'Because when you know you just know.'

CHAPTER THIRTEEN

IZZY WALKED DOWN to the community centre during her lunch break. She had arranged to meet Peggy McLeod there as well as Caitlyn Graham, who had finally agreed to work with Peggy in a mentor and mentee role. Peggy as a mother and grandmother with years of wisdom and experience working in the community was just what Caitlyn needed as a role model. Peggy had even offered to babysit Skylar occasionally when the boys were at school so Caitlyn could get a bit of a break. But when Izzy arrived at the centre Peggy was on her own.

'Where's Caitlyn?'

Peggy gave Izzy a miffed look over her shoulder as she placed a box of building blocks on the shelves one of the local farmers had made specially. 'Decided she had better things to do.'

'But I confirmed it with her yesterday,' Izzy said. 'She said she was looking forward to it. It was the first time I'd ever seen her excited about something.'

'Yes, well, she called me not five minutes ago and told me she's changed her mind.'

Changed her mind or had it changed for her? Izzy wondered. 'I think I'd better go and check on her. Maybe one of the kids is sick or something.'

'The boys are at school,' Peggy said. 'I waved to them in the playground when I drove past.'

'Maybe Skylar's sick.'

'Then why didn't she just say so?'

Izzy frowned. 'What *did* she say?'

Peggy pursed her lips. 'Just that she'd changed her mind. Told me she didn't want me babysitting for her either. I've brought up five kids and I'm a grandmother twelve times over. What does she think I am? An axe murderer or something?'

'Don't take it personally,' Izzy said. 'She's not used to having anyone step in and help her. I'll duck out there now and see if I can get her to change her mind.'

Izzy thought about calling Zach to come with her but changed her mind at the last minute. His car wasn't at the station in any case and she didn't want to make a big issue out of what could just be a case of Caitlyn's lack of self-esteem kicking in. She'd tried calling her a couple of times but the phone had gone to message bank.

Caitlyn's old car was parked near the house but apart from the frenzied barking of the dog near the tank stand there was no sign of life. Izzy walked tentatively to the front door, saying, 'Nice doggy, good doggy,' with as much sincerity as she could muster. She put her hand up to knock but the door suddenly opened and she found herself face to face with a thick-set man in his late twenties, who was even scarier than the dog lunging on its chain to her left.

'What do you want?' the man snarled.

'Um… Hello, is Caitlyn home? I'm Isabella Courtney, the locum filling in for—'

'Did she call you?'

'No, I just thought I'd drop past and—'

'She don't need no doctor so you can get back in your fancy car and get the hell out of here.'

The sound of Skylar crying piteously in one of the back rooms of the house made Izzy's heart lurch. 'Is Skylar OK? She sounds terribly upset. Is she—?'

'You want me to let the dog off?' His cold eyes glared at her through the tattered mesh of the screen door.

Izzy garnered what was left of her courage. She straightened her shoulders and looked him in the eye with what she hoped looked like steely determination. 'I'd like to talk to Caitlyn before I leave.'

Wayne suddenly shoved the screen door wide open, which forced her to take a couple of rapid steps backwards that sent her backwards off the veranda to land in an ungainly heap on her bottom in the dust. 'I said clear off,' he said.

Izzy scrambled to her feet, feeling a fool and a coward and so angry and utterly powerless she wanted to scream. But she knew the best thing to do was to leave and call Zach as soon as she was out of danger. She dusted off the back of her skirt and walked back to her car with as much dignity as she could muster. Her hand trembled uncontrollably as she tried to get her car key in the ignition slot to start the engine. It took her five tries to do it. Her heart was hammering in her chest and terrified sobs were choking out of her throat as she drove out of the driveway.

Zach was on the road when he got a distressed call from Izzy. 'Hey, slow down, sweetheart. I can't understand a word you're saying.'

She was crying and gasping, her breathing so erratic

it sounded like she was choking. 'I think Wayne's hurt Caitlyn. She didn't turn up at the playgroup. I heard Skylar screaming in the background. I think he'd been drinking. I could smell it. You have to do something. You have to hurry.'

'Where are you?'

'I—I'm on the road just past the t-turnoff.'

'Stop driving. Pull over. Do it right now.' He didn't let out his breath until he heard her do as he'd commanded. 'Good girl. Now wait for me. I'm only a few minutes away. I'll call Rob for back-up. Just stay put, OK?'

'OK…'

Zach called his colleague and quickly filled him in. He drove as fast as he could to where Izzy was parked on the side of the road. She was as white as a stick of chalk and tumbled out of the car even before he had pulled to a halt.

He gathered her close, reassuring himself she was all right before he put her from him. 'I'm going to check things out. I've called the volunteer ambulance and put them on standby. I want you to stay here until I see what the go is. I'll call you if we need you. It might not be as serious as you think.'

Her eyes looked as big as a Shetland pony's. 'You won't get hurt, will you?'

'Course not.' He quickly kissed her on the forehead. 'I've got a gun, remember?'

Izzy took a steadying breath as she waited for Zach to contact her. It seemed like ten hours but it was only ten minutes before he called her to inform her Caitlyn and Skylar were fine. 'Brody was his usual charming self,' he said. 'But Caitlyn insisted he hadn't hurt her or the child. She didn't appear to have any marks or bruises and the child seemed settled enough. She was sound asleep when I looked in on her. Apparently Brody was insisting she take a nap and wouldn't let Caitlyn go in to comfort her.'

'And you believed him?'

'I can't arrest him without evidence and Caitlyn swears he didn't do anything.'

Izzy blew out a breath of frustration. 'If he didn't hurt her today he will do sooner or later. I just know it.'

'Welcome to the world of tricky relationships.'

They can't get any trickier than the one I'm in, Izzy thought. 'Can I see you after work?'

'Not too busy with emails and video calls to your friends?'

'Not tonight.'

'Good,' he said. 'I happen to be free too.'

Izzy got back to the clinic in time to see her list of afternoon patients but just as she was about to finish for the day Margie popped her head into her consulting room. 'You got a minute?'

'Sure.' Izzy put down the pen she had been using to write up her last patient's details, mentally preparing herself for another emotional outpouring of Margie's unrequited love story. It wasn't that she didn't want to listen or support her. It was just too close to what she was feeling about Zach. How could it be possible to fall in love with someone so quickly? Did that sort of thing really happen or was that just in Hollywood movies? Was she imagining how she felt? Was it just this crazy lust fest she had going on with him that was colouring her judgement?

Margie rolled her lips together, looking awkward and embarrassed as she came into the room. 'It's not about Doug or anything like that… It's a personal thing. A health thing.'

'What's the problem?'

'I found a lump.'

'In your breast?'

Margie nodded, and then gave her lower lip a little chew. 'I've been a bit slack about doing my own checks but when you ordered that mammogram for Kathleen Fisher earlier today it got me thinking. I went to the bathroom just then. I found a lump.'

Izzy got up from her chair and came from behind the desk. 'Hop on the examination table and I'll have a feel of it for you. Try not to worry too much. Breast tissue can go through lots of changes for any number of reasons.'

Margie lay back on the table and unbuttoned her blouse and unclipped her bra. 'I can't believe I've been so stupid not to check my own breasts. I haven't done it for months, maybe even a couple of years.'

Izzy palpated Margie's left breast where, high in the upper part, there was a definite firm nodule, about the size of a walnut. 'You're right, there is a lump there. Is it tender at all?'

'No, it's not sore at all. It's cancer, isn't it?'

'Hang on, Margie. It could be any of several things. It could be a cyst, some hormonal thickening, maybe a benign tumour. It could possibly be cancer, but we have to do some tests in Bourke to tell what it is.'

'What do we do now?' Margie's expression was stricken. 'I'm worried. What am I going to tell the kids?'

'We'll do what we always do—we'll go step by step, figure out what the lump is and then fix it,' Izzy said. 'First we get a mammogram and ultrasound. Then, at the same time, we'll get the mammogram people to take a needle sample of the lump. That should give us the diagnosis. If it's a cyst, we just aspirate the fluid with a needle and that's usually the end of it. If the biopsy shows cancer cells, we get a surgeon to deal with it.'

'If it's cancer, will I have to have a mastectomy?'

'Mastectomies are very uncommon these days. Usually just the lump plus one lymph gland is removed, and then the breast gets some radiotherapy. If the lymph node was positive, possibly some more surgery to the armpit and maybe some chemo or hormonal therapies.'

Margie swung her legs off the examination table, her expression contorted with anguish as her fingers fumbled with the buttons on her blouse. 'I don't want to die. I have so much I want to do. I want to see my grandkids grow up. I want Doug to—' She suddenly looked at Izzy. 'Oh, God, what am I going to say to Doug? He'll never want me now, not if I've got cancer.'

Izzy took Margie's hand and gave it a comforting squeeze. 'No one's talking about dying. These days breast cancer is a very treatable disease when it's caught early. Let's take this one step at a time.'

'But who will run the clinic while I go to Bourke for the biopsy?'

'I'm sure I'll manage for a day without you,' Izzy said. 'I can divert the phone to mine, or maybe I could ask Peggy to sit by the phone. I'm sure she wouldn't mind.'

Margie sank her teeth into her lip. 'You know...the scary thing is if you hadn't been here filling in for William Sawyer I might not have bothered asking him to check me. I've known him so long it's kind of embarrassing, you know?'

'A lot of women feel the same way you do about seeing a male doctor for anything gynaecological or for breast issues, but all doctors, male or female, are trained to assess both male and female conditions.' Izzy wrote out the biopsy order form and a referral letter. 'I'll phone the surgeon and see if I can get you in this week. The sooner we know what we're dealing with the better.'

'Thanks, Izzy.' Margie clutched the letter to her chest. 'I don't mind if you tell Zach about this. I think Doug would want to know.'

'Why don't you call Doug yourself?'

Margie's eyes watered up. 'Because I'll just howl and blubber like a baby. I think it's better if he hears it from Zach. Will you be seeing him tonight?'

'He's dropping in after work.'

Margie's hand stalled on the doorknob as she looked back at Izzy over her shoulder. 'William is going to retire in a year or so. Maybe if you stayed you could job-share or something.'

'I can't stay. My home is in England.' She said it like a mantra. Like a creed. 'It's where I belong.'

'Is that where your heart is?'

'Of course.' Izzy kept her expression under such tight control it was painful. 'Where else would it be?'

Izzy opened the door to Zach a couple of hours later. 'Hi.'

He ran a finger down the length of her cheek in a touch as light as a brushstroke. 'You OK?'

She blew out a long exhausted-sounding breath. 'What a day.'

He closed the door behind him and reached for her, cupping her face in his hands and kissing her gently on the mouth. A soft, comforting kiss that was somehow far more meaningful and moving than if he'd let loose with a storm of passion. It was his sensitivity that made her heart contract. It wasn't because she was in love with him. That thought was off limits. Her brain was barricaded like a crime scene. Cordoned off. *Do Not Enter*.

He pulled back to look at her, still holding her hands in his. 'I've got some good news.'

Izzy gave him a weary look. 'I could certainly do with some. What is it?'

'Caitlyn Graham filed a domestic assault complaint an hour ago. That's why I'm late. Rob's taking Wayne Brody to Bourke to formally charge him.'

Izzy clutched at his hands. 'Is she all right? Should I go and see her?'

'She's gone to Peggy McLeod's place with the kids. I thought you'd had enough drama for one day.'

'What happened? I thought you were certain he hadn't hurt her when you went out there?'

'He hadn't at that stage,' Zach said. 'He'd verbally threatened her. Refused to let her leave the house, that sort of thing. But a couple of hours after we left, when the boys got home from school on the bus he started trying to lay into her. Apparently he's done it before but never in front of the boys. Jobe called triple zero.'

'Are you sure Caitlyn's not hurt? Are the kids OK?'

'Brody was too tanked to do much after the first swing, which Caitlyn luckily managed to dodge. She barricaded herself and the kids in the bathroom and waited for Rob and me to arrive.'

Izzy shuddered at the thought of the terror Caitlyn and the kids must have felt. 'I'm so glad she's finally out of danger. I felt sure it would only be a matter of time before he did something to her or one of the kids. He was so threatening to me. I thought he was going to assault me for sure.'

'If he had, he would've had me to answer to.' A quiver went through her at the implacability in his tone and his grey-blue eyes had a hard, self-satisfied glitter to them as he added, 'As it was, I already had a little score to settle with him.'

Izzy ran a gentle fingertip over the angry graze marks on the backs of the knuckles on his right hand. 'You wouldn't do anything outside the law, would you, Sergeant?' she asked.

He gave her an inscrutable smile. 'I'm one of the good guys, remember?'

She stepped up on tiptoe and pressed a kiss to his lips. 'I didn't realise they still made men like you any more.'

He threaded his fingers through her hair, gently massaging her scalp. 'You sure you're OK?'

Sensitive. Thoughtful. Gallant. What's not to love?

Izzy stepped back behind the yellow and black tape in her head. 'Margie has a lump in her breast.'

His brows snapped together in shock. 'Cancer?'

'I don't know yet. She has to have a mammogram and ultrasound and possibly a fine needle biopsy. I've managed to get her an appointment the day after tomorrow.' Izzy let out a breath. 'She wanted me to tell you so you could tell your dad.'

'Why doesn't she want to tell him herself?'

'I asked her the same thing but she's worried about getting too upset.'

He dropped his hands from her head and raked one through his own hair. 'Poor Margie. This town would be lost without her. My dad would be lost without her.'

'What a pity he hasn't told her that,' Izzy said on another sigh.

He gave her a thoughtful look. 'He will when he realises it.'

CHAPTER FOURTEEN

'CANCER?' DOUG'S FACE blanched. 'Why on earth didn't she tell me herself?'

Zach mentally rolled his eyes. 'You're the one who blew her off because she was getting too close.'

His father looked the colour of grey chalk. 'Is it serious? Is she going to die?'

'I don't know the answer to that. No one does yet. Izzy's organised a biopsy for her in Bourke. We'll know more after the results of that come through.'

'I need to see her. Will you drive me there now? I just want to see her to make sure she's all right.'

'What, *now?*'

'Why not now?' Doug said. 'She shouldn't be on her own at a time like this. Better still, I'll pack a bag and stay with her. I'll go with her to the appointment. She'll want someone with her. Might as well be me.'

Zach felt a warm spill of hope spread through his chest. 'You sure about this? You haven't stayed anywhere overnight other than hospital or rehab since the accident.'

Doug gave him a glowering look. 'I'm not a complete invalid, you know. I might not be able to do some of the things I used to do but I can still support a friend when they need me. Margie was the first person other than you to come to see me after the accident. She sat for days by my bedside. It's only right that I support her through this.'

Three days later Izzy opened the letter from the surgeon with trembling hands. Margie and Doug were sitting together in her consulting room, holding hands like teenagers on their first date.

'I want you to know I'm going to marry Margie, no matter what that letter says,' Doug said. 'I've already talked to Reverend Taylor.'

Izzy acknowledged that with a smile. Zach had already told her the good news. Now it was time for the bad news. She looked at the typed words on the single sheet of paper with the pathology report attached. She breathed out a sigh of relief. Not such bad news after all. 'It's not as bad as it could be. It's a DCIS—'

'What's that?' Doug asked, before Izzy could explain.

'DCIS is duct cancer in situ. It's not cancer but a step before you to get to cancer. It's like catching the horse just before it bolts.'

'So I don't have cancer? But you said duct cancer. I don't understand. Do I have it or not?' Margie asked.

'I'll try and explain it the best I can,' Izzy said. 'Think of it like this. Our body is made up of trillions of cells. Each cell has a computer program in it, telling it what to do. The computer program becomes damaged in some cell and the cell doesn't do what it's supposed to do. The worst-case scenario is when a whole lot of damage occurs, the cell goes out of control, starts multiplying too many copies of itself and won't stop. The copies spread throughout the body. That's cancer. But DCIS is where only a little bit of damage has occurred so far—the cell is a bit iffy when it comes to taking orders, but isn't yet out of control. If the lump is fully removed the problem has been cured.'

'Cured? Just by removing the lump? You mean surgery will fix this?' Doug asked.

'Yes, but the surgeon is still recommending radiotherapy afterwards because although the palpable lump of DCIS will be removed, there could be other unstable cells in the breast about to do the same thing. You'll need regular follow-up but it's certainly a lot better news than it could have been.'

Doug hugged Margie so tightly it looked like he was going to snap her in two. 'I can't believe what a fool I've been for all these years. We'll get married as soon as it can be arranged and go on a fancy cruise for our honeymoon once you've got the all-clear.'

Margie laughed and hugged him back. 'I feel like I've won the lottery. I'm not going to die and I've got the man of my dreams wanting to marry me.' She turned to Izzy. 'How can I thank you?'

'Nothing to thank me for,' Izzy said. 'I'm just doing my job.'

Which will end in two days' time.

Zach had been dreading the Shearers' Ball. Not just because too many of the locals had too much to drink and he had to be the fun police, but because it was the last night Izzy was going to be in town. Neither of them had mentioned that fact over the last couple of days. The drama with Margie and then the relief of his father finally getting his act together had pushed the elephant out of the room.

Now it was back...but Zach was painfully aware its bags were packed.

As soon as Zach arrived at the community centre where the country-style ball was being held he saw Izzy. She was wearing a fifties-style dress with a circle skirt in a bright shade of red that made her look like a poppy in a field of dandelions. He had never seen her look more beautiful. He had never seen *anyone* look more beautiful. Her hair was up in that half casual, half formal style, her creamy skin was highlighted with the lightest touch of make-up and those gorgeous kissable lips shimmered with lip-gloss.

The locals surrounded her, each one wanting to have their share of her. Caitlyn Graham was there with the kids, looking relaxed and happy for the first time in years. Peggy McLeod was cuddling Skylar and smiling at something Caitlyn had said to Izzy.

Jim Collis wandered over with a beer in his hand. 'She's something else, isn't she?'

Zach kept his expression masked. 'I see you got your tyres fixed.'

'Cost me a fortune.' Jim took another swig of his beer. 'Hey, good news about Margie and your old man. About bloody time. Look at them over there. Anyone would think they were sixteen again.'

Zach looked towards the back of the community hall where his father was seated next to Margie on a hay bale, their hands joined, his father's walking frame proving a rather useful receptacle for Margie's handbag as well as a place to put their drinks and a plate of the delicious food Peggy and her team had organised. 'Yeah. I'm happy for him. For both of them.'

'So…' Jim gave Zach a nudge with his elbow. 'What about you and the doc?'

'She's leaving tomorrow.' Zach said it as if the words weren't gnawing a giant hole in his chest. 'Got a new locum position in Brisbane. Starting on Monday.'

'Brisbane's not so far away. Maybe you could—'

'What would be the point?' Zach said. 'She's going back to England in July. It's where she belongs. Excuse me.' He gave Jim a dismissive look. 'I'm going to get something to drink.'

Izzy saw Zach standing to the left of the entrance of the community centre with a can of lemonade in his hand. He had his cop face on, acknowledging the locals who greeted him with a stiff movement of his lips as if it physically pained him to crack a full smile. She knew events like these were often quite stressful for country police officers. There were always a couple of locals who liked to drink a little too much and things could turn from a fun-loving party into an out of control mêlée in less time than it took to shake a cocktail. Friends could become enemies in a matter of minutes and the cop on duty had to be ready to control things and keep order.

Izzy had spent a few hours last night with Zach but the topic of her leaving had been carefully skirted around. She'd told him she was looking forward to the Brisbane locum but even as she'd said the words she'd felt a sinkhole of sadness open up inside her. It was like her mouth was saying one thing while her heart was saying another. *Feeling* another. But it wasn't like she could tell him how she felt. What woman in her right mind would tell a man she had only known a month that she loved him? He'd think she was mad.

It was a fling. A casual hook-up that had suited both of them. They had both needed to get over their broken engagements. Their short-term relationship had been a healing process, an exercise in closure so now they were both free to move on with their lives.

The trouble was it didn't feel like a fling. It had never felt like a fling.

Izzy went over to him with a plate of savoury nibbles Peggy had thrust in her hand on her way past. 'Having fun over here all by yourself?'

He gave her a dry look. 'You know that word "wall-flower"? I'm more of a wall tree.'

She smiled. 'I'm pretty good on a city nightclub dance floor but out here among the hay bales I'm not sure what might happen.'

'Are you asking me to dance with you?'

Izzy was asking much more than that and wondered if he could see it in her eyes. His expression, however, was much harder to read. He had that invisible wall around him but whether it was because he was on duty or because he was holding back from her for other reasons she couldn't quite tell. 'Not if you don't want to.'

He put his can of lemonade on a nearby trestle table. 'Come on.' He took her hand as the music started. 'One dance then I'm back on duty.'

As soon as his arms went around her Izzy felt as if everyone else in the community centre had faded into the background. It was just Zach and her on the hay-strewn dance floor, their bodies moving as one in a waltz to a poignant country music ballad.

Zach's breath stirred her hair as he turned her round in a manoeuvre that would have got a ten out of ten on a reality dance show. 'You know what happens if you play country music backwards?'

Izzy looked up at him with a quizzical smile. 'No, what?'

'You get your job back, your dead dog comes back to life and your girlfriend stops sleeping with your best mate.'

It was a funny joke and it should have made her laugh out loud but instead she felt like crying. She blinked a couple of times and forced a smile. 'I'm really going to miss Popeye. Do you think I could—?' She looked at his shirt collar instead. 'No, maybe not. I'm not very good at goodbyes.'

'What time do you leave?' The question was as casual as *What do you think of the weather?*

'Early. It's a long drive.' Izzy was still focusing her gaze on his collar but it had become blurry. 'I don't want to rush it.'

'Izzy…' His throat moved up and down as if he had taken a bigger than normal swallow.

She looked into his grey-blue eyes, her heart feeling like it had moved out of her chest and was now beating in her oesophagus. 'Yes?'

His eyes moved back and forth between each of hers as if he was searching for something hidden there. 'Thank you for what you did for my father.'

Izzy wondered if that was what he had really intended to say. There was something about his tone and his manner that didn't seem quite right. 'I didn't do anything.'

He stopped dancing and stood with his arms still

around her, his eyes locked on hers. It was as if he had completely forgotten they were in the middle of the community centre dance floor, with the whole town watching on the sidelines. 'You didn't give up on him.'

Izzy gave him another wry smile. 'I like to give everyone a decent chance.'

He looked about to say something else but the jostling of the other dancers seemed to jolt him back into the present. A shutter came down on his face and he spoke in a flat monotone. 'We're holding up traffic.' He dropped his hands from her and stepped back. 'I'll let you mingle. I'll catch you later.'

'Zach…?' Izzy's voice was so husky it didn't stand a chance over the loud floor-stomping music Bill Davidson had exchanged for the ballad. She watched as Zach walked out of the community centre without even acknowledging Damien Redbank, who spoke to him on the way past.

It was another hour before Izzy could get anywhere near Zach again. She got caught up in a progressive barn dance and then a vigorous Scottish dance that left one of the older locals a little short of breath. She had to make sure the man was not having a cardiac arrest before she could go in search of Zach. She found him talking on his mobile out by the tank stand. He acknowledged her with a brief flicker of his lips as he slipped his phone away. 'All danced out?'

Izzy grimaced as she tucked a damp strand of hair behind her ear. 'I've been swung about so energetically I think both my shoulders have popped out of their sockets.'

'The Gay Gordons not your thing, then?' It was difficult to tell if he was smiling or not as his face was now in shadow.

'I loved it. It's the best workout I've had since...well, since last night.'

He stepped out of the cloaking shadow of the community centre but didn't look at her; instead, he was looking out into the sprawling endless darkness beyond town. 'That was my mother on the phone.'

'Does she call you often?'

'Not often.' Izzy heard him scrape the gravel with the toe of his boot. 'That's probably as much my fault as hers.'

'Would you ever consider going over to see her again some time?'

He lifted a shoulder and then let it drop. 'Maybe.'

'Maybe you could look me up if you do.' As soon as she'd said the words she wished she hadn't. They made her sound as if she was content to be nothing more than a booty call. She wanted more. *So much more.*

'What would be the point?'

Izzy rolled her lips together. 'It would be nice to catch up.'

'To do what?' His eyes looked as hard as diamond chips now. 'To pick up where we left off?'

She let out a slow, measured breath. 'I just thought—'

'What did you think, Izzy?' His tone hardened, along with his gaze. 'That I'd ask you to hang around so we could pretend a little longer this is going to last for ever? This was never about for ever. We've had our fun. Now it's time for you to leave as planned.'

Izzy swallowed a knot of pain. 'Is that what you want?'

His expression went back to its fall-back position. Distant. Aloof. Closed off. 'Of course it is.'

'I don't believe you.' She held his strong gaze with indomitable force. 'You're lying. You want me to stay. I know you do. You *want* me, Zach. I feel it in every fibre of my being. How can you stand there and pretend you don't?'

His mouth flattened. 'Don't make this ugly, Izzy.'

'You're the one making it ugly,' she said. 'You're making out that what we've shared has been nothing more than some tawdry little affair. How can you do that?'

A pulse beat like a hammer in his jaw. 'It was good sex. But I can have that with anyone. So can you.'

Izzy looked at him in wounded shock. This was not how things were supposed to be. The flag of hope in her chest was slipping back down the flagpole in despair. It was strangling her. Choking her. He was supposed to tell her he wanted more time with her. That he wanted her to stay. That he loved her. Not tell her she was replaceable.

Somehow she garnered her pride. 'Fine. Let's do it your way, then.' She stuck out her hand. 'Goodbye, Zach.'

He ignored her hand. He stood looking down at her with a stony expression on his face as if everything inside him had turned to marble. He didn't even speak. Not one word. Even the ticking pulse in his jaw had stopped.

Izzy returned her hand to her side. She would not let him see how much she was hurting. She straightened her shoulders and put one foot in front of the other as she walked back to the lights and music of the community centre.

When she got to the door and glanced back he was nowhere to be seen.

'All packed?' Margie asked, her smile sad and her eyes watery, as Izzy was about to head off the next morning.

'All packed.' Izzy had covered the track marks of her tears with the clever use of make-up but she wasn't sure the camouflage was going to last too long. Fresh tears were pricking like needles at the backs of her eyes and her heart felt like it was cracking into pieces. She'd lain awake most of the night, hoping Zach would come to her and tell her he'd made a terrible mistake, that he wanted her to stay, that he loved her with a for-ever love. But he hadn't turned up. He hadn't even sent a text. But that was his way. She had only known him four weeks but she knew that much about him. Once his mind was made up that was it. Over and out. No going back.

Doug shuffled forward to envelop her in a hug. 'Thanks.'

Izzy knew how much emotion was in that one simple word. She felt it vibrating in his body as she hugged him back as if he too was trying not to cry. 'Take care of yourself.'

'Where's Zach?' Margie asked Doug. 'I thought he'd be here to say goodbye.'

Doug's expression showed his frustration. 'I haven't seen him since daylight. Didn't say a word to me other than grunting something about taking Popeye for a walk. Haven't seen him since.'

'But I thought—' Margie began.

'He said all that needed to be said last night,' Izzy said, keeping her expression masked.

'Should've been here to see you off,' Doug said, frowning. 'What's got into him?'

Margie gave him a cautioning look before reaching to hug Izzy. 'I'm going to miss you *so* much.'

'I'll miss you too.'

With one last hug apiece Izzy got into her car and drove out of town. She had to blink to clear her vision as an overwhelming tide of emotion welled up inside her; it felt like she was leaving a part of herself behind.

She was.

Her heart.

Zach skimmed a stone across the surface of Blake's waterhole, watching as it skipped across the water six times before sinking. His record was fourteen skips but he wasn't getting anywhere near that today. He had been out here since dawn, trying to make sense of his feelings after his decision last night to end things with Izzy.

He kept reminding himself it was better this way. A clean cut healed faster than a festering sore.

But it didn't feel better. It felt worse. It hurt to think of Izzy driving away to her next post, finding some other guy to spend the rest of her life with while he tried to get on with his life out here.

He had never been a big believer in love at first sight. He had shied away from it because of what had happened between his parents. They'd married after a whirlwind courtship and his mother had spent the next decade being miserable and taking it out on everyone around her.

He didn't want to do that to Izzy. She hadn't had

enough time to get to know herself outside a relationship. He had no right to ask her to stay. What if she ended up hating him for it after a few weeks, months or years down the track?

He skimmed another stone but it only managed four skips before sinking. It felt like his heart, plummeting to the depths where it would never find the light of day again.

He thought of Izzy's smile, the way it lit up her face, the way it had beamed upon the dark sadness he had buried inside himself all those years ago. Would anyone else make him feel that spreading warmth inside his chest? Would anyone else make him feel alive and hopeful in spite of all the sickness and depravity of humanity he had to deal with in his work?

Izzy was not just a ray of sunshine.

She was *his* light.

He'd wanted to tell her last night. He'd *ached* to tell her. The words had been there but he'd kept swallowing them back down with common sense.

She was young and idealistic, full of romantic notions that didn't always play out in the real world. He was cynical and older in years, not to mention experience.

How could they make it work? How did any relationship work? *Could* they make theirs work?

How could he let her leave without telling her what he felt about her? If she didn't feel the same, he would have to bear that. At least he would be honest with her. He owed her that.

He owed himself that.

Zach drove out to the highway with Popeye on the seat beside him. 'I can't believe I'm doing this.' Popeye gave an excited yap. 'I mean it's crazy. I never do things like this. We've only known each other a month. It's not like she said she loved me. Not outright. What if I've got this wrong? What if she says no?' His fingers gripped the steering-wheel so tightly he was reminded of his grip on the veranda rail all those years ago.

What would have happened if he'd called out to his mother that day? Would it have changed anything? If nothing else, at least it would have assured his mother he loved her, even if she'd still felt the need to leave. He had never told his mother he loved her. Not since he was a little kid. That was something he would have to fix.

But not right now.

Miraculously, he suddenly saw Izzy's car ahead. He forced himself to slow down and watched her for a while, mentally rehearsing what he was going to say. He wasn't good at expressing emotion. He had spent his childhood locking away what he'd felt. His job had reinforced that pattern, demanding he kept his emotions under control at all times and in all places. What if he couldn't say what he wanted to say? Should he just blurt it out or lead in to it? His stomach was in knots. His heart felt as if it was in danger of splitting right down the middle.

He loved her.

He *really* loved her.

Not the pedestrian feelings he'd felt for Naomi.

His love for Izzy was a once-in-a-lifetime love. An all-or-nothing love.

A grand passion.

A for-ever love.

He suddenly realised her car was gathering speed. He checked his radar monitor. She was going twenty kilometres per hour over the limit! Acting on autopilot, he reached for his siren and lights switch, all the bells and whistles blaring as he put his foot down on the throttle.

Izzy was reaching for another tissue when she heard a police siren behind her. She glanced in the rear-view mirror, her heart flipping like a pancake flung by a master chef when she saw Zach behind the wheel, bearing down on her. She put her foot on the brake and pulled over to the gravel verge, trying to wipe the smeared mascara away from beneath her eyes. If he wanted a cold, clean break then that's what she would give him. Cold and clinical.

His tall, commanding figure appeared at her driver's window. The rim of his police hat shadowed his eyes and his voice was all business. 'Want to tell me why you were going twenty over the limit?'

She pressed her lips together. So that was going to be his parting gift, was it? *A speeding ticket!* 'I'm sorry, Officer, but I was reaching for a tissue.'

'Why are you crying?'

'I'm *not* crying.'

'Get out of the car.'

Izzy glowered at him. 'What *is* this?'

'I said get out of the car.'

She blew her cheeks out on a breath and stepped out, throwing him a defiant look. 'See? I'm not crying.'

His gaze held hers with his inscrutable one. 'Either you've been crying or you put your make-up on in the dark.'

Izzy put her hands on her hips and stared him down. 'Is it a crime to feel a little sad about leaving a town

I've grown to love? Is it, Sergeant show-no-emotion Fletcher? If so, go ahead and book me.'

A tiny glint came into his eyes. 'You love Jerringa Ridge?'

She folded her arms across her chest, still keeping her defiant glare in place. 'Yes.'

'What do you love about it?'

She was starting to feel a flutter of hope inside her chest, like a butterfly coming out of a chrysalis. 'I love the way it made me feel like I was the most beautiful person in the world. I love the way it made me feel passion I've never felt before. I love the way it opened its arms to me and held me close and made me feel safe.'

'That all?'

'That about covers it.'

He gave a slow nod. 'So...Brisbane, huh?'

She kept her chin up. 'Yes.'

He took off his hat and put it on the roof of her car, his movements slow, measured. 'You looking forward to that?'

'Not particularly.'

'Why not?'

Izzy looked into his now twinkling eyes. 'Because I'd much rather be here with you.'

He put his arms around her then, holding her so tightly against him she felt every button on his shirt pressing into her skin. 'I love you,' he said. 'I should've told you last night. I almost did...but I didn't want to put any pressure on you to stay. A public proposal seemed... I don't know...kind of tacky. Kind of manipulative.'

She looked up into his face with a wide-eyed look. 'A proposal?'

His expression was suddenly serious again. 'Izzy,

darling, I know we've only known each other a month. I know you have a life back in England, family and friends and roots that go deep. I would never ask you to give any of that up. All I'm asking is for you to give us a chance. We can make our home wherever you want to be. I can employ a manager for Fletcher Downs. Dad and Margie will be able to keep an eye on things. We can have the best of both worlds.' He cupped her face in his hands. '*You* are my world, darling girl. Marry me?'

Izzy smiled the widest smile she had ever smiled. 'Yes.'

He looked shocked. Taken aback. '*Yes?*'

'Yes, Zach.' She gave a little laugh at his expression. 'I will marry you. Why are you looking so surprised?'

'Because I didn't think it was possible to find someone like you.' He stroked her hair back from her face, his expression tender. 'Someone who would make me feel like this. I didn't know it could happen so fast and so completely. I want to spend the rest of my life with you. I think a part of me realised that the first time we kissed. It scared the hell out of me, to tell you the truth.'

'I felt that way too,' Izzy said. 'I was so miserable last night. I couldn't believe you were just going to leave it at that after all we'd shared. Our relationship was supposed to be a fling but nothing about it felt like a fling to me.'

He hugged her tightly again. 'I was trying to do the right thing by you by letting you go. But I couldn't believe how the right thing felt so incredibly painful. I decided I had to tell you how I felt, otherwise I'd spend the rest of my life regretting it.'

Her eyes twinkled as she looked up to hold his gaze. 'Promise me something?'

'Anything.'

'No five-star destinations for our honeymoon, OK?'

His eyes glinted again. 'You want to go camping?'

'Yes, and I want to swim naked and make love under the stars.' She hugged him close. 'I don't even mind if Max comes along as long as he has his own tent.'

'No way, baby girl,' Zach said. 'Max will have to find another place to stay while we're on our honeymoon. I'm not sharing you with anyone. Where is he, by the way?'

She gave him a sheepish look. 'He's in the boot. He wasn't too happy about being stashed in there but your dad and Margie came to say goodbye and I didn't have time to let him down properly.'

Zach grinned at her and pulled her close again. 'Maybe if I kiss you right now I won't think I'm dreaming this is happening. What do you reckon?'

She smiled as his mouth came down towards hers. 'I think that's an excellent idea.'

* * * * *

HIS DIAMOND
LIKE NO OTHER

BY
LUCY CLARK

Published in Great Britain 2014
by Mills & Boon, an imprint of Harlequin (UK) Limited,
Eton House, 18-24 Paradise Road, Richmond, Surrey, TW9 1SR

© 2014 Anne Clark & Peter Clark

ISBN: 978 0 263 90758 2

Harlequin (UK) Limited's policy is to use papers that are natural,
renewable and recyclable products and made from wood grown in
sustainable forests. The logging and manufacturing processes conform
to the legal environmental regulations of the country of origin.

Printed and bound in Spain
by Blackprint CPI, Barcelona

Dear Reader

While I was writing HIS DIAMOND LIKE NO OTHER it was winter in Australia. The cold, the rain and catching the inevitable cold. I was lying in my bed, sneezing and snuffling and generally feeling sorry for myself, but thankfully I had Jane and Sean to brighten my day and keep me company. This also might explain why HIS DIAMOND LIKE NO OTHER is set in summer! Oh, I could just *feel* that glorious sun on my face as I entered their lives.

HIS DIAMOND LIKE NO OTHER is also my 60th Mills & Boon® Medical Romance™ title. I confess at times it was very difficult to write, because I wanted to make it extra-special, extra-memorable and extra-gut-wrenchingly heartfelt. I do love Jane—so very much—but the thing I love most is that even though she's experienced some emotionally distressing times she hasn't let it beat her. She's been forced to save herself, to become a strong, independent woman, and it's these very qualities that attract Sean to her.

Sean made me smile and laugh and clap my hands like a silly schoolgirl. He has such presence and drive, and a loving, supportive family. I delighted at his relationship with his son, as well as the closeness he shares with his parents and sisters. Family is important, and Sean is not only able to show Jane that, but to open up his world and share it with her. Now, *that's* being a true hero!

I hope you enjoy HIS DIAMOND LIKE NO OTHER.

Warmest regards

Lucy

DEDICATION

To Mum & Dad.

Even though I'm all grown up now,
I still need you both. Thank you for always
being supportive and generous and loving.
—Ps 103

Praise for
Lucy Clark:

'A sweet and fun romance about second chances
and second love.'
—*HarlequinJunkie.com* on
DARE SHE DREAM OF FOREVER?

HIS DIAMOND LIKE NO OTHER
is Lucy Clark's 60th book for Mills & Boon®!

These books are also available in eBook format
from www.millsandboon.co.uk

CHAPTER ONE

'SO. IT *IS* YOU.'

Sean Booke's deep voice vibrated through Jane's body, causing her insides to tremble. She closed her eyes for a split second and forced herself to remain calm, at least on the outside. It wouldn't do to allow her ex-brother-in-law to rile her. Pasting on a polite smile, she turned to look at him, unconsciously shifting her glasses and straightening her shoulders, tugging at the sleeves of her top to ensure they covered her wrists. It was a defence mechanism, developed over many years to hide the scars which were a permanent reminder of the darkest time in her life.

Sean Booke stood before her, more vibrant, more handsome, more intimidating than he'd been the last time she'd seen him, which had been three years ago at her sister's funeral. Back then he'd been dressed in a black suit, which had perfectly matched his mood, and at the wake she'd had little chance to speak to him as he'd somehow managed to manoeuvre his way around to the opposite side of the room to wherever she'd been.

Eventually she'd received the message. Sean hadn't wanted to speak to her and it appeared, given the gruffness of his tone, that nothing had changed. He carried a small, slim computer tablet as well as two sets of patient files. Jane cleared her throat.

'How are you, Sean?' She silently congratulated herself on her polite, impersonal tone as she headed into the paediatric ward conference room ahead of him, wishing she hadn't been adamant about being early for her first scheduled ward round. She was nervous enough, not only about starting her new job but about Sean's reaction to her presence at his hospital.

He ignored her question, his brow deeply furrowed as he followed her. '*You're* the new paediatrician?'

'Correct.'

She turned and looked at him, pleased they were alone for this conversation. It had been inevitable, especially when she'd accepted the position at Adelaide's Children's Hospital. There was no coincidence about it. She'd decided it was time for her to return to Adelaide, to work at this particular hospital, the hospital where, at the age of thirteen, she'd been a patient. It was time she made the effort to put her ghosts to rest but she had to admit that Sean Booke was far from a ghost, especially with the way his spicy scent seemed to wind itself around her.

'I couldn't believe it when I read the inter-office memo announcing your arrival. Specialist paediatrician in juvenile eating disorders.' He put his bundle of notes and computer tablet onto the table then stared at her, as though he really could not believe it. Jane tried not to tug on her baggy top, which hung rather low over her ankle-length skirt. Fashion had never been her thing; instead, she'd focused on studying and getting good grades.

'I mean, how many Jane Diamonds are there in the

world?' Sean shook his head, his words still filled with
an angry bitterness that was simmering just below the
surface. He turned and walked over to the window.
'How long is your contract?'

'Twelve months.' She wanted to tell him she hadn't
meant to cause him any pain but she didn't think he'd
believe her. As far as Sean was concerned, he'd tarred
her with the same brush as Daina. The fact that Jane
had always been the polar opposite of her older sister
clearly was of little concern to him.

'And you *chose* to come here? You knew this was
my hospital.'

'I was *invited* to come and work here, Sean. I just
didn't turn it down.'

'You?' He glanced at her over his shoulder, frown
still in place. 'You were head-hunted? By whom?'

'Luc Bourgeois.' Jane tried to be brave, tried to hold
his piercing blue gaze. She pushed her glasses onto her
nose and nodded. 'I guess my past experience working
with Professor Edna Robe has finally paid off.'

'Robe? World-leading specialist in the field of paediatric eating disorders?'

Jane raised her chin, telling herself she had no reason to hide her successes. 'I've co-authored five papers
with her and presented our findings two months ago at
an eating disorder conference in Argentina.'

He turned from the window, arms still crossed, and
looked at her more closely. 'Huh!' was all he said, leaving Jane to ponder what on earth that might mean.

They remained silent for a minute, Jane wondering
whether she should say something else, anything else,
rather than stand here and not speak a word. Sean was
the man who had been married to her sister, he was

the father of her only living blood relative—six-year-old Spencer. She was desperate to ask him about her nephew but wasn't sure, given the reception she'd just received, whether that was a good idea. Then again, perhaps he might think her strange if she *didn't* ask.

'You need more confidence in yourself, Jane,' Professor Robe had said to her late last year, hence why Jane had been the one presenting the paper in Argentina. Confidence? She had confidence in spades when it came to treating and caring for her young patients but a one-on-one confrontation with the man who had the power to refuse her request was bringing her inner doubts to the fore. She had to get past it.

'How's Spencer?' The words were out of her mouth before she could stop and analyse them any further.

Sean's frown returned but it wasn't as deep as it had previously been. 'He's fine.'

'How's he doing in school?' Now that she'd opened the discussion, she really did want to know more. She had so many questions about her nephew, along with the wish that Sean would grant her access to him.

'Fine.'

'Does he have any plans for his birthday? A present list? I'd rather get him something he really wants than have to guess.' Good heavens. She was starting to babble now.

The arms tightened defensively over his chest and Jane found herself momentarily distracted by the way his crisp white shirt pulled around his biceps. She tried to school her senses. Of course Sean was a dynamic, good-looking man. It was the reason her wayward sister had been attracted to him in the first place.

'Why do you want to know about Spencer? You've

never shown more than a passing interest in him before now.'

Jane felt as though he'd slapped her as that clearly wasn't true. 'I've sent Christmas and birthday presents every year,' she defended, feeling her temper beginning to rise. Usually, she was quite a calm and controlled woman but when she thought about facing her future, one of only work and loneliness, she was filled with desperation…desperation to make sure that *didn't* happen. Now she was desperate to make sure Sean realised just how much she loved her nephew, even though she didn't know him as well as she would have liked.

'And you've always been more than generous with your gifts. Still, you've never made any effort to see him.'

'Any effor—' She broke off her incredulous reply as two paediatric nurses walked into the conference room, greeting Sean with bright smiles. Jane boxed up her simmering anger at Sean and put it aside, pulling on her professionalism. When Sean made no effort to introduce Jane, instead immersing himself in setting up his computer and connecting it to the equipment in the room, Jane forced herself to step forward and hold out her hand. 'Hi. I'm Jane Diamond.'

'Oh the new paediatrician, the eating disorder specialist,' one of the women stated, shaking Jane's hand. 'Welcome. I'm Anthea. This is Romana. We're really glad you're here. Such a necessary sub-speciality you cover.' Anthea was still nodding as she spoke. 'Let us know if you need help settling in or finding your way about the hospital.'

Jane smiled, ignoring Sean's presence completely.

'I was actually a patient here, in this very ward, when I was thirteen.'

'Really?'

'Wow.'

'It doesn't seem like the general hospital layout has changed all that much since then.'

'Sad but true,' Romana said with a laugh.

'At least the equipment's been updated,' Anthea added, smiling. As more people came into the conference room, Anthea made sure Jane was introduced. Sean had moved to the corner of the room and she could almost feel him watching her, but every time she glanced in his direction he was either deeply engrossed in conversation with someone else or looking at a set of scans that were due to be discussed during the short prelude before the ward round.

The pre-ward round began with head of unit, Luc Bourgeois, introducing her. 'Jane and I worked together in Paris for twelve months and I have to say, when she finally agreed to my constant pleading to come and work here, I was relieved. Eating disorders, especially amongst children under the age of eight, have gone unchecked for too long. This hospital plans to change that. Jane will be undertaking a research project whilst she's here and I'm expecting everyone to afford her every professional courtesy with regard to patient care and participating with the project if required.'

'Absolutely,' Anthea agreed, and a few people even gave Jane a smattering round of applause. She felt highly self-conscious standing in front of everyone but forced herself to smile and nod. Standing in front of a lecture room full of people wasn't her favourite thing to do but she was forcing herself to get used to it. What made today's experience even more unnerving was the fact that she was so highly aware of Sean's presence.

He was standing at the front of the room as well, waiting to present an interesting case for discussion before they all headed out to begin the ward round. When Luc had finished successfully embarrassing her by listing all her accomplishments, as well as sharing one or two small anecdotes of the time they'd worked together in Paris several years ago, Jane went to move to the side of the room but somehow managed to trip over her own feet and slam straight into Sean.

His hands immediately came around her waist, steadying her. Jane was minutely aware of the way his warmth seemed to surround her, of the way his firm muscled torso pressed against her shoulder, of the way his scent danced about her senses, creating a heady combination and one she was far from immune to.

A few of the people in the room chuckled, not unkindly, and Jane quickly collected herself, shifting awkwardly, wanting to put distance between them, but instead she ended up staring directly into Sean's eyes. Everything in the room seemed to freeze. She could hear the flutter of her eyelashes as she blinked once, then twice, the pounding of her heart against her chest and the way his breath seemed to mingle with hers.

'Steady on.' His deep voice was filled with concern, or so it seemed, but that couldn't be right. Sean didn't like her. Sean had never liked her. During the course of his marriage to her sister, they'd rarely spoken.

'Er…sorry,' Jane muttered, the world around her returning to normal speed. It felt as though she'd been pressed up against Sean's warm body for quite some time, although only a few seconds had passed. She jerked from his hands and he dropped them instantly, mildly surprised, as though he hadn't even realised he'd been touching her.

'And now Sean's going to present us with a few case studies, which I'd like everyone to pay close attention to during the ward round,' Luc announced, as Jane shifted towards the rear of the room, leaning against the wall, desperate to hide herself away in an attempt to recover her equilibrium.

She watched as Sean stepped forward to talk, using a small remote to produce a radiographic image on the audio-visual screen that was linked to his computer tablet. How could she have tripped like that? Fallen against *him*? She tried to swallow over her dry throat, surprised to find she was actually trembling from the encounter with him. He was *Sean*, for goodness' sake, and he didn't like her.

She breathed in, needing to gain some level of control over her senses, needing to concentrate on what Sean was saying, but all she was conscious of when she breathed in was the lingering spicy scent she'd always equated with him. It was the same cologne he'd worn all those years ago when they'd first met. She'd been nothing more than a braces-wearing student of seventeen, studying furiously for her final school exams, when Sean had married her sister.

The two had met in the emergency department at a hospital in Sydney. Daina had been holidaying with friends, partying too hard, and had badly twisted her ankle. Sean had been the intern who had treated her. Daina had left the hospital with a perfectly bandaged foot, a pair of crutches and a date.

After a whirlwind romance Daina had eventually

told Jane that she wasn't coming back to live in Adelaide because she was married. Sean had accompanied his new wife back to Adelaide, met his new sister-in-law for the first time and casually suggested that with the subjects she was studying she could definitely get into medical school.

Even though Jane had been six months shy of her eighteenth birthday, Daina, who was her legal guardian, had upped and left, returning to Sydney with her new, handsome prize of a husband. Jane had seriously hoped that Sean would be able to fix Daina, that he'd realise she was suffering from some sort of multiple personality disorder, that he'd be able to get her the help she needed. But, almost six years later, after giving birth to a child she hadn't wanted, Daina had abandoned him and taken off. Three years after that, she was dead.

Jane was unable to believe the pain Daina had caused her, not only after their parents' death but prior to it as well. In fact, it had been Daina who had caused the car accident that had robbed Jane of her parents at the age of thirteen. For years Jane had bottled up the resentment she'd felt towards her older sibling and she'd thought that coming home to Adelaide, making an effort to get to know Spencer as much as Sean would allow, she'd hopefully be able to put her past pain to rest.

'Jane? *Jane?*'

Her eyes snapped open to find Sean standing before her, the rest of the medical staff who had been attending the pre-ward round meeting filing out of the small conference room.

'Would you care to join us?' His tone was filled with derision but she watched his eyes widen slightly as she carefully lifted her glasses and dabbed at her eyes, annoyed with herself for not paying closer attention during the meeting and for tearing up in front of *him*.

'Are you all right?' His tone was still gruff but there was also a hint of confused concern.

Jane sniffed and settled her glasses on her nose. 'I'm fine.'

'You're not. I can hear it in your voice.'

'Leave it.' She went to step around him but he moved and blocked her way.

'You look like Daina when you do that. That "don't mess with me" look.'

Jane tilted her head and glared at him. 'Then remind me not to do it again.' She moved quickly, effectively sidestepping him, and followed the last of the staff out of the room.

It wasn't exactly the beginning she'd hoped for but, really, had she honestly expected Sean to accept her presence, especially when she clearly did remind him, in small ways, of his deceased wife?

'It's no use, Luc,' she told her friend a week later as they sat in the hospital cafeteria, enjoying a quick morning cuppa before the hecticness of their day descended. 'Sean has made it quite clear over the past week that he resents me being here.'

'Nonsense.' Luc dunked a piece of croissant in his coffee before eating it. 'He's just…getting used to the idea, that's all.'

Jane levelled him with a stare of disbelief and Luc had the audacity to laugh.

'It's true, Jane. When you first mentioned to me, all those years ago when we worked in Paris, that a man

called Sean Booke was married to your sister, I thought
nothing of it.'

'Because back then you had no idea who he was,'
Jane pointed out.

'True, but then years later when I returned to Adelaide, who do I find myself working with? None other
than your Sean Booke.' Luc finished off his croissant
then spread his hands wide. 'It's one of the reasons why
I encouraged you to come back to Adelaide, to get to
know him. Sure, your sister has passed away but family is family. Plus, he's a nice guy, Jane.'

'To everyone but me.'

'So you admit he's good with the patients?'

Jane looked into her almost empty cup as she thought
back to the way she'd watched Sean interact with the
patients in the ward and she had to admit he was an
excellent doctor. He wouldn't rush the kids if they had
something to say; instead, he'd sit on their beds and
listen patiently while they talked. In clinic, she had
seen several of his patients coming out of his consulting
room with wide, beaming smiles on their faces, their
parents looking equally as pleased.

'Of course he's good with the patients,' she told Luc,
'otherwise you wouldn't have him working in your department.'

'Very true. I only employ the best—which is the
other reason you're here because even without the prospect of getting to know your nephew, I still would have
hounded you to work here. That was just my trump
card.'

'I know.' Jane finished the rest of her drink, grimac-
ing a little at the coolness of the liquid. 'We'd better go
or we'll be late for the pre-ward round meeting.' They

both stood and placed their cups on the dirty dishes rack before heading towards the ward. 'Will Sean be presenting another interesting case this week?'

'Yes. Why? Do you have an interesting case you'd like to share?'

'Not at this stage. I was just curious as to whether Sean always did the presenting or not.'

'He organises it so if you do have an interesting case, you'll need to speak to him.'

Jane filed that information away as they entered the room. This time, when Sean stood at the front of the staff at the meeting, discussing the noteworthy aspects of a newly admitted patient, Jane listened intently. She did her best to ignore the way his deep, smooth tones washed over her, and the way he gesticulated smoothly with his hands, pointing out the different methods of treatment that were projected onto the screen. He had lovely hands, she realised, gentle, caring hands, big and strong and able to support. The memory of him placing those hands at her waist the previous week, steadying her after she'd tripped, burst into her mind and it took all her willpower to dismiss it. She was here to concentrate on her patients, not on Sean Booke's hands!

During the following week Jane watched Sean help a ten-year-old boy come to a level of understanding with the diagnosis of leukaemia. She found him in the ward playroom, sitting on a chair that was way too small for him, colouring in with three other children, all of them laughing together. She also saw him agonising over the correct treatment plan for one of his older patients, a fifteen-year-old girl, Mya, whose lungs weren't responding to the usual asthma medications.

'How's Mya today?' Jane asked Sean a few days

later. She'd entered the nurses' station to write up some case notes and within a matter of minutes, with nurses heading off to tend to their patients, she'd found herself alone with Sean at the desk. Having been at the hospital for two and a half weeks now, and having had several professional patient-related conversations with Sean without any mention of their shared personal connections, Jane felt more confident in enquiring about his patient. What she still found difficult to ignore was the subtle spicy scent surrounding him, one that definitely held appeal.

'Still not stabilising.' Sean shook his head slowly, before closing his eyes and pinching the bridge of his nose with his thumb and forefinger. 'I've tried everything. She responds to treatment for one, sometimes two days and then the symptoms return.'

'She's not reacting as expected to the corticosteroids? Has this happened before?'

Sean opened his eyes and handed Jane Mya's file. 'If you can find something I've missed, be my guest.' He slumped forward onto the desk, resting his head on his hands. He was tired, bewildered and very concerned about his patient. He'd consulted with the respiratory specialists yesterday afternoon but it was becoming clear that the corticosteroids might be doing more damage than good.

'Were you here all night?' Jane's words were quiet and when he lifted his head it was to find her watching him with professional empathy.

'Arrived around three this morning, as you would have seen in the notes.'

'But you didn't head over to the residential wing? Catch a few hours' extra sleep?'

Sean was too exhausted to try and look for any sort of ulterior motive for Jane's questions. 'I was worried about Mya. I did have a shower and change not too long ago, hoping to clear my mind a little and for the solution to miraculously present itself, but that hasn't happened.'

Jane smiled, a soft, delicate smile that softened her green eyes. Sean stared at her for a long moment, amazed at the difference in her features, especially the lack of that wariness in her gaze that had often been present whenever they'd been in the same room together. This morning she'd pulled her long, luscious locks back from her face into a simple ponytail, her fringe neatly combed over her forehead. She wore a long-sleeved cotton top, which hung low over an ankle-length black and white striped skirt. She was neat and tidy, calm and professional, and yet this morning there seemed to be something different about her, and it wasn't just the soft smile she was giving him.

She nodded. 'Sometimes it is impossible to sleep, especially when there's a patient puzzle to solve.'

Sean couldn't believe the way her calm, peaceful tone seemed to wash over him, alleviating some of the stress that had built up in his trapezius. He forced himself to look away from her, not wanting to be drawn in by Jane Diamond and her pretty smiles. While it was true that he'd been impressed with the way she'd settled into hospital life over the past weeks, relating to staff and patients in an easy, professional manner, she also represented a connection to his past and it was a past he'd locked securely away and didn't really fancy revisiting.

'And with your puzzle, I'd like to offer a suggestion, if I may,' she continued, watching as he angled his neck from side to side, trying to work out some of the kinks in his muscles. She had to resist the urge to stand behind him and gently massage his shoulders, as she would naturally offer to do for any of her other colleagues. Sean was different and with him it was imperative she keep her professional distance.

'What's that?' he prompted, and it was only then she realised she was staring at him.

'Er...sorry.' Slightly flustered, she looked down at Mya's notes, adjusted her glasses, even though they were already perfectly positioned on her nose, and cleared her throat. 'Well, a few months ago, I was in Argentina at a paediatric conference—'

'I remember. You mentioned it on your first day here.'

'Oh? Good. Well, anyway, I bumped into a colleague who's presently conducting a research study into a new drug for asthma sufferers, especially ones who are dependent upon or having reactions to corticosteroids.'

Sean sat up a little straighter in his chair. 'Is that Dr Aloysius Markum?'

'It is.'

'I've just re-read his preliminary findings, which were published in the latest medical journal.'

'Yes.'

'But that study is closed. There's no way we could get Mya onto it and, besides, she'd have to go to Sydney.'

'That's not entirely accurate. The study has new funding to test the drug in different climates to see if there is any difference. Australia has a great range of temperatures with, for example, places like Tasmania being almost twenty degrees cooler than Adelaide at the same time of year, which is why he's received approval to expand the study.'

'Do you really think you can get Mya onto the study?' For the first time in their discussion there was a thread of hope in Sean's words.

Jane smiled warmly and nodded. 'Ninety-five per cent sure.' She looked at the clock on the wall, adding on the half-hour time difference for Sydney. 'He'll be at the hospital now. I'll give him a call.' Without another word she pulled out her cellphone and dialled Dr Markum's number.

'Hi, Al,' she said a moment later. 'It's Jane. I have a patient for your study.'

Sean watched as she gave Dr Markum Mya's immediate details before saying, 'I have her treating doctor here, my colleague Sean Booke.' She held her phone out to him and nodded with encouragement. 'He's interested.'

With that, Sean found himself discussing Mya's treatment with one of Australia's leading specialists in paediatric respiratory disorders, the man Jane Diamond had simply called 'Al'. Another fifteen minutes and it was all organised. He was to email through the relevant documentation but Dr Markum seemed more than happy at the idea of accepting Mya onto his new research study.

'I'll have my assistant email through what you'll need to discuss with Mya's parents and also the consent forms. I'm more than happy to talk to the parents either via phone or internet chat. Oh, and look after our Jane,' Dr Markum added, without breaking for breath. 'I'm still annoyed Luc managed to snatch her away from me.'

'I don't follow...' Sean remarked, looking across to

where Jane stood on the ward, chatting with one of their young patients.

'I offered Jane a job when I knew her contract with Edna Robe was almost up. Jane's not only a brilliant doctor but a brilliant woman. She helped my own daughter two years ago to recover from an eating disorder, which leaves me heavily in her debt, so just make sure you look after her while she's there and, hopefully, when her contract expires, she'll finally agree to come back to Sydney and perform her miracles here.'

With that, Dr Markum rang off, leaving Sean holding Jane's cellphone and watching her more closely. She laughed at something the young twelve-year-old boy had said as she straightened his bedsheets, her features radiating pure happiness.

She really was very natural with their patients and to hear such a glowing reference from a man of Dr Markum's repute, as well as the fact that Luc really had head-hunted her, made Sean consider Jane in a new light. During the past weeks he'd been so determined to keep his distance from her, not wanting to discuss or relive anything to do with his past, that he was now beginning to wonder if he hadn't under-estimated the woman Jane Diamond had turned into.

Still, the question remained—why *had* she turned down a man like Aloysius Markum? Surely working at a larger, more prominent hospital in Sydney was a better career move than coming here to Adelaide?

The question stayed with him for the next few weeks and he wondered if he had any right to ask her such a personal question. If he did, would it open the door to them discussing their past? Would it change the calm working relationship they'd managed to create, so much so that she no longer seemed on edge if they were left alone together?

'I see Mya's beginning to improve,' Jane remarked as they came off the ward after an intensive round.

'Are you heading up to the outpatient clinic?' he asked, and she nodded. 'I'll walk with you, if that's all right,' he added.

'Er...of course. We're both going the same way.' She shrugged her shoulders as though everything was perfectly normal.

Where they'd managed to form a calm, professional relationship during her time here, actually walking through the corridors together was something they'd avoided until now. Chatting at the nurses' station? Fine. Discussing patients in outpatient clinic? Necessary. But this? Jane racked her brain for something to say, determined to keep everything strictly on a professional level. She knew she still needed to ask Sean if it was possible for her to see Spencer, to hopefully, in the long term, spend a good deal of time with her nephew, but for the time being she'd been comfortable developing a firm grounding, a professional appreciation, before she hit him with such a request. Even the thought of asking him churned her stomach.

'Um, I'm so pleased Mya's parents were agreeable to her taking part in the study. A lot of people are quite skittish when they hear the words "research project".' She smiled as she spoke.

'It is good to see Mya improving.' Silence reigned, their footsteps echoing in the unusually deserted corridor. 'How's your own research project going?'

'Good. Thanks. Slowly at the moment but I've had two new patients sign up in the last week so that's good news.'

'Yes.'

Silence once more. She should talk more about her research project. That was a neutral topic. 'Actually, the two patients who have signed up are siblings.'

'Is that common?'

'With twins perhaps, but this is a brother and sister, different ages, with different types of eating disorder.'

'What does that tell you? Big trauma in their past?'

'That's the starting point.'

'Are they close? The siblings?'

'Not from our first interview.'

'You and Daina never really got along, did you,' Sean stated rhetorically, the words coming from his mouth before he could think about it.

Jane glanced up at him, a look of disbelief on her face, and when she answered her tone was clipped and brisk. 'No.'

'Why was that, do you think?'

Jane tried to control her rising temper. The one major topic that could easily rile her was the topic of Daina but, she rationalised, she knew that in returning to Adelaide, where Sean and Spencer had now made their home, it would eventually be something she'd have to discuss.

Reminding herself that it was necessary to remain on Sean's good side if she wanted access to Spencer, she tried to control her reaction. Even if she could see her nephew only once a month, that would be terrific. She could get to know him, tell him about the grandparents he'd never known and share some of her better, happier memories with him.

Jane took a steadying breath and paused in the corridor, Sean stopping beside her. 'Jane. I'm sorry, I shouldn't have just blurted out—'

'How well did you know Daina? *Really* know your wife?'

At her question, Sean's expression instantly changed to one of deep-seated pain before he quickly recovered and replaced his expression with one of benign detachment. 'Ex-wife. We were divorced soon after Spencer was born.'

'Really? I wasn't aware of that.' But she was aware of the bitterness he'd been unable to disguise from his tone. 'So if you know what she was really like, how can you ask me that?'

Sean clenched his jaw and gritted his teeth. 'Whenever I do let myself think of her, I try to remember her the way she was during those first few months of our marriage, before...' He stopped. 'I do it for Spencer.' He shook his head. 'He doesn't need to know the truth about his mother. Not now, at any rate.'

Jane nodded. 'I can understand that because the truth of who Daina really was, of the emotional pain she was capable of inflicting, is just too painful to remember, isn't it?'

'Yes.' His lips barely moved as he spoke, then he exhaled harshly and shook his head. 'Why did you come here, Jane? From what I understand, you had several job offers. Why dredge up all these old emotions? Daina is dead. There's nothing you or I can do to change the past.'

'I don't want to change the past, Sean.'

'Then what *do* you want, Jane?'

'I want to change my future…and I want that future to include Spencer.'

CHAPTER TWO

JANE LET HERSELF into her room, which was situated in the hospital's residential wing. At least she'd managed to obtain a room with an en suite and small kitchenette. At the moment it was ideal, living in such close proximity to the hospital, as it lifted the pressure of finding somewhere more permanent. She could concentrate on her patients and research project and not have to worry about traffic or where to garage a car. There were shops nearby, which provided everything she required, and a good public transport service to assist her if she needed more.

It was now the beginning of February and thanks to daylight saving there was no need for her to turn on the lights, but at the moment she wished the room were in darkness. It was half past seven in the evening and she was exhausted. Not only that, she couldn't believe she'd blurted out her sole purpose for returning to Adelaide to the one man who had total control over her request.

After she'd stated she wanted Spencer to be in her life, Sean had glared at her, his frown returning, before he'd shaken his head and walked away. Trembling with anxiety, Jane had found it almost impossible to shelve her own personal problems enough to concentrate on the clinic, highly conscious of keeping a safe distance from Sean at all times.

However, when she'd been introduced to Tessa, a young girl of six who she'd ended up admitting due to a bad urinary tract infection, one of the symptoms associated with eating disorders, Jane had pushed her own issues to the back of her mind. When the clinic ended, Jane quickly grabbed a bite to eat from the hospital's cafeteria, before heading back to the ward to see how Tessa was settling in.

'She's very quiet. Not speaking,' Anthea told her. 'She didn't want to stay but didn't want to go home either.'

'Hmm.' Jane processed this information. 'OK. Have the night staff keep a close eye on her and call me if there are any concerns. I'm staying in the residential wing so I can come right over.'

'I'll make a note in her file.' Anthea's words had been soft and the two of them stood there, watching the little girl, for a few more minutes, Jane's concern rising. With Tessa being so unsettled, as well as not feeling well because of the urinary tract infection, this first night might be hard for her.

Now as Jane lay down on the bed, taking off her glasses and kicking off her shoes, she couldn't ignore the niggling sensation that there was something going on with Tessa that no one was aware of. Little girls of six only had eating disorders if something else was very wrong in their lives.

Her phone started ringing and Jane sluggishly opened her eyes, reaching out her hand to the nightstand, patting around until she located it. It was only then she realised she'd dozed off, still completely dressed and lying on top of the bed covers.

'Dr Diamond.'

'Oh, uh…Jane, is it?'

'Yes.'

'I'm calling from the ward. There's a note in Tessa's file to call you if—'

'I'm on my way,' Jane interrupted, as she quickly disconnected the call and hunted around in the now-dark room for her shoes. Collecting her glasses and the hospital lanyard, which contained her hospital pass key as well as the key to her room, Jane headed back to the hospital, smoothing a hand down her hair to ensure it wasn't sticking out all over the place.

'Thanks for coming,' the night sister said. 'Tessa's been lying in her bed, whimpering and crying softly. Every time one of us gets near her, she stops, closes her eyes tight and completely ignores us.'

'OK. Thanks.' Jane nodded politely at the sister before heading to Tessa's bed. Although there were other children in the ward, she didn't want to pull the curtain around Tessa's bed for privacy because if the little girl had been abused in some way, which was the way Jane's intuition was leading her, then the last thing Tessa would want was to have herself 'cut off', as it were, from the rest of the ward.

Instead, Jane walked quietly over to Tessa's bedside, her heart almost breaking at the whimpering sound coming from the child. Just as the night sister had stated, Tessa immediately stopped the instant she realised there was an adult present.

'Hi, Tessa. It's me. Dr Jane. We met before.'

No answer.

'I'm really a bit tired. Do you mind if I sit down here for a minute or two?'

Again no answer.

'Thanks,' she remarked, and sat in the chair beside Tessa's bed. Jane remained silent to begin with then quietly began to sing, her soothing, clear voice audible to the rest of the small ward but not disturbing any of the other patients.

When one song finished, Jane would be quiet for a few minutes before starting another song. After an hour the night sister quietly walked over, handed Jane a bottle of water, gave her a thumbs-up and a nod of approval before leaving them alone.

Jane gratefully took a sip of the cool water before starting on another song. When she'd finished that one, she settled back in the chair and relaxed.

'Can I hear another one?' a little timid voice asked, when Jane hadn't started the next song for a good five minutes.

Jane's answer was to start singing again. No need for words or questions, the melodious sound of her voice was having a positive effect on Tessa and that was all that mattered. Another hour later Jane couldn't help but smother a yawn, pleased to note that Tessa was now in a deep, relaxed sleep.

Very slowly, Jane stood from the chair, stretching out her tired limbs before heading over to the nurses' station. She wanted to take a closer look at Tessa's case notes, eager to try and find something, anything, that would give her some clues as to what was really going on in the little girl's life.

'That was beautiful,' the night sister said, and Jane smiled her thanks.

'Agreed. I never knew you had such a lovely voice.' The deep words were spoken from directly behind her and Jane spun round, coming face to face with Sean. Unfortunately, she'd moved too quickly, making herself light-headed.

'Whoa.' Sean's arms came around her instantly, for the second time since she'd come back into his life. 'We've really got to stop meeting like this,' he murmured as Jane tried to steady herself. She wasn't sure if it was her imagination or fatigue but she could have sworn Sean's voice seemed kinder, gentler. Was this a good thing? She certainly hoped so. If he could see her for who she was, not just as Daina's sister, then perhaps she stood some chance of him approving her request to see Spencer.

Sean led Jane over to a vacant chair and helped her to sit down, trying to ignore the way her soft sunflowery scent captivated his senses. How could she smell as fresh as a daisy when it was almost six o'clock in the morning?

'I think all your beautiful singing might have drained your oxygen reserves.' The night sister chuckled. 'Although I have to say, you've made the night more pleasant to deal with.'

'That she has,' Sean agreed, immediately stepping back when Jane eased herself away from him, her hands held up in front of her in a defensive manner.

'I'm fine.' She tried not to snap, but it was difficult given she was cross with herself for being far too aware of Sean, of the way his warm hands had caused her to feel safe and secure, even for the briefest of moments. 'But thank you,' she added belatedly.

'At least Tessa's sleeping—*really* sleeping now.' The

night sister looked over towards ward room two, where she could hear giggling. 'Which is more than I can say for some of the other children.' With a sigh she left the nurses' station to go and deal with whichever recalcitrant patient dared to be awake at this hour in the morning.

Sean was left alone with Jane but she seemed more than happy to ignore him as she picked up Tessa's file and started reading it. After watching her for a moment, he decided to take a leaf out of her book and began reading his patient files, catching up on the notes the nursing staff had made during the night. If Jane wanted to play the professional card, so could he. They would sit there, ignore each other and do their work. The fact that he'd known her since she was a teenager, the fact that he'd been married to her older sister, the fact that her sister had ripped his heart out, cut it into tiny pieces and then set fire to them, in reality, had nothing at all to do with Jane.

And yet...he didn't seem able to keep his curiosity levels in check. She'd said she wanted to get to know Spencer. Why? Why *now*? Was she dying? Had something terrible happened to her...again? Sean closed his eyes on the thought. He knew all about the accident that had taken Jane's and Daina's parents from them, Daina annoyed that she'd been thrust into the role of responsible adult to care for her thirteen-year-old sister.

Jane had looked directly at him, her intent clear when she'd asked, 'How well did you know Daina? *Really* know your wife?' and he'd felt as though she'd slapped him. There was so much about his marriage that he'd shoved aside, promising himself never to think about it but with Jane returning, infiltrating his world, that resolve was becoming difficult to control.

Sean opened his eyes, glancing surreptitiously at Jane. Had her hair been that long, that deep chocolaty brown in colour, that silky, all those years ago? He clenched his hand into a fist to stop himself from wanting to reach out and run his fingers through it, wondering if it really was as glorious as it appeared.

He needed to stop thinking about Jane, to control his thoughts. She'd asked him how well he'd known his wife, and to begin with he had to admit he'd thought he'd known Daina fairly well...until he'd discovered, thanks to an ex-friend's guilty conscience, the number of other men who had also 'known Daina fairly well'. That confession had come after Spencer's traumatic birth and Sean, in his stubbornness, had insisted on a DNA test to reassure himself that Spencer was indeed his. Thankfully, Daina had been telling the truth for once and from that moment on Sean had devoted his attention and energies towards his baby son, rather than towards his wayward, cheating wife, serving her with divorce papers as soon as possible.

'Would you stop staring at me, please?'

Jane's voice cut through his thoughts and it was only then that Sean realised he was doing exactly what she'd accused him of. Her green eyes bored into his and he quickly looked down at the case notes in his hands. 'Er...sorry.'

Jane sighed heavily before returning her attention to Tessa's case notes, flicking back through the pages again, intent on reading everything possible about every admission, right back to her birth.

'Looking for anything in particular?' he asked.

'I'll know it when I see it.'

'Determined, eh?'

'And stubborn.'

'I'm sure those qualities have served you well over the years.'

Jane lifted her head and glared at him for a moment. 'What's that supposed to mean?'

Sean raised his eyebrows at her tone and when he looked into her eyes he was a little surprised to see them filled with repressed fire. 'You're…angry with me?' He searched her gaze again to ensure he'd read her emotion correctly.

Jane merely rolled her eyes at his words and returned her focus to the paperwork before her. 'Haven't you learnt not to tease women when they're frustrated because they can't find the answer to the problem plaguing them?'

'Er…actually, I have learnt that lesson, seeing as I have younger twin sisters, but sometimes, Jane, it's difficult to resist.'

Jane raised her head and stared at him for a moment. 'You have sisters?' Then, before he could answer, she shook her head as though to clear it from unnecessary distractions and returned her attention to the notes. 'There has to be something in here, some event, some incident, even a small one, that was enough to cause these disruptions in Tessa's life.'

'Disruptions?'

Jane stretched out her hand towards where Tessa was now sleeping soundly. 'She doesn't eat, she doesn't sleep, she whimpers any time an adult comes near her at night.'

'You think she might have been abused by an adult?'

'That's the most common assumption but it may not necessarily be an adult. She's scared, not of the dark but of the night.'

'What's the difference?'

Jane breathed in deeply, her eyes flashing with fire, and Sean could see her hackles were beginning to rise. He immediately held up one hand to stop her tirade before she began. 'I'm not teasing or trying to be difficult, Jane. I haven't had the training or life experiences you've had. I'm only enquiring because I don't understand your statement. Nothing more. I'm as concerned about Tessa as you are. Perhaps, if we head to the cafeteria and grab a cup of coffee, we can make some sense of the situation.'

Jane immediately shook her head. 'I'm happy where I am, thank you.' The last thing she wanted was to be sitting in close proximity to Sean in an almost deserted hospital cafeteria, listening to the sultry sound of his voice. It was bad enough that the night sister had left them alone at the nurses' station, forcing Jane to erect her automatic defences.

She'd had to protect herself from so much over the years, just like Tessa was doing now, not from physical or sexual abuse but from verbal and emotional abuse, which were every bit as damaging as the others. There had been one particular side to Daina only Jane had been privy to…and she couldn't stop the niggling question in the back of her mind as to whether or not Sean had also seen that side of her sister.

'Fair enough. In that case, would you mind explaining your statement? Why would Tessa be afraid of the night and not of the dark? I always thought the two were synonymous.'

'Look at the ward,' Jane invited. 'There are lights on. Small nightlights. It's not dark, not pitch black. Tessa's not afraid of the dark because that's where she feels the safest. It's dark in her mind, she can curl up into a corner in a dark room and no one will ever find her, but night-time…there's a real fear associated with that because the majority of people sleep at night and sleeping is when a person is most vulnerable.'

'You're saying that night-time makes her feel vulnerable?'

'Yes. How many times have you heard people saying they just wished for the night to be over, that they couldn't wait for the first rays of sunlight to start seeping through into the day? Insomniacs feel it all the time. All those hours they just lie there, not sleeping, just waiting. In Tessa's case, whatever has happened to her happens at night, which is why she refuses to sleep, which is why she whimpers, filled with anticipatory dread at what might or might not happen.'

'The mind is a powerful thing.'

'Most definitely.' Jane's voice was soft as she sighed, her previous annoyance having vanished as she once more stared down at Tessa's case notes.

'Do you want me to have a look?'

Jane handed them over without a word before standing and walking towards the edge of the ward where she watched Tessa sleep, the little girl's breathing still calm and relaxed. 'I wonder if this is the first decent sleep she's had in…well, I don't know how long.'

She continued to stand there while Sean read through Tessa's entire file. 'You're right. There's nothing that stands out.' Jane's shoulders slumped dejectedly at this news. 'But I do have a suggestion.'

'I'm open to it.'

'Why not task a few medical students to do a case study on Tessa?'

Jane raised an eyebrow at this. 'Go on.'

'For the next forty-eight hours they are to unobtrusively observe Tessa, her parents, her siblings, her friends—anyone and everyone who comes into contact with her, including all hospital staff, whether male or female, and also any interaction with other patients. I see you've already requested she have a consult with the dietician and the hospital's child psychologist, so once we have the data from the students, we can organise a conference and really see if we can't get to the bottom of this.'

'Wouldn't we need the parents' permission?'

'The medical students aren't treating Tessa, they're observing her. Tessa has been admitted to the hospital for observation as well as treatment for her urinary tract infection. Tessa wouldn't be a part of any sort of research study, she's just being observed in the interest of her health.'

Jane turned from watching Tessa and looked at Sean. 'I'll speak to Luc, and I'd also like her taken off the ward round during this time.'

'Agreed.' He nodded. 'It's a plan.'

'Yes. Yes, it is.' Jane couldn't believe how much lighter her heart felt now that there was a way forward, a way to hopefully figure out whatever was hurting Tessa. 'Thank you, Sean.'

He smiled at her then, a full-blown, twinkling-eyed smile that somehow pierced the barrier she'd so carefully constructed around her heart and flooded her world with light. She immediately returned to her seat, dropping down into the chair before her knees refused to support her weight due to the fact that they'd turned to jelly. Boy, oh, boy, Sean Booke's smile was lethal! 'You're more than welcome, Jane.'

He didn't seem to notice the effect he was having on her. Such a smile should be outlawed. The action had completely changed his features from ones she'd always considered to be dark and brooding to pure handsome sensuality.

When the night sister returned, Jane was more than thankful that Sean's attention was diverted as he asked about the patients who had been playing up but Jane didn't listen to half of what they were saying. She was still trying to gain control over her senses, swallowing over her suddenly dry mouth and fervently trying to quell the multitude of proverbial butterflies presently going haywire in her stomach.

No man...not even her ex-fiancé...had ever affected her in such a way. Things like this simply didn't happen to her. She wasn't the romantic, girly, lovey-dovey type so why had she been this affected by one simple smile from a man she wasn't even sure she liked?

'I know it's almost time for the ward to wake up and I'll make sure Tessa's not disturbed for as long as possible,' the night sister was saying, 'but I also think you need to get some rest, Dr Diamond. You're not due back on the ward until eight o'clock, so head over to the residential wing now and try to get some sleep.'

'You're staying in the res wing?' For some reason this news surprised Sean.

'Yes. It's convenient.'

'For the moment.'

Jane shrugged. 'I have no problem staying there for

the rest of the year.' She looked over at Tessa, who was still sleeping soundly. 'You'll—'

'Call you if there are any problems,' Sister interrupted, nodding her head. 'Absolutely.'

'I'll walk you over,' Sean stated, rising to his feet.

'It's fine. You don't have to do that.'

'It's a safety thing.'

For who? Jane wanted to ask, because even the thought of having Sean close to her as they walked through the quiet hospital was disconcerting enough for her. She gingerly stood, pleased to discover her legs were now going to support her. She looked from Sister to Sean, realising there was no way out. It was easier to accept.

'Right,' Sister continued. 'You two are organised, so off you go. I'd best go and receive updates from the rest of my staff before the breakfast trolleys are brought up.'

Sean swept a hand in front of his body, indicating Jane should precede him. 'Shall we?'

It was easier for her to accept his offer than to kick up a stink because she knew if that was the case, she'd have to explain exactly *why* she was kicking up a stink and the last thing she wanted to say to Sean Booke right now was that she found his spicy scent rather intoxicating.

Neither of them spoke as they walked through the deserted corridors, heading to the rear of the hospital towards the residential wing. Even after they'd entered the res wing and Jane had signed in, Sean still insisted on accompanying her right up to her room. The clerk behind the desk in the foyer was watching them intently and once more Jane decided it was easier to go with the flow than argue. She gritted her teeth, desperately trying to ignore her awareness of Sean's close proximity, and started for the stairwell. It wasn't until the door had closed behind them, their footsteps echoing around them, that Sean spoke.

'Jane?'

'Yes.'

'You mentioned that you wanted to change your future and that you wanted Spencer to be a part of that future.'

Jane swallowed over the sudden lump forming in her throat before answering, 'Yes.' Was this it? Was she going to find out that he didn't want her to see Spencer whilst walking up a flight of stairs in the residential wing? He didn't say anything else until she'd pushed open the door to the floor she was staying on. It was difficult for her to resist the urge to run the rest of the way, to disappear into the safety of her room before Sean asked the question she could feel was coming.

'Why now?' he asked, as they stopped outside her door.

Gathering her courage, Jane turned to face him, shrugging one shoulder.

'You're not sick, are you? Terminally ill? Or discovered you have some strange hereditary disease that Spencer might also inherit?'

That was not what she'd expected him to say and she couldn't help the way her lips curved upwards slightly in surprise. 'No. I'm not sick, or dying of some hereditary disease. Spencer is safe.'

Sean exhaled slowly and nodded. 'Good.'

Jane continued to stand there, waiting for him to ask another question, but none came. The awkwardness of the moment started to increase and she was very self-conscious about them both standing there and saying nothing. With jerky, almost robotic movements she pressed the electronic keycard on her lanyard against the door to open it. Sean still didn't ask her anything else.

'OK, then. I guess I'll see you later on this morning. Thanks for walking me over.' She pushed open the door, eager to escape the awkwardness, but Sean put his hand on her arm, stopping her.

'Jane. You didn't answer my question.'

She turned to look at him, her skin still warm from his touch even after he'd removed his hand. She wasn't used to being touched, especially not by handsome, brooding men such as the one who stood before her. She swallowed and slowly raised her gaze to meet his.

'Why did I come back now?' He nodded as she repeated his question. 'Well...' she faltered, before shrugging and deciding it was better just to be honest. 'Because...I've reached the end of me.'

He stared at her in puzzlement and she realised she needed to expand on her answer. The last thing she wanted to do was to completely bare her soul, to reveal to him just how lonely she was, but if she wanted to see Spencer then perhaps it was inevitable that she at least give him some information. She looked down at the floor and drew in a deep breath before meeting his gaze once more, her words rushing out quickly.

'I have nothing else, Sean. No one else.' She spread her hands wide in a gesture of openness. 'I've tried to fill my life with work and my patients and my colleagues and for a while there I thought I might actually be successful. I was even engaged for a short time, hopeful I'd be able to forget my past, to somehow pretend I was someone else.' She shook her head. 'I was wrong. Eamon...er...my fiancé, told me I never really opened up to him, always kept a part of myself hidden, secret, and he was absolutely right.

'It's been over twelve months since he broke our engagement, telling me I wasn't the woman he wanted any more, and during that time I finally realised that if I'm ever going to have any hope of a normal life, I need not only to address my past but to make peace with it. I hoped by focusing on the good things, like getting to know Spencer—my only blood relative left in the world—that I might actually come out of this journey in one piece.'

Jane looked down at the floor, annoyed that her voice had broken on the final words. She'd been doing so well, especially as being this candid with someone she really didn't know a lot about was extremely difficult.

Pursing her lips together in an effort to control the tears she could feel pricking at the backs of her eyes, she breathed out slowly and forced herself to meet his gaze. 'I have no one, Sean. No parents, no grandparents, no aunts or uncles. No cousins and…no sister. I've tried everything I can to find some level of happiness in my life but I've reached the end…and coming here was the only other option left.' She sniffed, her eyes now brimming with tears, and when one fell from her lashes, she impatiently brushed it away, not wanting to guilt him into feeling sorry for her. She didn't want his pity, she wanted his understanding and, hopefully, his permission to allow her access to Spencer.

'I have nothing else,' she whispered, before being unable to control herself any longer and quickly disappearing into the safety of her room, closing the door behind her.

CHAPTER THREE

JANE WASN'T SURE how she was going to face Sean after the way she'd all but blurted out her sad sob story, cried and then shut the door in his face. There was no way he was going to allow her access to Spencer now that he realised just how unglued she was. Worst of all, he might think she was like Daina, unstable deep down inside.

She wasn't. She'd worked hard to be nothing like her older sister, who had been manipulative, arrogant and, at times, downright cruel. Jane tried to close her thoughts to the memories that infiltrated her mind, memories she'd worked so hard to shield. Daina whispering in her ear that no one would ever love her because she was a scarred freak. Daina looking at Jane's high-school transcript and calling her weird because normal people didn't get top marks in every subject. Daina ignoring her, for weeks on end, pretending she didn't exist.

That had been the worst one of all. Daina had legally been Jane's guardian. They'd only had each other so when her sister had ignored her, not speaking to her or acknowledging her for long periods of time, the young teenage Jane had become very distraught.

More often than not, Jane would end up in her bedroom, sitting in the corner convinced there was something wrong with *her*. Then, out of the blue, Daina would change. She'd hug and kiss her little sister, cuddle her, tell her that everything would be all right. She'd take Jane out and lavish her with attention, buying her clothes and make-up and trinkets; they'd go to the movies and play games at the arcade. Jane had lived for those days, wondering whenever she went to the kitchen each morning to prepare breakfast for them both whether *this* would be the good day, the day where nice Daina came to visit.

Back then, her sister's erratic behaviour had definitely affected her but as soon as Daina had up and married Sean, leaving Jane all alone, she'd realised the only way to really deal with her sister and to avoid the negative effects had been to shut Daina out of her life as much as possible.

It had been clear, just from seeing Sean's expression when she'd asked him about how well he'd known his wife, that Daina had hurt him, too. Both of them had been left emotionally scarred and she accepted the fact that Sean would do anything and everything to protect Spencer. If he thought she was like Daina, there was no way he'd allow her to form any sort of attachment to the boy…and she couldn't blame him.

'Sean.' Jane spoke his name out loud and slowly shook her head from side to side. The fact that she found herself constantly thinking about her ex-brother-in-law was a little disconcerting but, she rationalised, there was a lot at stake. Spencer was important to her and at the moment she'd do almost anything to prove to Sean that she was a calm and controlled adult in the hope that he would give her permission to get to know her nephew.

She didn't want to think about the way Sean's powerful presence had turned her knees to jelly or the way his amazing smile had caused her insides to flutter or the way his blue eyes could be so incredibly expressive. She could simply sit and stare into them all day long and never get bored—and that realisation in itself was enough to startle her.

Any sort of romantic entanglement—with anyone— was the furthest thing from her mind and, besides, Sean was also her colleague for the next twelve months and if dating Eamon had taught her one major lesson, it was to never date colleagues.

She stared at her reflection in the small mirror above the bathroom sink as she slipped her glasses into place. 'Professional persona in place. Time to get to work. Focus on your patients and give them the best care possible. Do *not* think about Sean Booke and the way he can make your knees go weak with just one smile!' Her words and expression were stern and with a firm nod she turned and collected her hospital lanyard and phone from the bedside dresser.

Breathing in an air of professionalism, Jane left her room and headed back over to the hospital. She couldn't help but look around her, doing a double-take on any man who was six feet four inches tall and had short dark brown hair and blue eyes. Sean was the last person she needed to bump into right now, especially after she'd given herself such strict instructions to the contrary. Thankfully, she didn't bump into him and when she arrived on the ward she headed over to see Tessa.

The little girl was sitting up in bed, doing a jigsaw puzzle and not really wanting to talk or interact with anyone.

'Good morning, Tessa.' Jane smiled and wasn't

surprised she didn't receive a response from the girl. 'You've made a good start on that puzzle. Can I help?'

Tessa's answer was to shrug her shoulders but she didn't send Jane away neither did she lose interest in the puzzle.

'Which piece should I put in?' she asked, her fingers hovering over a few of the pieces. She waited a moment, pretending to be unable to choose, and when she finally picked up a piece, Tessa still didn't speak. 'Where does this one go?'

Again, there was no verbal interaction but Jane could see Tessa's gaze darting to exactly where the piece should go. Jane placed it in the right position and smiled. 'There.'

Tessa looked at Jane for a long moment, her brown eyes so deep and expressive, but only for a second. With a blink of her eyes the shutters came down but not before Jane had glimpsed that silent plea for help.

'I *am* going to help you, Tessa,' she told the girl quietly, her voice filled with promise. She also told Tessa that the doctors wouldn't be stopping at her bed during the ward round. 'They'd all want to help you with your jigsaw puzzle,' she said with a small laugh. 'All of us, the other doctors and the nurses and other people you might see while you're here, we *all* like to help people and we all want to help you.' Jane's smile was one of comfort and reassurance. Tessa's response was to look at her for another long moment, shutters still firmly in place, before returning her attention to the puzzle.

When Jane made her way back to the nurses' station, it was to find Luc talking to Sean. 'Good morning,' she murmured, glancing momentarily in Sean's direction, a little surprised at the way her heart rate started to increase. Why was she so aware of him?

'Did you get some rest, Jane?'

'Er…' She couldn't believe how flustered she felt at what would ordinarily be a normal question from any other member of staff but when Sean asked it, it was as though he really was interested, that he really cared. 'Yes. Thank you.'

'Good. And how's Tessa doing?'

'Silently begging for help,' Jane replied softly.

Anthea had just walked into the nurses' station as Jane spoke and the sister sighed with compassion at this news. 'The poor lamb.'

Luc shook his head. 'There's clearly something else going on,' he stated. 'Sean's been telling me about the plan to have some medical students observe Tessa for a few days.'

Jane nodded, her heart rate settling down now that they were talking about work. 'If we can figure out what's going on at home, we'll be one giant step closer to getting Tessa the correct help. That's one of the main focuses with eating disorders. Sometimes all the signs and symptoms point one way yet everything is the opposite. Monitoring Tessa's reaction to everyone who comes into contact with her will go a long way to hopefully providing us with that information.'

Luc pointed to Tessa's case notes on the desk in front of him. 'I read she had a difficult night, although it says she managed a few hours' deep sleep this morning, thanks to…' Luc picked up the case notes and read what the night sister had written '…"to…Dr Diamond's singing"?'

Sean immediately smiled at Jane, speaking before

she had the opportunity. 'She has an incredible voice. It soothed more people in the ward than just young Tessa.'

'Oh, I know *all* about Jane's beautiful singing, especially when she sings in French,' Luc remarked, winking at her. Jane ignored Luc's comment and instead tried to figure out her reaction to Sean and why his easygoing smile had caused her body to explode with tingles. She dropped her gaze down to where his tie was perfectly knotted, a bright coloured tie with popular cartoon characters on it, which was sure to delight the children.

Perhaps if she didn't look at his perfect mouth she wouldn't be as affected, but instead she became more aware of his Adam's apple moving up and down his perfect throat and how her peripheral vision clearly registered the width of his broad shoulders. Her senses were all too aware of his smooth, deep voice washing yet another wave of tingles over her. He'd spoken, asked her a question, and yet, due to his nearness, she had absolutely no clue what he'd said.

'Hmm?' Jane swallowed, forcing herself to move away from his overwhelming presence, needing distance, needing to control her rising panic. 'Er...' She couldn't believe how flustered she felt. 'Um...what did you say, Sean?' She picked up Tessa's case notes, holding them in front, using them as some sort of shield. When she dared to glance at him once more, it was to find him frowning in slight puzzlement.

'I...' He looked from her to Luc then back again, before shaking his head. 'It's fine.'

'OK. Well, I think I'll go and pore over Tessa's notes in the conference room before ward round starts,' Jane said to no one in particular, before hightailing it out of the small secluded area, which had made her far too aware of Sean's presence.

She entered the conference room, unable to believe the way Sean's nearness, his presence, his voice, his… everything was turning her into a tongue-tied schoolgirl, much as she'd been when they'd first met all those years ago.

After taking a few deep breaths, she walked over to one of the chairs at the back of the room and sat down, opening Tessa's notes.

'Why didn't you say something before?' Sean remarked as he stalked into the conference room, heading directly towards her and stopping close to where she sat.

Slightly startled, Jane looked up from the case notes. 'Sorry?'

'Luc.'

'What about Luc?'

'You…and *him*.'

'I'm not sure I understand.'

'*You* and *Luc*. You told me you'd moved to Adelaide solely because of Spencer.'

Jane's eyes widened as she grasped his meaning and quickly shook her head. Her glasses slid down her nose and it wasn't until she went to push them back that she realised her hand was trembling a little. 'What? Me and Luc? No. We're friends. Colleagues. Sean, I'm not involved with Luc.'

'It certainly looks that way.'

'It does?'

'You're very…chummy and it's clear he likes you.'

'What?' Jane frowned, positive Sean had the wrong end of the stick. 'Luc is a colleague and a friend.' She spread her hands wide, desperate for him to believe her.

'So why did Dr Markum tell me that Luc managed to persuade you to come and work in Adelaide?'

'Perhaps because Luc *did* manage to persuade me to come and work here.'

'So he could be close to you?'

'What? No.' Jane was confused how things had become so muddled. 'So I could be close to Spencer.'

Sean opened his mouth to say something then closed it again, thinking for a moment. 'But…that implies that Luc knew you and I had a personal connection.'

Jane nodded. 'Yes.'

Sean scratched his forehead. 'How?'

'One night, when we were working together in Paris…' She stopped and started again. 'It was a terrible night. There'd been a multiple MVA and a family of six, four children, two parents, had all been admitted. Both parents passed away and two of the children. It was horrible, having to tell those two kids—one nine and one fourteen—that the rest of their family had died.'

'That is terrible.' Sean pulled up a chair and sat down next to her, his previous annoyance dissipating.

'Afterwards, Luc and I started talking about our families. He told me about his brother, Pierre, and his sister, Nicolette, and her husband, Stephen. He told me about his nieces and nephews, his aunts and uncles and I, for all intents and purposes, had no one.' She shrugged as she said the words. 'No parents, no aunts or uncles or cousins.'

'How long ago was this?'

'Just before Daina passed away.' Jane looked down at her hands, which were clenched tightly together. 'I told Luc about a nephew I'd never seen and I must have mentioned your name because he remembered it. So when the job here came up, Spencer became the cherry Luc needed to secure my services here at the hospital.'

'You're just friends.'

'Friends,' she agreed.

'I didn't mean to jump to conclusions.'

'Would it matter, though?'

'What? If you were dating Luc?'

'Or anyone else, for that matter. Would it impact your decision regarding my request to spend time with Spencer?'

'It might. It would depend on who you were dating and whether or not that relationship might inadvertently affect Spencer.'

Jane nodded, thinking through his words before sitting forward in her chair and meeting his gaze. 'I am not Daina, you know. I am nothing like my sister and I hope you can see that.' Her words were imploring. 'I would never do anything to hurt Spencer and indeed...' she sat up a little straighter in her chair, her green eyes flashing with determination and strength '...I would do everything in my power to protect him.'

There was something about the way she spoke, about the way she'd said the word 'protect', that caused Sean to think there was a lot more she *wasn't* saying. She would protect Spencer. Why would Jane think Spencer needed protecting?

Jane's cellphone beeped and she checked the message. 'It's the child psychologist about Tessa. I might not be available for the ward round this morning.'

'I'll let Luc know.'

'Thanks.' Jane stood and gathered her files. 'I hope we're clearer about a few things now, Sean.'

He nodded and with that he watched her walk from

the room, head held high, her long plait swishing from side to side as she moved. How was it possible her green eyes could look so…intense? Didn't she have any idea just how passionate she looked when she was determined?

She'd been absolutely correct at guessing his response to her easygoing relationship with Luc. The way the two of them interacted so naturally—which, of course, they would do if, as she'd said, they'd spent a fair amount of time working with each other in the past—had indeed reminded him of the way Daina would flirt and tease with other men.

Jane had clearly realised the track his thoughts had taken and she'd called him on it, indicating she was not only intuitive but direct. From what he'd seen during the past month, she wasn't anything like Daina but, then, Daina had done an excellent job of deceiving him for quite some time.

Jane hadn't been deceptive, though. She hadn't tried to go behind his back and find out information about Spencer. Instead, she'd told him directly that she was hoping for access to his son…and yet he was finding it difficult to trust her.

In fact, he found it difficult to trust any woman, especially one he was attracted to, after the way Daina had treated him.

Attracted? Was he attracted to Jane?

There was no doubt that she had a certain…style to her, one that he was sure many people had underestimated, just as he'd done. She'd shown herself to be highly intelligent as well as caring, two qualities he admired. She definitely didn't tailor her wardrobe, as Daina had, his ex-wife often wearing outfits that he'd considered far too alluring out in public. Was that why Jane dressed the way she did? To prove to herself that she *was* the opposite of Daina?

As the day progressed, Sean found himself unable to stop thinking about what Jane had said about being all alone. Was it true? Did she really have no other family? None?

Daina had never really spoken of any other relatives, except Jane, and even then she'd almost ignored her younger sister's existence, much preferring to concentrate on herself. The thought stayed with him at the back of his mind during outpatients, his sub-committee meetings and even while he was driving home. What was it like to be all alone?

When he pulled into the two-storey house where he lived with his parents and his son, Sean imagined what it might be like to arrive home to a dark, empty home with no one waiting inside. As he scooped Spencer into his arms and tickled the boy's tummy, as he chatted with his parents, who had always been there to help him look after his son, Sean felt such enormous pangs of pain at the thought of all these wonderful people being taken from him.

How would he feel if that extended to his twin sisters and their families? His grandparents? His aunts, uncles and cousins? The emptiness, the void, the loneliness that would be left in his life would consume him. Was that what had happened to Jane?

'Are you all right?' his mother, Louise, asked him as she joined him in the bathroom while he checked his son's teeth.

'Hmm? Sure.' He kept his attention off his mother and on his son. 'There you go, bud. Rinse and spit, wipe your mouth and go and choose some stories for us to read.'

'Yep. 'K, Dad.' Spencer did as he was told while Sean tried not to let his mother see that anything was wrong. Even the briefest thought about losing the people he loved so very much was making him feel uneasy and as Spencer raced from the bathroom, Sean dipped his head and pressed a kiss to his mother's cheek.

'Thanks, Mum.'

'For?' she asked, a little surprised by his action.

'Everything. Being a great mother and grandmother. Always supportive.' He shrugged, feeling highly self-conscious but glad he was saying these words to her.

'Of course.' Louise eyed him cautiously. 'Sean? What's going on?'

Sean raked a hand through his hair and looked past her to make sure Spencer wasn't within earshot. 'Do you remember meeting Daina's sister?'

'Er…Jane?'

'That's it.'

'I spoke to her at the funeral. It was odd. She didn't seem all that upset about her sister's death but at the same time she was very sad.' Louise shook her head. 'I can't explain it.'

'That's probably because she and Daina didn't ex-actly get along.'

'Not surprising.' His mother's tone was flat, both of them clearly understanding what wasn't being said— that it had been difficult for *anyone* to really get along with Daina.

'Jane's working at the hospital.'

'Your hospital?'

He nodded. 'She's a paediatrician.'

'Oh, yes. I remembered her saying she was a doctor.' Louise frowned. 'Why? What does she want?'

'To see—'

'Daddy!' Spencer called out brightly. 'I'm ready for stories now.'

'Spencer?' Louise guessed. 'She wants to see Spencer?'

'Yes.'

'Are you going to let her? Can you trust her?'

Sean shrugged as he headed towards his son's room, the image of Jane seated beside Tessa's bed, her sweet, angelic voice filling the air. He could recall the song she'd been singing and how it had made not only Tessa but the night staff feel. Surely someone whose intention it was to help others could be trusted just a little bit. Right? Besides, Jane would accept any time he would allow her to spend with Spencer. She was leaving it up to him decide and orchestrate. Surely that was a good thing. Right?

'Can you trust her?' Louise repeated, and Sean met his mother's gaze.

'I hope so.'

The next day, Sean had firmly decided he was going to allow Jane limited access to Spencer to begin with.

'Are you sure?' his mother had asked when he'd informed her of his decision.

'Yes. Jane is very different to Daina and, besides, you've seen the gifts she's sent Spencer every year for his birthday and at Christmas.'

'They're always his favourite,' Louise agreed.

'Although he has no idea who this "Aunty Jane" person is, he's always enjoyed the presents she's sent.'

'What will you tell him?'

'The truth. She's his mother's sister and she's moved to Adelaide.' With the decision firmly made, Sean started to imagine what Jane's expression might be like when he told her the good news. Would she be excited? Happy? Apprehensive? Worried?

Ever since she'd told him about being so incredibly lonely, Sean had wanted to remove that forlorn look from her eyes. He hoped his affirmative answer would accomplish this. How could any person really be filled with sorrow and yet still have the strength to keep on going, to keep on forging ahead, making a difference in other people's lives? The thought of him being able to make a difference in *Jane*'s life filled him with a sense of happiness he hadn't felt in a very long time, and as he arrived at the hospital he decided to find Jane and tell her the news immediately.

He grinned to himself as he entered the ward, an extra spring in his step as he headed to the nurses' station, but much to his chagrin Romana informed him that Jane had already been in to see her patients and had left.

'Oh.' Sean was disappointed. 'Do you know where she is? We don't have clinic today so I'm not quite sure where I can find her.'

'Are you looking for Jane?' Luc asked as he came onto the ward.

'Yes.'

'She's in the research labs all morning.'

'Huh.' Sean frowned and Luc picked up the phone receiver on the desk and handed it to Sean.

'Call her.'

Sean looked from his friend to the phone and back

again, catching the very interested look in Luc's eyes. 'It's OK. I'll catch up with her later. It's no big deal.'

But it was, he told himself as he sat in his small office and worked steadily through his pile of paperwork. He had news, important news that would make Jane smile. The longer he couldn't pass on the news, the more urgent his need became. He had it in his power to see her green eyes shining with happiness rather than sadness.

Feeling as though the walls of his office were starting to close in on him, he stalked out of the department and out into the hot Adelaide sunshine. It was a scorcher of a day and he rolled up the sleeves of his white shirt, immediately missing the air-conditioning, as he headed towards the North Adelaide shopping district.

It was only as he noticed the increase of people in the area that he realised it was lunchtime and as he hadn't yet eaten he decided that would be next on his list. It might even improve his disposition. He wasn't the sort of man who liked to be at odds with himself and he'd been that way far too often in the past.

Marrying Daina had most certainly taken him out of his comfort zone and although their marriage had been far from smooth, he'd gained a son from the union. Spencer was a constant source of delight and blessings and Sean knew how fortunate he was to have such a wonderful child.

'Sean. Mate. Good to see you,' came the friendly greeting from Ronan, the proprietor of the café Sean preferred to frequent. 'Usual table?' Ronan didn't even bother to collect a menu as Sean knew the selection off by heart. 'Oops. Sorry, mate. Looks as though someone's already sitting at your table.'

'Never mind. By the win—' Sean stopped as he saw exactly who was seated at his table. His grin widened and he unconsciously straightened the knot of his tie. 'Actually, Ronan, don't worry about it. My usual table looks…just perfect.'

There, sipping a cup of coffee while reading a toy catalogue from a nearby toy shop, sat the one woman he'd spent all morning wanting to talk to.

CHAPTER FOUR

'HELLO, JANE.'

Jane looked up from poring over the toy catalogue directly into the face of Sean Booke.

'Sean?'

'I've been looking for you,' he remarked as he pulled out the chair opposite her and sat down. Jane shifted in her seat, sitting up a little straighter.

'Oh?' She immediately pulled her cellphone out of her pocket to check if she had any missed calls.

'I didn't leave a message. Luc said you were in the research labs so I didn't want to bother you.'

'But the patients are all right? Tessa?'

'The patients are fine.' He was impressed at just how much she really cared about them. 'I hope you don't mind me joining you.' He was calm and polite. 'Have you ordered any food yet?'

She frowned at him, unsure what he wanted. Why had he been looking for her? Had he reached a decision regarding Spencer? Did he have more questions?

'Er...no.'

Sean put his arm in the air to get Ronan's attention. The proprietor came over. 'Ready to order?'

Sean looked at Jane. 'Antipasto and another coffee?' he asked, and before she could think what she was doing, Jane had nodded her consent, rationalising that if she was nibbling on some food, perhaps it might assist her with not being so distracted by every little move the man opposite her made.

'Antipasto for two and coffees,' Ronan confirmed, before nodding. 'I'll see to it immediately.'

'Thank you, Sean,' she said, once they were alone again. 'I guess eating something isn't such a bad idea, especially as I want to spend some time with Tessa this afternoon before the meeting to go over the medical students' preliminary results.'

'What's your gut telling you?' he asked.

Jane shrugged. 'A few different things.'

'Do you trust your instincts or do you prefer to deal with cold data and facts to make your decisions?'

'Both.'

Sean grinned. 'Me too.'

They continued to discuss a few more patients, Jane determined to keep the conversation nice and professional for the moment so she could regain control over her wayward senses. Sean had the ability to shatter her usual calm. It wasn't just his good looks and charm, it was the way he genuinely seemed to care for others, not only the patients but the staff as well. In fact, just last week she'd overheard him talking to Romana, reassuring the nurse, who'd been upset because her dog had been ill.

'Did you take him to the vet I recommended?' Sean had asked gently.

'Yes. He was very nice, very caring.'

'He's a good vet.'

'I know. I'm just worried.'

'He'll take care of little Kelad,' he'd promised, his tone so absolute there was no way even Jane had doubted him and, thankfully, Romana had come in just a few days later and announced that little Kelad was much better.

With the arrival of their food and drinks, she was glad, not only of the delicious morsels before her, only then realising just how hungry she was, but also the welcome distraction eating provided. Sitting opposite Sean, seeing him away from the hospital setting, sharing a plate of food with him, Jane found herself becoming more and more intrigued by him. With his dark hair and blue eyes, he was still as incredibly handsome as she remembered and she wondered whether he had a girlfriend or partner. Had he been able to move on to a more successful and healthy relationship after his disastrous marriage?

If she knew he was involved with someone else, it might help her to curb the increasing desire she felt for him...but how did she ask him such a thing without it becoming awkward, especially when they seemed to have only just found a more even footing to build on?

Sean pointed to the toy catalogue beside her on the table as he swallowed his mouthful. 'Looking at investing in some new toys?'

Jane flicked her fingers over the pages and smiled. 'Actually, I was hoping to get some ideas for Spencer. It's only seven weeks until his birthday.'

'Yes, but you don't have to factor in posting time this year. You can give him your present in person.'

'I can?' Jane shifted in her seat, sitting up a little straighter at this news.

'Jane.' He put his knife and fork down before looking

at her. 'First of all, I'd like to apologise for questioning you about Luc. Even if anything was going on, it still wouldn't have been any of my business.'

Jane stared at him, blinking once then twice.

'What is it?' he asked, when he realised she was looking at him with a confused expression.

'I...just hadn't expected you to be so—' She quickly stopped what she saying and looked down at her hands.

'To be so...what?' he probed, the small curve returning to the edge of his mouth. 'So...gracious?' Jane stared at him. 'So...reasonable?' Jane's lips began to twitch into the beginnings of a smile. 'So...perfunctory?'

Jane's smile increased as she slowly shook her head from side to side. 'So *honest*.' Good heavens. When this man turned on the charm, he *turned on the charm*!

Sean gave her a quizzical look. 'You hadn't expected me to be honest?'

Jane spread her hands wide. 'Our few dealings in the past haven't always been the most straightforward.'

'True, but hopefully we've managed to clear the air a little.' He gestured to the empty plates before them. 'As well as clearing the plates,' he continued with a chuckle. The warm sound washed over her and she sighed out loud. 'I think today's been a good start.' Plus it had helped to solidify his decision in allowing her to visit Spencer. The fact that she was poring over toy catalogues, wanting to find the perfect present for a little boy she didn't even know, gave him some indication that she did have Spencer's best interests at heart.

Jane smiled shyly, bring her hair forward to hide her face a little. The action on some women might look coy and practised, but on Jane it only made her appear more genuine. 'So do I,' she told him.

'Jane, I want you to meet Spencer. I want him to get to know you and for you to spend time with him.' For what seemed like an eternity Jane didn't say a word, only stared at him across the table.

Finally, she managed to clear her throat and ask, 'Are you sure?' She needed to check, needed to make sure because she'd been let down too many times in the past. She had to double-check before she allowed her elation to burst forth. 'I don't want you to think I'm pressuring you into this.'

Sean closed his eyes for a second, trying not to be disappointed that she hadn't instantly exploded with happiness, hugging him and smiling brightly up at him with those rich, green eyes of hers.

'That's not the case, Jane. I really do want you to know your nephew. Family is important. I understand that. Spencer *is* your family so it shouldn't matter whether we're friends or colleagues or…whatever.'

Whatever? Jane wondered what he might mean by that comment. Whatever?

'Jane?'

'Huh?' She blinked quickly, clearing her wayward thoughts. 'Sorry. You were saying?'

'I was saying I think it's only right for you to have access to Spencer.'

'And you're really sure?'

Jane stared at him for a moment, his words slowly sinking in. Sean was going to allow her to get to know Spencer! It was as though all her dreams had come true. Slowly, very slowly, she allowed her emotions to shine out.

'That's…' She sighed with relief as the smile continued to spread over her face. 'That's very good news. Thank you, Sean. *Thank you*.'

Sean stared at her, unable to believe the utter delight reflected on her face. He'd wanted to see a bright beaming smile and she was definitely giving him one. He'd wanted her eyes to twinkle with delight and that's exactly what was happening. But what he hadn't counted on was the way the two combined would make her look so incredibly beautiful, it momentarily robbed him of breath.

Inner beauty, he'd learned, was far more important than external beauty. Daina had been a knockout on the outside and broken on the inside. Not that he was comparing the sisters, but to say Jane's natural radiance was presently knocking him off balance was an understatement.

The other thing he hadn't counted on was the fact that, a moment later, she seemed to be struggling to keep tears at bay. She bit her lower lip, her cheeks becoming tinged with pink as she tried to suppress her emotions. 'Thank you, Sean,' she whispered, and this time he heard the pure gratitude in her voice. She clutched her hands together at her chest. 'I don't think I've ever been this happy.'

'Really?' He was astonished by the statement but didn't pursue it. Something so simple had made her happy?

'And you won't change your mind?'

Sean couldn't help the tingling of annoyance he felt at her question and was about to tell her that he was a man of his word and that she could rely on what he said when he remembered she'd endured years of Daina's behaviour. One minute nice, the next horrible. Perhaps Jane wasn't questioning *him* but rather seeking reassurance because she'd been let down too many times in the past.

Sean reached over and took her hand in his, noticing she gasped a little at the action, her green eyes flashing with something...was it repressed desire or just surprise? He hoped it was the former because ever since he'd met her he'd had a difficult time removing her from his thoughts. 'Jane.' His tone was slightly husky and he quickly cleared his throat. 'I promise that I'll always try to be open and honest with you—I think it's what we both need after the way we've been hurt in the past.'

'Uh-huh,' she agreed, completely mesmerised, not only by his touch but by the way his gaze seemed to see right into her heart, stripping her of all her defences, leaving her naked and vulnerable before him.

Was that a good thing?

'All finished here?' the waiter asked, as he came over to clear their plates.

'Oh.' Jane quickly jerked her hand out of Sean's grasp and looked down at her empty plate and cup. 'Uh...yes. Yes. Thank you.'

Had she just been staring across a table into Sean's eyes, holding his hand...in public? This place was so close to the hospital that anyone could have walked in and seen them together and not have understood that it was all quite innocent and that nothing was going on between them except for the fact that he was granting her wish, that he was allowing her to see—

'Jane?'

'Hmm? Huh? What?' She looked across at him to find him smiling brightly at her, as though he could see the redness she could feel staining her cheeks. She looked away, dipping her head, using her hair as a shield against her embarrassment.

'When would you like to see Spencer?'

Jane wiped her face with her napkin before picking up the toy catalogue from the table as the waiter cleared everything away. She thanked him then opened her purse to get out some money. Sean quickly held up a hand to stop her.

'It's fine. I have an account here.'

'You do? You eat here that often?'

Sean nodded, instructing the waiter to put the food and drinks on his account. 'The food is made fresh and it's healthy. Besides, Ronan's daughter goes to school with Spencer so why not eat at a place you can trust?'

'Why not indeed,' she said. 'Well…then, thank you for lunch, Sean.'

'You sound surprised,' he remarked as he stood and came around the table to hold her chair for her.

'Thank you again,' she murmured, wishing he wouldn't be so chivalrous and gorgeous smelling and close and warm and inviting. It stalled the logical thought processes in her mind.

'You're welcome.' His smile was smooth, teasing and a little inviting, and Jane quickly picked up her bag and the catalogue and started for the door. She remembered to thank Ronan and his staff and to compliment the chef before she headed out of the cool air-conditioning into the heat.

'What time's the meeting about Tessa?' Sean asked, swatting away a fly.

'Not for another hour.'

'OK.' He nodded. 'Then, if you're not needed at the hospital, what would you like to do?'

Jane stared at him, surprised he hadn't simply made an excuse to leave. Did he *want* to spend more time with her? 'We could go to the toy store.' She held up the catalogue. 'Take a look around, see if there's anything there Spencer might like.'

'Great. Mind if I tag along?'

'You really want to?'

'He is my son after all, so I'll definitely be able to give you some pointers as to what he might like.'

Jane's smile was bright and her eyes twinkled. 'OK, then.'

'Every year you send him the most wonderful presents. He loves them.'

'He does?' She hadn't been sure whether Sean was passing on the gifts or whether he preferred Spencer not to have any contact whatsoever with her.

'It must be difficult, buying for someone you don't know.'

Jane shrugged. 'I just buy him what I wanted when I was his age. I know we're different genders but I was never really girly.' She'd left that to Daina. 'I loved cars and model aircraft and chemistry sets. Boys always have the better toys, as far as I'm concerned.'

'Well, you've always picked winners.'

'Wow. Yay, me!'

That gorgeous beaming smile was back and Sean drank it in. To say Jane was captivating him more and more with each passing second he spent in her company was an understatement.

'You're always so good with remembering his birthday,' Sean said. 'Never once have you forgotten.'

'It's a bit hard to forget Spencer's birthday.'

'Why?'

'Because it's the same day as mine. We share a birthday.' Jane delivered the line as though she was telling him the weather.

'You—? Wait. Spencer was born on your birthday?'

'He was.' Jane smiled up at him. 'That's why I've always felt such a strong connection with him. He's my birthday buddy. He'll turn seven and I'll turn thirty.'

Sean shook his head in astonishment. 'I had no idea. Daina…she never—' He stopped, both of them still strolling along. Jane looked up at him.

'She never talked about me, right?'

'Not really.'

'And I'll bet when she did it was usually derogatory in some way.'

'In the beginning, well, I guess I took everything she said as gospel.'

'But after that?'

'Do you mean when I realised my wife had serious mental health issues?' They stopped at a set of traffic lights and Sean pressed the button, both of them waiting for the lights to change. Jane turned to face him.

'How long did it take for you to realise?'

'About twelve months, I'm sorry to say. You'd think as a doctor I'd have picked up the signs and symptoms sooner.'

'You were no doubt very busy at the hospital, working all hours, and, believe me, Daina could be quite convincing when it suited her.'

Sean nodded. 'You sound as though you know exactly how I felt.'

'Let me guess. Whenever you tried to question her

about things, she'd tell you that you were overreacting
or that you'd grasped the wrong end of the stick. She'd
give you just enough attention, indicating she understood what was happening, then she'd expertly turn the
tables so that you were the one in the wrong, making
you feel guilty and filled with remorse.'

'*Yes.*' Sean was astounded at just how well Jane ar-
ticulated what he'd experienced, living with Daina.

'It's very difficult when you're emotionally involved
with someone, when you love them, to realise they're
manipulating you.'

'Yes.' He nodded slowly and exhaled. 'It wasn't until
Daina started trying to turn me against my parents and
siblings that I began to realise there wasn't something
wrong with *me*, it was *her*.' He spread his hands wide.
'I knew what she'd said about my sisters couldn't possibly be true. I know them so well, we're a very close-
knit family and when I discussed things openly with my
sisters…well, it was then the blinkers finally came off.'

'But you were still married to her for almost six
years, Sean.'

'She was my wife, Jane. She was mentally ill. I
couldn't just abandon her.'

'I doubt she felt the same way about you.' The words
were out of Jane's mouth before she could stop them
and as the pedestrian light finally turned green she set
off across the road. 'I'm sorry if that sounds harsh,' she
continued as they started walking down the other side
of the street, 'but I know Daina. I know the way she
could manipulate and twist the situation and I know
that even if you loved her, even if you tried to get her
help, she would have done little to actually help herself.'

Jane glanced across at him, hoping she hadn't overstepped the mark of this new level of friendship they seemed to be building. 'I'm sorry if what I've said offends you but—'

'No. You're absolutely right,' he interjected. 'But I've been raised to appreciate the value of family and, as my wife, Daina was my family. I wouldn't have been able to live with myself if I hadn't done everything I could to help her.'

'What did you try?' Jane asked as they neared the toy store.

'I organised appointments for her with mental health specialists. The first few times she refused to turn up and would often disappear for days or even weeks, not coming home and worrying me to the point of despair.'

'Yeah.' Her words were soft and she stopped under the shade of a nearby tree and looked up at Sean, who stood with his hands shoved into his pockets, his face drawn with remembered pain. 'Hiding from the truth.'

'A few times, though, I did manage to get her admitted to a clinic where she stayed for a few weeks, receiving medication for her condition, and it looked as though it was working.'

'But the instant she was discharged, after convincing everyone that she really was fine, things would begin to change again?'

'Yes.' Sean raked one hand through his hair. 'I tried everything I could to get her help but her problems, and she received so many diagnoses over the years, weren't easy to overcome if she wasn't willing to help herself.'

'Instead, everyone around the person suffers.'

Sean looked at Jane with concern as she spoke. She was looking down at the ground and when he reached out, lifting her chin so he could see her eyes, he saw pain reflected there. 'She hurt you a lot, didn't she?' It was a statement more than a question but Jane shrugged one shoulder, stepping back from his touch. Sean dropped his hand back to his side and watched her for another moment, seeing the years of unhappiness Jane had probably endured at the hands of her sister.

'So what finally ended it? You've already told me you were divorced before Daina passed away. What was it that made you end that toxic relationship?'

'Toxic. That's a good word for it.' Sean shoved both hands into his trouser pockets again and shifted his feet. 'She was pregnant with Spencer and at first she kept telling me how delighted she was, how this baby would change everything, make everything better between us, but it was just another one of her lies.'

Jane remained silent, watching the different array of emotions cross his face. Confusion, hurt, dejection, anger.

'I came home one day to find her gone. Usually when she left, or ran away, she'd pack a bag but this time nothing was missing. I checked the usual places, the different friends she relied on, but none of them knew where she was. Then two weeks later she came back home and seemed to be all right. She said she'd been confused, that she wanted to have the baby and that she loved me.'

Jane sighed. 'I know where she went during that time, Sean.'

'You do?'

She nodded. 'Daina came to see me. I was living in Melbourne and she'd somehow found me and turned up on my doorstep, saying she needed a place to stay for the night. As usually happened when Daina was around, all she talked about was herself, that to start off with she'd thought she'd wanted a baby, that it might be fun, but that she'd been in the shopping centre where a baby had been crying. Constantly crying, not stopping, and she realised she didn't want a baby after all. She said she'd tried to get an abortion but she was too far along with the pregnancy. The abortion clinics had turned her away.' Jane sighed heavily. 'That was why she'd come to see me.'

Sean gulped. 'She wanted you to do an abortion!'

'Yes.'

'What did you say?'

'That she was a fool. That she was too selfish to see that she had it all. She had good looks, a loving husband and was now going to have a child. I told her I was jealous of her. That seemed to feed her ego enough and she started talking about keeping the baby. It was all I could think of to ensure she didn't do something else to try and terminate the pregnancy.'

'How many weeks gestation was she?'

'Thirty-one.'

'What happened after that?'

'She left, telling me she was going to return home to her wonderful life with her loving husband. I hoped it was the truth.'

'And at thirty-three weeks I returned from a late shift at the hospital to discover her lying at the bottom of the stairs.'

'Oh, no.'

'She was drifting in and out of consciousness and she was cold. She'd sustained a concussion and at one point it did look as though she might lose the baby.'

'Obviously, Spencer managed to pull through.'

At the mention of his son, Sean smiled. 'He's a tough

little lad. Resilient.' The smile slowly faded as he met Jane's gaze. 'After his birth, Daina admitted to me that she hadn't accidentally fallen down the stairs as I'd presumed.'

Jane gasped, covering her mouth as she whispered, 'She'd thrown herself down voluntarily.'

He nodded. 'Yes.'

'What happened?'

'I finally saw the real Daina. After almost six years of my life, during which I'd tried everything I could to make her happy, to give her what she wanted, to try and please her, I saw her true self. She admitted that she'd continued drinking and even taking drugs throughout the pregnancy in the hope that the baby would abort spontaneously, but it hadn't so, in her mind, terminating the pregnancy herself was the next logical conclusion.'

'She always had such a convoluted way of thinking.'

'Yes.' He looked at Jane. 'You understand completely.' He reached out and took her hand in his. Jane tried not to react to the warmth that shot up her arm and burst into a mass of tingles throughout her entire body. Why on earth did one simple touch from him affect her in such a way?

'I've never been able to talk to anyone else about Daina,' he continued, completely unaware of how she was feeling. She wanted to pull her hand away but knew that would raise more questions than anything else. Instead, she focused on what he was saying. 'Not even my parents, as close as we are, really grasped the full level of Daina's vindictiveness. Sure, they could see she was a little unstable at times but she was quite the actress and played us all.'

'Yes.' Jane shifted back a little, the action causing

Sean to casually release her hand. She quickly grasped the toy catalogue from her bag, needing something to hold onto, trying desperately to concentrate on what he was saying rather than the way he was making her feel.

Even her own parents hadn't understood the full extent of Daina's moods, hadn't seen the way she'd emotionally bullied Jane for years prior to the accident. Now, with Sean, Jane was finally coming to realise, just as he was, that someone else *truly* understood. It provided them with an instant bond, even though it was formed through negative experiences.

'Spencer,' Sean continued, 'was in the neonate intensive care unit for the next three months but he was a fighter. After the delivery Daina was kept in overnight for observation and was then discharged, but before she left the hospital I told her our marriage was over. I would be filing for divorce as soon as possible and that if she didn't agree, if she did anything to contest it, I would have her charged with attempted manslaughter of our child.'

'You were angry.'

'I was livid, not only at her but at myself. I couldn't believe I'd been such a fool and for such a long time.'

'You made up rational excuses for her behaviour,' Jane offered.

'Exactly.' He spread his arms wide. 'I can't believe how…freeing it is to talk to you like this, Jane. You understand.'

'I do.'

Sean paused for a moment, looking at her as though he was seeing her for the time. She was not merely Daina's sister or Spencer's aunt…she was Jane, a woman who had clearly been through some terrible emotional experiences but instead of allowing them to make her weak had drawn strength from them, working hard and specialising in treating children with eating disorders who were also lost. She was trying to make a difference in the world and that realisation made him appreciate her even more.

CHAPTER FIVE

'WELL,' SEAN SAID after a long moment. They'd stood there, staring at each other, and Jane found herself becoming a little self-conscious, especially as Sean seemed to be looking at her as though he'd just discovered a rare treasure. Surely that couldn't be right. Jane had never classified herself as a rare anything. 'We have to do something,' he continued as he started walking again.

'For what?'

'For your birthday,' he stated, as though it was completely obvious.

Jane realised he was changing the subject and she was more than happy for that to occur. Still, the thought of having someone actually plan something for her birthday was more than she could contemplate right now. 'Oh, no. It's fine.' She brushed his words away. 'Focusing on Spencer is better. You only turn seven once and it's a big deal in a boy's life…or so I've gathered from my young patients over the years.'

For some reason he felt a strange sense of responsibility for Jane's happiness. Although Daina had torn his life to shreds, he'd had the support of his parents and siblings to help him through, especially where Spencer was concerned. Jane had had no one. If he didn't do something for her birthday, who would? Sean decided it would be best not to pursue the matter at the moment but he also made a note to ensure that this year Jane would have a birthday she wouldn't forget.

'So when would you like to meet Spencer?' Sean asked, as they continued down the street towards the toy store.

'I was going to leave that up to you. I don't want Spencer to be all nervous and worried about meeting a new aunty. I don't want it to be a "Surprise! You have a new relative" sort of thing.'

Sean laughed at her words. 'It wouldn't be like that. He knows he has an Aunt Jane, he's seen a picture of you—'

'Really? You have a picture of me?'

'I believe you were in a few that were taken at the funeral.'

'Oh.'

'Spencer's not completely in the dark about your existence.'

'Good to know…and thank you, Sean.'

'For?'

'For telling him about me. For not allowing me to be overlooked, even though things didn't work out with Daina.' Her words were filled with gratitude. As he held the door for her to enter the toy store, he thought it odd. Of course he wasn't going to hide her existence from his son. That would not only be dishonest but also cruel. Why would Jane even think he'd do—?

He stopped his thoughts. Daina. She'd said some terrible things to him about Jane, so no doubt she'd said some terrible things about him to Jane. Jane had

grown up in the shadow of her very pretty, very domi-
nant big sister and he had the distinct feeling that she'd
been overlooked more than once during her childhood.

It made him want to introduce her to Spencer this afternoon but perhaps she was right and that he should at
least prime his son first, even though he knew Spencer
would do nothing except accept the situation his father
presented. He was a very well-adjusted boy and if his
father said it was OK, then it would be OK. The knowledge filled Sean's heart with paternal pride.

As he watched Jane walk around the toy store, picking up things here and there, he quickly went through
the rest of his weekly schedule in his mind.

'How about Friday afternoon?' he said as he came
up behind Jane, who was looking at a remote-controlled
dinosaur and giggling.

'Friday afternoon? To meet Spencer?' She gulped.
'That's in…two days' time.'

'Well, I was going to suggest this afternoon but I
know you have meetings so it wouldn't work out.'

'This afternoon?' She gulped and stared at him with
wide eyes.

'But then I thought that perhaps both of you might
need to get used to the idea.'

'I would do it,' she said quickly, in case he thought
she was backing out. 'I would come this afternoon.
Don't think I wouldn't. It's just that I've thought about
this and wanted this for so long that to actually have a
dream come true and—'

Sean chuckled and reached out to put a hand on
Jane's shoulder. 'It's fine, Jane. I understand you need
a bit of time to mentally prepare yourself. So…Friday?

You can come with me to pick him up from his drum lesson.'

'He plays the drums?' Jane's earlier panic disappeared and she smiled brightly. 'I've always wanted to learn.'

'Perhaps he can teach you a thing or two although at the moment it's more a matter of him trying to gain some upper-body strength in his little almost-seven-year-old arms.' Sean laughed.

'That's fantastic. I'd love to hear him play.'

'Oh, you'll get the chance. One basic beat after the other. He loves to practise, although I'm not sure my parents or the rest of the neighbourhood are all that happy about it.'

'Your parents?'

'They live with us.'

'They do?'

Sean nodded as they continued to browse around the toy store. 'It's the only way I can work at the hospital, be available at all hours of the day and night and still give Spencer the relatively normal upbringing he deserves. We converted a house into two apartments. One upstairs, one downstairs.'

'Sounds ideal. What time does his drum lesson finish?'

'Five-thirty. You don't have a car, do you?'

'No.'

'OK. We both have clinic on Friday afternoon so, once we're finished, I'll take you to meet my son.'

Sean nodded with finality as though the deal was done. Jane swallowed as the realisation sank in. She was going to meet Spencer. It was happening. Things were working out as planned, instead of going pear-shaped, like they usually did, especially when it came to her private life. Spencer. She'd loved him ever since she'd been aware of him and now she was finally going to meet him…in two days' time!

Should she get him a present for when they first met? A sort of a 'Hello. How are you?' present? Was that crass? Perhaps she should buy some sweets or take some cake but she had no idea if Spencer had any food allergies. What about a book? Should she get him a book? Her mind went into overdrive as she walked around the store, settling in front of the music section and looking at all the different types of drumsticks available.

'I should get him a present for Friday,' she stated, taking a pair of drumsticks off the shelf.

'He doesn't need presents, Jane. He's already spoilt enough.' Sean took the sticks from her and put them back, before meeting her gaze. 'Your presence will be present enough.'

His words were soft yet intense and the way he stared at her made her wonder if he, too, could feel this strange and overwhelming tug of desire that seemed to exist between them. How? Why? She didn't understand how it was possible for her to be so attracted to Sean. The man had been married to her sister and—

No. That was in the past. The past couldn't be changed. The past was irrelevant. She'd trained her mental thought processes to stop looking back, to seek out the future but also not to miss the present…and at the present moment she couldn't deny the way Sean's intense gaze was making her feel.

She needed to say something to break the moment, to try and remember how to breathe again. 'OK,' she murmured, and forced herself to blink, to turn away and head to the rear of the store, where a model train was presently manoeuvring its way around the track.

Jane stopped, staring at a doll on the shelf in the back corner of the store. She frowned as memories flooded through, unbidden. A moment later Sean joined her and casually pointed to the doll.

'Now I know you like to buy Spencer different presents for his birthday but I know for a fact that dolls just aren't his thing.'

'I used to have one of these.' Jane reached out her hand, belatedly realising she was trembling a little, and picked up the boxed doll. 'If you pressed her belly button and gently pulled on the hair, the hair would grow. At the back, there was a winder to crank the hair back inside.' Jane trailed her fingers down the plastic packaging of the box. 'Mine was called Cinnamon.'

'You don't still have the doll?'

'No.' Jane sighed. 'Daina had one of her tantrums—I can't remember what it was all about—only that she was so mad she punished me by cutting off all of Cinnamon's hair so it didn't grow or shrink any more. I was upset but I could still play with the doll. However, a few weeks later, when she realised I hadn't abandoned the wrecked doll, she took it and hid it. I looked everywhere and then three weeks after Cinnamon had gone missing I found the doll all over my bedroom floor, in pieces.'

'How old were you?' Sean had listened to the way she'd spoken, so calm and controlled, as though she was reliving the memory of someone else.

'Eight.'

'What did your parents say?'

Jane slowly shook her head. 'They didn't know. I learned at a very early age that if I attempted to involve my parents when Daina acted out, the retribution was ten times worse.'

'She hit you?'

'No. She never laid a finger on me. She had other ways of making my life miserable.' Jane put the doll back on the shelf then walked away.

They continued to look around the store until Jane picked up a little torch that had small covers you could put over the light, causing it to make different shapes on the wall. Without a word, she headed to the register to make her purchase, asking them to gift wrap it for her.

'I'd best head back to the hospital. There are some case studies I'd like to read before the meeting about Tessa.'

'Of course.' They walked back to the hospital, both lost in their own thoughts but also quite comfortable with the silence. It was odd to feel so comfortable with Sean but perhaps, now that she had an answer to her question, now that she'd been granted access to Spencer, the previous tension she'd felt between the two of them had disappeared. No. Not disappeared...changed. She pushed the thought away, knowing she'd give it due consideration later when he wasn't affecting her senses as much as he was doing now.

'Regarding Tessa,' Sean said after a while, swatting away another fly as they drew closer to the hospital, 'she's being abused, isn't she?'

'There's always a reason why kids don't eat and it's usually the biggest cry for help they can give us doctors. Besides, there are many different forms of abuse. It's just figuring out which one.'

'You obviously have an idea what might be happening.'

'I have a theory but I don't want to say anything until there's further proof.'

'Gut instinct?'

'Uh-huh.'

'It's good to know you follow your instincts. It can be a doctor's most valuable tool.'

'I'm glad to hear you think that way,' she said, turning to smile up at him. Again, Sean was struck by how lovely she was, how real, how natural.

When they entered the building, they both sighed with relief at being surrounded by the air-conditioning. Jane headed to the ward and found the medical students seated at the nurses' station, the notepads in front of them filled with different observations and notes. Jane stopped and spoke with them for a moment before she went over to where Tessa was sitting up in her bed, reading a book.

Sean stayed where he was, watching closely as Tessa's expression seemed to soften when she saw Jane. He'd never noticed Tessa do that with anyone else. He checked the notes the nurses had written, noticing that Tessa hadn't eaten anything all day but, thankfully, hadn't made any attempt to pull out her drip, as she had once before.

There was a gasp of surprise and he looked over to see Tessa's big eyes widen as she opened the present from Jane. Within another minute she'd flicked the torch on and off several times, discovering that if she turned the rim, the light would change colour. She put the different covers over the bulb, testing each one, clearly enthralled with the gift. Then she put it down on the bedside table and shook her head. Sean edged closer, wanting to hear what Jane was saying to the girl.

'There are no strings attached,' she told Tessa softly. 'I know what it's like to accept a gift from someone who later demands payment—often a payment that's too high for you to give.'

Tessa watched Jane for a moment then asked, 'Who hurt you?'

The colour instantly drained from Jane's face and Sean watched as she bit her lip and swallowed three times before answering. 'My big sister.'

'Where is she now?'

'She died.'

'Did you kill her?'

'No. She was in a car crash.'

'I wish my sister was in a car crash.' The words were out of Tessa's mouth before she could stop them and she quickly covered her mouth with her hands, her eyes wide and wild with fear. 'Don't tell anyone. Don't say anything.' Her pleading was an urgent whisper.

Jane looked directly at Sean and it was only then he realised she'd known he was there the whole time. Had she just said all of that to Tessa in order to get the little girl to confess? To let them know exactly who was hurting her? This information would certainly help the medical students to hone their observation skills now they knew exactly what they were looking for.

'I'll come back and see you later tonight,' Jane promised, before pointing to the torch. 'There are no strings attached to this gift, Tessa. It's just something to help you not to be so afraid of the night.'

'How did you know it was her sister?' Sean asked Jane as they re-entered the nurses' station.

'I didn't, but sometimes sharing your own stories with these kids, to let them know you really do understand what they're going through, even though the circumstances of the abuse might differ, is an important step in forming a connection. I've chosen to utilise the bad things that have happened to me throughout my life in order to help me bond with my patients, because when eating disorders are involved, it's been proved through extensive research that if a true connection can be made between doctor and patient, there's far more opportunity for a successful recovery.'

'That must be very draining for you.'

Jane shrugged. 'It helps abate the loneliness.' She spoke to the medical students, asking them if Tessa's sister had come in to visit and to highlight those sections when they gave their report. 'I need to prepare for the meeting,' she murmured, and Sean nodded, still reeling from everything he'd learnt about her today.

As she walked away, he couldn't help thinking back to the things Daina had said about her younger sister. It wasn't that she'd talked about Jane or her parents much at all, but if she had had something to say, it had always shown *her* in the best light, to ensure he was left with a positive opinion of her.

'I took Jane in.' He could hear Daina's voice in his head. 'I was only eighteen when our parents died but I was there for Janey throughout her time in hospital and I cared for her, stepping up and being her legal guardian to ensure she wasn't put into the foster system. It wasn't easy. I was grieving for our parents and looking after a confused teenager who was terribly sick, both physically and mentally. It was tiring and exhausting but I managed, by the grace of God, to get us through that difficult time.' And of course every word Daina had spoken had been delivered with the dramatic flair of an award-winning actress, oftentimes with tears.

As he returned to his office to try and once more distract his mind with paperwork, he instead found himself looking Jane up on the internet. Surprisingly, he was able to access several of the papers she'd co-authored with Professor Robe and soon he was reading his way through them. He shook his head in stunned amazement. Jane was clearly an expert in her field, as well as being incredibly intelligent and sensitive. The hospital had been right to head-hunt and secure her professional services for twelve months.

Twelve months. She'd been here for one already. Eleven months of her getting to know Spencer, and of spending more time with her away from the hospital. Sean couldn't deny the delight he felt at that thought. He would brush away everything he could remember Daina saying about her sister and start afresh.

'A clean slate,' he told his cramped office. 'For both of us.'

CHAPTER SIX

THE MEETING ABOUT Tessa went well, with the medical students able to provide data about Tessa's behaviour when her parents came to visit, bringing her older and younger siblings with them.

'She was fine with the toddler,' one medical student reported. 'Pulling him onto her bed and hugging him close.'

'She wants to protect him,' Jane murmured. 'And the older sibling?'

'The older daughter, who is approximately nine or ten years of age, was almost...' The medical students looked at each other, both a little unsure.

'Go on,' Jane encouraged.

'Well, she wasn't mean at all. In fact, she was really nice to Tessa. She'd even brought Tessa in a present and was making Tessa laugh.'

Jane clenched her jaw and tried to keep her own feelings under control. 'Passive aggressive,' was all she said.

'But Tessa was laughing,' one of the students said, completely perplexed.

'No. Tessa was playing the part she needs to play in order to protect herself and her baby brother.' Jane looked at the data provided by the students. 'See here?'

she said, pointing to an entry made half an hour after Tessa's family had left. 'She went to the toilet then went back to her bed, curling up small and almost hiding beneath the covers.'

'Do you think she was trying to vomit in the toilets?' Sean asked.

'Trying to purge herself of the way she was feeling? Yes. At the moment the drip is keeping her fluids up and the antibiotics are treating her urinary tract infection but the act of physically trying to purge the negative emotions is quite common in such cases.' Jane picked up the articles she'd photocopied and handed them around to the dietician, social worker and nurses also attending the meeting.

As Jane continued to point out different case studies, Sean listened with half an ear, admiring the way she understood not only the psychological but physical implications of what her patients were going through. Did that mean that Jane herself had suffered from an eating disorder as a young child? Had Daina's bullying caused Jane to try and purge the negative emotions from her body? Was that why she wore such loose-fitting clothing? Did she still suffer from an eating disorder?

Concern flooded through Sean as he watched her move. Her long hair swished down her back as she moved over to the white board and began breaking down Tessa's symptoms. The fact that Jane had also managed to prise a confession out of Tessa only served to corroborate the signs and symptoms.

'So what do we do?' Anthea asked. 'How can we help poor little Tessa?'

'Excellent question,' Jane replied, and for the first time since they'd entered the meeting she smiled. The action lit up her features and Sean was once more struck by her inner beauty. Did she have any idea just how beautiful she was?

For the rest of the meeting they formulated a plan of action to help Tessa, as well as getting some help for the older sibling. Had the parents noticed anything? Were they also afraid of their oldest daughter, unable to impose any parental control on her? It did happen. Jane had seen it with her own parents. Oftentimes they'd found it much easier to placate Daina than stand their ground. She hoped that with this early intervention for Tessa the situation would be defined and coping strategies put in place for all concerned.

After the meeting Jane couldn't believe how drained she felt and so she slipped away quietly, not bothering to say goodbye to anyone. Back in the residential wing, she put her phone and hospital lanyard onto the table beside the bed and kicked off her shoes. She lay down on the bed and allowed the cool air-conditioning to soothe her.

No sooner had she closed her eyes than her phone rang. 'Not happening,' she moaned, as she reached out to pick up her cell and answer it. 'Dr Diamond,' she said, trying to hide the tiredness in her voice.

'Jane? Where are you?'

'Sean? I'm in my room. In the res wing.'

'You're OK.'

'Of course I'm OK. Why wouldn't I be?'

'Well, you just disappeared.' There was a hint of annoyance as well as relief in his tone. 'I would have walked you over to the res wing. Although it's in hospital grounds, that doesn't mean it's one hundred per cent safe. I was worried.'

'You were worried?' Her eyebrows hit her hairline.

'Of course I was.'

'About me?' she asked, disbelief lacing her words.

'Look, Jane. I know you haven't had a normal up-bringing so this may come as a shock to you, but families look after each other, care for each other. I may have driven my twin sisters crazy with my over-protective big-brother routine while we were growing up but they also knew it was only because I cared.'

'You…care?' Her words were hesitant.

'About you? Yes. You're Spencer's aunty. So are my sisters and, as such, you deserve the same consideration as them.'

Jane tried to process his words, still unsure what this 'consideration' might entail. Did that mean Sean saw her in the role of a surrogate sister? Had she misinterpreted those long, lingering looks they'd shared?

'Oh. Well, I apologise for not saying goodbye. I was tired and I'm not really used to having people…care about me in that way. You know, concerned for my safety and all that.'

'Well, you'd better start getting used to it. Family is family and I'm very protective of mine.'

'As you should be.'

'That now includes you, Jane.'

'It does?'

'Yes!' The word was filled with exasperation and Jane couldn't help but smile. Sean cared about her? He considered her as part of his family, even though she hadn't even met Spencer yet? The sensation of being so accepted overwhelmed her and she pursed her lips together in an effort to stop the tears of happiness she could feel welling up inside her. Sean cared.

'I've never had anyone, protective or otherwise, really care, so you'll have to forgive me if I don't follow protocol.'

'That's all right,' he said, his tone more calm. Sean leaned back in his chair and put his feet up on the desk. 'I'll guide you through any rocky waters.' He smiled as he spoke. Jane had such a soothing voice, sweet, calm and controlled. He'd seen those gorgeous green eyes of hers flashing with anger or glowing with complete happiness, but how would she look, how would she sound when she was filled with desire?

He closed his eyes on the thought and immediately pushed it away. He shouldn't be thinking about her in such a way and yet he didn't seem able to stop himself. All those years ago when he'd met Daina, things had moved incredibly fast and he'd been married before he'd known which way was up. He knew now that that had just been Daina's style, but with Jane he had the sense that a slowly-slowly approach would no doubt benefit both of them.

He'd only started to really get to know her a few days ago but what he was seeing, the inner character she was revealing, was…breathtaking. He was beginning to realise just how much she'd missed out on, not only during her childhood but also as an adult. She'd been so incredibly lonely that she'd risked moving to Adelaide. She'd put her heart on the line, almost begging him to allow her access to Spencer. How could any man not be affected by her genuine heart? How could he not want to wrap his arms about her and protect her from any future hurts?

'Any big dinner plans for tonight?' he found himself asking, imagining arriving at her door with take-out, the two of them eating and chatting amicably together in her small, intimate room.

'Toast and jam.' Her answer was accompanied by a big yawn and the image in Sean's head evaporated. She was tired, exhausted.

'Do you have trouble sleeping?'

'Sometimes. It's another reason why I'm more than happy to stay here, close to the hospital. If I can't sleep, at least I can catch up on some work or check on my patients.'

'Or sing to them.'

'Or that.' She chuckled.

'You have a lovely voice. Soothing. Relaxing.'

'Well, any time you're stressed, give me a call and I'll sing you a lullaby.'

'I'm stressed right now.' The words were out of his mouth before he could stop them. Why had he said that? To hear Jane's pretty singing voice coming down the line would only serve to intensify the emotions he was attempting to keep under control. Before he could say anything else, Jane immediately began to sing.

Her lilting voice surrounded him and he leaned back further in his chair, letting the lyrics and melody blend together. He could feel the tensions of his day begin to disappear, his breathing deepening as he completely filled his lungs with oxygen before inhaling slowly.

At the end of the first verse and chorus, Jane stopped to yawn and he couldn't help but laugh. 'You're de-stressing yourself as well.'

'I think you might be right.' She yawned again. 'I think I'd best say goodnight before I fall asleep with the phone glued to my ear.'

'Wise move.' He chuckled. 'Goodnight, Jane. Sleep

sweet,' he murmured, before disconnecting the call, *and* before he gave in to the urge to rush to the res wing and haul her into his arms. How could one short song make him feel as though he'd just found the most perfect place to call home? He didn't need any new complications in his life, especially as he'd worked hard since Spencer's birth to maintain a certain level of detachment from romantic relationships. He'd tried dating once or twice but with the distrust Daina's antics had instilled deep within him he had become naturally suspicious of the most innocent actions.

So why didn't he feel that way with Jane? How could he be absolutely certain she was as genuine as she appeared? He frowned, not wanting to listen to the doubting voice. 'Meeting Spencer will be the true test,' he said, as he took his feet off the desk and stood. Spencer had a good intuitive sense about him, most children did because they weren't as fooled by deception as adults could be.

As he collected the papers he needed to work on and locked up his office, Sean found himself wishing it was Friday afternoon already. Seeing Jane face to face with his son would help give him the reassurance he was looking for.

After clinic on Friday afternoon, Jane couldn't believe how jittery she felt.

'I'm as nervous as a long-tailed cat in a room full of rocking chairs,' she told Sean, as she finished writing up the last set of casenotes.

'You'll do fine.' He checked his watch. 'We have a good half an hour before we need to pick Spencer up.'

'Really?' She checked the time on her cellphone. 'We

finished clinic on time? How miraculous.' Sean chuckled at her words and she felt a wash of tingles spread down her spine at the sound. She'd made him laugh and the thought filled her with a bit more confidence about the important meeting awaiting her.

'Do you think I have time to change?' She stood. 'If you bring your car around to the res wing car park, I could meet you there.'

'Sure, but for the record you look lovely just as you are.'

Jane stared down at her long, ankle-length skirt, flat shoes and baggy shirt, her hair pulled out of the way in a loopy sort of ponytail. 'I do?'

'Yes.' His smile was genuine as he realised she truly had no idea just how lovely she was. He wanted to ask her if she wore the baggy clothes because she was self-conscious about her body. He wanted to know if she'd had an eating disorder as a child. She didn't seem to be suffering from it now but what would he know? Apart from having lunch with her the other day, he hadn't seen her eat much. He brushed the thoughts aside for now. 'OK, you head over to the res wing and I'll meet you there.'

It didn't take him long to move his car from one car park to the next and he headed inside the residential wing's lobby, sitting down in the cool air-conditioning and taking the opportunity to read the latest hospital news circular. No sooner had he started reading the lead article than he realised Jane was standing in front of him. He put the circular down and slowly stood up, his gaze travelling over the woman before him.

Dressed in jeans, flat shoes and a long-sleeved T-shirt that was still a little big for her, there was no doubting that she had a beautiful feminine shape. Add to that the fact that she'd plaited her long luscious locks into pigtails, making her look more like the seventeen-year-old he remembered, and Sean's previous warnings to himself to take things slowly seemed to disappear.

When she shoved her glasses onto her nose, a move he was coming to realise indicated she was nervous, he belatedly realised he'd been staring at her.

'Er…sorry.' Sean cleared his throat and thrust his hands into his pockets.

'Is this OK? Not too casual? I wasn't sure how formal or informal I should be.'

Sean smiled. 'Just be yourself and, if I might say so, you look lovely.'

'Lovely?'

'Yes, Jane.'

She lowered her head again but not before he'd seen the disbelief reflected in her eyes. 'How can you not know how beautiful you are?' he asked softly, stepping a little closer to her so others in the lobby didn't overhear what he was saying. 'Your hair is…glorious. When it's loose, I want to touch it, to watch as the silky strands slide through my fingers. And your eyes…' He exhaled slowly as he looked deeply into her eyes. 'So sad and intense. A man could lose himself in your eyes.'

'Uh…' Jane stumbled, breaking her gaze from his and looking down at the floor, feeling completely out of her depth. No one had ever spoken to her like this before, not even Eamon. Why was he saying these things to her?

'You're caring, intelligent and have the voice of an angel.' Sean reached out, placing his fingers gently beneath her chin, lifting her head so their eyes could meet once more. 'You're a person of worth, Jane Diamond. Far too many people have told you otherwise and it's time for that to change. You are a person of worth,' he repeated. 'And I for one am proud to call you my friend.'

'Friend,' she whispered, as though she were just learning to speak a new language. 'You're right, Sean.' She swallowed over the dryness in her throat. 'No one's ever told me that. Thank you.'

As she stared up at him, he knew what he'd said was completely true as her green eyes seemed to be inviting him to stare into them for ever. Such an odd sensation and one he was all too tempted by. However, the last thing either of them needed right now was any sort of romantic attachment. Logically, he accepted that. Emotionally, he didn't seem able to stop thinking about her.

Tonight he should be focused on keeping her calm, helping her through the apprehension he could already see was buzzing through her. He dropped his hand and took a step back, before forcing a smile. He held his hand out towards the door. 'We don't want to keep Spencer waiting. Shall we?'

Jane nodded, as though she were no longer capable of speech. Thankfully, his car wasn't too far from the entrance to the res wing so they were effectively going from one cooled place to another. Neither of them spoke for a while as Sean navigated the evening traffic, but once they were away from the hospital he glanced over at her.

She was tense. Both hands clenched tightly together in her lap. Her gaze was directly ahead, watching the traffic. Was she tense because she was in a car or was she nervous about the upcoming meeting? Sean decided it didn't really matter which one it was but tried his best to relax her a little.

'I read the last paper you published with Professor Robe.'

'Really?' She seemed surprised.

'Yes. It was very interesting as well as thorough but there are a few things I'm still not one hundred per cent sure about. You mentioned in the article the initial methodology required further investigation before you were able to employ the present model.'

'That's right.' There was a stronger note in her words, as though her mind was definitely shifting to more comfortable ground.

'What was the initial methodology you used?'

'Well…' And throughout the rest of the drive to the place where Spencer had his drum lesson, Sean kept asking questions and Jane kept answering them, her smooth voice combined with her intelligent words definitely assisted in focusing his train of thought, although once or twice when he stopped at red lights, he wasn't able to resist watching her mouth as she spoke. Such a perfectly shaped mouth as well.

'And here we are,' he said, as she just finished explaining the negative side effects of the medication doctors had previously used to treat urinary tract and bladder infections, which were common ailments associated with eating disorders.

'What? Here?' Jane looked at her surroundings, astonished. Then she looked back at Sean. 'You distracted me.' It was almost an accusation and Sean couldn't help but laugh. She looked so indignant it was adorable.

'It was clear you were over-thinking things and, besides, I really did want to know about your initial methodology.'

Jane slowly exited the car and looked over at him. 'Hmm. I guess I'll believe you.'

'Oh, thank you. Very much.'

There was a wonderful, natural smile on his face, such as she hadn't seen before. Combined with the delight in his eyes and the way his deep laughter vibrated through her, it was a wonder she could stand. Now, however, was not the time to be thinking about Sean or about the way his nearness affected her. She was here to meet Spencer.

Jane tried to calm her breathing. She'd looked forward to this day for so long…well, almost from the day Spencer was born. How she'd longed to be a part of his life and now, thanks to Sean, she was getting that opportunity.

'Coming?' Sean asked, and it was only then she realised he was walking up the path towards the house where loud drum beats could be heard. She slowly moved away from the car.

'Does he know I'm coming?'

'Yes. He's very interested to meet you.' He waved away her concerns as he pushed open the door and walked right in. 'You'll be fine,' he called, speaking a little louder over the drum beats.

To her surprise, the house they entered had a large practice room with a baby grand, a drum kit, keyboards and several other instruments set up, ready to play. But it was the boy sitting behind a set of drums that looked far too big for him, hammering out a steady beat in time to some rock music, who really caught her attention. The boy was a mini replica of his father, except that Spencer's hair was a little longer, curling slightly at the back.

Spencer finished playing the song, doing a drum-roll

flourish at the end and hitting the cymbal loudly. Jane couldn't contain herself and let go of Sean's hand before she started clapping. Sean joined in and, in the next moment, Spencer's face lit up at the sight of his father.

'I'm so purple at it.' He held his drumsticks high in the air and they clapped louder. Jane beamed from ear to ear, unable to believe this moment had finally arrived.

'Purple?' she asked, momentarily looking towards Sean.

'It means brilliant.' He shrugged. 'Don't ask me more than that. Kids nowadays make up their own lingo and sometimes I think it's purely to keep us adults in the dark.'

Jane giggled, unable to believe how happy she felt, and she hadn't even spoken to Spencer yet. She didn't have long to wait as the boy wriggled out from behind the drum kit and raced over to his father.

'Dude.' Sean held up his hand and Spencer dutifully gave his father a high five. 'That was so purple.'

'I know, right!' Spencer grinned at his father then turned and looked at Jane, before angling his head to one side. 'Are you my new aunty? Aunty Jane?'

Jane pushed her glasses up the bridge of her nose and nodded. 'Yes. Yes, I am.'

'That's *totally* purple!' he yelled jovially, and within the next instant the young almost-seven-year-old had launched himself at her, wrapping his arms about her waist. Tears flooded into Jane's eyes as she put her hands on Spencer's back then looked over at the boy's father.

'It is. It's totally purple.' She laughed, happier than she could ever remember being.

CHAPTER SEVEN

THE HUG DIDN'T last long at all. In fact, it was over and done with as Spencer seemed to jump around the room, shifting from foot to foot as he told his father about his day. He kept looking at Jane, accepting her so instantly that her heart was overwhelmed with a pure love she'd never felt before.

After a moment he stopped still in his tracks, tipped his head to the side and looked at Jane intently. 'Hang on. You're the Aunty Jane who always sends me those cool presents for my birthday and Christmas, right?'

'That's right.'

'We did discuss this last night as well as this morning,' Sean gently reminded his son, but it appeared Spencer only had eyes for his new aunt at the moment.

'I love the microscope you sent for Christmas. Dad and I looked at a drop of blood on a slide and I wrote you a letter to say thank you but I didn't know where you lived so I didn't get to send it but now that you're here, I can give it to you.'

Jane's heart turned over with delight. 'I'd like that.'

'Super green. Did you want to come to my house?'

'Uh…yes. I'd like that very much. Thank you, Spencer.'

'Green,' he said with a nod. 'I've gotta pack up my

stuff.' He took a step towards the drum kit then stopped and turned to look at her. 'Hey, because you're here and it's my birthday soon, does that mean I'm not gonna get a cool present?'

'Spencer!' Sean immediately chastised his son.

'It's all right, Sean. It's a fair question,' Jane interjected. 'Perhaps we can work something out. Perhaps we could go shopping together?'

'Really?' Spencer's eyes lit up.

'It means the present wouldn't be a surprise but you could definitely choose what you wanted.' And she'd get to spend time with him. 'If it's OK with your dad,' she added, looking at Sean. Although he was willing to give her access to Spencer, Jane still didn't want to overstep any boundaries. She needed to keep things on an even keel lest Sean retract his permission. Jane was very good at not rocking the boat, at realising where her boundaries were, but with Sean…when he was close to her, speaking in those deep and sensual tones, telling her she was lovely…when that happened, she had no idea where the boundaries were!

Being around Sean was unsettling but in a good way. He had definitely ignited a spark when he'd confessed he wanted to run his fingers through her hair. How was she supposed to take a comment like that? How was she supposed to keep things on an even keel so she could continue to see Spencer, when Sean continually knocked her completely off balance?

Spencer picked up his music books and put them into his bag. 'It'll be OK, won't it, Dad,' he stated with confidence. 'Aunty Jane and I can go shopping, can't we?' He looked pleadingly up at his father. 'And after the shops we can all go home and play with whatever I get and you and Dad can have a coffee.' Spencer slung his music bag over his shoulder, looping the bag across his body, and spread his hands wide, as though everything seemed organised and perfectly normal.

Jane was still holding onto the way the words 'Aunty Jane' had rolled so easily off his tongue. Oh, to be so innocent, to be so secure in parental love. It was clear, even after just a few minutes of meeting Spencer, that Sean had done a wonderful job of raising his son.

'I love meeting new aunties,' he remarked with an air of superiority, as though he had relatives popping out of the woodwork every single day of the week. 'I already have two aunties, two uncles and three cousins and two grandparents and Dad, and now I have *another* aunty. This is so purple.'

Spencer waved goodbye to his music teacher, remembering to thank him for the lesson before his father scolded him for having bad manners, then headed to the door.

'Are you all right?' Sean asked softly. Jane had been unaware he'd moved to stand beside her, the warmth emanating from him surrounding her like a comfortable, snuggly blanket, safe and secure. She blinked and smiled, then laughed through the blend of emotions. Happiness, joy, confusion, acceptance, awareness. It was all too much for her so, instead of trying to figure things out, as she usually did, she was simply going to accept that this was the way she felt and there was nothing else to do except go with it.

'I'm purple and super green and all the other colours of the rainbow. I have no real idea what any of it means but I'm quite impressed that the younger generation understand their colours so well.' She laughed again, delight filling her, and then, because her emotions were so overwrought from being on edge for far too long, she followed Spencer's example and threw her arms around Sean's neck, hugging him close.

'Thank you. Thank you. *Thank you*.'

Sean's arms came easily around her waist and he closed his eyes, allowing her addictive scent to wash over him. He'd watched Jane throughout her first encounter with Spencer and to be able to offer her such joy and happiness, to unite her with her only living relative, filled Sean's heart with a sense of completeness. As a child, his mother had often told him about the power of giving, of how it made the giver feel happier than the receiver.

Closing his eyes, he tried to commit every second of this spontaneous embrace to memory before Jane pulled back, still grinning up at him, and turned to follow Spencer. There was no doubt in Sean's mind, seeing Spencer talk in his usual animated way, telling Jane all sorts of superfluous things, that it had been the right decision, both for woman and boy. The fact that he himself was drawn to Jane, admiring her intelligence, appreciating her gentleness, accepting her shyness, was the bigger problem.

With Jane now having been introduced to Spencer, it meant that Spencer would classify her as part of his family. It meant that they'd be inviting Jane to their family get-togethers, that he'd be seeing her more and more away from the hospital, in a relaxed, casual setting, and while he was definitely on board with the concept of her enjoying everything his family could offer her, and while he was happy to jump at any excuse to get to know her better, at the back of his mind was the niggling thought that all of this could end in disaster.

The attraction between himself and Jane was very much a fact. At first, he'd thought it was only on his side but after the way she reacted when he'd told her how lovely she was, staring at his mouth and trembling slightly from nervous awareness, Sean was interested to see what would happen if he kissed her.

Even the thought of touching his lips to Jane's made his heart rate increase and yet he questioned himself about the logical implications of such an action. If he were to pursue a romantic relationship with Jane, what would happen if everything went sour? Would he be able to bear seeing her interacting with his family? With his son? Would it be difficult for the two of them to be in the same room together? It would be bad enough at the hospital but at least there they could focus on their patients. However, seeing Jane at his home with Spencer…could he do that? Perhaps it would be better to keep their relationship on a friendly, platonic and professional level to avoid hurting all concerned?

Sean's thoughts continued to spin as he drove home, thankful that Spencer kept up a steady stream of chatter, telling both adults about his day and how Johnny Madalzinski had got into trouble because he'd brought a water squirter to school and squirted the teacher.

'But before he got in trouble we all had a go at lunchtime and when I did it it went the longest and nearly squirted Lanie, and all the boys were jealous because I was the best at it.'

'Does he ever stop for breath?' Jane murmured, and Sean instantly smiled, returning his thoughts to the present.

'Not often.'

As soon as they pulled up in the driveway and Sean garaged the car, Spencer was out of the vehicle like a tornado, picking up his school bag and music bag but dropping bits of paper, a pencil and a lunch wrapper on the ground as he raced into the house. Jane could hear him calling out, 'Grandma? Grandpa? I'm home!'

'He certainly is vibrant and energetic,' Jane remarked as she helped Sean pick up all the things Spencer had dropped.

'He's a healthy, happy, almost-seven-year-old boy.' Sean gestured to a stool at the kitchen bench. 'Please, have a seat.'

'I can see that.' Jane shook her head in bemusement. 'I just hadn't expected...' She stopped and shrugged as she sat down on the bench stool, watching him turn on his coffee-maker. 'I don't know what I expected.'

'That he'd be like Daina?' Sean asked the question quietly as he took two mugs from the cupboard.

'I don't know. I guess so.' She frowned for a moment. 'It's all so different from how I grew up.'

Sean smiled. 'Not for me. Growing up with two younger sisters in a rowdy but happy home was my normal.'

'It's nice you're able to provide that for Spencer.'

'Some days it's not easy but I have a lot of help and support and that makes all the difference.' He pressed buttons on his impressive coffee-machine and within a minute or two was placing a fresh latte before her. 'I'm guessing your upbringing wasn't exactly normal?'

'No.' Jane stirred the drink and scooped some milk froth up to her lips. She didn't elaborate any further and Sean had to quash his impatience.

Thoughts and questions about Jane had kept him awake for several nights now and maybe if he had some deeper level of understanding of what made Jane Diamond tick, of why she appeared to have such a hold over him, then he'd be able to control the way she made him feel. Sean watched her scoop more milk froth from her drink before licking the spoon. She did this a few times, and one time ended up with froth on her upper lip.

'Wait a sec,' he murmured, and leaned across the bench, brushing her upper lip with his thumb. Jane gasped at the contact, her gaze never leaving his. 'You had a little bit of…' Sean stopped and swallowed, desperately wanting to follow the action with his mouth but knowing that was impossible. Jane was…family now. That was the only way he could allow himself to think of her and yet it was a struggle to do so, especially when she sat there, staring at him with those big, hypnotic green eyes.

He reached out with his other hand and touched her mouth again, his fingers caressing her cheek, his thumb rubbing gently across her lips. Jane sat still, her gaze fixed on his. She was unable to breathe, his touch such a soft caress. His gaze dipped to her mouth. 'I find you quite remarkable, Jane Diamond.'

Before she could say a word he brushed his thumb over her lips again but this time the action was slower, more sensual, more intense. There was no excuse of milk froth, this was just pure desire. It was as though he wanted to touch her, to excite her, to let her see herself through his eyes. But could she trust him?

Jane pushed the thought away, intent on focusing on the here and now as Sean's thumb tenderly traced her lower lip, causing Jane to draw in breath, her entire body flooding with tingles and anticipatory delight.

'I wish you—' She stopped, unable to speak, unable to concentrate, unable to do anything else but feel. Her eyelids fluttered closed. 'You…we…shouldn't,' she whispered, her words barely audible.

'Why shouldn't we?' Sean's words were husky and when she risked opening her eyes to look into his she was stunned to find him looking at her with intense desire. No. That couldn't be right. For so long, for too many years, she'd always believed bad things about herself. She'd been told all her life that she was nothing special, but seeing the way Sean was looking at her… was it possible for her to believe him?

'Jane.' He breathed her name and before she knew what was happening he'd bent his head and brushed a light, feathery kiss across her cheek. 'You clearly have no idea just how much you've infiltrated my thoughts.' He continued to kiss her face, edging his way towards her ear, and Jane couldn't help the tears that instantly sprang to her eyes and began to slide down her cheek.

Sean kept kissing her face, working his way up to her forehead, before he looked at her. 'Jane, you're a beautiful woman.'

She shook her head but he stilled the movement, wiping away her tears. 'Say the words,' he instructed softly. 'Say, "I am a beautiful woman."'

'I can't.'

'But it's true and I think you need to start believing it. I wouldn't say it otherwise.'

'Ha!' She laughed without humour.

'If you don't believe I'm telling the truth, you must think I'm lying.'

Jane's answer to this statement was to shrug her shoulders.

'So you think I'm lying.'

'Men have lied before in order to seduce a woman.'

'You think I'm trying to seduce you?' His eyebrows hit his hairline.

'Aren't you?'

'With my son and parents not too far away?' he said, and she had to concede his point.

'You still didn't answer the question,' she said softly.

He chuckled softly and she edged back from his tender touch, trying to block out his sweet words. She knew there was no way he could really mean them and she'd learnt long ago not to build up false hopes.

'You're a smart woman, Jane, so how come, when it comes to affairs of the heart, you just clam up?'

'Sean...' There was the hint of protest in her tone, indicating she wasn't sure about the course this conversation was taking, but when he smiled at her she found her mind turning to mush and she completely forgot what she'd been about to say. How was it possible he could make her do that? She'd always been able to maintain a certain level of control over her emotions as far as men were concerned. Even with Eamon she'd been the one to call the shots in the relationship, which had been one of the reasons he'd cited when he'd broken their engagement.

'Hmm?' He exhaled slowly, his gaze flicking from her eyes to her lips, the action causing Jane to feel all tingly inside, her heart rate increasing. 'You are stunning.'

'Don't look at me like that,' she protested weakly.

'Like what? Like a man who's very interested in you?'

He wanted to kiss her. He wanted to kiss her and the desire was increasing with each passing second, especially when she continued to stare at him with those gorgeous eyes of hers.

'Don't be interested in me.'

'Why not?'

'Because I...' She stopped and swallowed, her gaze lingering on his mouth for just a fraction of a second longer than it should have. It was enough to let him know that even though she was saying no, deep inside her heart she was saying yes. It was enough to give him hope and he hadn't felt hope about a relationship for a very long time now. He also knew it was important for Jane to steer them through these tentative waters at her own pace. Rushing would only result in her rejecting him and he'd been rejected enough to last a lifetime.

'Jane—' he tried hard not to stare at her luscious lips as he spoke '—I want you to know that I take my commitments very seriously and—'

'Stop.' Jane placed a finger across his lips. 'Don't say anything, Sean. Don't make any promises.' She quickly removed her finger, the intimate contact doing nothing to quell the simmering fires of desire burning through her entire body. She really did want to believe what Sean was saying, wanted to accept him at his word, but how could she when she'd trusted in the past and been hurt? If Sean knew the truth of her secret, if he comprehended that she really wasn't beautiful at all, if he saw her terrible sca—

'Jane?' he queried.

'I...I'm just not sure I can deal with reje—'

'Through here!' came Spencer's loud, excited voice, heading in their direction. 'You'll never believe it, Grandma. *Another* aunty!'

Within a split second of hearing Spencer's voice Jane had pushed Sean away, needing to put as much distance between them as possible, and slipped off the stool. She tried to quieten her frantic thoughts. How could she have possibly allowed Sean to get so close?

She tugged at her top, making sure it was in place, instantly wishing she hadn't come dressed so casually. She combed her fringe with her fingers and pulled the long plaits, which Sean had pushed back, to the front. It was her armour and right now. With the impending prospect of meeting Sean's parents, she needed it more than ever. She had no idea what sort of reception they might give the sister of the woman who, from the few things Sean had said, had caused their son a fair amount of emotional stress. Would they tar her with the same brush?

'Look. See?' Spencer ran towards where his father and Jane were standing. 'Another aunty! From my mummy's side.'

The little boy sounded so excited, not at all perturbed that his words might cause painful memories to resurface. He ran right up to her, glancing back now and then to ensure his grandparents were following.

Jane, now satisfied that her 'armour' was on, stood her ground, ready to be introduced to the two people walking towards her. Sean's mother had short dark hair with red and gold streaks through it, and his father was the spitting image of his son, only thirty years older. If he was any indication of how Sean would age, Jane

had to admit that there were some excellent genes in
the Booke family gene pool.

'You were right, Spencer,' Sean's mother remarked as
she walked over to where Jane stood. Sean just leaned
against the bench top and watched as his mother smiled
brightly. 'Hello. Sean told us you'd be stopping by.'

Jane squared her shoulders and lifted her chin, pasting a professional smile on her face. 'I hope it's not an
inconvenience?'

'Oh, tush,' his mother said, and brushed Jane's words
away. Still, Jane wasn't exactly sure what to do or say
next so she held out her hand. 'I'm Jane. It's a pleasure
to meet you, Mrs Booke.'

'Good heavens. Call me Louise. We're hardly that
formal, isn't that right, Barney?' she said, glancing at
her husband. Barney shook hands with Jane after Louise, the two of them staring at her for what seemed like
an eternity but which in reality was only a few seconds.

'I do hope you're able to stay for dinner, Jane.' Louise glanced at Sean, who shrugged. 'You haven't even
asked Jane to dinner yet? Where are your manners?'
Louise swatted playfully at her son.

'Yeah, Dad,' Spencer took the opportunity to chime
in, a cheeky grin on his face. 'Manners!'

Jane couldn't help the bubble of laughter that over-
flowed and she quickly clapped a hand over her mouth.
A split second later both Sean and his parents laughed
as well and Spencer just stood there, grinning, pleased
the adults were laughing but not at all sure why.

'So...dinner?' Louise persisted, leaning in closer.
'Let me give you a little tip. I won't take no for an answer.'

'Then I guess...' Jane said, quickly glancing at Sean

to make sure it was all right with him. When he gave her a small nod she realised he was more than happy to have her stay. 'I'd better not say no.'

'Excellent. OK, Spencer, we need to set the table.'

Spencer raced off, calling loudly, 'But I can do it by myself. I'm nearly seven, you know.'

'I'll help him,' Barney said, and Jane had to admit that for a man in his seventies he was quite spry.

'Now, why don't I show you the house,' Louise stated, and then, before Jane knew what was happening, Louise had linked her arm through hers and was leading her towards the staircase. 'We live in the upstairs part of the house and Spencer and Sean live downstairs. That way, if Sean gets called to the hospital in the middle of the night, he doesn't need to disturb Spencer,' Louise said, and Jane turned and glanced back at Sean, her eyes wide with uncertainty. Sean's answer to her unspoken question was to give her a friendly wave.

At first she felt as though Sean was feeding her to the lions but after a few minutes in Louise's company she realised the woman was gentle and genuine. She talked about how Sean had insisted they all live together. 'It works well for all of us because Barney and I aren't getting any younger and it pays to be living close to a doctor should we need him.' She laughed and it was only then that Jane realised she was joking.

'Come and help me with dinner.'

'Are we ready to eat yet, Grandma?' Spencer asked, and Jane was amazed not only at his manners but also his easygoing relationship with his grandmother. Jane couldn't even remember meeting her grandparents and never had she interacted with her own parents in such a relaxed and friendly manner. Children had been treated very differently in her family.

She watched as Spencer helped his grandmother, the two of them laughing easily together. When Sean and his father joined them, the atmosphere only became more relaxed. She sat quietly throughout the meal, only really speaking when spoken to but watching with pleased astonishment the genuine familial love demonstrated by the Booke family.

'So, Jane,' Louise asked, as she and Spencer dished up a dessert of fresh fruit and home-made ice cream, 'what is it that's brought you back to Adelaide?'

Jane instantly looked at Sean, wondering if she should confess she'd moved here because of Spencer, that she was all alone in the world and he was all she had left in the way of family. If she said that, however, she knew Louise and Barney would feel sorry for her and, besides, she didn't want Spencer to feel obligated to get to know her.

'Uh…'

'She was head-hunted by the hospital,' Sean put in, holding Jane's gaze firmly. 'You see, Mum, Jane's a brilliant paediatrician who has been involved in extensive research with juvenile eating disorders.'

'Really? Head-hunted?'

'That's impressive,' Barney added.

Jane wasn't used to so much positive attention and quietly thanked them before eating more of her dessert so she didn't have to answer any more questions.

'So, are you married or have a steady boyfriend?' Louise asked.

'Mum!' Sean's reaction was one of instant mortification.

'What?' Louise spread her arms wide, feigning inno-
cence. 'Jane's part of our family now and I have a right
to know a bit more about the members of my family.
It's not an uncommon question, Sean.'

Jane's spoon clattered to the table and she swallowed over the instant lump in her throat. 'Part of...'
She stopped, unable to believe how warmed her heart
became at those words.

'Our family,' Louise finished, with a wide smile.
'You're Spencer's aunt. That makes you family and we
Bookes take our family ties very seriously. We like
being involved in each other's lives and helping out and
caring and loving. It's what families do.'

Jane could feel Sean watching her closely. He knew
the truth. He knew why she'd really returned to Adelaide. To hear his mother welcome her so openly, so
freely, especially after only having met her less than an
hour ago, made Jane feel a warmth flood through her,
a caring, loving warmth such as she'd never felt before.

'You might be smothering her a bit, Mum,' Sean
murmured under his breath, but Jane set her shoulders
straight and looked at Louise.

'No. This isn't smothering. Not in the slightest. I
guess I'm just a little surprised that you're so interested in me.'

'Why wouldn't we be?' Louise asked.

'Because...' Jane paused and glanced once at Sean
before drawing in a deep breath, his small nod of encouragement giving her strength to continue. 'Because
I've been on my own ever since Daina died. I came from
a very dysfunctional family and have no idea what a
normal family is supposed to be like. I have no husband,
no fiancé and no boyfriend. In fact, I have no other fam-

ily except Spencer.' Her gaze fell on the small boy and she smiled warmly. 'He's my only relative.'

'Only? Oh, my dear,' Louise said softly, her tone filled with maternal concern. She immediately came around to where Jane was seated and tugged her to her feet. 'Jane, Jane, you poor thing.' Louise held both of Jane's hands in hers. 'You may have been alone and without family when you walked in this door tonight, but right here, right now, that changes.'

'Yes,' Barney agreed, coming to stand by his wife.

'*We* are your family.' And with that Louise put her arms around Jane and hugged her close. Barney put his arm around both women and in another instant Spencer was wrapping his little arms around her waist.

Jane, a little startled from such open displays of affection but also absorbing every moment of it, looked across to where Sean sat, a big, wide grin on his face.

He winked at her. 'Welcome to the family, Jane.'

CHAPTER EIGHT

JANE INSISTED ON taking a taxi home after dinner, especially as Sean still needed to settle Spencer down after his exciting evening, gaining a new family member.

'Mum and Dad can put him to bed and I can drive you back to the res wing,' he offered, but she put her phone away after dialling the number for the cab company.

'It's fine. You've already given me so much today and I don't want to overstay my welcome.'

'Impossible.'

'Still, I can't thank you enough, Sean.' Her face was radiant as she looked at him and he clenched his jaw and shoved his hands into his trouser pockets to stop himself from hauling her close into a warm and comforting hug.

'It's good to see you smiling, Jane.'

'Why wouldn't I smile?' She spread her arms wide. 'This is close to being the best day of my life.'

'Really?'

'Well, I don't want to say it's the very best day because who knows, there may be better ones yet to come, but for now this day is definitely first.'

'I'm glad.' And he was. What she must have been

through over the years and yet she'd managed to con-
quer so many negative emotions, and all on her own?

Jane watched him closely, noticing a slight frown
mar his brow. 'You don't…you know…mind, do you?'

'Mind?'

'Sharing your family with me,' she answered.

Sean's smile was honest and forthright. 'It's a pleasure, Jane.' It also meant that because his family had
welcomed her, effectively adopting her as one of their
own, he would need to work better at controlling his
wayward senses whenever she was around. Even now,
the desire to hug her, especially when she was just
standing there, looking up at him as though he'd given
her the moon, was still difficult for him to resist. From
what he'd seen and from what she'd shared, Jane clearly
needed stability in her life and any sort of romantic attachment he may feel towards her was null and void.

Colleagues. Friends. Family. That would be his relationship with her from now on.

'Did you want to say goodnight to Spencer?' Sean
offered as he took a step back from her, and Jane immediately nodded. The little boy begged her to read
him a story while she waited for her taxi to come and
this she did, unable to believe the joy she felt at being
able to do such a simple, ordinary task.

When she'd finished, he put up his hands to her, indicating he wanted her to pick him up. She put her arms
around him and he gave her the biggest, squeeziest hug
she'd ever had in her life.

'I'm so excited to go shopping for my birthday present,' he said, and Jane almost toppled backwards from
the way he was leaning in to her.

'So am I,' she returned, the warmth inside her increasing when Spencer kissed her cheek. When the taxi pulled up, Sean stepped forward and lifted his son up and into his arms, Spencer more than comfortable resting his head against his father's broad shoulder. Jane wanted to pull out her cellphone, to take a photo of man and boy, especially given their similar colouring. Instead, she smiled at them both, before turning and walking out into the waning late February sunshine to where the taxi was waiting.

'See you tomorrow morning for ward round,' Sean called, and she turned to wave.

'See you next weekend at the beach,' Spencer called, giggling as he tried to imitate his father's deep tones.

'The beach?' Jane was confused.

'I'll talk to you about it tomorrow at ward round,' Sean told her, and she nodded, excitement filling her at the prospect of seeing more of the Booke family.

Jane couldn't help but giggle a little herself as she waved one last time and climbed into the back seat of the taxi. She gave the driver the address then buckled her seat belt and closed her eyes, allowing the wonderful warmth of memories to wash over her. For so long she'd imagined what it might be like to be included in such a close-knit family unit, fanciful dreams she'd had throughout childhood, and tonight, thanks to Sean's graciousness, she had felt the full power of familial love.

Not only that but somehow she'd found herself drawing closer and closer to the man himself, still unable to believe he'd almost kissed her. Was it possible she'd finally found a man who really could see beneath the shields she'd taken great pains to erect? The fact that he knew some things about her past had helped. It had provided them with a bond, right from the start, and even though they'd both been a little sceptical of the other, they'd somehow managed to find common ground.

The butterflies in her stomach took flight as she recalled the way Sean had stared longingly into her eyes, of the way his gaze had dipped to her lips as though he'd wanted nothing more than to cover them with his own. And perhaps he would have, if they hadn't been interrupted.

Would she have pushed him away? Would she have welcomed his embrace? Even just thinking about it now was causing her to tremble with anticipation. What if he had kissed her and it hadn't been any good? What if the sensual tension she felt when she stared into his beautiful blue eyes only affected her and not him?

She stopped that thought before it could take root. Negative thoughts only bred negative emotions. That was something she'd learned a long time ago and she wouldn't allow them to infiltrate the happiness she'd found tonight. Sean was a handsome and wonderful man and perhaps, at some point in the future, there might be the possibility that he would give in to the repressed desire she'd witnessed in his eyes and capture her lips with his own. When he did, she wanted to be ready, wanted to let him know that he was exciting sensations and feelings within her she'd never really felt before. To let him know that how he made her feel was unique.

When she arrived at the residential wing, she paid the taxi driver and entered the building with a definite spring in her step and a wide smile on her lips. Happiness was an emotion she'd searched hard to find and yet tonight she felt as though she'd been given a huge dose and it was a sensation she was determined to hang onto.

* * *

For the next week Jane felt as though she was walking on air. Sean had spoken to her about his family's plans to head to the beach the following Saturday.

'As part of the family, you're expected to attend.'

'Oh. Uh…OK.'

He'd laughed at the uncertainty reflected on her face. 'Relax, Jane. You'll be fine. Trust me.' Then he'd winked at her and headed to his next meeting. In fact, throughout the week Sean had definitely appeared to be treating her in a more brotherly way. He made no effort to touch her again and she started to wonder whether he still found her attractive?

He kept to his word about Spencer and so far she'd seen her nephew three times during the week, dining again with them on Wednesday night. This time, Spencer had insisted she read him three stories and when Sean told his son that Jane had a lovely singing voice, Spencer had insisted she sing to him.

'You have to be lying down, teeth brushed and ready for bed,' his father had ordered, and Spencer had quickly gone through his night-time routine, eager to have Jane sing to him. Spencer had asked her to lie down on the bed next to him and with an encouraging nod from Sean, who'd been watching from the doorway, she'd kicked off her shoes and rested her head on the pillow beside Spencer. Then the boy had surprised her even further by wrapping his little arms about her neck and snuggling in close.

'OK, Aunty Jane. I'm ready for you to sing now,' he'd told her, but it had taken Jane a moment or two to clear the sudden lump of emotion from her throat before filling the room with her beautiful song. Spencer's easy acceptance, his easy love was going a long way to opening up a heart she'd kept closed for a very long time. And it wasn't only Spencer who was working his magic. Thoughts of Sean seemed to be her constant companions and she'd started to realise it was pointless to deny them. She *wanted* to think about him, she *liked* thinking about him, but most of all she desperately hoped that he was thinking about her in return.

She sang three songs to Spencer and at the end of the third one realised the boy was asleep, his breathing nice and steady.

'Uh...Sean?' she whispered.

'Yeah?'

'I'm stuck.' Although he was sleeping soundly, Spencer's arms were still firmly around her neck. 'How do I get up without waking him?'

Sean's soft chuckle washed over her before he came to her rescue, shifting his son out of the way before helping Jane to her feet. The two of them were standing very close, her hands on his upper arms, her fingers tingling from the feel of his firm biceps beneath his shirt. He placed his hands at her waist to steady her and as she stood there, her toes curling into the soft rug, her knees threatening to fail her, Jane stared into his face with a feeling of homecoming.

The two of them, standing here, close together, beside Spencer's bed, the little boy sleeping—it all felt as though this was where she was meant to be. It felt right. Although his face was half-lit by the shadows created by Spencer's nightlight, Jane had the sense that Sean felt it, too. They stayed there, neither of them moving, for half a minute, the character clock on the wall ticking in time with her heartbeat.

There was no panic, no questions, no need to search for ulterior motives. The moment was…perfect. Even when Sean took her hand in his, letting her slip on her shoes before he led her from the room, Jane felt no sense of apprehension or fear. Yet when the bright artificial light from the kitchen made them both squint, Sean dropped her hand before heading around to fill the kettle, offering her a cup of tea.

'No, thanks,' she said, realising he was once more trying to inject some distance between them. 'I'd better call for a taxi.'

'OK.' He didn't try to talk her out of it, didn't offer to drive her home, and when he walked her to the taxi and shut the door, she saw him shove both of his hands through his hair before sighing heavily and heading back inside. What the action had meant she wasn't sure but his happy, brotherly attention towards her had continued, leaving Jane feeling quite confused.

On Friday, just after she finished morning clinic and was on her way to the ward conference room for a progress meeting about Tessa, her cellphone buzzed in her pocket. Jane was astonished to find it was Louise.

'Hello, Jane.' Louise's bright tones came down the line. 'Just wanted to let you know about the plans for tomorrow at the beach. Barney has a great gazebo he likes to put up on the sand so we'll have some shade and the girls have some lovely recliner chairs, which means you don't get sand all over you when you lie down. Now, with regard to food,' Louise continued, before Jane could get a word in edge ways, 'we figured cold cuts of meat and salad should be the order of the day. Sean's bringing the drinks and I was hoping you'd be able to provide some sort of dessert, perhaps a fruit bun or some fresh fruit, nothing that's going to melt or go stale too quickly in such extreme heat. What do you think?'

Jane gaped a few times as Louise talked and then quickly agreed. 'I'd be delighted to provide something for dessert. Thank you for the suggestions.'

'All right, dear, no doubt you're as busy as anything so I'll let you go. See you tomorrow—patients willing.'

Jane couldn't help but giggle with happiness as she said goodbye, ending the call and slipping her phone back into her pocket.

'That sounded like a nice phone call,' Sean's deep voice said from just behind her. Jane turned and looked over her shoulder, waiting for him to catch up.

'That was your mother.'

'Oh?'

'Yes. Organising tomorrow's *family* event.' Jane grinned as she enunciated the words clearly, the smile on her face growing brighter. 'She wants me to provide something for dessert.' The pride in her words was clearly evident.

'Excellent. Make it something chocolate.'

'Chocolate?' Jane frowned. 'But won't that melt?'

'Not if you put it in the drinks cooler I'm bringing. I'll have lots of ice in there.'

'Oh. Well, Louise suggested a fruit bun or some fresh fruit and I don't want to take the wrong thing.' Her frown increased. 'This is the very first time I've ever been asked to contribute something to a *family* event and I don't want to mess it up. It means I'm included, not just a guest joining in for the day.' She paused. 'Perhaps I should bring fruit bun and fresh fruit and chocolate.'

Sean chuckled. 'You're over-thinking this, Jane.'

'Well, wouldn't you?' she asked as they entered the ward.

'It won't matter what you bring, everyone will be appreciative. Trust me. Both of my sisters are health freaks and their children and husbands will thank you for bringing along a bit of chocolate.'

Jane shook her head slowly. 'You think you're helping me, Sean, but you're just making me even more confused. The last thing I want to do, the very first time I meet your sisters, is to get them off side.'

'Impossible. They'll love you.' He winked at her and the resident butterflies in her stomach took flight. Stupid butterflies.

'Good. Then *you* bring the chocolate,' she remarked, and again his warm chuckle filled her with pleasure. She really had to figure out how to get better control over her senses, especially when it appeared Sean really did think of her more as a sister than anything else. She pushed the thought away and focused on the meeting, eager to receive progress reports about Tessa's situation.

After the meeting Jane went to have a chat with Tessa, pleased when the little girl smiled warmly at the sight of her. Sean watched as Tessa leaned in close to Jane, talking softly but earnestly, opening up more, confiding, confessing.

There was certainly something engaging about Jane, about the way she gave you one hundred per cent of her attention when she was talking to you or listening to you. Even his mother had remarked about it.

'She's so…interested in everything,' Louise had said yesterday morning at breakfast. 'You did the right thing,

Sean, inviting her to be a part of Spencer's life. You didn't have to.'

'It was the right thing to do.' Even though it meant he'd been unable to get her out of his mind ever since. Last night, for instance, he'd found himself waking up at three o'clock in the morning from a dream where he'd been holding her close, in one of the outpatient clinic rooms, kissing her perfect mouth, unable to resist her any longer.

He told himself he was happy she'd been accepted by his family; both his sisters were very eager to meet her. Getting his own urges under control was paramount, especially when Jane kept smiling brightly at him simply because she'd been asked to bring some food to a family picnic.

Yet when he knocked on her door on Saturday morning to pick her up and take her to the beach, it was a very different, less composed Jane who opened the door.

'I've bought an Esky and packed the food into it, as you suggested,' she dithered, not bothering to invite him in but leaving the door wide open, indicating he should feel free to cross the threshold. The large red insulated cold box was by the door, ready to just pick up when they left.

'I bought a sun hat,' she continued, pointing to the large, almost sombrero-like hat on the bed. 'And some strong sunscreen, but now I can't find where I put it.' She opened a drawer and searched inside, before closing it and opening the next one. 'You would think, in such a confined space as this, I wouldn't lose anything!' Exasperation laced through her tone as she once more did the rounds of the room, stopping for a brief moment to look at and around him. 'Where's Spencer?'

'He's going with my parents. I wanted to stop by the ward and check on some patients.'

'Oh. Of course.' Jane tried to disguise her disappointment at not being able to spend even a few more minutes with Spencer. She opened her wardrobe doors and looked in there for the sunscreen, although why she would have put it in there, she had no clue.

Sean scanned the room as well, trying not to be intrigued by what she was wearing. Most people, on such a stinking hot day as this, would wear fewer clothes. Shorts and T-shirt or, for a woman, a light cotton sundress with flip-flops, but not Jane. She was dressed in a pair of light-coloured three-quarter-length trousers, a pastel top and a thin cotton long-sleeve shirt over the top. Her hair…even as he watched her flit around the room…mesmerised him. Her fringe was, as always, combed over her forehead, coming down to meet her eyebrows, but the long, luscious locks were contained in some sort of messy braided low bun, little wisps of hair falling out here and there, framing her face and making her look…angelic.

His gut tightened with the urge to stop her, to pull her close, to calm her nerves—which were clearly on display with all her dithering—and enfold her in his arms. He wanted to reassure her that she was safe, that he would never let anyone hurt her, and he wanted to follow the lead of the constant dreams he'd been having of her where he would tenderly capture her lips with his.

'Jane, I have some sunscreen,' he told her softly, as she checked beneath the bed.

'But this is special stuff. I burn so easily,' she told him, and when she straightened, meeting his gaze, he realised the extent of her nervousness. She looked terrified and he realised that although she was excited to be a part of a family, it was also very new and unsettling to her. He instantly stepped forward and gathered her hands in his. It was the first time he'd touched her in so long that he felt like he'd been struck by lightning. What this woman did to him, how she affected him, was becoming even more powerful than before.

Sean quickly settled his thoughts before speaking. 'Jane, it's no drama.'

His calm, easy words, the warmth from his touch, the way he gave her that handsome half-smile instantly melted her nerves. How was it possible that in the blink of an eye Sean Booke was able to quell her fears and to make her feel so incredibly safe?

'It isn't?'

'No. We can buy some more along the way. You're supposed to be relaxing today, on your day off from the hospital, not stressing about sunscreen.'

'But—'

'Shh,' he interrupted and placed a finger across her lips. He knew it was a stupid move the moment his skin made contact with hers because even touching her in such a way made it nigh on impossible for him to continue to keep his distance, for him to try and view her as some sort of distant relative.

The sensations he'd been doing his best to quash for the past week came bursting forth. 'I've tried so hard to keep my distance, to see you as just another family member but...' he shook his head slowly '...it isn't working. I can't stop thinking about you.'

'Oh.' She sighed, trembling slightly at his words, her body tingling with delight. She licked her lips then swallowed.

'Why do you think I haven't touched you? And made sure I wasn't alone with you in a room? I just couldn't control my reaction to you.'

Was that why? Was he telling the truth? Jane swallowed, unable to speak for a moment while her mind processed this information.

'But, Sean...' She stopped, staring into his eyes and taking a deep breath as she realised it was time to perhaps ask some tricky questions, to take a few bricks out of the protective wall she'd carefully constructed around herself. 'Sean, are we...I mean, do we...you know, *feel* the way we do simply because of that past connection?'

'Or are we *attracted*—' Sean spoke the word clearly and pointedly, indicating he knew what she'd been trying to say and that he wasn't afraid to name what they both clearly felt '—to each other because we're so much alike?'

Was that the reason? She'd never thought of it like that before but, then, she'd been attempting to school her thoughts where Sean was concerned. She had such an innate fear that if she gave herself permission to really explore this attraction and then somehow messed things up, he would cut her off from ever seeing Spencer again.

'You're trembling,' he pointed out, rubbing his thumbs over her hands.

'I'm nervous about meeting your sisters, of making a good impression, of having this day go well,' she babbled, looking away from his hypnotic gaze in case he saw the truth, that she was frightened of the way he made her feel.

'You don't need to worry about my sisters. They're predisposed to like you.'

'Why? How do you know that?' Jane tried to gently tug her hands free from the touch that was setting her senses on fire.

Sean chuckled softly, the sound warming her through and through. 'Because I know my sisters and I know you.'

'No, you don't.' This time she did pull away and turned her back to him. Sean immediately put his hands on her shoulders, rubbing her arms as he spoke in that soothing voice of his.

'I know you better than most,' he countered. 'And I like what I see, Jane. I like you...a lot.'

CHAPTER NINE

By the time they arrived at the beach, Jane was a mass of nerves. Not only was she about to meet Sean's sisters and their families but he'd just confessed to her that he liked her—a lot. He was attracted to her and she had no present concept of what that meant, what he now expected of her, and whether or not she'd be able to fulfil it.

She decided to focus on the immediate problem of making a good impression on Sean's sisters, Rosie and Kathleen, but, as Sean had predicted, they were already enamoured with her from the start, both of them coming forward to hug her and welcome her to their family. Spencer's greeting was to launch himself at her like a cannon ball, give her a firm hug before wriggling from her arms to run off and play with his cousins, who were tossing a ball to each other.

Barney and Louise also welcomed her with hugs and after a few hours of sitting around, chatting and eating and laughing, Jane couldn't help but smile brightly.

'I could get used to this,' she remarked to Sean, as he sat down beside her on the towel she'd spread on the golden sand. Louise and Barney were nearby, lounging on the chairs, chatting with one of their daughters, so Jane spoke softly.

'What? Sweat all day because the sun's too hot? Or having to reapply sunscreen every few hours? Or craving salty foods due to the sea salt in the air? Or perhaps it's the constant swatting of flies you could get used to?'

Jane laughed. 'All of the above, as well as being surrounded by people who are happy to be with me.'

These words told him far more about her upbringing, about the loneliness she'd faced as an adult, than if she'd told him directly. He wanted to reassure her, to let her know that her days of being alone were over. 'We are, Jane. We all are and it's genuine.'

She turned to look at him and even though she was wearing prescription sunglasses, she knew the lenses weren't dark enough that he couldn't see her eyes. 'I really want to believe that, Sean. It's been very difficult for me to take that leap of faith and to trust but today I really do feel accepted.'

'I'm glad.' He stared at her for a moment before forcing himself to look away, her smiling mouth far too tempting, and here was most definitely not the place for their first real kiss. He knew it was inevitable, that soon he would kiss Jane, and he wanted it to be perfect.

Spencer came running up, interrupting the moment, demanding his father come into the sea and 'toss him around'.

'Toss him around?' Jane looked at Sean as he stood, trying not to stare as he pulled off his T-shirt, revealing a very broad, very brawny, very beautiful chest. Her fingers instantly began to tingle, wanting to touch it, to feel the light smattering of hair on his chest. She unconsciously licked her lips and breathed out slowly as she carefully raised her gaze back to meet his. It was only then she realised he'd been more than aware of her visual caress and that he'd enjoyed every second of it. The gorgeous little half-smile that set her heart racing once more was firmly in place. He raised one eyebrow, indicating he was very interested in her interest in him.

'Why don't you come and join us?' Sean asked, scooping his son into his arms, mainly to stop Spencer from excitedly jumping up and down and spraying sand all over Jane, and also because to have her look at him in such a way had been extremely alluring.

'Yeah. Aunty Jane, Aunty Jane, Aunty Jane. Come in the sea with us!' Spencer clapped his hands and giggled with anticipatory delight.

'Uh…' Jane quickly shook her head and looked away from the perfect picture of man and boy, two sets of perfect blue eyes enticing her to join them. 'I don't like the water.' And as she said the words she unconsciously adjusted her glasses and tugged at the hem of her cotton shirt, before ensuring the sleeves of the shirt were still secured at her wrists.

'Aw. Why not?' Spencer was clearly disappointed and it was the last thing Jane wanted. She thought fast and knew she had to do something to appease him but she was not going into that water. Wearing a swimsuit would only expose the rest of the people on the beach to her body. She didn't want to be stared at or thought a freak. She'd suffered through enough of that for years and now that she was her own, strong, independent self, she was the one deciding what she would and wouldn't do, and she would not go into that water and swim.

'Why don't you come and stand in the shallows?' Sean suggested, and when she looked at him, she re-

alised he'd been watching her entire internal struggle.
'Just roll your trousers up a bit and paddle in the shallows.'

'Yeah!' Spencer clapped his hands in agreement.

Jane nodded, realising Sean had provided the perfect solution. She'd get to join in, to find out what 'tossing Spencer around' consisted of. She quickly located
her enormous hat and placed it on her head, before following Sean's suggestion and rolling up her trousers
to just above her knees. She stood and brushed sand
from her clothes.

'Ready?' Sean asked, before putting Spencer down
and holding out his hand to her.

'Ready,' she stated, and took his hand, drawing in a
cleansing breath. Sean was asking her to join in but he
wasn't forcing her to do anything she wasn't comfortable with. Did he have any idea just how much that en-
deared him to her? It let her know that he was willing
to accept her for what she could give. Wasn't that what
she'd been searching for? Acceptance?

Smiling brightly at him, she walked quickly across
the hot sand to where the water was lapping. Spencer
ran full pelt into the water, splashing with the waves
and laughing brightly. Sean raised Jane's hand to his
lips and pressed a kiss to it before letting her go and
following his son, scooping the giggling boy up and
wading with him to the deeper water.

Jane clasped her hands together, her thumb con-
sciously rubbing the spot where he'd kissed her as she
allowed the delight to wash over her. Did he realise that
such a small, respectful and charming gesture as that
would only make her like him even more?

When the water was up to Sean's waist, and he had

made sure that the coast was clear, Jane watched as Sean faced Spencer away from him and then, on the count of three, tossed his son into the air, the little boy whooping with delight before he splashed into the water not too far away.

Sean turned to face Jane and spread his hands wide as if to say, 'Ta-dah!' She laughed and clapped and gave him a thumbs-up as Spencer swam back to his father, ready for a repeat performance.

'Hey! Look!' she heard some of Spencer's cousins say. 'Uncle Sean's tossing Spencer. Come on.'

'It's my turn after Spencer,' one of them called.

'I'm after you,' the other yelled, as they made their way out to Sean. Jane laughed, more than happy to watch. After a while Louise came and stood beside her, the two of them both cheering and clapping as Sean patiently 'tossed' his son, his nephews and niece into the water.

Jane couldn't believe how relaxed she felt around this close-knit family, how accepted she felt, and she knew it was all because of Sean. Even later in the afternoon, as he drove her home, the conversation was easy and relaxed.

'Does Spencer often go to his cousins' house for sleepovers?' she asked as Sean concentrated on the heavier-than-usual traffic.

'At least once a month, or I have a few of them at my house on the weekend, depending on sporting schedules. It's good for Spencer to mix with his cousins, especially being an only child.' He frowned a little as he slowed the car. 'Fair dinkum, I think everyone left the beach to head home at the same time,' he murmured a moment later.

'Would you like more children?' she asked with soft intrigue, pleased he'd provided her with the perfect opening to ask the question.

'I like being a father,' Sean commented as he changed lanes. 'But raising a child, especially when my parenting career began with having the sole care of a sick, premature baby, wasn't at all easy. That's when my parents and I came up with the living arrangements we now have. We both sold our places and converted the house, ensuring they had their own separate living quarters and I had mine but that Spencer's needs could easily be met.'

'So what happens when he wakes up in the morning and you're at the hospital?'

'There's a message board in my parents' kitchen. You might have seen it. I usually leave a message on there, letting them know I'm not home. My dad's an early riser so if Spencer wakes up and I'm not in my bedroom, he just goes upstairs and his grandparents look after him.' Sean shrugged. 'It's the best solution we could come up with.'

'I think it's a wonderful solution and I'm sure your parents love spending so much time with their grandson.'

Spencer grinned. 'They do, and vice versa. We all just wanted to make Spencer's life as easy and uncomplicated as possible.'

Jane paused before asking the question that had been bothering her for some time. 'Does he ever ask about Daina?'

'Not really. He was three when Daina passed away but she left home soon after he was born, and he doesn't remember her.' They were silent for a moment, Sean inching the car forward in traffic then stopping due to the gridlock. 'Jane…when was the last time you saw her?'

Jane looked out the window for a moment, not really seeing the sea of cars before them but instead calling up her old memories. The topic of her sister was hardly her favourite subject but if she wanted things to progress with Sean, perhaps it was best they dealt with questions when they arose naturally.

'I believe it was about four months after she'd come to see me about wanting me to terminate her pregnancy.' She stared down at her hands, surprised to find them quite relaxed. Usually when she spoke about Daina her hands would be clenched tightly together, but not this time. Was it because she knew that, whatever she said, Sean would accept her words as truth?

'She turned up on my doorstep in Melbourne, no baby in tow. Figure back to perfection. She said she was flying overseas the next day and just needed to stay for the night. She was more than happy to show me one or two pictures of Spencer, to rub in the fact that she still had everything. She was married and she had a baby and I was still her weird freak of a sister, who would always be alone. That was the first I knew of Spencer's name and his birth date. She said he was still in hospital and she didn't have time to sit and wait around. That she'd met a modelling producer and he wanted to do a professional photographic session with her in Bali. She left early the next morning and I heard nothing else until two days before her funeral, and even then it was quite by accident.'

Jane shook her head. 'I found out my sister had died because I bumped into a friend of hers. She was distraught, calling me unfeeling and ungracious, especially after everything Daina had done for me. I had no idea what she was going on about until she told me Daina had been killed in a car accident.'

'Jane.' Sean looked to her, a worried frown on his brow. 'I'm sorry. I would have told you but I had no idea where you lived or how to contact you or anything.'

Jane shook her head. 'It's over. Her death made it over. As horrible as it is to say, with Daina gone I knew she wouldn't be able to hurt me any more.'

Sean reached over and cupped her face with his hand, the warmth of his touch, the caress of his fingers making her heart soar with possibilities. 'It is over,' he agreed. 'And we are free to move forward with our lives.' His smile was encouraging, promising and with a small hint of excitement in his eyes. He dropped his hand and looked back at the traffic before them. The light had turned green but no one had moved, the intersection blocked with other cars. 'Something's wrong.'

Jane noticed the change in his tone of voice and when she looked out at the gridlocked traffic, she frowned. 'Roadworks?'

'Or an accident.' Sean reached for his cellphone and called through to the Adelaide General Hospital. He spoke for a moment to a colleague in the emergency department. 'The ambulances can't get through,' he told Jane as he waited another moment for further information. 'We're close,' he told the person on the other end of the phone. 'Right. OK. No problem.' He made sure they had his cellphone number before he disconnected the call and drove his car up onto the wide grassed median strip in the middle of the road.

'We'll have to help out,' he told Jane as he unbuckled his seat belt.

Jane swallowed as she felt all the colour drain from her face, dizziness swamping her. 'A car accident?' Her words were barely a whisper.

Sean shifted in his seat to look at her. 'Jane, I know attending a car accident must be difficult for you because you lost your parents in a car accident, didn't you? Or was that another one of Daina's fabrications?'

'No. That was true but…' Jane swallowed her words. How could she explain to Sean what she'd endured? All those surgeries, being in and out of hospital…the pain. She closed her eyes and tried to focus her wayward thoughts. Facts. Focus on the facts. There was a car accident. People were hurt, they were in pain, just as she'd been. Jane knew if it hadn't been for the paramedics who had attended her at the accident site, using their knowledge and expertise to save her, she would not have survived. Wasn't it only right that she now did the same for others who needed her, used her own knowledge and expertise to make a radical difference to someone's life?

She opened her eyes, looking directly at Sean. 'Those people need our help,' she stated, more to get the words through her own foggy mind than to point out the obvious.

'Yes.'

Jane clutched her trembling hands together, surprised when Sean put his hands over hers, channelling his calmness into her. 'You're an amazing woman and an amazing doctor, Jane.'

Jane nodded, unable to reply to his words.

'Ready?' he asked, and she could see the urgency

in his eyes, his desperate need to get to the people who were in trouble and to help them. He wanted to help others, just as he'd been helping her by introducing her to Spencer and his family.

'Ready,' she confirmed.

His smile was bright and he winked at her before releasing her hands. 'Atta girl.' He turned and climbed from the car, retrieving his medical kit from the boot. 'I'm glad I had the presence of mind to shower and change before we left the beach,' he remarked when Jane came to stand next to him. He was pleased she was coming with him, pleased she was offering her expertise and proud that she was pushing through whatever mental blocks she still had about car accidents. Even though he'd watched her go incredibly pale, had seen the internal struggle within her, she was fighting past whatever barriers were in her way. She was doing what she knew in her heart was right. He took her hand in his. 'You're extraordinary, Jane Diamond.'

She opened her mouth to reply but no words came out. Speechless. He'd left her speechless with his lovely, heartfelt words. Sean believed in her.

Together, they made their way through the stopped traffic, hearing sirens in the distance. 'The accident couldn't have happened any longer than five minutes before we hit the gridlock,' Sean pointed out, and Jane noticed his tone was becoming more clipped, more detached, more professional.

She was the same usually, all brisk and professional...but not around car accidents. They were her weakness. However, she now had Sean to help provide her with the strength she needed and as they made their way briskly towards the wreckage, Jane tightened her grip on his fingers. He didn't pull away, didn't let her go, and as they came closer to where they could begin to see what had happened, Sean gave her hand a squeeze, stopping her for a moment.

'What is it?' she asked, her already heightened senses bringing worry into her tone.

'If you're not able to handle things, just tell me, Jane. Nothing wrong with that. Remember, I believe in you. You're far stronger than you think.' His words were soft yet still quick, as though he wanted to give her that final reassurance.

Jane stared into his eyes for what seemed an eternity yet was no more than a few seconds. 'I've got your back.' She nodded, realising that, no matter what they were about to face, she wasn't going to let Sean down.

'Let's do our jobs,' she said. He let go of her hand and led the way closer to where a few other people had climbed from their cars and were attempting to help out in whatever way they could.

'Two cars. No, three cars, but one is parked and empty,' Sean commented on first glance as he scanned the area. It appeared that one car and a mini-van with three occupants had crashed into the parked car. The other car had one occupant but the battered front windscreen and dented bonnet indicated that something had hit that car with force. Jane scanned the area and it was then she saw the figure of an elderly man supine on the road.

'One patient on the road. Hit by car,' Jane said to Sean.

'The paramedics are almost through.' Sean pointed to where the ambulance was driving up the grassy me-

dian strip towards them. 'Do a quick triage on this patient, instruct the paramedics and find me.'

'OK.' Jane nodded and headed towards the man lying
on the road, arriving a whole thirty seconds before one
of the paramedics.

'I saw the whole thing,' one woman said. 'I was
walking to my car and this man was just too slow crossing the road. It wasn't the driver's fault. He didn't see
him until it was too late and then that other car swerved
and—'

'Thank you,' Jane said. 'Please give him some room.'
She quickly introduced herself to the paramedic while
he opened the emergency medical kit for her. She pulled
on a pair of gloves and addressed the patient. 'Can you
hear me?' she said to the man. 'My name's Jane. I'm
a doctor.'

'I can hear. I can hear,' the man returned.

'What's your name?' The man started to move but
she quickly put her hand firmly on his shoulder, wanting to keep him still. 'Just stay there. It's all right.' Her
tone was now calm and placating, needing him to understand but also to be reassured by her words. 'What's
your name?' she asked again.

'Roderick.' His words were slightly slurred but she
understood him.

'How old are you, Roderick?' the paramedic asked,
as Jane started to feel bones, trying to ascertain if he'd
broken anything.

'Eighty-five,' he slurred again.

'Have you been drinking, Roderick?'

'No, no drinking. My tongue.'

'Your tongue is sore?' she asked, as she checked his

pulses, pleased there didn't seem to be any problem
with his circulation.

'Yes.'

'You might have bitten it.'

'Too slow. I was too slow on the road.'

'No need to worry about that now,' she remarked.
'It feels as though you may have done some damage
to your left leg but nothing that can't be fixed. I think
you may have landed on your right wrist. Stay still,
Roderick.'

The paramedic held Roderick's head still while Jane
quickly looked at Roderick's tongue, listened to his
breathing and ensured his pupils were equal and reacting to light. 'Stabilise and transfer,' she instructed
the paramedics, feeling more comfortable with her role
at the scene.

'Can you check out the driver of the car? He's over
there.' She pointed to a man sitting on the grassy median
strip, a few people gathered around him. 'I'll be over
with the other patients in the mini-van.' Jane looked
around for Sean but couldn't see him. The police and
fire-brigade vehicles were making their way through,
the police determined not only to assist with the accident but to get traffic sorted out as soon as possible.
Good. At least that part of the accident scene was under
control. Jane looked around for Sean, expecting to see
him over at the mini-van, but he was nowhere in sight.

'Sean?' she called.

'Over here,' he replied, and Jane went up onto the
footpath near the row of parked cars and it was then
she saw him, attending to another person who was
also lying on the ground. It was a woman of about
twenty-two and she was clearly pregnant. 'Where did

she come——?' As Jane asked the question she looked towards the road and it was then that she realised the mini-van's front windscreen was practically missing and that was because the young woman before her had gone all the way through it.

'She's been thrown from the car!' The words were a horrified whisper and when Jane closed her eyes she could see far too clearly, *feel* far too realistically the way the woman would have exited the car, head first, her face and arms scratched from the exploding glass, the dreaded sensation of being airborne and knowing there was nothing you could do to stop the impending pull of gravity as the ground loomed closer.

'Jane. *Jane.*'

Her eyes snapped open and she stared wild-eyed at Sean.

'Jane?' From her expression, Sean began to realise just what had happened to Jane in the car accident. 'You were thrown out,' he said softly, his words a statement of fact. He also knew that if he didn't manage to get Jane to focus on him rather than on the situation, she'd be of no use to him whatsoever and right now he really needed her assistance.

'Breathe, Jane. Breathe. Look into my eyes. Focus on my words.' He held her gaze, his words calm but firm. 'It's OK. You can do this. Just…breathe.'

Jane stared into his beautiful blue eyes, eyes that had often managed to turn her insides into mush, but this time they were silently telling her that he believed in her, that he needed her help and that she could get through this. He wouldn't leave her alone. He would be right beside her every step of the way and, to her utter amazement, she felt the panic and fear that had gripped her beginning to subside.

'That's it.' Sean glanced at his patient then back at her. 'Better?'

'Yes.'

'Good. This is Carly. She's twenty-two years old and thirty-three weeks pregnant. She's lying as still as possible, waiting for the next ambulance to make its way through.' Sean smiled down at the young woman, who seemed to relax a bit more beneath his soothing gaze. Jane couldn't blame her. Sean had a gorgeous smile and comforting eyes.

He lifted his head and looked at Jane again but this time something changed in his eyes. Worry. He was clearly worried and he wasn't worried for her but for Carly. This realisation helped Jane to take a deep breath and pull on her professionalism. If she could help Sean, if together they could help Carly, do everything they could to save this young woman's life, then she knew it was one enormous step towards healing the hurt she'd been carrying around for far too long.

Sean angled his head slightly, indicating he wanted her to come over and give him a second opinion on Carly's injuries. 'What's the situation? Police on the scene yet?' His tone was still calm and she picked up on the fact that he was trying not to scare or worry Carly too much, especially in her present condition.

'Just arrived. First ambulance is through. Paramedics attending.' She kept her words calm, logical, professional. Sean was right. She could do this. She stepped forward and reached into his medical kit, pulling on a pair of fresh gloves. 'Hi, Carly. I'm Jane. Just stay as still as possible.' She hoped her tone sounded reassuring and when she glanced at Sean and saw that proud smile on his face, her confidence soared.

'We have some cuts and abrasions to the legs and face.' Jane felt Carly's arms and checked her hands. 'Both wrists need splinting and possibly right elbow.' She took the stethoscope he proffered and listened to Carly's breathing. Then she pressed the stethoscope to Carly's abdomen and listened closely for ten seconds. She looked up, staring directly at Sean, realising that what she heard were the sounds of a baby going into distress. 'Carly, we need to check your blood pressure before we can get you stretchered up.'

Jane stood up and spotted a paramedic, carrying one of the usual large emergency kits they always used, heading in their direction. 'Over here,' she called, and within a moment the paramedic was putting a cervical collar around Carly's neck while Sean took Carly's blood pressure and Jane found an extra blanket.

'We need to put a blanket beneath her hip so we can keep the baby off the vena cava and stop the risk of de-oxygenated blood.'

'Agreed.' Sean called over a few of the police officers to help.

When Carly was stabilised with her neck brace and a non-rebreather mask fitted over her mouth and nose, Sean put his hands on either side of Carly's head. 'On my command,' he said as the emergency workers and Jane got into position, 'we'll brace and roll.' Sean looked at the team before giving the command. With brisk but careful movements they rolled Carly to her side while Jane placed the blanket into position before Sean gave the command to roll Carly back.

'Carly, have you felt the baby kick since the accident?'

'Yes,' the frightened woman replied, her words a little muffled beneath her mask.

'That's very good news,' Jane reassured her. 'I'd just like to have another feel of the baby. OK?'

'Yes,' Carly said again.

Jane concentrated, carefully feeling around Carly's abdomen, visualising the different body parts of the baby, checking where they were. 'Head's definitely engaged,' she remarked a moment later.

'OK. I think we can get Carly stretchered up,' Sean said, 'then off to the hospital. I'll phone ahead and speak to the obstetric registrar.'

The paramedic nodded and started taking Carly's observations. Sean and Jane stood and ripped off their gloves, walking a little way away from their patient. 'The baby's not liking this at all,' Jane remarked.

'Carly's BP is not where I'd like.'

'We'll need to watch her,' she agreed. 'Perhaps get a cannula in now.'

'Good idea. We'll need to put it in her ankle as both wrists are fractured.'

They turned and went back to Carly, letting the paramedics know they needed that extra line in, just in case. Jane took Carly's blood pressure again and agreed with Sean's assessment that it was a little low. She assisted the paramedics as they shifted Carly to the stretcher, Jane once more doing obs and checking the portable baby sphygmomanometer, which showed Jane that the baby wasn't taking too kindly to what was happening to its mother.

When they had Carly safely in the ambulance, the

paramedics doing observations once more, Jane inserted the cannula into Carly's ankle.

'I'm going to get an update on what's happening with Carly's friends in the mini-van,' Sean told her. 'She keeps asking and the information might help to settle her down if she knows her friends are all right.'

'Yes. Good thinking,' Jane replied, and pointed to a nearby police officer. Sean jogged over and spoke to the sergeant then headed back.

'Hi, Carly,' Sean said as he came into the ambulance and sat next to her. 'Your friends who were travelling with you are fine. The driver, Kieran, has a broken nose and a few cuts and bruises. The people in the back have seat-belt bruises and a bit of whiplash. That's it.'

Carly seemed to relax at this news, closing her eyes and breathing out with relief. 'They're OK,' she murmured.

'Let's monitor oxygen saturation and repeat fifteen-minute obs,' Jane instructed. 'I want to take a closer look at the baby.' She used an amplified stethoscope to obtain a more accurate reading of the baby's heartbeat, not liking what she heard. She felt the outside of Carly's abdomen and decided it might be best to do an internal.

'Carly, I'm going to need to check to see if you've started dilating.' There was no response from Carly and Jane called to her, 'Carly? Carly?'

'BP?' Sean asked, reaching for his stethoscope. He listened to her breathing.

'Dropping,' the paramedic replied.

'There's blood,' Jane remarked a second later. 'I think the uterus might have ruptured.'

'Push fluids,' Sean ordered. 'Carly? Can you hear me?' he asked, his tone firm and insistent.

'Baby's going into distress,' said Jane.

'Carly?'

'Mmm?' The tone was weak, as though Carly really didn't have the will to fight any more. 'Tired,' she mumbled.

'Come on, Carly. You've got a lot to live for. Are you having a boy or a girl? Do you know?'

'Boy,' she whispered.

'BP still dropping.'

'We need to get the baby out.'

'It hurts,' Carly complained, but at least her words were stronger.

'Carly, your uterus has ruptured. The baby is not doing well. We need to get him out *now*. Do you understand?' Jane asked, as she prepared the instruments she would need.

'I'll organise an anaesthetic,' Sean stated and together with the paramedic they began to get Carly organised.

'Carly, we need to get the baby out. If we don't, we risk losing both of you. Do you understand?'

'Yes.'

Sean and the paramedic sedated Carly. 'Review BP,' Sean requested.

The paramedic nodded, carrying out the instructions. 'Improving,' he remarked.

Jane looked to Sean. 'I'll deliver. You be ready to receive.'

'Agreed.'

It didn't take long for the administered anaesthetic to take effect and soon Jane had the scalpel in hand and was making an incision along the Caesarean line.

'I need more exposure. Retract,' Jane called, and

Sean duly inserted the retractors. 'Scalpel,' she said again, unable to believe the amount of blood. They worked seamlessly together as though they'd been doing it for years, Sean able to pre-empt everything she required. 'Something has definitely ruptured,' she remarked.

'We can keep her stable and once the baby's out you can take a closer look around.'

'Agreed.' Jane concentrated on the present scenario, visualising it in her mind before she reached in to grab hold of the baby's head. She'd assisted with several Caesarean section births over the years but never in circumstances like this. Thankfully, they had a lot of equipment in the ambulance but still she was having to improvise as she went along. 'I've got him.' She kept a firm grip on the little fellow and gently brought him out.

'BP steady and holding,' the paramedic reported.

'Ready and waiting,' Sean said, holding out a sterile towel ready to receive the baby.

'Out you come, mate,' she said, and in another moment Jane lifted the baby boy from his mother's womb and into Sean's large, capable hands beneath the sterile towel.

'Clamp and cut,' he instructed the paramedic, as Jane set about delivering the placenta. It was her job to look after the mother but she was acutely aware of the fact that the baby was not breathing.

'No tone. Bag him. Begin cardiac massage.' While Sean and one of the paramedics worked on the baby, she tried to focus her thoughts on discovering the source of the bleed.

'BP?' she asked, and the paramedic quickly took the observation.

'Steady.'

'Keep maintaining fluids. That's it, Carly. You stay with us,' she encouraged the unconscious mother. 'How's the baby doing?' Jane asked.

'Check pulse,' Sean said, and the paramedic pressed his fingers to the baby's groin, everyone silently praying the pulse was there.

'It's there! Faint but there.'

Jane breathed a heavy sigh of relief. 'He's a strong one.'

'He's still having a little difficulty breathing but he *is* breathing. We'll intubate and get this ambulance under way to the hospital.' Sean continued to attend to the baby and Jane continued to investigate the source of Carly's internal bleeding.

'Swab,' she instructed the paramedic who was assisting her. 'I need more light.' As she'd commanded, a strong beam of torchlight was directed where she needed it. 'Ah. There it is. Clamp.' She accepted the instrument and thankfully soon had the bleed under control. 'How's the baby?'

'Colour returning. Five minute APGAR is seven.'

'Excellent. Let's get moving.' And with Carly and the baby now in a more stable situation, one of the paramedics exited the back and headed around to the driver's seat, all of them thankful that the police had managed to control the traffic so the area wasn't as gridlocked.

It wasn't until they arrived at the hospital, the obstetric registrar and neonatal team waiting to take over, that Jane started to feel fatigue beginning to set in.

'Well, that wasn't the sort of ending I'd had planned for our day together,' Sean remarked after they'd

cleaned up. They were in the A and E staffroom, Jane
sipping the cup of relaxing tea Sean had made for her.

'What *did* you have in mind?' she asked, resting
her head back against the wall, watching Sean through
heavy-lidded eyes.

He shrugged and came over, sitting beside her and
brushing her fringe from her eyes. 'A quiet chat, a nice
cuppa.'

'Isn't that what we're doing now?' Jane couldn't disguise the huskiness in her tone and knew Sean was
aware of it from the way he raised one eyebrow. That
slow, irresistible smile started to appear on his lips.
There was nothing she could do to control her emotions.
She was exhausted, worn out, the emergency having
zapped all her usual shields.

'Not exactly the venue I'd imagined but I guess so.'
He brushed his fingers down her cheek, tenderly caressing her skin. 'Jane, you're tying me in knots. I can't
seem to think straight when I'm around you and I can't
seem to concentrate at all when we're apart.'

'I think you're exaggerating.'

His smile increased. 'Perhaps.' He brushed his thumb
over her lips, just as he'd done previously. 'You're remarkable. So strong and valiant.'

'I don't—'

'Shh. I'm trying to compliment you.'

'Oh. Sorry.' She was instantly contrite but somewhere, deep down inside her, she started to feel bold,
started to feel that perhaps, with the way he was looking at her, with the way he seemed to be looking into
her eyes as though she were the most precious person
in the world to him, she might be able to take a chance.

She gave him a little smile. 'I thought you might be wanting to kiss me.'

'Well…' His eyebrow rose in interest. 'That, too.' He swallowed and brushed his thumb once more over her lips, before edging back slightly to remove the teacup from her hands and place it on the table. He used the opportunity to move in even closer, leaning towards her, pleased when she didn't pull back but instead seemed to welcome his nearness. 'Is that what you want?'

'Yes. Yes, Sean, it is.' Her lips parted to allow the pent-up air to escape.

He exhaled slowly and came closer. 'Am I dreaming?' he whispered, his breath mingling with hers.

'If you are, then it's a dream we're sharing,' she returned, her tone equally as soft, equally as intimate.

'A shared dream,' he murmured, before his lips finally made contact with hers.

CHAPTER TEN

JANE COULDN'T BELIEVE the way it felt to be kissed by Sean. His mouth was gentle on her own, tenderly moving, testing, allowing her to pull away at any given moment, but that was the last thing she wanted. It was only now that she realised *this* was what she'd been yearning for for so long.

It wasn't just the fact that Sean wanted to kiss her but the fact that it was *Sean* kissing her. As though waiting for her to make the decision whether to pull away or to continue with this gloriousness, he pressed small butterfly kisses to her lips until Jane reached out to thread her fingers through his hair, encouraging him to stay as close to her as possible.

Even then, even after she'd put more urgency into her kiss, wanting to show him that without a shadow of a doubt she wanted this as well, Sean still hesitated, pulling back and opening his eyes to gaze down into her upturned face.

'Are you sure?' he whispered.

'Yes.'

'This could change…everything,' he murmured.

'Yes.' Her eyelids fluttered open and she gazed at him

with desire in her eyes. Could he see the desire? Could he see just how much she wanted him? Needed him?

Unable to stop herself, she suddenly yawned and then smiled sheepishly at Sean. 'Sorry.'

He shook his head and brushed one last kiss across her mouth. 'It's my fault for not realising how exhausted you must be.'

'We helped out in the same emergency,' she pointed out, annoyed with herself for breaking the moment. 'Why aren't you tired?'

'You've faced far more than an emergency today. First meeting the rest of my family—'

'They're wonderful people, Sean. You're very lucky.'

'And if that wasn't nerve-racking enough, having to face the demons of your past, putting your own personal trauma aside in order to help out someone who was in a similar situation.'

'I couldn't have done it without you. You were my anchor,' she murmured, as he carefully removed her hands from his hair, entwining his fingers with hers.

'I'm thinking we're good together.' He gave her hands a little squeeze, before edging back and pulling her to her feet. 'I also think it's best if we get you back to the residential wing before you fall asleep right here in the staffroom.'

'If I did, would you be my knight in shining armour and carry me back to my castle?' The words were that of a constant fairy-tale, one which she'd dreamt of over the years, desperately hoping that one day she would meet the man who was able to see the *real* her, to want the *real* her, to love the *real* her. Was it possible that Sean was that man?

'Without a doubt,' he murmured, dropping a kiss to

the tip of her nose before letting go of her hands in order to quickly tidy the staffroom, tossing out the remainder of their drinks and washing the cups.

'You're quite adept in the kitchen,' she remarked, when he linked his hand with hers and led them out into A and E.

He pointed to himself with his free hand. 'Single parent, remember? Adept at a lot of domestic duties.' He led her through A and E, completely oblivious to the curious glances they were receiving from a few of the staff because they were holding hands. Jane hated being the source of gossip, but at the moment she had to admit that she felt sort of…delighted that Sean wasn't afraid to show the world—or at least the A and E staff—that he cared for her. She only hoped she wasn't making a grave mistake.

She pushed the negative thought aside as they continued towards the residential wing, Sean continuing to hold firmly to her hand until they stood in the corridor outside her room.

He turned her to face him, quickly enveloping her in his arms and holding her close. 'Thank you for coming today.' His words were thick with repressed emotion and Jane received the distinct impression that although he wanted to come in with her, he was also leaving the decision up to her.

She swallowed. Could she do this? Could she let him in? Not only into her room but also into her heart? True, he was already there in an emotional sense but was it possible for her to let him see the *real* her? For him to see her scars? With Eamon, she'd been incredibly reserved, avoiding intimacy with him for as long as possible, until that one night when she'd made the mistake of opening up to him, showing him her scars and watching the revulsion cross his face.

She'd known, as soon as she'd witnessed his expression, that he would find some excuse to leave, find some reason for calling off their engagement, and forty-eight hours later that was exactly what had happened.

If things were going to progress with Sean, if there was any hope for any sort of future for them, then she preferred to know sooner rather than later. If she showed him her scars tonight, if she unveiled herself, she'd know as soon as he saw the deformity of her skin whether or not he truly cared about her. It was a risk but this way, if he did reject her, she'd be able to start the healing, start to find an even footing where she could quash the love she was beginning to feel for him and treat him as nothing more than a colleague and friend.

'The sooner the better,' she murmured against his chest.

'Hmm?' he asked, his big, strong arms still holding her close. Jane eased back and looked at him.

'Come in.'

Sean stared at her for a long moment as though she'd just spoken a foreign language and his sluggish mind was trying to translate. 'Wait. What?'

Jane fished around in her bag for her hospital lanyard, which held her room keycard, and quickly opened the room before she could change her mind. 'Come in,' she invited, holding the door for him.

'Jane? Are you sure? I mean…' He hesitated at the threshold. 'I want to… Don't get me wrong but—'

'Shh.' She quietened him, holding up one finger for silence. Then beckoned him forward and without another word from either of them Sean walked in, letting

Jane close the door behind him. 'There's something I want to show you and I want to show you before I lose my nerve.'

'Jane?'

'I like you, Sean.' She pointed to the chair near the small breakfast table, indicating he should sit down.

'I like you, too, Jane.'

'OK.' She stepped forward after he'd sat down and pressed a finger to his lips. 'If this is going to work, I need you to be quiet.'

He frowned and whispered against her finger, his eyes filled with questions. 'If *what* is going to work?'

'Shh.' She bent her head and brushed a kiss across his lips, before drawing in a deep breath and stepping away from him. 'This is important to me and...' She closed her eyes and started to unbutton her long-sleeved cotton shirt.

'Jane. No. Wait.' Sean shot to his feet.

Her eyes snapped open and she stared at him. 'What?'

'I don't think you should... I mean...just wait a minute and, uh...' He raked an unsteady hand through his hair, his confusion evident in his concerned blue gaze. 'I thought we could just talk and perhaps...well, if things escalated to that but...even then...' He stopped, belatedly realising he was beginning to trip over his words.

Jane was family. He'd invited her to become a part of his family so she wouldn't have to be alone any more, so that she could spend time with Spencer and finally feel that after all these years she was no longer alone, and while he was most definitely attracted to her, and had been pleasantly surprised when she'd taken charge just now, the last thing he'd expected from her was some sort of striptease! Was this how the men in her life had previously treated her? Like some sort of possession to do with as they wished? Did she consider only their pleasure but not her own?

He didn't treat women in this way. He'd been raised to respect women, to cherish them and to treat them as equals.

'I do want to talk,' she said, but that didn't stop her from unbuttoning her shirt. 'Please, sit down. I need to get through this now before…before…' She stopped, unable to voice the way she felt about him. It was definitely different from any other feelings she'd had in the past. Even with Eamon, the man she'd been about to marry, she hadn't felt so comfortable or accepted, but she knew if there was any hope of a future with Sean, any hope at all, she needed to be completely open and honest with him, and that meant showing him her hideous body.

'Please sit,' she urged again, and it was the hint of veiled desperation in her voice that made him do as she asked. He swallowed, watching her every move, and when she'd finished undoing all the buttons on the shirt, she took off her glasses and put them onto the table, the shirt still remaining closed.

'Today was difficult for me, in many ways. Meeting your family…' She smiled warmly at him as the memories of her wonderful time at the beach—feeling so included—washed over her. 'That has definitely been the highlight. But the accident, facing what had happened to me all those years ago, being in A and E—a department I avoid at all costs if possible—was…confronting.'

'You did so well, Ja—'

'Shh.' She spoke the sound softly before drawing in another breath and holding his gaze. 'I remember everything about the accident, every minute detail as though it happened only yesterday. I want to tell you, Sean. I want you to *know* me, the *real* me, and to do that I need to open myself, open my past up to you, to let you into my deepest, darkest secrets.'

Sean didn't speak this time but instead nodded once, wanting to convey to her that he now understood more of what she was trying to do…and he was incredibly impressed by her strength.

'We were driving home from a wedding, which had been up in the hills. I used to get carsick if I sat in the back so my mother had insisted that I sit in the front and she and Daina would sit in the back seat. Once we'd come down off the hills, the road now not so winding, Daina declared that it was her turn to sit in the front but my father refused to pull over. It had been raining, there was quite a bit of traffic on the road and he'd been drinking at the wedding. He was agitated and annoyed. He also had a very short fuse. My mother was trying to keep both Daina and my father under control by yelling at them to stop yelling at each other.

'Then Daina decided we could just switch places at the next red traffic light. It would have to be quick, she said. I was to climb into the back while she ran around the outside of the car. I didn't realise…' Jane stopped and swallowed over her dry mouth, her words still quiet and straightforward with only the mildest hint of disbelief '…until it was too late that she'd already unbuckled my seat belt. A dog ran onto the road, between our car and the car in front, and because of my dad's slower reflexes he swerved late and smashed our car into an enormous tree, as well as collecting a few other cars along the way.'

Jane wanted to close her eyes, to hide from him as she recalled the next bit, but if she did, she'd miss gauging Sean's reaction to her disfigured body. She didn't want to witness the repulsion she knew would come but if she didn't put herself through this now, it would only make it more difficult for her to get over him later.

She pursed her lips together and forced her breathing to remain calm as she continued. 'I felt as though I'd been sitting on an ejector seat. One moment I was looking back at Daina and the next I experienced searing pain as the windscreen glass cut into my face, arms and hands. I could see the ground beneath me, as though I was frozen in time, but it loomed closer and closer until I thudded down, skidding a little. The pain in my hands, my wrists was the first wave I felt. It was blindingly agonising and yet another pain made itself known.' She paused and gripped the edge of the shirt with both hands, slowly removing it to reveal the thin singlet top beneath.

She saw Sean's gaze dip to look at her arms, seeing the scars running up her arms. Would he realise that these scars were why she always wore long-sleeved tops and shirts? She heard his sharp intake of breath as she lifted the singlet top to reveal the large area around her side and abdomen, covered in scars and three different skin grafts.

'I landed on a large stick, which did quite a bit of internal damage.' She turned slightly so he could see the full effect. Her skin was disfigured and stretched, looking like a very bad patchwork quilt. 'I required kidney surgery and bowel surgery to fix the internal organs and then the skin grafts began, not all of them working the first time.' She twisted her shoulder to show him the ten-centimetre-long scar that had, over time, faded to become a paler shade of pink.

'Not only was I disfigured on the outside, I was broken on the inside. My parents died in that accident, my father of a fatal blow to the head and my mother bled out internally. And although they may not have been the best of parents, certainly having their fair share of problems, they were still my parents and I grieved deeply for them.'

Sean continued to stare at her, and she continued to carefully watch his expression. His brow was puckered in a slight frown but she hoped it was a frown of empathy rather than one of disgust. Was he looking at her with a clinical eye? Switching his mind from sensual mode to practical mode? Would he ever be able to regard her as a desirable woman? An object of beauty? A woman he wasn't too repulsed to touch and caress? Could he accept her? Would he ever tenderly caress and touch her badly stitched-together skin?

Jane held her breath, trying desperately to figure out what he was thinking. She simply stood there before him, not only baring her body but baring her soul. Couldn't he see how important this was to her? How she needed to be reassured? To be told that her life wasn't going to remain as lonely and as devoid of personal emotional connections as it had been for far too long? Was he the man who might love her as she hoped?

'I don't remember Daina having any scars.' His voice was deep yet distant and Jane's eyelids fluttered closed as horrified pain pierced her heart. She'd made another mistake. She'd opened up the box that contained her darkest fears and exposed herself to him...and all he could think about was Daina.

She worked hard to control the tears that were rising up within her, her head feeling incredibly heavy with the instant headache pounding against her temples. *You idiot. You stupid, disfigured nobody.* She couldn't stop the voice that penetrated her mind, the voice that always sounded exactly like Daina's. *Whatever made you think a man, especially one like Sean, so handsome and sexy, could love you?*

'Jane?'

She paused the voice in her head, knowing it would definitely continue later, and opened her eyes, glaring at him as she quickly pulled her clothes back over her body, turning her back to him as she attempted to button up her shirt, even though her trembling fingers made it nigh on impossible. She forced herself to concentrate on the menial task, to push away those other thoughts, to push away the answer to her initial question. Would Sean be able to accept her for who she was, scars and all? Clearly, he could not.

'She had bruises and cuts but they quickly disappeared,' Jane remarked woodenly. All she wanted now was for Sean to go, to leave her alone, to let her deal with the wounds he'd just inflicted. Why had she hoped for tender words? For a level of understanding about why she'd needed to literally bare her soul to him?

He was the same as all other men. More interested in himself, his world, his life. Why had she thought he might be any different? Couldn't he see, didn't he understand that she needed reassurance? She knew she was broken but she wasn't relying on him to *fix* her, she was relying on him to accept her, to not care about Daina or any other woman, not here, not right now.

The first tear rolled down her cheek and she impatiently brushed it away. She didn't want to guilt Sean with her tears, to have him hold her, offering insincere comfort. Not now, not when he'd shown his true nature.

She must have stood there with her back to him for longer than she'd realised because when he spoke her name, she heard the questioning urgency in the tone.

'Jane?' He placed his hand on her shoulder but she shrugged away from his touch, not realising he'd moved from the chair. 'Jane, what is it?'

'What *is* it?' she asked, her words angry, her tears choking in her throat. She shook her head and sniffed, knowing she should get control over her emotions but realising she might have passed the point where logical thought was possible. 'How can you even ask me that? I…' She walked stiffly away from him, her movements stilted as though her brain was having difficulty sending signals to her limbs.

'I'm not sure I underst—'

'Of course you don't.' She rolled her eyes and shook her head. 'Why? Why did I even bother?' she whispered, more to herself than to him.

Sean stepped forward and placed both hands on her shoulders, wanting her to look at him. 'Jane?'

'Get your hands off me,' she growled, her voice low but steady. He gazed down into her face for a whole three seconds before doing as she'd asked. He stepped back and thrust both hands into his hair before placing them on his hips and looking at her as though she were a puzzle he simply couldn't figure out.

Jane drew in a breath, trying to muster as much civility as she could. The emotions were beginning to erupt and she knew of old that if she tried to quell them too much, it only made matters worse.

'I think you should leave.'

Sean shifted his stance, still staring at her in utter confusion. He opened his mouth to say something then closed it again before shaking his head. 'If that's what you want.'

'It is.'

'Then I'll go.'

Although he said the words, he still didn't move for a good ten seconds, the two of them standing there, staring at each other. There was no way she could decipher his expression and right now she was too distraught to care. The only thought that kept spinning around in her mind was that although she may have felt some sort of bond with Sean, although they may have acknowledged an attraction to each other, that attraction had abruptly come to an end the instant he'd seen her disfigurement.

He nodded and shoved his hands into his pockets. 'I'll go.'

With that, he walked past her to the door and without looking back opened it and left.

As the door slowly closed behind him, the rush of pain, anguish and loneliness, all the emotions she'd been fighting for far too long, washed over her like a raging torrent, flooding her mind. With her legs no longer able to support her, she crumpled to the floor as the first sobs of heartbreak began to rack her body.

Despite the way Sean loved his family, despite the way he loved his son, there was no denying the fact that he could never love a freak like her.

CHAPTER ELEVEN

FOR THE NEXT three days Sean had the distinct impression that Jane was doing her best to avoid him. Initially he'd thought she was embarrassed at having shown him her body, that she needed some time to come to terms with her vulnerability, but every time he walked onto the ward, she would leave at her earliest convenience, not even bothering to utter an excuse.

He knew she'd been to Maternity to check on both Carly and the baby because when he'd gone to see how mother and baby were doing, Carly had sung Jane's praises, letting Sean know how wonderful she was.

'She told me that when she was a teenager she was also in a car accident like me. She opened up to me, she told me she knew *exactly* what I was feeling and why it was important for me to speak to a psychologist about it now, rather than letting the emotions build up and get the better of me.'

'Wise words,' Sean had remarked, already having read in Carly's file that she'd bluntly refused to see the psychologist.

'I can't believe she opened up to me like she did. She didn't have to but because she did I can see that she's not just spouting hospital rules at me but that she really does care because she *understands*.'

'Yes.' Sean knew Carly wasn't the only patient to be saying such things about the wonderful Jane Diamond. Tessa, who was beginning to show definite signs of improvement as far as her eating habits went, continued to be glued to Jane's side as much as possible. He'd read in Tessa's notes that Jane had sat in on every counselling session with the parents, offering helpful suggestions as to ways they could support both their daughters—the one who was bullying and the one who was being bullied.

Jane had also dropped around to spend some time with Spencer, or so his mother had told him late yesterday evening. Sean found it interesting that Jane had chosen to see her nephew on the evening when she knew he'd be in departmental meetings. In fact, it seemed that Jane had time for everyone…except him.

Perhaps the kisses they'd shared had been enough to scare her off? Perhaps she now wanted to just be friends and not be romantically involved…but if that was the case, why had she shown him her scars in the first place? He couldn't believe how amazing she was, how brave and incredibly beautiful, and now she seemed to want nothing to do with him.

He'd left her messages on her phone. Some jokingly jovial, telling her he couldn't sleep and needed her to sing him a lullaby over the phone, and when she hadn't returned any of his calls he'd left messages that were filled with concern and confusion. No reply.

He still wanted to pursue the attraction he felt for her, to figure out what had gone wrong and why she was bent on avoiding him. He knew she felt the same way, too, or at least she had. So why had she shut him out? What had he done? Said? He was at a loss to figure it out and it had been constantly at the back of his mind for the past three days, ever since she'd asked him to leave her room.

Sean flicked back the bed sheet and stalked from his bedroom, deciding it was better to give up on attempts to sleep and try and catch up on some paperwork. 'At least the bureaucracy of the hospital will help get your mind off Jane,' he murmured as he made himself a cup of tea.

He worked solidly for half an hour, the light over his paper-strewn dining-room table sufficiently illuminating the area as the clock in the hallway ticked steadily towards dawn.

'Sean?'

He heard his mother's voice at the top of the stairs. 'Are you awake?'

'Mum? Come on down.'

Louise did as he asked, coming into the room, her summer dressing gown pulled tight around her. 'Can't sleep either?' she asked rhetorically. Sean's answer was a shrug of his shoulders. 'Problem at the hospital?'

'Not really.'

'Problem with Spencer?'

'No. He's fine.'

Louise settled herself at the table and looked closely at her son for a moment. 'Problem with…Jane?'

Sean eyed his mother cautiously. 'What makes you ask that?'

'Oh, I don't know. When she was here she kept changing the subject every time I mentioned your name.'

Sean put his pen down and groaned, resting his head

in his hands. So she really was avoiding him, not just being super-busy and efficient at work. He'd hoped it was the latter, he'd hoped he was reading the signals incorrectly, but if his mother had picked up on something—and she was usually incredibly astute—then there was definitely something wrong.

'I thought the two of you were getting along very well,' Louise stated. 'It certainly looked that way when we were at the beach.'

'The beach.' He lifted his head from his hands. 'That seems so long ago now.'

'I'm sorry if you think I'm prying, son, but how *do* you feel about Jane? Tell me to shut up and mind my own business if you want but I only ask because I care about you, and about Jane and about Spencer. Whether you like it or not, your son became very much involved in all of this the instant you gave Jane access to him.'

'You think I should have kept her away?'

'No. Heavens, no. From what I can observe, Jane hasn't had the easiest of lives and it's a credit to her that she's such a strong survivor.'

'Yes.' Sean thought back to the way she'd bravely revealed her scars to him, the way her big eyes had been wide with fear, like a scared little rabbit, and yet she'd done it. She'd conquered her fear and shown him her deepest, darkest secret and then...

'It's as though she sometimes gets swamped with the emotions from her past,' he said out loud, standing and pacing the room. 'I thought she was steering clear of me because she...well, she opened up to me.' He stopped pacing and raked a hand through his hair. 'But if she was avoiding talking about me, then it must have been... But what did I do?'

'How did she open up to you?' Louise asked.

Sean looked at the floor then met his mother's eyes. 'She showed me her scars.'

'From the car accident when she was a teenager? The one where her parents died?'

'Yes.' He shook his head. 'What she must have endured.'

'And what did you say?'

'Huh?'

'After she'd bared her soul to you—because that's what she was doing, darling—what did you say?'

Sean frowned. 'I didn't…say…' He tried to recollect what had happened next. 'She showed me her scars, she told me her parents had died in that accident. I was surprised that Daina hadn't been scarred in any way, given the severity of the accident.'

Louise gaped at her son. 'Tell me you didn't mention Daina.'

'What? I just said I didn't remember Daina being scar—' He stopped talking and closed his eyes, slowly shaking his head from side to side. 'She thought I was comparing them. Her and Daina.' And that had been when she'd turned away from him, that had been when she'd finally stared at him with the eyes of a stranger and told him to leave. He'd only done as she asked because he'd thought it had all been too much for her and that she wanted to be alone.

'Has Jane ever had a serious relationship before?'

'Yes.' The answer was a whisper as he quickly recalled what she'd told him. 'She said he broke off the engagement because she kept herself hidden, that she was secretive, and that in the end she wasn't the woman he wanted.' Regret pierced Sean's soul at the thought of the pain he'd caused Jane.

If she was under the impression that he thought her scars ugly and disfiguring then he had to change her mind. He had to show her that she'd become important to him, that she'd somehow managed to open his heart, helped him to heal from his past pain and to risk loving again.

'Loving?' His eyes widened as the word tripped off his tongue. He glanced at his mother to find her watching him intently.

'I don't know what just went on inside your head, son.' She chuckled as she stood and tightened the belt of her dressing gown. 'But it was funny watching a multitude of emotions work their way across your face.' She leaned up and pressed a kiss to his cheek. 'Let me know if your father or I can be of any help.'

'Can you look after Spencer when he wakes up in about half an hour?' Sean's mind was working at a rate of knots. 'I need to fix this. I need to let Jane know that's not how things are, that's not how I feel, and I think I know exactly how to accomplish that.'

Louise nodded. 'I'm still only getting half the picture but that's all right. I'll wait until the ending's written.' She pointed a finger at him, her tone filled with mock warning. 'Just make it a happy one.'

As Louise headed back up the stairs, yawning as she went, Sean looked at the clock on the wall. 'Half past five.' He walked to his phone, his gut telling him that Jane would not be asleep, that she'd no doubt be somewhere in the ward, helping her patients through the night. 'Anthea?' he said when the phone on the ward was answered. 'It's Sean. Is Jane on the ward?'

'Yes, she is. Do you want me to get her for you?'

'Er…no. No. It's fine.' He was about to say goodbye but added quickly, 'Don't tell her I called. OK?'

'OK.'

'And if possible, can you keep her on the ward until I get there? Shouldn't be more than half an hour or so.'

'OK,' Anthea said again, her tone a little curious. 'Are you feeling all right, Sean?'

Sean grinned as his plan began to solidify. 'Anthea, I've never been better in my life!'

Jane sat by Tessa's bedside, pleased with the progress the young girl had made over the past few weeks. It made her feel wonderful to be able to help someone because it was a small way of righting the wrongs that had been done to her. Tessa was due to be discharged tomorrow and was naturally apprehensive at going home.

'I'm safe here. Why can't I stay here?' she'd asked Jane only a few hours ago, the rest of the ward quiet as the two of them had talked softly.

'Because you need to grow stronger at home. Staying here will do nothing for you, Tessa. Facing your darkest fears is…' Jane had stopped, as the image of Sean's gaze on her disfigured body, the look of disbelief in his eyes, had come immediately to mind. She'd pushed it aside. 'Is how you become strong. Your parents know what your sister was doing to you and they've been able to find out what was wrong with your sister, why she felt it necessary to bully you.'

'But what about you?' Tessa had held Jane's hand. 'Will I see you again?'

'You're seeing me in three days' time in my clinic.'

Tessa had looked at Jane then, caution entering her

eyes. 'Are you for real or are you just being my doctor?' Blunt and to the point. Jane's smile had been bright because two weeks ago Tessa wouldn't have had the courage to ask such a thing.

'I'm both. I'm your doctor first and foremost but I'm also your friend.'

'So we can, you know, go the park one day or something like that?'

'What about the movies?' Jane had suggested, and Tessa's eyes had brightened with absolute delight.

'Really?'

'Of course.' Jane had laughed at the reaction and Tessa had joined in before sighing as though a huge weight had just been removed from her shoulders. Fifteen minutes later, the child had drifted off into a calm and comfortable sleep.

Jane sat there, envying the little girl. Yes, things had been bad but Tessa was getting help and, most importantly, was responding to that help. If only her own life could be as easily fixed, but that wasn't to be. She had to somehow figure out a way to endure working alongside the man who had stolen her heart but rejected her body.

Closing her eyes, she couldn't help but remember the way he'd held her so tenderly, the way he'd kissed her, murmured that he thought her beautiful. If only it had been true. At least she'd found out early on, at least she hadn't spent months of her time here in Adelaide fixating on the hope that something might happen between Sean and herself. The fact that he'd generously included her in his family circle, allowing her access to Spencer, was something she would be forever grateful for, and where she'd thought he'd accepted her for who she was, that he might be able to see past the scars on her body to the real her, cowering inside…well, she'd been mistaken before and she shouldn't have been surprised that it had happened again.

Realising if she sat here allowing her thoughts to continue in this manner, she'd probably end up bursting into tears and waking Tessa, she uncurled herself from the chair. Quietly standing up and heading to the nurses' station, she found Anthea busy filling in paperwork, getting ready for the hand-over.

It was just after six o'clock in the morning and while Jane had managed a few hours' sleep prior to coming and checking on Tessa, she was starting to feel fatigued. Even if she wanted to sleep, she knew as soon as her eyes closed, all she would see would be Sean's grim face, his eyebrows drawn together as he stared at her grotesque body.

'Not a bad night,' Anthea murmured, then gestured in Tessa's direction. 'Is she anxious about going home this morning?'

'Yes. Listen, I might head back to my room, shower, change, have something to eat and then be back here in time for her nine o'clock discharge.'

'Uh…sure, Jane, but, uh…would you mind just having a quick look at these files for me, please? I'm not sure if the medication dosages are correct.'

Jane sighed and nodded. 'Sure.' She accepted the files from Anthea, noticing the other woman kept checking the clock on the wall and then glancing over Jane's shoulder towards the doors to the ward. 'Something wrong?' Jane asked ten minutes later.

'What? Oh. Uh. No.' Anthea shifted uncomfortably and couldn't help glancing at the clock once more.

'These dosages look fine.'

'Great. Good. Thanks.' Anthea glanced frantically around the nurses' station as though looking for something. 'Uh, actually, I can't...er...find...Tessa's discharge forms. Have they been prepared?'

'I filled in all the preliminary details only a few hours ago. They should be in her notes.' Jane went over to where the casenotes were kept and was surprised when she couldn't find Tessa's notes. 'They were right here.'

'Oh. I'll help you look for them,' Anthea quickly volunteered, once more glancing at the clock and then the doors to the ward. Jane frowned but decided that perhaps the fatigue of working through the night was starting to get to Anthea. Jane looked around the place and eventually found the notes under a different pile of papers, not at all where they should have been.

'Here they are.' She opened the notes and checked the discharge papers were in there. 'There you go.'

'Oh. Thanks. One of the enrolled nurses must have moved them. Thanks, Jane.' There was a look of concern on Anthea's face.

'Are you sure you're all right? You're acting a little...strangely.'

Anthea laughed nervously. 'I'm just no good at this.'

A prickle of apprehension worked its way down Jane's back. 'No good at what?' she asked cautiously.

At that moment the ward doors opened and Anthea breathed a sigh of relief. 'Stalling,' the ward sister replied, before pointing.

Jane turned around slowly, sensing before she saw him that Sean had just entered the ward. Why had Anthea been stalling? Had Sean realised she'd been doing her best to avoid him? Had he employed the help of the ward sister in order to make her feel even more uncomfortable than she did? What had he told Anthea? Did the entire ward know about her scarred body?

The questions flooded her mind, one tripping over the other, her breathing becoming uneasy. She quickly looked behind Sean at the closing ward doors, wondering if there was any way she could escape, but with Anthea behind her and Sean walking towards her it appeared she was trapped.

Jane immediately pulled her sleeves down, then crossed her arms over her chest and lifted her chin, her eyes flashing defiantly. If she was going to be cornered, she was going to do her best to project an attitude of defensive fake nonchalance.

Sean took one look at her then glanced past her to Anthea. 'Thanks,' he remarked, which only made Jane more annoyed.

'What do you want, Sean?' she asked, completely failing to keep her emotions under control, her tone laced with annoyance.

'I want you.'

Her eyes opened wide at his words. 'Pardon?'

'I want you to come with me. Please.' He held out his hand, waiting for her to put hers into it. Instead, Jane shook her head and stepped around him, stalking out of the ward, hoping against hope that he wouldn't follow her.

'Jane.' He was closer than she'd realised and fell into step beside her. Thankfully he didn't try to stop her as she made her way through the hospital corridors, heading towards the residential wing. 'I'm sorry.'

'Sorry? About what?' Again, she hadn't managed to keep her tone absolutely devoid of emotion and she silently berated herself. She needed to get control over her emotions, not remember the way his big strong arms had held her, his fingers had caressed her, his lips had brushed tenderly and provocatively over her lips. She was not in love with him. She was *not*. She had to keep telling herself that because right now she knew it was an absolute lie.

'About walking out the door the other night.'

Jane faltered for a moment and Sean took the opportunity to place his hand on her arm and stop her in her tracks. 'Please, Jane. Just hear me out. If you want nothing to do with me after that, I promise I'll leave you alone.'

'Will you? Really?' She gazed up into his eyes, stunned and amazed to find him looking not only desperate but extremely contrite.

'Probably not.' He smiled and shrugged his shoulders. 'It's difficult for a man to leave the woman he's in love with, even if it's what she wants.'

Jane's throat went dry and she tried to swallow. 'Love?' she squeaked.

'Yes, Jane. I love you.' The words came easily to his lips and where he'd practised long and convincing speeches on the drive to the hospital, all that mattered right now was that she understood exactly how he felt. He tugged her into a small nook, out of the way of the main corridor, for a bit of privacy. 'I *love* you,' he repeated, emphasising the middle word. 'You've managed to unlock the pain from my past and make it disappear as if by magic. You've shown me I'm not only capable of trusting again but also of loving. You've been so incredibly brave, opening your heart to me, showing me your scars, and I...' He looked down into her face, overcome with love at her inner strength.

'It's all right, Sean.' She hung her head, her long hair hanging like a veil around her. 'I know my skin is grotes—'

'What? No. No.' He shook his head and lifted her chin so he could once more look into her eyes. 'You misunderstand me. I don't find your scars horrible or ugly or anything like that.'

'But...' Jane was unable to believe and accept what he was saying. 'You found me distasteful and...compared me to...to...'

'I'm sorry you took it that way. I wasn't comparing you to Daina. I was...astounded that she'd walked away with nothing and that you, so strong and so brave, had lost everything. She was... Her behaviour towards you was...' He shook his head. 'I don't want to talk about the past, about Daina. It's over and done with and there's nothing we can do to change it. What we *can* do is to move forward with our lives...together.' He took her hands in his and held them tightly.

'Sean?' His name was a whispered caress on her lips and in another moment he'd dipped his head and was brushing the sweetest of sweet kisses to her mouth.

'I love you, Jane. Scars and all.'

'But—'

'No buts. I love you, Jane. *Scars and all.*'

Tears instantly sprang to her eyes as she desperately tried to accept what he was saying. She bit her lip but the action only caused him to kiss her once more.

'I love you, Jane, scars and all. And I am going to keep telling you that until you believe me. I love you, Jane. Scars and all.'

'Oh, Sean. Really?'

He smiled. 'I love you, Jane. Scars and all.' With that, she leaned into him and he immediately put his arms around her, drawing her close. 'Now, I have something special planned for us this morning.'

'You do?'

'Yes.' He looked down at her, unable to resist brushing another kiss to her lips. 'So would you do me the honour of trusting me? Of not asking too many questions and allowing me to follow through with my initial plan?'

'You have a plan?'

'Yes, but somehow, where you're concerned, they never seem to work out exactly as I imagined.'

'Why is that, do you think?' Jane reached out and brushed her fingers through his hair, delighted that she had the right to touch him. He loved her. Sean loved her—*scars and all*.

'Because you twist me into knots and no one's ever been able to do that before.'

Jane looked at him with a hint of doubt still in her eyes.

'No one,' he emphasised. 'You don't react the way women usually do. You march to the beat of your own drum and I adore that. You are unique, Jane.' He brushed the hair from her eyes and bent to kiss her lips once more. 'And you're doing it again. You're derailing me from the plans I have by being so incredibly wonderful.'

'And what are these "plans" that you have?'

'I want to take you back to my house so you can have breakfast with Spencer and me, so I can have the perfect setting where I can get down on one knee and ask you to become my wife.'

'Wife?' she squeaked.

'I love you, Jane. Why wouldn't I want to marry you?'

'But...I... Are you sure?'

'Never been surer of anything in my life.' Sean took her scarred arm in his hand, gently pushing up the sleeve. Next he brushed kisses up the length of her scar, wanting her to know that, beyond a doubt, he wanted her, needed her, loved her. He didn't care that she was scarred. The realisation made her feel foolish for having read his expression incorrectly the other night.

'Oh, Sean.' She shook her head. 'I'm sorry.'

'Sorry?' He met her gaze.

'Sorry for making you leave the other night. I thought you were disgusted by my scars, I thought you were like...other people.'

'Your former fiancé may not have been able to see past the physical to the stunningly beautiful woman that you really are—inside and out, as far as I'm concerned,' he quickly clarified, lest she take his words in the wrong way. 'But I'm not him. I love you, Jane. Scars and all.'

She nodded, starting to accept that what he said was the truth. He'd professed his love for her, he'd told her he wanted to propose to her, that he wanted her for his wife, and yet hadn't pressured her for any type of answer...giving her time to process and to think things over. Perhaps Sean did understand her, better than she understood herself.

'I...er...need to be back at the hospital by nine, so I can be here for Tessa's discharge,' she said, by way of explanation.

'Then we'd best get moving,' he told her, bending to kiss her lips again before slipping an arm about her waist and walking through the hospital, once more not caring who saw them or the tongues they set wagging.

During the drive to his house Sean chatted easily with her, as though it was quite normal for him to have professed his love for her, while she couldn't help feeling more and more nervous the closer they drew to his home.

'What if Spencer doesn't like me enough to have me for a stepmother?' Jane blurted out the instant he pulled into the driveway. 'I mean, he barely knows me and... isn't this all moving a bit too fast?'

Sean removed the key from the ignition, before unbuckling his seat belt and turning to face her.

'Jane. For a start, Spencer hasn't stopped talking about you since he met you.'

'He hasn't?'

'He thinks you're fantastic.'

'He does?'

'And, besides, it's clear to me—and to anyone who's seen you with him—just how much you care about him, how much you love him.'

'I do. He's the reason I came back to Adelaide.'

Sean took her hand in his and kissed it then instructed, 'Wait there.'

'Why?'

His smile broadened. 'I want to be chivalrous. Is that OK?'

'Oh. Uh...sure.' And so she sat in her seat, waiting for him to come around the car and open the door for her. Although the sun had only been up a short while, the heat was starting to make itself known, but it was nothing compared to the way Sean warmed her through and through when he smiled lovingly down at her.

'You still have your seat belt on,' he murmured when she looked up at him. 'Allow me.' He instantly leaned into the car, his face coming incredibly close to hers, his breath mingling with hers as he reached across to unclip the belt.

'Mmm,' he murmured, as he took the opportunity to press a few kisses to her cheek, Jane delighting in his tender touch. She angled her head so their lips could meet and when they did, with her finally starting to accept that he truly did love her, that he wanted to spend the rest of his life with her, that all her dreams did actually seem to be coming true, Jane kissed him back with all the love in her heart.

'Sean?' she murmured, caressing his face with her fingertips.

'Yes, my love?'

'I want you to know…that I don't like long engagements.'

At her words, a slow smile spread across his face. 'Duly noted.' He kissed her again, before helping her from the car and slipping his arms about her waist. 'I take it that your answer to my impending proposal will be yes?'

'How could you doubt it? Before I met you—this time around…' she quickly clarified, and he nodded, indicating he understood what it was she was saying. 'My life was…hollow. I'd look in the mirror and not recognise myself because I never really smiled any more. Sure, I'd smile for my patients, doing everything I could to help them. I'd smile for my colleagues, wanting to show that I could work alongside them, but I wasn't smiling for *me*.

'I guess, given my upbringing, that doing things for myself, rewarding myself, being kind to myself, wasn't something I'd ever thought possible. But now, thanks to you and your generosity in allowing me to become a part of your family, I no longer feel faceless or hollow. I can keep on living my life, surviving in the world I've built for myself, but…I don't want to.'

She placed both her hands to his face and looked directly into his eyes, his beautiful, blue hypnotic eyes. 'I want to be with you, Sean. With you and Spencer. I want to become a family. The three of us. I…I…' She stopped and sighed heavily.

'It's OK if you're not ready to say it, Jane. I don't need the words because I can see it in your eyes and, really, the other night you said all that needed to be said—I just didn't realise it. You bared your soul to me, you allowed me into your deepest, darkest secret and I am not only honoured, I'm humbled by it.' With that, he released her from his hold, took her hands in his and went down on one knee.

'This still isn't the way I'd planned to propose but it doesn't matter. It's the *right* time to ask you and believe me when I say, Jane—to me, you are perfect. In every way. Please, my love, consent to be my wife and Spencer's mother?'

'Oh, Sean,' she gasped, quickly tugging him to his feet. 'Yes.' She rose up on tiptoe and placed a kiss firmly to his mouth. 'Yes. Yes and yes again. You can propose to me as many times as you like and I will always say yes.'

Sean gathered her close, dipping his head down to claim her lips. 'I might just hold you to that.'

No sooner had he pressed his mouth to hers than they heard the front door open and Spencer came running out.

'Aunty Jane. Aunty Jane. You're here!'

Sean released Jane to briefly scoop his son into his arms. They looked across to the doorway where Louise was standing, dabbing at her eyes with a handkerchief, a big, bright smile on her face.

'Have you come for breakfast, Aunty Jane? There's a huge feast on the table inside and Grandma said I wasn't allow to touch *any* of it until you got home—but I sneaked a strawberry when she wasn't looking,' he confided in a stage whisper.

Jane couldn't help but laugh, unable to believe how happy she was.

'Shall we go in?' Sean asked Jane as he let the wriggling Spencer go, securing his arm around Jane's waist once more.

'Yes, *my love*, we shall.'

CHAPTER TWELVE

DURING THE NEXT few weeks after she'd accepted Sean's proposal Jane couldn't believe how happily her life had turned out. Not only had Louise and Barney well and truly accepted her as part of their family but they'd asked her to move into their guest room.

'Just until the wedding,' Louise had stated. 'That way, you'll be close to Sean and Spencer.' This arrangement suited Jane down to the ground as she wasn't used to making life-changing decisions in a rush.

'You could just sneak downstairs and stay with me,' Sean had said temptingly on more than one occasion, but he'd also understood Jane's need to take things slowly.

'Falling in love with you in such a short time has been enough of an emotional education,' she'd told him, before kissing him with all the love in her heart. 'Slowing things down isn't a bad idea, Sean. For all of us.'

'I know,' he'd agreed, but he had held her close while they'd waited for Spencer to finish getting ready for bed. 'I just never thought I'd feel this way, so...content. I want you, Jane. I want you to be my wife and I want it soon. Although things have happened faster than either of us probably imagined, it also feels so incredibly right. You said you don't like long engagements and neither do I.'

'But Spencer…'

'Feels the same way. He's already started calling you "Mum".'

Jane grinned widely; her heart burst with love every time Spencer did so. 'I never knew it would feel so… perfect.'

'We *are* perfect. The three of us.'

'I know but just the thought of organising a wedding, of actually setting a date—' She stopped. 'Sean, every time I've tried to make arrangements in the past, things have always gone wrong.'

He'd pondered her words for a moment before asking, 'What if I surprise you?'

'Surprise me?'

'Surprise wedding.'

'What? Like a surprise party?'

'Why not? That way you don't have to be stressed about it at all.'

She looked at him with surprise. 'You never fail to amaze me.' She kissed him quickly yet lovingly. 'Promise me you won't ever stop.'

'So I can organise a surprise wedding for you?'

'Um…' It would stop her from worrying and stressing about things. 'Are you sure you want to do it?'

Sean's answer had been to capture her mouth with his own. 'Absolutely.'

And so for the next few weeks, Jane simply released all that extra tension from her shoulders, amazed at how wonderful it was to have someone else to care about her burdens. What she *was* able to focus on was helping Louise plan Spencer's seventh birthday party.

'I know you wanted all the attention to be on Spencer and not on you, but I'm glad you're letting us make this a combined birthday party,' Louise said the day before the event as Jane helped her to put the finishing touches on Spencer's character birthday cake. She'd never made a birthday cake before, and certainly not one for the little boy who now called her Mummy.

'Spencer insisted. He said he wouldn't have a party at all if I didn't agree to have one with him.' Jane laughed as she licked a bit of the icing from the knife before putting the mixing bowls into the sink. 'He's so excited to be sharing his birthday with me. He told me it's our special bond.' And on hearing those words from the almost-seven-year-old, Jane had let go of the last tie she'd been holding onto from her past. No longer was Spencer her sister's son; instead, he was her birthday buddy. 'He's quite a charmer—just like his father.'

'It's hereditary,' Louise agreed, then glanced at the clock behind her. 'Good heavens. Is that the time?'

'Oh, I need to go and pick Spencer up from school,' Jane said, glad Sean had insisted she take a few days' annual leave before the birthday party.

'You'll enjoy the build-up to the party even more if you're not having to stress about patients and rush around at the hospital,' he'd said, and Jane had to admit he'd been right.

When Spencer got into the car, he was buzzing with delight about his party tomorrow.

'And we can't wait to go laser tagging and we've already decided who's going to be on my team and who is going to be on Tessa's team,' Spencer remarked.

'Tessa's looking forward to it, then?' It had only been after Tessa's discharge from the hospital that Jane had learned the little girl not only went to the same school as Spencer but was in his class. In true Booke family fashion, and without any prompting from the adults, Spencer had sought Tessa out, befriending her, and when Jane had seen the girl only a few days ago she'd been amazed at the transformation. A rosy glow had infused Tessa's cheeks and the smile on her face as she'd chatted animatedly with Spencer had filled Jane's heart with joy. 'These Booke men are quite wonderful,' she murmured.

'What did you say, Mummy?' Spencer asked.

Jane smiled at him. 'I said you and your dad are quite wonderful.'

'What does wonderful mean?' He tipped his head to the side and looked at her intently, as though he completely trusted her to know all the answers.

'Uh…' Jane thought for a moment. 'It means purple and green together,' she told him.

'Ohhh. Yeah. I get it now.' Spencer paused for one quick breath before continuing with what he'd been saying. 'And anyway Tessa and I both wanted you on our team but she said that as you were my new mother that you could be on my team. I can't wait until we have the cake. Is it finished? Did you and Grandma finish it?'

Jane laughed at the way he wasn't to be derailed from the topic at hand and listened intently as she drove them home in her new car. Home. How perfect that word sounded. True to his word, Sean hadn't said anything more to her about the wedding but when he'd asked her if she wanted to wear an engagement ring, Jane had shrugged.

'Not really. I mean, nine times out of ten I can't wear rings at the hospital so I don't see the point.'

'Were you always this practical?' he'd asked, with a wide smile on his face.

'I had to be.'

'And rightly so.' Sean had also had the impression that Jane didn't want the traditional wedding service with all the trappings and trimmings because that was exactly the wedding he'd had with Daina. If Daina had been a Bridezilla, then Jane was the complete opposite. It was one of the reasons he loved her so much. She was simply perfect for him. 'Well...' he'd said a moment later, having thought about it. 'How about we have your wedding ring made up with a few diamonds inset?'

'I guess so but I'm not really a diamond sort of girl. I guess having a surname like Diamond all these years has put me off. However, I do like the idea of getting some stones inset. What's your birth stone?'

'I believe it's tanzanite.'

'And Spencer and I are both aquamarine so why not have a piece of tanzanite inset with an emerald either side? One for each of us.'

'And if we happen to blessed with more children in the future?'

Jane had glanced over at him, realising this was his way of asking her if she wanted children. She'd smiled reassuringly and nodded. 'Then I'll have to get the ring adjusted.'

Sean had reached over and kissed her hand. 'Sounds perfect.' He'd then told her he'd need her ring size and once that had been achieved, she'd gone back to simply enjoying her new world, the world of love and laughter and family. She'd been able to get to know Kathleen and Rosie much better and was enjoying playing a nightly game of chess with Barney. She really was part of the

Booke family and when Sean came home from work that night she couldn't help but slip her arms about his waist and tell him just how much she loved being with him, being a part of his family.

Sean kissed her as though he hadn't seen her for weeks, rather than only since that morning. 'And tonight, my gorgeous Jane, I'm going to take you out for a special pre-birthday dinner because, believe me, although Spencer says he's happy to share his birthday with you, the day will still be all about him.'

'And I'm more than happy to have that happen.' She laughed.

'Go on up and get dressed. We have reservations in an hour.'

'Oh. Is it a fancy place? I'm not sure I have anything suitable to wear.'

'It's all taken care of.' He smiled and kissed her again. 'I love you, Jane. Every single part of you.'

'I believe you, Sean. I really do.' It was a few more minutes before she was able to head up to her room, excited that she was getting to enjoy a special, secret dinner for her birthday *just* with Sean.

On the bed, she found a garment bag and when she unzipped it, inside was the most wonderful cream-coloured dress she'd ever seen in her life. Simple in design, the straight skirt came to mid-calf while the bodice had small daisy flowers embroidered around the waist and a scooped neckline. The dress was sleeveless but also in the garment bag was a light shawl, embroidered with daisies. She stared at the dress for a whole minute, unable to believe something so beautiful was being given to her.

At the knock on her door, she jumped. 'It's only me,'

Louise called, opening the door a little. 'Sean told me he's taking you out for a special dinner. Can I come in?'

'Look what Sean bought me!' Jane pointed to the dress as Louise came into the room, closing the door behind her.

'Oh, Jane. It's gorgeous.'

'I know.'

'Here. Let me help you put it on.'

Jane was pleased with the help because when she tried to undo the zipper she was surprised to find her hand trembling. She didn't even have time to think about the scars on her body or that Louise might see them. She was far too excited to be self-conscious. When the dress was on, Jane stared at herself in the mirror, gobsmacked at her reflection.

'I look…beautiful.' She spoke the word as though she'd never thought of herself in that way before.

Louise laughed. 'Of course you do, darling.' She pointed to Jane's feet. 'You need shoes and, do you know, I think I have just the pair. Good thing we're the same size. Be right back.'

Jane turned one way then the other, unable to believe it was really her in the reflection. She looked at her hair and held it up from her neck, bunching the long locks, trying to figure out what sort of style suited the dress. Finally, she pulled half of it back, leaving the rest hanging loose down her back. 'That works.'

Louise returned a moment later with the shoes and also a small necklace which was made from diamonds and sapphires in the shape of little daisies. 'Look what else I found. It was Sean's grandmother's.'

'Blue daisies,' Jane gasped, and when Louise clasped

the necklace around her neck, Jane couldn't believe how perfectly it all fitted. Even the borrowed shoes matched.

'I like what you've done with your hair,' Louise said. 'Perfect. Now, how about a little bit of make-up? Just a touch of blush and a bit of lip gloss?'

Jane nodded deciding that as tonight was going to be her very special pre-birthday dinner with Sean, and he'd gone to such trouble to buy her the dress, she wanted to be the perfect princess for her very own prince.

When Louise had finished applying the make-up, giggling that she felt very much like the fairy godmother getting Cinderella ready for the ball, Jane slipped her glasses back on and stared at her reflection in stunned disbelief.

'Oh, my. I really *am* a princess.'

Louise laughed. 'I can't wait for Sean to see you.'

'Me neither.' Jane smoothed her hand down the dress.

'Well, go on, then,' Louise prompted, pointing to the door. 'I'm sure your chariot awaits.'

Jane laughed and headed for the door, walking with more pride and self-assurance than she could ever remember feeling before. It was Sean. He had come into her life, enhancing it beyond measure.

As she descended the stairs, it wasn't Sean but Spencer, who was dressed for bed, who saw her first.

'Mummy!' he gasped, unable to stop himself from staring at her.

The word made Jane's moment even more complete.

'You're so beautiful,' he breathed.

'That's an understatement, son,' Sean remarked, walking over to take Jane's hand in his, bringing it to his lips and kissing it in a gallant gesture. 'Stunning.'

She smiled shyly. 'Thank you for the dress. It's…the prettiest thing I've ever worn.'

Sean seemed genuinely choked up at the sight of her and simply nodded, acknowledging her words.

'You two had better get going,' Louise interjected a moment later as the two of them just stood there, staring into each other's eyes.

'Yes.' Sean was the first to snap out of it. 'Let's say goodnight to Spencer.'

Jane bent down and held out her arms to Spencer, who immediately ran to her. He wrapped his arms about her neck and kissed her cheek. 'I can't wait until you're my real mummy. It's so exciting,' he squeaked, before his father scooped him up and blew a raspberry on his tummy, peals of delighted laughter filling the air.

'Don't razz him up too much,' Louise complained, glaring pointedly at her son.

'True. True.' With that, Sean pressed one last kiss to his son's cheek and put him back on the floor. 'Brush your teeth and remember to do exactly what Grandma says, OK?'

'Yes, Dad.' Spencer rolled his eyes as though he'd already been through this drill.

'Right, then.' Sean crooked his arm towards Jane who immediately placed her hand around his elbow. 'Shall we?'

'We shall,' she returned, and it wasn't until she was walking out the door that Louise gave her a small fabric bag, which she slipped over Jane's wrist.

'Has a bit of lippy in it in case you need a touch-up later on.'

'Oh. Thanks.'

'Happy birthday.' Louise and Spencer waved, Barney coming to join them as they all waved the birthday girl off on her adventure.

The instant Sean had reversed out of the driveway, Louise turned to her husband and grandson. 'Action stations!' she declared, and they all quickly set about putting the rest of the night's events into motion.

It wasn't until after dinner, eaten by candlelight in a secluded gourmet restaurant, that Jane looked across the table at Sean and realised that something was going on.

'Is that your phone buzzing again?'

'Yes.'

'I hope it's not an emergency, although if it is, we'll deal with it.'

'It's not the hospital,' he replied.

'Oh.' Anxiety marred her features as she watched him read the text message. 'Is it Spencer?'

'No, no.' Sean smiled at her. 'Everything is fine... except for the little surprise I have for you.' He motioned to the waiter and a moment later a box wrapped in pretty birthday paper with daisies all over it was placed in front of her. 'Happy birthday, Jane.'

'A present? I thought the dinner was my present.'

'Open it,' he encouraged, watching her closely.

'OK.' Jane smiled as she ran her hands over the box that looked as though it contained a bottle of wine. Carefully she peeled off the paper, pleased when Sean didn't try to rush her. Finally, she removed the paper and looked at what was inside. 'Cinnamon!'

'No one's going to wreck this doll,' Sean said softly. 'Her hair is almost as long as yours but I have to say yours is much more impressive, and silky and soft and...' He breathed out, repressed desire in his eyes.

'And you know I want to run my fingers through it right now.'

Jane held his gaze and nodded, the doll still firmly in her hands. 'Then we'd better get out of here,' she suggested, and he nodded. 'I can't believe you remembered the doll. This is the most perfect present, Sean. Thank you.'

He stood from his seat and came around to hold her chair, and she instantly pressed her lips to his. 'Thank you,' she said again.

'You're more than welcome,' he remarked, letting his hands trail slowly through her free-flowing locks.

Jane sighed. 'I guess it is almost pumpkin time.'

'Pumpkin time?'

She smiled at him as they said goodbye to the proprietor. 'Midnight,' she tut-tutted as they walked to his car. 'You have two sisters who no doubt dressed up as fairy-tale princesses when they were younger and yet you have no idea what "pumpkin time" means?'

He shrugged. 'My sisters were always a puzzle to me when we were growing up.' He held the car door for her, pressing a kiss to her lips before quickly going around to the driver's side. Even there, he seemed a little pre-occupied and almost...nervous.

'Sean? Is everything all right?'

'Of course it is. Why wouldn't it be?' he said as he drove them away from the city, towards Port Adelaide. 'I just have one more little surprise for your birthday and then we can think about heading home.'

'OK,' she said, her nerves settling with his reassuring tone. She dug around in the little handbag Louise had given her and reapplied the lip gloss, before closing her eyes and allowing herself to listen to the soothing classical music Sean had switched on.

'I'm having such a wonderful time,' she said dreamily, her words relaxed and floating away on the breeze. 'I can't believe how much I love you, Sean. How much you mean to me. I never want to let you go. I never want to be apart from you. You've made my world.'

'That's good to hear,' he said as he slowed the car and finally brought it to a stop. It was only then she realised he'd parked the car and that they were at the port. Outside her window was a small cruising yacht, covered in fairy-lights.

'Wow. Will you look at that? It's gorgeous.'

Sean came around the car to help her out before pulling her close and dropping another kiss to her lips. 'Happy pre-birthday surprise,' he whispered, gesturing to the yacht.

'Huh?' But it was only as her eyes adjusted to the light that she was able to see the people who were already on board the yacht. Louise was there with Barney and Spencer, Sean's sisters and their families, as well as Luc, Anthea, Romana and a score of their other friends from the hospital.

'Sean?'

'Happy surprise wedding,' he said, then took her hand and led her towards the gangplank. 'It's all organised.'

Jane gasped. 'The dress.'

'Something new,' he commented.

Jane touched the blue sapphire necklace at her throat. 'And this?'

'Something old and something blue.'

A giggle worked its way up as she looked down at

the shoes. 'And, of course, my something borrowed.' She nodded in appreciation. 'Very clever,' she said as she allowed him to escort her onto the yacht, where they were greeted by a round of welcoming applause.

'I think my mother deserves an award for her performance,' Sean said.

'And Spencer. How did he keep this a secret?'

'He nearly didn't. Not when he saw you looking so beautiful,' he replied as he continued to lead her through the parting crowd towards the bow, where a marriage celebrant stood waiting for them. 'As difficult as it's been to keep the secret, wanting to share so much of it with you, your reaction, your appreciation, your trust in allowing me to do all of this for you, to give you the most perfect night of your life, has been wonderful.'

'No. Not wonderful, Dad. *Purple*,' Spencer interjected, rolling his eyes.

They both laughed. 'It *is* purple, Sean.' She grinned as she said the words. 'The most perfect purple and green night of all time.'

They stopped before the marriage celebrant and she turned to face Sean, holding his hands tightly in hers, doing her best not to cry from overwhelming happiness.

'Dearly beloved,' the celebrant began, but Jane couldn't contain her love for Sean any more and stood on tiptoe and kissed him passionately, in front of everyone.

'I haven't got to that part yet,' the celebrant murmured, but neither Sean nor Jane cared. Against all odds, they'd found each other, bonded together in a love that would last a lifetime.

* * * * *

A sneaky peek at next month...

MEDICAL
ROMANCE™

THE ULTIMATE IN ROMANTIC MEDICAL DRAMA

My wish list for next month's titles...

In stores from 2nd May 2014:

☐ 200 Harley Street: The Proud Italian – Alison Roberts

& 200 Harley Street: American Surgeon in London
   – Lynne Marshall

☐ A Mother's Secret – Scarlet Wilson

& Return of Dr Maguire – Judy Campbell

☐ Saving His Little Miracle – Jennifer Taylor

& Heatherdale's Shy Nurse – Abigail Gordon

Available at WHSmith, Tesco, Asda, Eason, Amazon and Apple

Just can't wait?

Join the Mills & Boon Book Club

Want to read more **Medical** books?
We're offering you **2 more** absolutely **FREE!**

We'll also treat you to these fabulous extras:

- Exclusive offers and much more!

- FREE home delivery

- FREE books and gifts with our special rewards scheme

Get your free books now!

visit www.millsandboon.co.uk/bookclub
or call Customer Relations on 020 8288 2888